To CO[...]

From one vet to
another, thank you
for your service! I

Ghosts of the
Mountains

know that this was a
different time and place
from your experience in
Italy, but I hope it
brings back only fond
memories. Best Wishes,
VR/ Mark Bowlin

Also by the Author

The Texas Gun Club
2010 Winner, Gold Medal Award, Military Writers
Society of America

Victory Road
2011 Winner, Gold Medal Award, Military Writers
Society of America

For God and Country
2013 Winner, Silver Medal Award, Military
Writers Society of America

Ghosts of the Mountains

A Texas Gun Club Novel

Mark Bowlin

The 1630 Press
Flower Mound, Texas

Ghosts of the Mountains
A Texas Gun Club Novel

Cover by ACDbookcoverdesign.com

Manufactured in the United States of America

For information, please contact:
Mark Bowlin
The 1630 Press
Flower Mound, Texas
mark@markbowlin.org

ISBN-13: 978-0-9908904-0-9
ISBN-10: 0990890406

In memory of my brother-in-law Jim Thorp.
By God, he was one hell of a Texan.

Acknowledgments

As always, I would like to thank Susan and Alex Bowlin for their support during the writing of *Ghosts of the Mountain*. It was more of a challenge than the previous novels, and I apologize for taking so long to get it complete. It was begun after a year spent in Northern Iraq, and, well, mine wasn't the first personal timeline disrupted by that unhappy country. I always have amazingly unselfish help from many people during the course of putting together my books. I would like to thank my father, Stan Bowlin, who was my primary reader, as well as Michele di Lonardo of Cassino, Italy. Michele's been a wonderful resource and is a great tour guide of the battlefields along the Gustav Line. Many thanks to CAPT Doug Grossmann, USN, and CAPT Doug Peabody, USN, who donated their names to one unsavory character. Likewise, thanks to Toni Bernardi Rose, whose mother Kay Bernardi once told me, "That's not the Toni I raised." Indeed.

I'd like to express my appreciation to COL David Harmon, TXARNG (Ret.); CDR Bob Rose, USN (Ret.); LTC Kevin Smith, TXARNG; the current commander of the 1-141st, LTC Ross Davis, TXARNG; Lt Cdr Robert Hawkins, MBE, RN; SFC Aaron Hodgson, USA; Gary B.G.E. Beams; Joyce Gilmour; Patti Stickle; and Bob Wranosky.

The Assault on Hill 593
11–12 Feb '44
Cpl. Ed Kulis

The Abbey

Hill 569

Hill 468

Hill 593

Snakeshead Ridge

Cassino

Caira

Mt. Cairo

Prologue

January 21, 1944
1100 Hours
Able Company Command Post, West Bank Rapido
River, Italy

The time had come.

The lieutenant could hear the squeal and clank of the tracks, but through the smoke and the fog, he could not yet see the tanks. It was only a matter of minutes.

He blew his breath out and shook his head sadly. It was all over. There would be no reinforcement from the other side of that bloody river, and his first command—less than four hours old—was coming to an inglorious end.

Surrender.

It was inconceivable, but…there it was. To fight on would accomplish nothing. Nothing, he thought. They would all be dead within minutes, and the lieutenant knew that there couldn't be an attempt to rescue his company for hours. Maybe days.

The company commander was dead, not that he'd been any help, and the company had less than a platoon, maybe a squad, left of soldiers that were able to fight. *But fight with what? Fists against armor?* The ammunition was nearly exhausted and consisted entirely of a few rifle magazines and a handful of grenades. There were no more rounds for the machine guns and the mortars. The precious bazooka rounds hadn't even survived the crossing. Even if they were fully armed, a platoon or a company, or even a whole battalion, would not even scratch the German defenses. It was such a terrible waste.

First Lieutenant Sam Taft had contemplated death— both before and during this terrible battle, but he didn't dwell on his mortality. He was an optimist by nature and had always focused his thoughts on going home after the war was won. He had never before considered giving up, his pride had never even countenanced the notion, but he found that however distasteful, he really had no choice.

Sam didn't think of himself as a soldier. He was a rancher, ripped from his life in South Texas by the war, and he wanted with all his heart to return to his wife and never set foot on a battlefield again. At least he didn't want to think of himself as a soldier, but he was. A good one, and a good, conscientious combat leader despite his disdain for military life. He had never before shied away from difficult decisions, and he wouldn't now.

"Sergeant Kenton!" Sam called out over the shattered valley floor to his platoon sergeant, who was now the acting top sergeant of the company.

"Yes, sir?" called back Kenton from his shell crater.

"It's time."

The sergeant slammed his fist into the mud, cursed, and then nodded. He had come to the same conclusion.

So had the Germans. A tank entered the battlefield from somewhere out of the haze and then at first cautiously, then openly, panzer grenadiers emerged from the smoke and began to round up the Texans. Any will to fight further melted away.

Deeply ashamed, Sam laid his rifle next to the body of Mark Christian, his radioman, and stood up with his hands over his head. For the soldiers of Able Company, the Battle of the Rapido River was over.

Chapter One

January 24, 1944
0830 Hours
Clearing Station, 111th Medical Battalion,
Mignano, Italy

Consciousness slowly returned to Captain Perkin Berger. At first, all he could note were the sounds: professional sounding voices, the gentle moans of patients who hadn't been evacuated, the clatter of a dropped tray.

Perkin's second sense to return was smell. The tent smelled mostly of alcohol and wet canvas. There seemed to be other aromas, but he couldn't put a name to them until he detected the smell of coffee, which cautiously prompted him to open a single eye. He couldn't remember where he was, and as he had been dreaming of Sam, he thought for a second that he'd been taken prisoner as well.

He hadn't been. A passing soldier was clearly American, and that encouraged Perkin to open his other eye and attempt to sit up. That was when the sense of touch returned to Perkin, and he gasped as his entire torso erupted in pain. Perkin reflexively dropped back down onto his cot, and he reconsidered his rash movement. *Bad idea…maybe I'll just lie here for a spell.*

"Good morning, Cap'n," a cheerful voice greeted him.

Perkin rolled his eyes backwards and saw a tall boy barely out of elementary school wearing a white lab coat and standing over him at the head of his cot.

"I'm Dr. Poynter. How are you feeling?" The doctor moved around to the side of Perkin's cot and Perk could see that maybe the imposter was a teenager.

"What'd you do with the real doctor?" Perkin mumbled.

"I'm sorry, I didn't catch that," Poynter said. "I asked how you felt."

As Perkin's thought processes continued to evolve concerning the young doctor, he said truthfully, "I ain't sure. Where am I?"

"You're at the clearing station at Mignano. Do you know how you got here?" Poynter pulled a stool over and sat down next to Perkin's cot.

As the doctor began his examination, Perkin thought for a moment and then shook his head. "No, Doc, not exactly. I was at Paestum. No…that can't be right. I was…" Perkin shook his head again and said thickly, "I can't remember right now."

The doctor nodded, "Not surprising. As I understand it, you were wounded by artillery and then thought it would be good idea to swim in an icy contaminated river, after which you decided to go back on the line for a couple days. Does that sound about right?"

Perkin didn't know, so he asked instead, "I didn't kill General Clark, did I?" Perkin had a vague memory, or maybe it had been a dream, of placing Mark Clark in the crosshairs of a borrowed sniper rifle.

Poynter laughed, "You don't see any medals on your

chest, do you? Heavens no, you didn't kill Clark…do you think you did? You know as a medical man, I can't advocate generalcide, but I'd sure make an exception for that son of a bitch."

The doctor waved an orderly over, and together they rolled Perkin onto his side and began to check his sutures. A few minutes later, the doctor spoke again, "You look a lot better today, Captain. When you were brought in yesterday afternoon, you were running a 103 fever, and your stitches were really red and inflamed. We pumped you full of penicillin, and knocked you out. Miraculous duo, penicillin and sleep. I'd guess you slept for about seventeen or eighteen hours. No wonder you're groggy, but the sleep has probably helped as much as the penicillin. I know you fellas haven't had much over the past four days."

"I think that the last time I slept was a couple of hours at the aid station on Friday. I hadn't slept for some time before that. What day is it now?" Perkin asked.

"Monday." The doctor stood up. He had plenty more patients to see. "You take it easy. We're gonna see if you can hold food down, and then get you on your feet and see what kind of mobility and range of motion you have."

"Say, Doc? You haven't heard any word of Lieutenant Taft, Sam Taft, have you?"

The young doctor smiled sadly and shook his head, "Your cousin? Your battalion commander, Major Spaulding, told me this morning that you'd ask. No, and he hasn't heard anything either. He also said, and I'm quoting, 'Perk probably thinks that without his full participation, the outcome of the war likely hangs in the balance, but tell him the division will survive for a day or two longer without his hand at the helm.'"

1015 Hours
1st Battalion HQ, Mount Trocchio, Italy

The battalion headquarters was a mud-covered truck. There was little need for anything else because the battalion had been destroyed, and offensive operations were off the table for the foreseeable future.

Despite the trauma of the previous days, two young soldiers leaned casually against the truck and shared a cigarette. Next to the soldiers, a single crutch belonging to the taller of the two men rested on a fender. Private Roscoe Pfadenhauer, the owner of the crutch, leaned his head back and turned his face toward the sun hoping to share in its warmth, but he was disappointed. The sun was hiding behind a deep thick layer of clouds and little of its bounty reached southern Italy that morning.

"Do you think that they'll let you come back to the company after you're healed up?" asked the smaller soldier, a scarred seventeen-year-old corporal named Eddie Kulis.

"I don't know. It may take a spell...the doc here says that they'll likely have to reset my arm, and maybe set my ankle. They should've moved me out the first day, but I guess there were just too many fellas worse off than me. The word is that after the docs are done with you, you get sent to a replacement depot, and then shipped out to God knows where. Hell, I might end up in England with some conscript division and a bunch of guys who don't know shit from Shinola."

"Well, you'll have English girls to look forward to then." Corporal Kulis thought of little else beyond women, and he believed that as the troops stationed in the United Kingdom weren't in combat, they had plenty of spare time to pursue women.

"If I could get one like Cap'n Berger's nurse, I'd die

happy. You said she was a real peach."

Kulis smiled at the thought of Helen, a beautiful English nurse that had become Captain Berger's de facto girlfriend. "She is, but you're more likely to get the one that they tried to set Lieutenant Bear up with. She'd snap you in half with her thighs alone—eight feet tall, Charles Atlas arms with a full-grown mustache, and thick ankles."

"What do I care about ankles? I can't fu...oh, good morning, sir!" Private Pfadenhauer and Corporal Kulis came to attention and saluted in unison as their battalion commander drove up in his jeep.

"Mornin', boys! Are you heading out, Private Pfadenhauer?" asked Major Bill Spaulding. He reached into his mouth with his good hand, his other heavily wrapped in fresh gauze bandages, and pulled out an exhausted quid of tobacco which he tossed on the ground.

"Yes, sir. There's a truck comin' that'll pick us up in fifteen minutes over yonder. Then we'll head down south on murder alley." The road leading to Mount Trocchio was under German observation, and sometimes the artillery tucked back into the mountains behind the Gustav Line would fire at vehicles.

"They took a shot at my jeep this morning on my way down to Mignano. I had to go see a doc about my hand and check on Captain Berger. Their aim ain't bad, but their time on target thankfully needs work. They missed me by at least a football field." Major Spaulding produced a pack of cigarettes from his jacket pocket and passed it around as he added, "I gotta say though, it's a good feeling when you make the bend and are outta sight."

The younger soldiers grinned momentarily at the thought of the excitement, and then getting back to business, Corporal Kulis asked, "Sir, what's the word on Cap'n Berger?"

"He's doing better. They were able to bring his fever down, and I understand some of the stitches on his side might have to be redone. I swear he's gonna look like a jigsaw puzzle by the time the war's over. I also got a better accounting on our casualties. You guys wanna hear it?"

The smiles dropped from the faces of the two young soldiers as they nodded. The battalion had been severely mauled, and many of their friends were missing and believed dead.

"I came across a few of the boys from Able in the clearing station this morning. Froman was there. He came across the river after the fight was over. Said that since he was Jewish, he preferred to take his chances with the river rather than become a German prisoner. I guess he was carried past San Angelo and well into the 143rd's sector before getting pulled out. He's being treated for hypothermia, but we should get him back before long."

"Sir, did he have any word about what happened… at the end?" Kulis asked quietly.

Spaulding nodded sadly. "He said they were out of ammo, and the Krauts were bringing up armor when Lieutenant Taft surrendered the remainder of the company. By his reckoning, there was less than a dozen or so left who weren't wounded or already taken prisoner. He said that Sergeant Hawkins was killed, as was Vince Fratelli…" An involuntary groan from Private Pfadenhauer stopped him.

Spaulding grimaced as he reached into a pocket and pulled out a folded sheet of paper. In his raspy smoker's voice, he said, "I'm sorry, boys. I know Vince was a buddy. We lost a lot of good men at this terrible place. I heard this morning that the regiment was reduced by fifty-four percent, but that don't tell the whole story. It ain't like the remaining forty-six percent could fight—I doubt that I could put together an effective platoon at this point." Spaulding stared at the paper, swallowed hard, and then handed it to Kulis. "It's the butcher's bill. You two can look it over, just bring it back when you're done. Good luck getting fixed up, Howie. I'll fight tooth and nail to get you returned to us if you like."

As Kulis silently took the piece of paper from Major Spaulding, Private Pfadenhauer nodded and said, "Yes, sir. I'd like that very much. Good luck to you as well."

Major Spaulding returned the salutes of the soldiers and started to walk away, but he hesitated and turned back to the young soldiers. He looked at them through moist eyes and said, "You and a handful of the boys are all that are left of the old company. It's hard to account for the time, but we've been together for years, and now I got one in-bound officer and seventeen troops left in Able." Spaulding sighed, and said, "I don't know of a single regular army unit that was as good as that company. And now it's gone, and it surely breaks my heart."

Spaulding stopped speaking, and turned to the northwest to face distant Rome. He shook his head as he thought about what they had paid to get only halfway to the Eternal City. It was an appalling muster. Spaulding turned back to Kulis and Pfadenhauer, looked the soldiers over and he nodded reflectively as he concluded his thoughts and said, "Eventually, the army will see fit to send us a levy of replacements, but we'll have to make do with what we got until then. And when they get here, we'll still be on the line, and them boys will be just about overwhelmed. I'm going to have to count on the old Hammers to make this work for a long time to come, and when the new boys come in, you'll have to mold them as best you can into the soldiers and officers that we want them to be. My image of that soldier is Vince Fratelli or Bob Hawkins. My new officers will be green as well, and we'll have to guide them just as they strive to guide you. My image of that officer is Sam Taft."

1015 Hours
Six Miles Northwest of Terni, Italy

Sam would have laughed had he known that Major Spaulding regarded him as a model soldier. He was wet and shivering, and more than a little confused and afraid. Other than a hunk of black bread handed out by German soldiers when he'd been captured, he hadn't eaten for more than a day. He'd had a restless night without much sleep, and that was on top of two or more days without sleep before then. Sam knew that they wouldn't last long without shelter, food, and good uninterrupted sleep.

At least two motorcycles had ridden past in the last fifteen minutes, and while Sam didn't dare lift his head up to see, they almost certainly were ridden by German soldiers. Perhaps they were looking for Sam and his comrades, but that was a question he'd prefer not to address with them personally. If they were caught, they would almost certainly be executed on the spot.

Their hiding spot in the ditch was less than ideal, but it had been the best that they could do at the time. Lieutenant B.G.E. Beams was in sad condition, and Sam was certain that he had a concussion. He and Sergeant Kenton had carried Beams for most of the way since they escaped from the Terni train station in the dark morning hours the day before.

Sam laid his head down in the tall grass and thought over the events again for the thousandth time.

The time from surrender to escape had been dramatically short—less than a day. An old friend, Captain Waller Finley-Jones, the regiment's British liaison officer, had once told Sam that most successful escapes happen before the prison camps, and that possibilities for escape are numerous for those who know how to look for them. Once at a *stalag*, though, Finley-Jones said that escape was exponentially more difficult: "We've had some very celebrated escapes from the Nazi camps. Chaps who made it over or under the wire, and made their way to Switzerland or to the resistance in Vichy France or Spain and Portugal or even to Sweden. But they're only a handful of good fellows compared to the hundreds of thousands left behind in the stalags. Now, we had hundreds who escaped from Jerry in France in '40 and from North Africa, but they almost all did it while at collection stations or in transit. If I'm ever captured and manage to escape, I plan to lay low, as you chaps say, for a few days and then make my way to the coast. I'll steal a boat and be back in Swansea for breakfast."

Despite Finley-Jones' advice on looking for ways to escape capture early, escape had not been on Sam's mind. Sam had dozens of wounded soldiers that he wanted to see to, although he had been pushed by two German soldiers into a column of American prisoners and marched to the rear of the German lines.

Even through the smoke and the fog of the battlefield, Sam was stunned by the thoroughness of the German defenses. He passed row after row of concertina wire that separated open patches of ground that he surmised were heavily mined. Trenches with prepared fighting positions were interlaced with more trenches that served as communication and resupply avenues for the frontline German troops. Heavily fortified bunkers and pillboxes dotted the landscape like miniature steel and concrete castles, and Sam had thought he'd even seen Panther turrets mounted in the ground.

There were signs that the American bombardment that preceded the crossing attempts had done some damage, but Sam's professional eye uncovered no sign that the German defenses had even been slightly disrupted. It would take much more than a few hours' worth of artillery and two understrength regiments to force a breach in the Gustav Line. It was simply too well defended.

A German officer, later that morning, had unconsciously reinforced that same notion to Sam when he remarked to the American officer, "A reconnaissance in force like that is seldom worth the effort."

A reconnaissance in force? Sam had thought. It had been a full-scale assault—the best the Fifth Army could throw across the river—and it had barely caught the Germans' attention. Sam had said nothing, but nodded his agreement and declined the cigarette offered by the German officer.

They had been marched to a collection point some miles behind the Rapido River, where Sam again noticed the magnitude of their defeat. There were scores of prisoners, maybe even hundreds of prisoners—and that was just from the Texas division. At the collection point, he was searched for a second time. He had been disarmed entirely on surrender and all of his military gear save his helmet, overcoat, and uniform had been confiscated. His personal items, which were little more than a small sewing kit and two letters from his wife, Margaret, were returned.

Sam saw soldiers that he knew from his regiment, the 141st, as well as from the 143rd, the other infantry regiment that had crossed that night. He saw medics, chaplains, engineers, and even a soldier that he knew to be an anti-aircraft artilleryman, although there had been no need for him to be close enough to the river to be captured. But the vast majority were riflemen, and Sam had never seen a collection of men that were simultaneously so downcast and angry.

It was at the collection point that Sam began to organize the remains of his company. They had been placed in a former wheat field that was now enclosed by several strands of barbed wire. He had found the bulk of the company in varying stages of wholeness, with some members barely walking wounded, and some seemingly without a scratch. Sam had been beginning to think that perhaps he was the only company officer to survive when a limping B.G.E. Beams slapped Sam on the back and had offered his hand.

"Goddamn, I'm glad to see you alive, Sam!" Beams said. He had offered a tired smile, which was quickly replaced by a dark scowl, as Beams demanded, "What took you fellas so long? We were alone for a long time, amigo. B.G.E. almost stood for Beams Got Eighty-sixed."

Sam nodded in sympathy and said, "Ebbins got us lost in a minefield. I told him he was turning us in the wrong place, but guess what? He wouldn't listen. When we got to the river, we crossed as soon as we could, but it was too late. I'm sorry." Sam shook his head in disgust over the memory of his former company commander's conduct on the night of the crossing.

Lieutenant Beams likewise shook his head in disgust. With his hands on his hips, he spat in the mud and said, "Wasn't your fault. Where is that son of a bitch, anyway? Sippin' schnapps with the field marshal? Or did he run back to Africa?"

"Naw. He didn't make it. Eddie Kulis crossed the

river and told me that he came across Ebbins' body. No doubt with a bayonet between his teeth," Sam said dryly. Sam was entirely indifferent to Ebbins' death. He had known Ronald Ebbins since high school, but had never respected him as a man or a soldier.

Beams however looked disappointed for a moment, and then shrugged. "Sounds like Ebbins—too dumb to know that the bayonet goes on the rifle. It's ironic, though."

"How's that?"

"I was hopin' to kill him myself with a bayonet. B.G.E. stands for Beams Gutted Ebbins."

Sam had looked around the muddy wheat field, and as he listened to the constant boom of artillery, he said tiredly, "Life's full of lost opportunities. Any idea what's next?"

"Yeah…seein' as I was one of the first prisoners, I've had the chance to make friends. A Kraut officer told me that we'll be pulled from the combat zone and sent to a dulag in what he said was 'Compliance with Article 7 of the Geneva Convention.' Snotty son of a bitch. I ain't ever heard of a dulag so I asked him what it was. It's a Durchsomethingorother. Means a throughway camp or somethin' like that…"

"Yeah. It's a transit camp." Sam had said grimly. Talking about it made it seem even worse.

"Yeah. So, we'll be registered there with the Red Cross as prisoners of war, get to send our postcard home, and then we'll be sent onward to a stalag in Germany or wherever until the war's over and we get repatriated."

Sam's mind drifted from recent events, and despite the cold and drizzling rain, he slid into sleep as he lay against the bank of the deep ditch. His nap was less than five minutes.

"Sir!" Sam felt his shoulder being shaken, and when

he opened his eyes, he saw Sergeant Kenton kneeling next to him. "We ought to be movin', sir. We need a little more distance."

Despite the imperative need for more sleep, Sam was instantly awake and relatively alert. As he raised himself up, he looked over at Lieutenant Beams, who was curled up in a tight ball underneath a bush. Sam raised his eyebrows at Sergeant Kenton.

"Yeah, I know. He ain't in much shape to be moved, but I figure that we've only gone seven or eight miles. Maybe less. I'll carry him first," Kenton said as he stood up.

Sam leaned over and took a long drink of water from the ditch. The ice-cold water was like a sword pushed through his empty stomach, but he drank until he couldn't stand any more.

"All right Bill, let's wake up Sleepin' Beauty here, and we'll keep pressin' to the northwest. If we can do this for another day or so, we'll be outside their probable search radius, and we'll see about getting some help or doublin' back to the south."

1635 Hours
Nine Miles Northwest of Terni, Italy

It had been slow going, and Sam had little idea of how far they had traveled since awakening Lieutenant Beams that morning. Maybe seven or eight miles like Kenton said, but Sam thought it more likely that they had only gone four or five miles. It was his experience that people invariably overestimated their distance when moving overland.

There were no roads, towns, and few farms in sight. Perhaps more importantly, thought Sam, there were no telegraph, telephone or electrical wires to be seen either. They had finally dropped from exhaustion while following an old path through forested hills. There was a stream nearby for fresh water, plenty of pine boughs to build a lean-to shelter, but no food to eat. They could get by for another night, but it would be a long one.

Lieutenant Beams was in rough shape. His knee had been banged up during the battle, although he had told Sam at the collection point that he couldn't remember being scratched. The knee was swollen and it made walking uncomfortable, and running painfully awkward, but it still worked. More concerning to Sam though was the state of Lieutenant Beams' face and head. Sam thought it certain that Beams had a concussion, and it would take an extensive set of dentures before the lieutenant smiled normally again.

As Sergeant Kenton gathered the pine boughs and looked for kindling, Sam sat down next to Lieutenant Beams and gave his friend an examination. Brushing away Beams' attempt to stop him, Sam looked at the gash on Beams' head, then moved his examination to the lieutenant's broken nose and smashed lips.

"Knock it off, would you?" mumbled Beams with some asperity. He gingerly inserted a finger past his crushed lips and winced as he realized he was missing teeth. "I hurt all over. What'd you guys do to me? Kenton's not using me like a woman, is he?"

"What if he is?" said Sam with a slight grin.

"Well, tell him I'm saving myself for marriage. B.G.E. stands for Beams Gets Engaged." Beams tried to return the grin but all he could produce was a macabre grimace.

Sam managed his first laugh since the surrender. "I think he prefers somethin' a little prettier. Although if Perk was here, he'd say he's seen you look worse. So, you seem to be a little more alert than earlier. Things clearin' up some?"

"I don't know that I'd go that far, Sam. Where the hell are we?" Beams' speech lay somewhere between a clumsy mumble and a whistling lisp and Sam had to lean in close to understand.

"We're in some woods. Beyond that, I don't know. I ain't even sure what part of Italy we're in to tell you the truth. We'll sort all that out as we go."

"No, Sam. I mean where are we as in what happened?"

"You don't remember what happened at the train station?" It was an event that Sam would never forget.

"No. I feel like I just came off a three-day bender in Galveston. The last thing I remember is we were in a forty and eight...and now it appears I'm missing some of my nibblers. What happened? Did the train derail or something?"

Sam thought back to the previous morning and shook his head. A forty and eight was a boxcar designed for either forty soldiers or eight horses. It had seemed more packed than forty men. "No. We were at some train station and being moved across the tracks from one train to another in the middle of the night. Do you remember that? Most of the boys were already up in the railcar, and it was you, me, and Kenton left to load. All of a sudden, an air raid alarm goes off and everyone turns to look at the sky. I don't know...I guess you saw an opportunity to escape in the dark and the rain, and you ducked under the car." Sam had puzzled about this since the escape. Neither he nor Sergeant Kenton had seen Beams leave. "A Kraut saw you, grabbed your ankle and dragged you back under. I knew he was up to no good because he looked to see if any of his sergeants were watching before he started pounding your brains in with his rifle butt. Me and Bill stopped it."

"You stopped it?" Beams' eyes were wide.

Sam nodded, but said nothing. It was a memory that would be hard to live with. There had been just two soldiers supervising the loading of their boxcar, and when the soldier began beating Beams, the other guard instantly slammed the boxcar door shut so no other prisoners would attempt to escape. As Sam and Sergeant Kenton stood paralyzed, the first German soldier slammed the rifle butt twice into the face of the prostrate Beams, and in the forest, Sam winced as the sound of the butt smashing his friend's face stirred his memory.

When the German raised his rifle again to strike the unconscious officer, Sam was no longer paralyzed. A memory flashed through Sam's mind of an Australian officer that he had met only a month before who had likewise been abused as a prisoner of the Germans. The image of that nervous, mute officer in his mind had enraged the even-tempered giant like never before, and without thinking, Sam stepped forward, wrapped his massive arms around the German's head from behind, and wrenched it as hard as he could. With a sickening snap, the soldier's neck broke and he dropped to the ground instantly without further sound.

The other German soldier who had been watching the beating with a grin on his face fumbled for a whistle kept on a lanyard around his neck. Instinctively, he began to back rapidly away from Sam. He backed into Sergeant Kenton. Had the soldier shouted for help, Sam knew, they'd be dead already, but the German hadn't been fast enough. Sergeant Kenton seized the other soldier from behind and clapped his hand hard over the second soldier's mouth. Kenton, who was nearly as large a man as Sam, stretched the German's head back farther and farther until Sam thought he would snap this soldier's neck as well, but it didn't break. After a second's hesitation, Sam lunged toward the struggling German soldier, and with all his weight and strength, crushed his exposed larynx with a single punch so hard it made Sergeant Kenton stagger.

Sam, who had never wanted to be a soldier, much less a killer, would later reflect that he had killed two men with his bare hands in less than ten heartbeats.

1645 Hours
1st Battalion HQ, Mount Trocchio, Italy

"Welcome to Able Company, sir. I'm Corporal Kulis. In addition to being a battalion intelligence NCO, I'm assigned additional duty to Able as your executive officer, senior NCO, your first, second, third, and weapons platoons as well as your cook, driver, and headquarters element. When Captain Berger returns, I'll turn over command of the 1st Platoon to you, which will then consist of me."

It was a bold opening to the man who would be running Able Company until Captain Berger was released from the clearing station. Corporal Kulis was as close to a fearless person as existed, but his first look at the new lieutenant had left him a little nervous. An old, thick, white scar crossed over the lieutenant's nose and a smaller parallel scar ran below it on his left cheek. His hazel eyes and reddish brown hair softened his facial features somewhat, but Kulis thought the lieutenant's build to be a little intimidating as well. The de facto commander of Able Company was obviously muscular on a scale relative to Lieutenant Taft, although he was considerably shorter, and his wide shoulders gave him an appearance as being nearly as broad as he was tall.

The lieutenant's name was Alexander Ryan, and

he had reported to the battalion headquarters upon his arrival that afternoon with orders to Able Company. The problem was, as Ryan had discovered, that the company didn't exist except on paper.

Second Lieutenant Ryan appeared to be searching his memory for something, but he apparently gave up and when he smiled at the young corporal before him, the smile reached his eyes and belied his otherwise hard appearance. Ryan said, "That's a hell of a lot on your plate, Corporal. How about I relieve you of cooking responsibilities?"

"That's probably best for all parties involved, sir," said Kulis, who was inwardly relieved. The officer had a sense of humor and Kulis's snap judgment was that Ryan would fit in well in the company. Kulis had seen a mixed bag of officers in his time in the army, and Kulis believed that officers with a sense of humor tended to be the best ones. It was his observation in life that humor and intelligence were correlated, and if any officer responded to Kulis's introduction with anything other than panic, he might actually have some promise—or he was too dumb not to know better.

"Do you mind if I ask about your background, where you've served, where you're from?" asked Kulis. "You don't sound like a Texan." The real question was service. Corporal Kulis was hoping to learn that the new officer had prior combat experience or had been previously enlisted.

"I'm not a Texan. I'm a farmer, Corporal…"

"Hey! Me too, sir! At least I used to be." This was at least some good news as far as the young corporal was concerned, as he believed that farmers had far more common sense than city dwellers could possibly possess.

"…from Sperry, Iowa. It's near the Mississippi in the southeast corner of the state. I was a student at Iowa

State before the war. Studied agriculture. Obviously not much service to tell you about. I went through my officer training, then the infantry school where I got my orders to the division. I spent the last six months at Camp Bowie overseeing the hand-to-hand combat course before being sent out here. How about you? Where are you from?"

"Like about half the boys here, I'm from Texas. If you're from Iowa, you should be in the 34th Division, sir. Ain't they from the Midwest? I understand they just crossed the Rapido by Cassino town today. Poor sons-a-bitches. That's their guns you're hearing." Kulis paused for a moment so the new lieutenant could listen to the distant machine-gun fire. "My daddy has a farm between Rosebud and the Brazos River, which is the Texas version of the Mississippi...you know...when it has water in it. I ain't goin' back to farmin' though, I'm goin' to stay in after the war. Speakin' of which, I take it you've been briefed by Major Spaulding?"

"I have but I'd like to get a rundown from your perspective. Let's walk around our little encampment here and you can point out the places that I need to know while we talk."

"Yes, sir. Umm...what was it that you were thinkin' of a few minutes ago?" asked Kulis. His hesitations were gone, and he was willing to accept the new officer into what he regarded as his company.

"I was trying to remember if they taught me how to build an infantry company up from scratch at Benning."

"Did they?"

"I don't think so. Maybe I slept through that lecture."

They hopped out of the back of the heavy truck that was serving as the battalion headquarters, and began to walk down the newly established paths of the American encampment behind the shelter of Mount Trocchio.

As Kulis pointed out the mess tent and latrine, he gave the new lieutenant an overview of the campaign to date. "Sir, we landed at Salerno on September 9th, and established the beachhead there at Paestum. They're still using that beachhead to land supplies as I understand it. We were in heavy combat for a month, we lost two platoon leaders there by the way, and then we were moved off the line for refit and training. Cap'n Berger was a platoon leader at Paestum but was promoted and given acting command of the divisional recon troop. We came back on the line in mid-November for the San Pietro and Mount Sammucro operations, which were real ball-busters, and then we were off the line for, I don't know, three weeks or so at the end of the year for training."

Kulis pointed out the regimental command post and continued, "I was transferred over to the battalion intelligence staff along with Cap'n Berger, and Cap'n Ebbins took over command of the company as Major Spaulding took over battalion when the battalion commander moved to regiment when most of the regimental staff was killed at San Pietro—I guess I should tell you that promotion seems to be mostly based on superiors bein' killed off, sir."

Ryan stared at the corporal and then shrugged. "It's the time-honored method, I suppose. As long as you don't covet my job, Corporal, I guess we're good to go."

"I don't, sir. As you said, I got enough going anyways. So, you know the story of the crossing so I won't go into detail, but we lost all of our officers there. Lieutenant Bear, I mean Lieutenant Taft, was taken prisoner, and the rest of the Able Company officers were killed including the company commander." Kulis allowed himself a slight smile in the darkness. "Captain

Berger, when he gets out of the hospital, will come back as the acting commander, or maybe permanent commander of the company, and hopefully, some more replacement officers like you are in-bound."

"Yeah…Major Spaulding told me not to hold my breath. Casualties were so high at the river that there aren't enough replacement officers and NCOs to go around to the battalions that need them. He said not to count on any more until we're off the line."

"Did he tell you when that would be, sir?"

"No. Until further notice, we're to reinforce our defensive position here, and be ready to resume the offensive across the Rapido. Whatever comes our way."

"Did he say what we're to resume the offensive with?" Corporal Kulis asked incredulously.

"Well, as you explained it to me, we're Able Company. So…if it comes down to it, follow me."

1800 Hours
1st Battalion HQ, Mount Trocchio, Italy

Lieutenant Ryan nodded at the other officers and took a seat on one of the side benches in the headquarters truck. He had just met the other company commanders, and just as quickly, their names faded from his overloaded memory.

Yesterday morning, he had been at the replacement depot at Caserta awaiting his orders. He'd had a huge breakfast and had taken a walk around the palace grounds with a pretty USO volunteer. Less than thirty-six hours later, he was in a combat zone for the first time and found himself the acting company commander of a unit that realistically existed only on paper. Now, he was receiving his first briefing and he struggled to pay attention. There had been so much to learn on his first day in the battalion and he felt he was absorbing only an infinitesimally small percentage.

The briefer was a filthy first lieutenant from Charlie Company. The lieutenant, whose name had also escaped Lieutenant Ryan, wiped a grain of dirt from an eye, and said, "We conducted a patrol on the west side of the river, and Major Spaulding asked me to give you a rundown on what we learned. We tried to cross last night but couldn't. We ran into a minefield on our side of the river, and it took us some time to egress the field. We had one casualty there." The lieutenant took a deep breath, pointed at a map and said, "The minefield was here. I don't know the boundaries though. Anyway, by the time that we backed out, we were coming into conflict timewise with the regimental demonstration that was scheduled last night. So we withdrew, waited until the demonstration was over and then attempted to cross at a different spot. This time we got pinned by machine-gun and mortar fires before we even got to the fucking river, and so we called it off for a second time. We had another casualty here."

Major Spaulding interrupted, "Bob, show us where the machine guns and mortars were sited."

The lieutenant pointed out the approximate machine-gun positions, noted that he had no fucking idea where the mortars were located, and then continued: "We finally crossed this morning just to the north of the Able crossing site from last Friday. The enemy minefield just opposite the crossing site has been reconstituted, but they haven't restored the concertina wire at the crossing yet. The minefield itself wasn't as thick as the original belt, so I think that they're restoring their first line as they get to it. We neutralized the mines, chucked 'em into the river, and then moved inland. A couple hundred yards from the river, we came to a little hollow that I think some Able personnel had been at. We found the body of the Able top sergeant and a few others."

Spaulding interrupted again, "Did you see the body of Lieutenant Taft?"

"No, sir, but I found that rifle, the Johnson, that he carried. It was next to the body of his radioman. We found Lieutenant Hoar on our way out. I don't know how he was still alive, but he was. We brought him back with us and my boys took him to an aid station."

"Thank you. How far did you penetrate?" Spaulding asked.

"We got maybe three hundred yards beyond the river. We came under observation from a pillbox located here..." The lieutenant pointed to the map again, and said, "They opened fire on us, and we withdrew. As you know, sir, the battalion provided smoke and artillery to mask our withdrawal, and we returned at 1600, mission complete."

Spaulding nodded. "Your thoughts on this site? Can it support bridging?"

The lieutenant shrugged, "Yeah. It's no worse than anywhere else along the river..." The soldier's face was hard and he clearly wanted to say more on the subject of the river, but stopped himself and said, "I mean, yes, sir. In the four patrols that I've conducted or tried to conduct, this is the best site. There's a small defilade at the crossing that gives you some cover, and the defenses aren't hard until you get inland some. The problem is that the Krauts almost certainly tracked us back to where we crossed. The defenses will be more prepared tonight, I'd reckon."

Ryan watched as Spaulding nodded again. Then the battalion commander spoke to the lieutenant from Charlie Company, "Yep. They don't miss a trick. Good patrol, Bob. Thanks for the rundown." Spaulding now addressed the small group of officers, "The regiment's going to do another demonstration tonight. It's intended to keep the Germans fixed on the sites that we attempted last week, while the 34th Division continues to try to establish a beachhead upriver. The first demonstration is at 0030 hours and a second demonstration at the battalion crossing sites three hours later. We're in regimental reserve so there should be no action for us, but they're going to pull a company from the 760th Tank Battalion ahead of our battalion and let the Shermans do the talking for a while."

Spaulding spoke for a few more minutes about the defensive positions of the regiment, including his concern that the Germans might counterattack in the division's sector in response to the 34th's assault tomorrow, and then the briefing ended.

Ryan was getting ready to drop out of the truck, when Spaulding called him back. "Lieutenant, did any of that make sense to you?" Spaulding asked.

"Yes, sir. Most of it anyway." It was a fairly honest answer. Theoretically, Ryan understood the entire briefing, but while the training that he'd had at Fort Benning and Camp Bowie had allowed him to visualize the information that was being conveyed, it wouldn't make true sense until he had seen it for himself. Ryan was in no hurry to be in combat, but he was ready for the professional fog to lift.

Spaulding instinctively understood. He spit a long stream of tobacco out of the back of the truck, narrowly missing Corporal Kulis who was standing by to escort Lieutenant Ryan, and said, "You're not gonna get a lot of sleep tonight with the demonstrations, but try. Come see me first thing in the morning and we'll start your education."

1815 Hours
Nine Miles Northwest of Terni, Italy

A small fire had been made in a hollow in the woods. Both Sam and Sergeant Kenton had carefully walked a perimeter around their campfire, and decided that the woods and the hollow were sufficient to hide the light beyond about twenty-five yards away.

They pooled their resources, and found that they had five letters among them—three death letters and Sam's two personal letters. Sergeant Kenton had a small Zippo lighter that had not been confiscated with his cigarettes when he surrendered, and Sam had a small sewing kit with two small needles bound tightly against a piece of cardboard by brown thread. When Lieutenant Beams rolled his eyes upon discovering that Sam had gone into combat with two love letters from his wife and a sewing kit, Sam retorted, "Better those letters than the fifteen 'Dear Johns' that you get every week. How many women are you currently engaged to?"

"More than one, less than a hundred," replied Beams. "It's a numbers game for after the war. What about the sewing kit? Thinking about self-suturing?"

"Not in this lifetime. My uniform's so worn out that I've had to sew the knees up twice. I thought it might be handy."

"Well, if you're interested in takin' up needlepoint in the stalag, maybe it will be."

"We ain't goin' to a stalag," Sam snapped. The lighthearted banter was over.

Sergeant Kenton had looked carefully through the woods for something approaching dry kindling, and after some searching had found an old fallen maple tree that had given up enough reasonably dry wood that he was able to start the fire with the use of only one of the just-in-case letters—his own letter, which was addressed to a brother in Chillicothe, Texas. He was grateful to have found the maple. Most of the nearby trees were pines, and the wood would have been smoky whether it was dried or not.

Surprising everyone, Sergeant Kenton also produced two pockets filled with small tubers that he claimed were the bulbs from dead soldier orchids. He placed them on a flat rock and slid the rock close to the fire. Every minute or so he would snake his hand in quickly to turn the tubers as he swore about the heat, and he repeated this process until the bulbs were brown and smoking.

"They'll taste just like potatoes—only different," he promised with a grin.

He was half-right. They weren't like potatoes, but they weren't bad to the hungry soldiers either. Although Lieutenant Beams was in great pain, he was so hungry that the small bulbs went down largely bereft of mastication. Kenton had also picked up a handful of acorns that he said came from a scrub oak. "I hear these kermes acorns ain't very tasty, but they've got some nutrition. If I had some more light, I'd go about gettin' some of them squirrels we seen."

"I thought acorns were poisonous," said Beams suspiciously. He picked one up and looked at it doubtfully.

"Naw," said Sam. "That's just what the pecan industry wants you to believe. They're okay to eat but it depends on the variety. They're like women...some are right sweet, and some are pretty damn bitter." Sam flicked the cap off an acorn, and carefully cracked it with a rock. He bit down on the meat of the nut, and then spit it out. "This is one of those. Too bitter. If I hadn't lost my helmet at the train station, I suppose we could have stewed some of these up though with one of

Bill's imaginary squirrels."

"Maybe I can get us some real chow tomorrow for breakfast, and it ain't gonna be nuts and squirrels. All I need is your sewing kit." Kenton grinned as he held his hand out for the kit. In response to Sam's puzzled look, he said, "You'll see."

Sergeant Kenton would say no more about breakfast, and instead set to work digging three shallow parallel trenches with his hands. Periodically, he would stoke the fire and then scrape the hot coals into the trenches with a rock. When he got the coals where he wanted them, Kenton covered them over with dirt and tamped it down lightly. While Kenton was preparing their beds for the night, Sam prepared a lean-to with the pine boughs.

The boughs were propped against a fallen pine tree, and when they were finished, the soldiers had a shelter that dramatically reduced the cold wind. As they lay huddled together with their feet toward the fire, and their bodies on the coal-warmed ground under the shelter, Beams asked, "What's our plan, sir?"

Sam had given this a great deal of thought since they pulled Beams under the boxcar and began a shambling run on the far side of the train down a spur line in the darkness. He found that a plan as such didn't really exist, but he said, "The Church is our ticket home, or our way to finding safe houses with families that'll take us in until our lines have passed us by—wherever that is."

"Lieutenant, what do you mean 'the Church?'" asked Sergeant Kenton.

"When Perkin and I took that R&R on the Adriatic coast over New Year's, part of that was work. His kind of work. Spook stuff. We were tasked with hauling a priest past German lines and into occupied territory. From

there, he was going to head for Rome when the snow
in the mountains allowed. I don't know all the details
about what Perk was doing, but this farmhouse that
we stayed at was part of an underground railway of the
Vatican's through the central mountains. We dropped
this priest off and picked up two Australian officers who
were working their way home." Sam blew his breath out
unconsciously as he wondered for the thousandth time
if Perkin was okay. "Damn, it's hard to believe, but that
was only three weeks ago."

There was more to the mission than that, Sam
knew, although he was truthful when he told his
comrades that he didn't know all the details. It was
Sam's deduction from the bits and pieces that he knew
that Father Patrick Riley, the priest in question, was
working for British intelligence in a scheme to capture
or turn a German-American intelligence officer named
Grossmann.

2115 Hours
Avezzano, Italy

Major Douglas Grossmann sat in the office chair
with his feet unceremoniously propped up on the
church's sole desk. He was beginning to hate this
assignment and if the priest wanted to kick him out for
either poor manners or questionable posture, well, that
was fine with him.

He shook his head at his weakness and lit another
cigarette. Grossmann smoked more when he was bored,
and there was no question that he was bored now. The
Abwehr major had been undercover for the better part
of the past month, and he had been sequestered in the
church's office for too many days now. Even worse, he
had been told that he wouldn't be moving for maybe

more than a month.

It was nearly unbearable. Grossmann tried to remember the British adage from the Great War and decided that it was "War was months of boredom punctuated by moments of sheer terror." He couldn't remember it exactly, but he had nothing better to do than to think about it, so he did until his thoughts strayed again.

Grossmann's war had generally been interesting. He was a German-American intelligence officer who had avoided the months of sheer terror on the Eastern Front, and had been posted in Paris and Rome for the majority of his service since the war began five years before. He had been able to do some things that sent his pulse racing, such as infiltrate the Fifth Army's headquarters, but there had been very little of the sheer terror part of the war for him. He could forgo the terror he reasoned, but a little excitement now would be welcome.

Grossmann enjoyed human companionship. He wasn't cut out for solitude. He particularly enjoyed female companionship, and if he had been a more sympathetic man, he might have felt a great deal of sympathy for his celibate host. As it was, he felt only the pain of his own loneliness, and he frequently thought about abandoning his mission to return to Rome and his lover, Antoniette Bernardi.

The thought of Antoniette led to a sigh, which was just like the thousand sighs that preceded it, an expression of longing, loneliness, and of deep intense anxiety. As he inhaled deeply of his cigarette, he sardonically reflected that a German soldier was supposed to be a superman and above such weaknesses, and yet, he thought, even Clark Kent pined for Lois Lane.

To an outsider, the source of his anxiety would not have seemed complex, yet it was to him. At its most fundamental level, Grossmann was not certain of his position with Antoniette. She worked for him, was a magnificent intelligence collector, and, was the most effortlessly deceptive person that he knew. He loved her deeply. No, he corrected himself. He was deeply infatuated with her, but when she kissed him, *he knew* that the moment and the emotion were real. The energy that was transferred from something as simple and dangerous as her kiss was numbing. Almost magical. His pulse quickened and he became nervous.

Yet, at another, more intellectual level, he suspected that not everything was as it seemed. Antoniette was playing him. He just didn't know for whom she was working, or whether she was just toying with him for her own amusement. Even if he was convinced that he was being played, and he wasn't, he was not convinced that he possessed the power to do anything about it. Maybe she wasn't on the job. Maybe he wasn't being toyed with...*maybe she really loves me*, he thought as his musings came full circle again.

In the few days that he had been at the undistinguished church in the southernmost part of the mountain town of Avezzano, Grossmann had been exiled to the church's office. A dark cold room with a single dirty window, and a sole lamp on the priest's desk. A musty-smelling folding cot, apparently donated to Catholic charity by Constantine's army countless centuries before, was his bed. The priest, Father Carlo, was a decent fellow who was full of zeal for the defeat of fascism and Nazism, but was nevertheless overly restrictive from Grossmann's point of view. Grossmann wasn't allowed out except to use the nearby bathroom, and he hadn't bathed since his arrival.

Parishioners who were part of the priest's network of confidants provided food and wine for Grossmann, and although it was meager fare due to rationing, it was always welcome. Grossmann had approached the priest that morning out of bored desperation and tactfully asked if it might not be better if he were moved to a private home to lessen the risk to the church. Alas, no, was the response. With another escaped prisoner of war unaccounted for, the priest felt that it wouldn't be right to put his flock at risk. Not for the first time, Grossmann regretted having killed the Australian captain. He had been very enjoyable company.

Grossmann thought frequently about Captain Tim Mullen and his death. Mullen was an Australian soldier who escaped from an Italian-run camp when Italy entered into the armistice with the Allies. He had made his way to the Vatican where he had been housed with other escapees in safe houses run by a senior Jesuit, Monsignor Hugh O'Flaherty—another man in this network opposed to the Nazis that Grossmann liked very much. Grossmann was posing then, and now, as a downed American pilot named Doug Peabody.

Grossmann met Mullen in a safe house just yards away from the Rome Gestapo headquarters, and the two had become friends while waiting for the opportunity to be moved out of Rome. Mullen was trying to get home to Australia; Grossmann was trying to discover the key terminals of the Vatican's underground railroad.

Just before their departure, the two men had been visited by Monsignor O'Flaherty, who entrusted them with Church information on the German program of genocide for the Jews of Europe. Grossmann and Mullen had been made to memorize the extermination camps and their locations, and they were instructed to carry the information to the American and Australian governments.

During their transit out of Rome, Mullen had

discussed O'Flaherty's directive with Grossmann, and the German intelligence officer had felt compelled to kill Captain Mullen. It was regrettable but inevitable— he would have had to kill Mullen at some point in his journey anyway. Just as he would have to kill the priest and anyone else along for the journey before making his way back to Rome.

Chapter Two

January 25, 1944
0630 Hours
1st Battalion HQ, Mount Trocchio, Italy

"Good morning, Lieutenant Ryan. How was the first day on the job? Get a good night's sleep?" Major Spaulding's fatigue undermined the intended cheerful tone.

"Not exactly, sir. It wasn't hard falling asleep, just staying that way. You know, sir, I've tried to learn something new every day that I've been in the army. Yesterday, I learned that an infantry company could consist of two guys." Ryan was ordinarily a confident man, but his first day on the line had left him a little unnerved. The last action of the unit to which he was now assigned had led to the death, wounding, or capture of nearly all its personnel. He had known, of course, that such things happened; he just didn't expect to encounter it on his first day in a combat zone.

"The good news is that the company will muster about twenty or so by the close of the day. Of course, the bad news is that's still less than fifteen percent manned. Cigarette?" Spaulding offered as he pulled a pack from his jacket pocket.

"No thank you, sir," Ryan said. "I smoke cigars and I try to limit myself to one a day. My girl back home says too many leaves my breath smelling like the cow lot."

Major Spaulding motioned to the lieutenant to join him at a small map table as he said, "That's why I've always been an advocate of women smoking. They don't mind your breath so much then, although I think a woman with a cigar or a chew is vulgar. Take a look at this."

Spaulding traced his finger along the map and said, "Normally, one of the S-2 eggheads or Cap'n Berger gives the orientation to new officers, but today you get me. So, here's your crash course on the geography of the battlefield, and the progress of the battle. You probably remember from your basic geography that the Italian peninsula runs north and south from the European continent into the Mediterranean Sea."

When Lieutenant Ryan nodded, Major Spaulding said, "That ain't quite right. It runs from the northwest to the southeast, and when people say 'north to Rome,' they ought to be sayin' 'northwest to Rome.' So, we can have a river like the Rapido come out of the mountains on a north-south axis and cut directly across our route to Rome. That leaves us on the east bank of the river, and the Krauts on the west. The Rapido comes down from some mountain peak about 5,000 feet above sea level and it drops to the Tyrrhenian Sea some twenty-five miles to the southwest of here. For it to drop 5,000 feet in that short of a distance, it has to move along right smartly, hence the name 'Rapido.' We found during our crossing that some guys who were competitive swimmers got washed hundreds of yards downstream while they only had to swim laterally some twenty yards. The other thing is that it's damn cold. More than a few good men were taken down by exposure this past week."

Spaulding poured himself and Lieutenant Ryan a cup of coffee as he continued, "We're in the opening of the Liri Valley, which runs all the way to Rome. The boys call it 'Death Valley,' but then, that's been the name of every valley so far in the Italian campaign. Overlookin' the valley is Monte Cassino, which means Cassino Mountain, and the town of Cassino lies at the base of the mountain to the east. Atop the mountain is the Abbey of Monte Cassino, which Perkin tells me has been around in one form or another since St. Benedict opened up a chicken stand here in the sixth century or so. Actually, what he told me was that Benedict tore down a pagan temple of Apollo and built his chicken stand there, and that there used to be a big sign on the mountain that said 'Eat at Benny's' but it got burned by Ostrogoths...or somethin' like that."

Seeing an uncomprehending look in Ryan's eyes, Spaulding coughed out a raspy laugh and said, "I'll tell you about Perk in a minute. So, where was I? Oh yeah, the abbey. It looks over the battlefield, and there's no doubt that the Krauts are sittin' up there fat and sassy watchin' us down here in Death Valley..."

"So, we're going to level the joint?" interrupted Ryan.

"I gather there's some debate goin' on about that now. One school of thought is what you just mentioned. Level the joint, as you said, and remove it as a Kraut sanctuary. You know, when in doubt, burn the abbey. The other school of thought, to which I and the illustrious Professor Berger hold, is that it won't make a lick of difference one way or the other. We reduce it to rubble and they still have the mountaintop to spit on us from, plus about a million new fighting positions in all the rubble we create. So what do we gain by it?"

Spaulding shrugged and answered his own question, "Probably not much other than it'll feel good to wipe the smugness off their faces for a while. I'd pay for that, but since the flyboys are almost certainly gonna bomb us by mistake, there's less fun in it for me than you might imagine. I don't know, Alex. I guess the bottom line is that if all other things are equal…well, I cain't see how it's in the interests of the Allies to destroy one of the oldest institutions of western civilization."

0645 Hours
Nine Miles Northwest of Terni, Italy

Sam yawned and stretched, and thought about rolling over and going back to sleep again. It had been a wonderful night's sleep, and he would later reflect that it had been the best night's sleep he'd had since learning they were going back on the line three weeks before.

It was a cold morning and he had used a pile of scratchy leaves for a pillow, but it hadn't rained overnight. Sergeant Kenton's buried coals had kept him warm and comfortable, and the lean-to had given the three soldiers a sense of security.

The fire had been allowed to die out overnight, and they had made a conscious decision that a solid night's sleep would have more benefits than posting a security watch. The three men fell instantly asleep, and their snores had been consumed by the natural nocturnal sounds of the forest. As Sam slowly awoke from his deep slumber, he could sense that the fire had been revived. More importantly, he thought he could smell chicken. He sat bolt upright, hitting his head on a pine bough, and looked around startled.

Sergeant Kenton grinned at him. He was kneeling next to the fire, which had been re-kindled, but was not blazing. His hands were red with blood and the large soldier had bits of feathers stuck to his uniform.

"Good mornin', sir!" Kenton said with a quiet, yet intense delight. He nodded toward Lieutenant Beams who was still sleeping.

Sam crawled over to the fire and looked at Sergeant Kenton with something approaching awe. The sergeant's bloody hands were moving rapidly between several maple skewers, each holding a large unrecognizable piece of what appeared to be chicken. Every few seconds, Kenton would turn a skewer, and Sam could see that the skin was being to crisp. His stomach growled loudly and Sergeant Kenton grinned even broader.

"Where in God's name did you get that?" Sam asked in an excited whisper.

"There was a farmhouse about a half mile back that we passed yesterday. This is their old rooster. I reckon that he might be a bit chewier than one of their hens, but I took what I could get."

"How'd you get him without waking up everybody?"

Kenton whispered back, "In '37, I rode the rails for a bit. Some of the hobos who did it for a livin' taught me a few things—like, you can catch a chicken with a worm on a hook easier than you can catch a fish. Once he gets a hook in his gullet, he can't make any noise. So I made a rig with your needle and thread, dug up some worms under a rotten log, and went fishin'. Or chickenin', I suppose. I hate to report though, sir, that I also broke into a toolshed and took a machete. It's not exactly a filet knife, but it worked."

Indeed, it had. Sam woke Beams up, and then took over the cooking responsibilities while Sergeant Kenton and Lieutenant Beams washed their hands in a nearby creek. Sam studied the woods while he waited. The impression of a densely forested wood was less so today than it had been the day before. Then, it had been overcast, which heightened their sense of isolation. Now, the sun was coming up and some of the light was filtering through to their campsite. If light could come in then smoke could trickle out, Sam thought—even with the hard wood that they were burning.

As the other two soldiers returned, Sam propped the chicken skewers against a rock, and pushed a large mound of dirt over the fire. It smoked more intensely while he was burying it, but then the smoke was quickly contained.

The smile faded from Sergeant Kenton's face. "You afraid of us bein' seen, sir?" When Sam nodded, Kenton said, "Yeah, maybe my little farmhouse raid wasn't such a good idea. We'll need to be careful moving in light like this. Maybe we ought to stay here for the day, and move out tonight."

"Screw that." Beams spoke for the first time. The swelling on his face was even pronounced, and the bruises looked more severe in the brighter light. His speech seemed even worse as he painfully mumbled, "I was gonna die if I had to eat acorns. I know you country boys say they're safe, but I don't have the gums for them any more. I needed some real food, but we gotta keep movin' away from the station or we'll eventually be found."

The chicken was divided into equal parts while Sam washed up, and when he came back to the campsite, he found to his delight that he had a thigh, a drumstick, back, and neck waiting for him. Even though the rooster was stringy and was served without salt or other seasonings, it tasted wonderful to Sam.

The three soldiers devoured their chicken, although Lieutenant Beams could only manage by tearing small pieces of chicken from the bone with his fingers and pushing them to his remaining teeth in the back of his mouth. He later confessed to Sam that he nearly gave up on the chicken, it being so painful to eat, but his hunger trumped the pain.

0645 Hours
1st Battalion HQ, Mount Trocchio, Italy

"Sir?" The briefing had largely run its course, and while Lieutenant Ryan had a thousand questions on his mind, he wanted to follow up on something the battalion commander said. "What's the story with Captain Berger?"

Major Spaulding was in the process of stuffing a wad of tobacco into his cheek. When he got it tamped into place, he said, "Perkin's my best friend. He's simultaneously my smartest officer, and my dumbest. There's no one who can think through a problem like the Professor—he has a Ph.D., you know—but the problem is that when it comes to himself, his judgment can sometimes be as sharp as a bowl of pudding. Assuming that he doesn't die in the clearin' station and he's back here in a couple days, I plan to make him the acting CO of Able Company until division gets me a qualified captain or first lieutenant."

"If you don't mind me asking, sir, why acting?"

"I need him at battalion." Spaulding was tempted to say that he was also reserving the billet for Lieutenant Taft, but he didn't want to go into an explanation why he believed that Sam had escaped. "He has significant combat experience, is a good tactical officer, and he may be the bravest man I know, all of which make him an ideal company commander, but I also need good staff officers who have those attributes as well."

"Yes, sir. When are we going to get replacements?"

"There should be a trickle of men over the next couple of days, but there aren't going to be many until we're off the line for refit. And before you ask, I don't know when that will be. In the meantime, we have requirements that we have to fulfill, including patrolling along the river. If that means you, me, and Kulis patrolling, well, so be it."

"Yes, sir. Speaking of Corporal Kulis, is there a way to get him another stripe? I asked around and he's got a solid reputation." The reputation that he had heard was of a cold-hearted killer, but Ryan wasn't one for rumors. "Unless we get NCOs in with combat experience, we'll need him as a squad leader, I would think."

Spaulding smiled. "A week ago, he was a PFC. Now you wanna make him a sergeant? I think he's about as promising a soldier as I've ever seen, but in cased you haven't noticed, he's awfully young. I ain't gonna question the army about how old he is, but if they come back next week and tell me he's underaged, I wouldn't be surprised. So, how about we use him as an acting squad leader as soon as we get a squad formed, and then we'll see. If he does well, we'll see about another stripe. And if we get some experienced NCOs, he stays where he is."

"Yes, sir. What do you want me to do in the meantime?"

"Three things. First, I'd like for you to become intimately familiar with the geography here along the river. Second, I want you to do the same to the mountain ridges northeast of Cassino. Kulis can help you with both of those. Finally, I'd also like for you to draw a jeep and introduce yourself to Cap'n Berger in the clearing station in Mignano. I'm sure he's miserable down there. Do that today."

0815 Hours
Clearing Station, 111th Medical Battalion,
Mignano, Italy

Perkin sat in silence on the edge of his cot. He was awaiting Doctor Poynter's verdict on his future, and even if he'd had a friend at the clearing station, he was so shocked by what he'd seen in his short time there that he didn't much feel like conversation.

Most of the worst cases in the clearing station had been transferred to the evacuation hospital over the past twenty-four hours. The trickle that began early on the night of the assault had quickly become a deluge but had since subsided. A few new cases continued to come in but they were mostly victims of land mines or artillery bursts, or rarely, self-inflicted wounds. The wounded of the battle were either patched up and released back to their units, or sent farther to the rear.

Perkin had been lucid for more than a day, and he couldn't wait to leave the facility and get back to the battalion—or anywhere else for that matter. He had been witness to the heroic efforts of the five doctors and the handful of nurses and medics who had worked almost without sleep since the battle began five days before. The wounds that they treated were shocking, and they frequently could do little more than stabilize the most seriously wounded before sending them onwards to a hospital. Nevertheless, significant surgeries were taking place, and on a short walk to the latrine the day before, Perkin had passed a cave near the clearing station tent that had been marked "Parts." It was a temporary repository for amputated legs and arms. Both the imagery and the smell were appalling and Perkin couldn't leave the area quickly enough.

Perkin was still in deep pain. He was also incredibly

stiff. His numerous stitches were beginning to pull and itch as he moved, but the doctor had told him that it was unlikely he would require further surgery. Penicillin and rest were all he required he was told again, with the addition this time of therapy.

He was unsure what would happen next. He should have been sent to the Fifth Army evacuation hospital in Caserta, but the casualties had been so severe on the Gustav Line that the evacuation hospital was full. In a moment of personal candor, he recognized that he wasn't fit to return to duty, but he knew he couldn't stay here.

"Good morning, Captain!" Doctor Poynter was cheerful as he walked up to Perkin. He'd been able to grab six hours sleep the night before on an empty cot.

"Mornin', Doc, how are you?" Perkin was unsure of Doctor Poynter's rank as he didn't seem to be wearing any insignia under his lab coat, but he felt that unless any army doctor had white hair he was safe in going with the more informal salutation. Poynter not only did not have white hair, Perkin was unsure whether the youthful doctor had yet to begin shaving.

"Swell. Wonderful morning. So, the nurse tells me that your fever is gone, you've gotten plenty of rest, and that your bowels and bladder are functioning in accordance with army regulations."

Perkin grinned. "Is that all that's required? If so, I'm ready to return to the front."

Poynter laughed back at the young captain. "Isn't this the front? I've been telling everyone back home that's where I am. How disappointing. Well, let's see now. Lift your right arm over your head."

Perkin tried but couldn't. His right side was too stiff.

The doctor watched Perkin wince, and said, "The

nurse over yonder told me you were itching to get back and that you asked her to help."

"No, doc. I told her my back itched and then I asked her to help. I could have scratched it myself, but she was lookin' a little lonely and I thought she might enjoy it." Despite his understanding with himself that he shouldn't return to duty, Perkin had indeed asked for the nurse's help in getting out of the clearing station.

"Oh, guess I misunderstood. Lift your left arm over your head," Poynter ordered.

Perkin tried his left arm, but likewise failed.

"That's about what I thought. Look, I don't think that there's any permanent damage but since you can't even wipe your own butt, let alone carry a weapon or a field pack, I can hardly sign off on your return to full duty. You've got some slight muscle damage with both your shoulder and abdomen injuries. It's more extensive over your left shoulder. Now, I would think you'll get your full range of motion back, but that will require therapy. At a minimum, we'll have to make sure that you stretch and exercise as much as possible without pushing too hard. I think you'll need supervision, and that's the trick…you need professional help but we can't do it here. Until beds free up, I can't send you to Echelon 3 care in Caserta, and if I send you to Echelon 4 in North Africa, or even England or North America, there's a one percent chance at best you'll come back to the 36th. That's just a fact, and unfortunately for you, my friend, these aren't million dollar wounds. You'll be healed up and likely sent to another division in Europe or possibly the Pacific. Shoot, you might end up in this new Pentagon they've built."

Perkin was stunned. His wounds couldn't possibly send him home. In his mind, Bill Spaulding's loss of a fingertip was far more traumatic. It was unthinkable that he would leave the division until he knew what had happened to Sam.

1145 Hours
Pieta, Italy

The transaction for the sheep rental had taken longer than Lieutenant Ryan had expected, but he'd had little experience in Italian price-setting negotiations. His first experience at haggling with the Italian sheepherder had been edifying, and although he haggled for nearly half an hour, he was not convinced that he had made a good deal.

There had been some difficulty in finding an Italian farmer who was willing to part with any or all of his stock, particularly under the unusual circumstances of a short-term lease. Sale prices had been going up in real terms for the first time in years since the Allied army had arrived in the Liri Valley. The British and Americans paid for the livestock whereas the Germans simply confiscated the sheep and cattle of the unfortunate farmers. Consequently, the Italian farmers and sheepherders had decided that as the Americans would be on the banks of the Rapido for months to come, prices would continue to rise. No one wanted to miss out on the good days of the war, they had been a long time in coming.

Ryan was persistent, however, and after Kulis drove the lieutenant and an interpreter to a couple of farms in the valley, he found a smallholder willing to contemplate the temporary release of his stock to the American. Ryan, while intimately familiar with livestock and appreciative of its relative value, was Anglo-Irish to his core. He was unprepared for Latin negotiations.

His first hurdle was the issue of how many sheep to rent. Ryan wanted as many sheep as he could manage, but when he explained what he wanted them for, the sheep's owner balked. It was an award-winning flock after all. Certainly the finest between Taranto and Rome, and had not the smallholder raised each one by hand from baby lambs?

Ryan had a vague notion that Taranto was somewhere distant, but he was under no illusions about the quality of the flock. He was unimpressed with the dirty thin animals and he thought he saw bluetongue in several of the ewes. They were fine for his needs, though, even if they had blue tongues and not blue ribbons.

The farmer began with his price, which would have been outlandish for an equivalent-sized herd of cattle. Ryan shook his head and an offer was made and refused. Another offer followed with a counter-offer proffered by the shepherd. It was still too high. Several times, the negotiations broke down altogether, and had the smallholder been an American, Ryan likely would have punched him on general principle. He hated arm-waving theatrics.

Ryan grew exasperated but increased his offer. The shepherd was on the verge of refusing again, but money finally exchanged hands and the deal for the sheep was struck, along with a guaranteed delivery time of 0600 hours. Although Ryan was unaware of the fact, the money exchange was facilitated by a heavily armed Kulis who glared at the sheepherder while he incessantly cocked and uncocked a Colt .45.

1345 Hours
Eleven Miles Northwest of Terni, Italy

Progress had been slow since leaving the small

forest. Lieutenant Beams could only walk for short distances before requiring help or resting. His knee buckled several times, and he slipped and fell hard while walking up a gravelly hill. Although Beams protested, Sam and Sergeant Kenton took turns helping the wounded soldier.

They had made the decision to leave the forest. Concern that an angry farmer might call a constable over his missing rooster or track Sergeant Kenton's footprints to the woods prompted a quick cleanup of their camp and a hasty departure. The boughs that they had used as shelter were dispersed through the woods, and leaves had been kicked over their campsite. Sam knew that it would not pass close inspection, but he hoped that perhaps their cleanup had been good enough to avoid attracting attention.

They had no plan other than to keep moving away from the train station in Terni, although the town's name and location were unknown to them. Eventually, Sam told his companions, they would have to seek help from the Italians, but he wanted to put enough distance between themselves and their point of escape that perhaps the local populace would be unaware of the incident. Sam believed instinctively that the Italians would be sympathetic to their plight, but he didn't want to test their sympathy against a reward for their capture.

They had passed a few small farms but didn't stop. Sam's eyes roamed over the stone houses with thin smoke coming from chimneys and saw no vehicles or draft horses, and only small feedlots with very few animals. Either the fascists or the Germans had confiscated virtually everything. Come spring, the Italian farmers would be hard pressed to plant their farms and they would be in dire need of assistance next year—if they weren't already.

Even in their relatively remote area of the peninsula, the war was present. Heavy bombing to their southeast suggested that the train station that they had escaped was being struck again. Contrails were visible in the cold clear air and distant dark puffs of smoke high in the sky indicated that Axis flak batteries were defending the switching yard. The noise rumbled through the hills and mountains of Italy, and the soldiers stopped and watched. Months ago such a battle would have held their attention endlessly, but they watched for only a minute before turning their backs to the giant plume of smoke and dust, and to the angry puffs of smoke in the sky. They had seen it all before, and so they kept moving.

1345 Hours
Avezzano, Italy

"Father, you are a wonderful host, but I'm going stir-crazy." Seeing that the Italian priest didn't understand, Major Grossmann tried a different tack. "We also call it cabin fever…the sense of going crazy because you can't get outside and walk around. See daylight. Smell fresh air. Go for a walk."

Father Carlo sympathetically looked at the man he knew as Doug Peabody. He gave a very Italian shrug and asked, "Doug, my friend, you think that this office is like a prison cell, and you wish to leave?"

"Leave? No. We leave when the snows have melted for us to walk the mountain ridge out of here. But get outside? Absolutely. I don't know if I can handle another day," Grossmann said truthfully.

"Would you not be imprisoned much longer if you were caught by the occupiers?"

Is there no one in this damn country that speaks plainly?

Grossmann thought. Instead of voicing his displeasure, and rather than answer the priest's question directly, Grossmann said, "My Italian is nearly flawless. You said so yourself. I'm even dreaming in Italian. I won't make a mistake. Look, Monsignor O'Flaherty trusted me in Rome to run errands. To walk around unescorted. Why can't you?"

"When I become a monsignor, maybe I'll have a different outlook on things. A monsignor..." He sighed, "*Allora*. Anyway, I have a congregation to tend to, he doesn't. And you should forget his name, Douglas. It puts a good man...no...a great man, in jeopardy." The priest smiled again sympathetically. "Here, have one of my cigarettes, and we'll talk no more about it today."

1540 Hours
Clearing Station, 111th Medical Battalion,
Mignano, Italy

Perkin stiffly walked another lap around the encampment, being careful to avoid the cave marked "Parts." There were several large tents that made up the clearing station, and there were several other tents and Italian buildings that were being used by various aspects of the 36th Division headquarters.

There was really nothing interesting to see from Perkin's perspective, and he had yet to meet anyone interesting that he didn't already know. He had already walked by and said hello to all of the wounded soldiers that he knew who remained at the clearing station, but they had been informed that they were being moved soon as well.

Some of the soldiers that he knew from the regiment were being moved to newly-available beds in the hospital in Caserta, while others were being sent back to their units. Those that were going onward to the hospital down south were worse off than Perkin, and those that were going back to their units were in better shape. He felt like he was in a living purgatory.

Another conversation with Dr. Poynter had left him with the impression that he would eventually be sent back to North Africa or maybe even to the States for rehabilitation. It would not happen, he vowed to himself. He had heard many stories of soldiers checking themselves out of hospitals and returning to their units, and that was what he was prepared to do. He would see about taking leave and then head to the mountains to see about finding Sam.

Perkin rounded a small bend in the path that he was walking, and as he saw two men walking toward him, his face broke out in a wide smile. Finally, he knew someone worth talking to.

"Corporal Kulis!"

"Hey, sir!" The smile on the face of the young rifleman was just as wide. "You're looking good. Last time I seen you, you weren't moving so well. Hey, Cap'n, let me introduce you to Lieutenant Ryan. Lieutenant, this is Cap'n Berger."

Perkin looked at the squat muscular officer, and saw with some amusement that the lieutenant was debating whether to salute the man before him in a bathrobe and slippers. As returning the salute would be painful if not impossible, Perkin preempted the younger man by cautiously sticking out his hand.

"Lieutenant, nice to meet you. If you have Eddie with you, I assume that means that you're in 1st Battalion. Would that be a fair guess?"

As he shook Perkin's hand, Ryan said, "Nice to meet you as well. Yes, sir. Until your return or until we get some replacements, I'm the sole officer in Able

Company. And you're looking at pretty much the entirety of your command as it stands right now."

Perkin got a delighted look on his face and he turned excitedly to Kulis, "Eddie, am I getting Able Company?"

The teenager laughed and said, "Yes, sir. I reckon you've been tolt that at least twice. But you had a pretty high fever at the time. I'll leave it to Major Spaulding to give you the details. I understand that he wants you to come back to the battalion staff eventually, but I'm sure you can work out the timin' with him."

"Goddamn, that's the best news I've heard in ages!" Then as a thought occurred to him, Perkin's face fell.

"What's the matter, Cap'n?" Corporal Kulis was struck by the sudden change in demeanor. Captain Berger suddenly looked ten years older.

"The doc here is sayin' that they're gonna ship me to North Africa or back home for rehabilitation. If that happens, it's unlikely that I'll come back to the Gun Club and I may not be able to help Bear out."

Lieutenant Ryan looked puzzled for a moment, and then asked, "They can't do the rehabilitation here? In Italy?"

Perkin shook his head. "No. The inn's full here. There aren't the beds or the doctors. My doc told me that one in six beds at the military hospitals in Italy is taken up by a gonorrhea patient. Can you believe that? Some dogface gets the clap, and I get shipped out 'cause there ain't room for me. The kicker is that my wounds aren't even that serious. They just need to help me recover a full range of motion in my arms. I don't see any solution other than goin' AWOL and headin' back to the line."

Corporal Kulis thought furiously for a second. He didn't want Captain Berger leaving the division, and he certainly didn't relish the thought of being perhaps the only combat veteran in the company. Then the scarred young soldier smiled and said, "Let's not worry about this now, sir. What's the name of your doctor, by the way?"

1715 Hours
Twelve Miles Northwest of Terni, Italy

The slow and easy movement through the gentle rolling hills to the northwest of Terni had come to an end. The geography hadn't changed as much as the demographics. Late in the afternoon, Sam's party came across the first people they had seen for the entire day.

They had been walking through a long gully that gave them a degree of cover and a bit of protection from the wind when the gully sloped up to a lip and ended. Sergeant Kenton climbed the short distance to the rim of the gully, and laying on his belly, peered into the distance.

"We got some kind of activity here. No military that I can see, just some industrial stuff," he called down to Sam.

Sam crawled up the slope and lay in the brown winter grass next to Sergeant Kenton. The light was dying quickly, faster than Sam thought possible, but he could make out a handful of men standing next to an antiquated steam shovel. The men appeared to have wrapped up the workday and were preparing to go to home. There was no sign of an incoming shift.

The "industrial stuff" that Sergeant Kenton spoke of consisted of several dirty buildings, including what looked to Sam to be a stable. The ground to the south of the buildings had been excavated but was open country on the far side of the mine, which is what the site appeared to be to Sam. One thing that confused him, though, was a collection of huge upright cylinders spread throughout the excavated land. It was unlike anything that Sam had seen before at a mine.

Sam motioned to Kenton and they slid to the floor of the gully where they found Lieutenant Beams taking a nap. Sergeant Kenton looked at Sam and asked, "Do you wanna just stay here for the night, sir?"

Sam had been thinking about that since he climbed to the edge of the gully. There had been lights emerging to either side of the mining operation suggesting that there were villages to the north and the south of their path. So unless they were prepared to enter a village, they'd have to double back on their track and do a wide sweep around the little towns. On the one hand, as they didn't know where they were and didn't have a destination, why not double back a little bit? On the other hand, Sam desperately wanted to put more distance, a lot of it, between themselves and the train station.

"No. I want to give them some time to clear the area, then scoot through to the other side. A half mile or so beyond and we can call it a day. Maybe we'll come across a barn or shed that we can occupy for the night."

Lieutenant Beams had opened his eyes when the discussion began and asked, "What do we have here, Sam?"

"A small mine, I think. It looks like a little lignite mine that I saw while hunting whitetail over in Zavala County."

"Oh." Beams thought for a moment and lisped, "Three questions."

"Shoot."

"First, what the hell's lignite?"

"Coal," Sam replied.

"I thought coal came from mountains like in West Virginia."

"Well, I don't claim to be an expert about coal mining, but the one I saw in Zavala was a surface mine, which looked a lot like this operation."

"Oh. Okay, that leads me to my second question. Where the hell's Zavala County?"

Sam smiled. "It's between San Antonio and Old Mexico to the southwest. What's your third question?"

"With a name like Zavala, why weren't you hunting brown tail?" Beams laughed an odd laugh that seemed to barely squeeze through his scabbed and swollen lips. The pain didn't dampen his amusement, and for the first time since the escape, Beams seemed a little more like his old self.

Sam smiled at the joke, but said nothing as he helped Beams to his feet. He had made the decision to cross the quarter-mile site, and he wanted to look it over again and imagine a path before it was completely dark.

1800 Hours
Near Dunarobba, Italy

The rapid darkness that Sam had witnessed was the end of the day coinciding with the first partial solar eclipse of the year. Had he known of the eclipse, it would have meant little to Sam but the new moon that accompanied the event lent no light to their crossing of the mine site. It occurred to Sam that there might be abrupt drop-offs in the terrain or even mine shafts, although he saw no indication of such things, and they walked slowly using a long stick as their guide.

Their movement, while slow, still advanced them across the open mine where broken pieces of coal crunched under their feet—despite considerable efforts to be quiet. Several times Sam stopped the small party as he listened to the night sounds, but he heard nothing of concern.

They had traversed nearly half the distance across the mine site when Sam's walking stick hit something hard. Straining his eyes in the darkness, Sam realized that they had run into one of the strange cylinders that dotted the site.

Sam tentatively reached out and touched it. The cylinder was cold and hard, and felt more like stone than concrete or metal. The surface was covered with coal dust, and Sam could feel long vertical ridges that seemed somehow familiar. As the party moved around the large stone, it struck Sam that he felt like he was walking around a large tree. He turned back and touched the surface again. It felt exactly like a stone tree.

Sam grinned in the darkness as he figured out the mystery of the cylinders, and he whispered to his companions, "Do you know what this is?"

"I have no idea, Bear," Beams said.

"What about you, Bill? Any thoughts?" Sam asked of Sergeant Kenton.

"I don't know, sir. Something like Stonehenge, maybe?"

"I don't think so. I think it's the remains of a petrified forest. Probably was buried here, and the miners uncovered it." Sam touched the ridges again for confirmation.

"Well, I'll be goddamned. I read about the one in Arizona in a newspaper. The scientists said that it was millions of years old, even though my grandma Kenton tells me the earth is only about 6,000. Those scientists are goin' straight to hell accordin' to her. I thought I might go see it some time. I wish it was light now, I'd save myself the trip," Kenton said wistfully.

"I seen one in Mississippi in '25. Dad took me and Perk on a trip back east and we went there after stoppin' at Vicksburg. Mississippi's a damn muggy place." Sam had a momentary pang of anxiety about his cousin, and shaking his head, he said, "Let's go."

It was only ten minutes to the end of the site, and as they passed the low building that Sam had identified as stables, he smelled the horses. It was a deep rich respectable smell to Sam and he surmised that the coal mine wasn't modernized. It was likely that the horses pulled wagons of coal to a railhead somewhere nearby, although he hadn't heard any trains all day. Then again, he thought, as he put the pieces of the day together, perhaps the bombings that they'd seen earlier in the day had brought a stop to all rail traffic in that part of Italy.

The smell of the horses wasn't lost on the others either. Sergeant Kenton grabbed Sam's arm and whispered in the dark, "Should we take some horses? We could be miles away by morning."

Sam shook his head emphatically in the dark—stealing horses simply wasn't in the realm of his being. If there was an old Model A Ford he could take that could get him home quicker, he wouldn't have hesitated for long, but a horse was another matter. Besides, he knew the coalmine wouldn't have anything other than slow workhorses, if it even had any of those left. It might have just had mules, and Sam didn't want to take the risk to find out. He didn't respect mules at all.

"Naw. I can't take someone's horses. Besides, they ain't gonna have cow ponies or quarter horses. Let's keep moving," Sam said.

"What's a cow pony?" a deep Italian voice said in English from four feet away as a light on the side of the stables came on and illuminated the three American soldiers.

1830 Hours
Near Dunarobba, Italy

Their interrogator was a tall thin man in a gray overcoat. He wore a crumpled black hat over white hair and he wore a thick white mustache, although he didn't strike Sam as being old enough to warrant the white hair.

The Italian looked the Americans over closely, and then walked up to Sam and bowed his head slightly. "Edgardo Bazzini. Just like the president of the Roma Football Club, except no relation, thank God. That man is an idiot and a disgrace to football." Bazzini seemed unperturbed by the sight of three American soldiers, two of whom were very large men.

"Pleased to make your acquaintance," Sam said reflexively as he shook hands with Bazzini. Looking to see if there were more people in the shadows, Sam introduced himself and his companions.

After introductions were concluded, and Bazzini had shaken everyone's hand with vigorous pumps up and down, he said, "I saw you earlier and thought that I would wait to see what you wanted. I gather you don't want my horses, which is good, because the Germans have only left me with two. I think that you are Americans, not English, yes?"

"Yes, sir, we are," Sam answered.

"You smell worse than Americans normally do, but not as bad as the English. Are you from the landings at Nettuno? Have you driven the occupiers back this far?" asked Bazzini with keen interest.

"I'm sorry, sir. I don't know what you're talking about. What's Nettuno?" Sam asked.

"It's a town south of Rome on the water. The BBC says that American and British troops landed at Nettuno and Anzio three days ago. I thought you had come from there."

"No. We were taken prisoner at Cassino, and we escaped." Sam started to say more about their escape, but figured there was no sense in offering up information.

"Oh." Bazzini sounded disappointed. "I was hoping that you being here meant that Rome had been liberated. Where are you going?"

"Sir, I don't rightly know. We don't even know where we are. We were just moving towards the coast. Are we close to Rome?" Sam asked.

Bazzini shrugged and said, "Yes and not. It's close in peacetime. No so close now. Maybe...ninety kilometers to the south. It's far enough if that's your destination. And in the wrong direction."

"Wow. We're a lot farther north than I thought. We escaped from a train station to the southeast of here." Lieutenant Beams spoke for the first time.

Bazzini stared at Beams and asked, "What happened to your face? Were you attacked by a dog?" Without waiting for an answer, he said, "That was probably the Terni station. The rail yard was destroyed this morning. By your people. You were probably on the way to Dulag 226. It's a German camp for prisoners. Does anyone have a cigarette?" When the Americans shook their heads, Bazzini shook his head sadly and said, "No tobacco. No coffee. No sugar if we had coffee. It's like the Depression, but worse."

"Mr. Bazzini, where'd you learn to speak English?" Sam felt it was impolite to ask too many questions, but he was puzzled by this Italian who spoke very under-standable English.

"Dallas," Bazzini said proudly.

"You lived in Texas?" Sam asked with delight.

"Dallas isn't in Texas, it's in Pennsylvania. No so

far from Shavertown. I'm a mining engineer, or I used to be. More of a manager now. When I was young, I went to the States and learned anthracite mining in America. Too many Huns and Polacks in Pennsylvania. And now, too many Huns in Italy." Bazzini pointed to a distant building that was next to a road on the north side of the mine site. "I have a German civilian who, *come si dice*, uh, oversees my operation. He comes in twice a month to check on my production, and stays in a room over there. He's probably drunk already. Germans drink quite a bit you know."

"That doesn't surprise me," Sam said with an inward grin as he imagined Perkin talking to this unusual Italian. "Do we need to be moving on? Are we putting you at risk by being here, Mr. Bazzini?"

"From him? No. Tomorrow he will wake up hung over, and demand that I work faster, while he threatens to confiscate my remaining horses and my steam shovel. None of which he will do, because the Germans need my lignite. This is my mine, and the Germans take my entire output for their factories and camps in Italy."

"Oh." Sam couldn't think of anything else to say.

"So, don't worry about him. Or about me. Are you hungry? My wife will have *ribollita* tonight, I am sure."

2100 Hours
Near Dunarobba, Italy

Ribollita, as it turned out, was on the menu, and was an amazing treat for the starving soldiers. Bazzini described it as "peasant food, bread soup," but it was a meal fit for a king in Sam's opinion.

Mrs. Bazzini appeared much older than her husband did, and while she was much shorter than Mr. Bazzini, Maria Bazzini also had white hair and was very thin.

She had gasped when the three Americans walked into their stone house, but after a rapid-fire exchange in Italian with her husband, she worked hard to make their guests feel at home.

Through her dark eyes, she watched with some amusement as the Americans drank glass after glass of that evening's milking, and the amusement was replaced by pride as her ribollita was consumed with great praise. Neither she nor Bazzini ate any of the soup, but instead simply shared a small piece of hard white cheese that was kept in a wire basket and hung from a ceiling pulley by a rope. No amount of argument by Sam and the others would change their minds. The Bazzini dinner was for the guests, and that was that.

As the soldiers began their meal, Mrs. Bazzini left the dining room and the Americans could hear water running. When Sam looked quizzically at Mr. Bazzini, the Italian explained that his wife was running a bath for the first of the soldiers.

"I am an engineer. I designed and built my own heating system for this house, powered by coal, of course, and I have a coal-fired water heater. It is an amazing thing, and I take it with me every time I move to a new mine. It's English, of course. They are a mean little people, but they understand coal."

Sergeant Kenton was the first to bathe, and when he returned to the sitting room, he was clean, freshly shaved, and had a huge grin on his face. "I haven't felt this good for weeks," he exclaimed to a beaming Mrs. Bazzini.

Lieutenant Beams went next, and when he was finished with his bath, Mrs. Bazzini gave him two cloves to suck on. The cloves, she explained through her husband, would help with the pain of his gums and missing teeth.

Sam was the last to bathe, and like Sergeant Kenton, he hadn't felt that good for some time. The bath was also the only time that Sam had been by himself since before the river assault. He had thought about the attack on the Gustav Line many times since then, but for the first time since surrendering, he questioned his actions that morning. Not that Sam cared much about what the army thought of him, but he cared deeply about Margaret's opinion. Would she think him a coward for surrendering? Would she be ashamed? He had no way of knowing. Then he started thinking about Perkin. The last news that he had of his cousin was that he'd be all right—if he didn't bleed out first.

It occurred to Sam as he scrubbed his body with lye soap that when he was with Beams and Kenton that he didn't have the luxury of self-doubt and pity—there was no time for anxiety because he was always focused on keeping the others moving and thinking about the next step. It also occurred to Sam that they had been very fortunate with meeting the Bazzinis. They could have run into the German overseer just as easily. Then he would not be taking a steaming hot bath, he was sure.

Chapter Three

January 26, 1944
0600 Hours
East Bank, Rapido River, Italy

The two men moved slowly on a parallel path roughly 300 yards away from the Rapido River. The sheep had a tendency to head toward the water, which was not in the interests of the two men, and from time to time one of the soldiers would have to run forward and drive the animals away from the river.

Corporal Kulis and Lieutenant Ryan were dressed in a manner closely mimicking the sheeperder from yesterday: wool hats, black overcoats, and boots. Under the overcoats, they wore their uniforms—not because they were afraid of being caught out of uniform, but for the simple reason that they had limited means with which to acquire a more convincing disguise.

Both men carried long sticks, which they used to push and prod the reluctant animals. Although Kulis and Ryan both came from farming backgrounds, neither possessed any experience with herding sheep, and they frequently commented that they preferred working with cattle. Both whistled at the fifteen sheep from time to time, and Corporal Kulis tried calling out, "Hup! Hup!

Hup, y'all! Hup!" with no appreciable success.

Despite the animals not going exactly where they wanted them to go, the evolution had been so far worthwhile. It was a crash course in the geography of the battlefield and was far superior to the maps, aerial photographs, and sand tables that Ryan had reviewed in the regimental headquarters.

The idea to use the sheep as minesweepers had been his, and Ryan was relieved when Captain Berger had grinned delightedly at the plan when briefed the afternoon before. The only proviso of the company commander had been to stay farther than 150 yards out from the river, and to be prepared to drop everything and run when they were shot at. Major Spaulding had been more skeptical of the plan, but as he had been ordered by regiment to conduct a patrol, he grudgingly gave his approval. Spaulding moved the minimum standoff distance back to 250 yards, and generously offered to pay for the sheep from battalion funds.

The scene along the river that Lieutenant Ryan took in was one of utter devastation. Tens of thousands of artillery rounds had been fired at targets on both banks of the icy river and huge craters indicated where scores of rounds had impacted the very same spot. There was very little living vegetation on the east bank where they drove their small flock of sheep—only lifeless stumps and branches remained of ancient olive groves and vineyards.

Twice, the soldiers passed shattered wood boats covered in dried blood. Ryan didn't want to stare at the wreckage, nor reflect on what might have happened, yet he found himself unable not to look in their direction. Two minutes later, he came across what he thought was the remains of a decapitated head, but he could not bring himself to look at it closely.

"Come on, sir. We need to be nonchalant about this."

Ryan looked over at his companion with some surprise. "Nonchalant?"

"Yes, sir. It means that we have to act casual." Kulis's solicitousness changed quickly. "Keep movin', ya damn fuckin' sheep! Goddamn, I hate these things!"

The whole exchange tickled Ryan, who knew the meaning of nonchalant but couldn't recall it ever being used in a conversation. Putting the wreckage and the head behind him, he asked, "What exactly did Captain Berger mean when he said he needed to be here to help Bear? That's his cousin, Lieutenant Taft, isn't it?"

"Yes, sir. That's Lieutenant Taft." Kulis understood the gist of the question, but didn't offer any further information.

"Okay. So...how can he help Lieutenant Taft? I thought he was captured at the river."

"He was, sir. Just over there and a few hundred yards inland, in fact." Kulis nodded with his head toward the river where the 1st Battalion had been destroyed trying to cross. "Sir, with all due respect, Captain Berger is the smartest man in the division, and he's also an excellent intelligence officer. If he believes that he can help Lieutenant Bear, maybe we should just leave it at that."

0610 Hours
One Mile West of Dunarobba, Italy

They had been on the move for more than an hour. Mrs. Bazzini had awakened Sam at 0430, and according to a plan they had agreed on the night before, the soldiers were on the move half an hour later.

Mr. Bazzini had explained to Sam that they needed to get away from the mine before daylight. He wasn't

overly concerned about the German overseer, but he
didn't want his workers seeing them. Some of the
workers might be on the fascist state payroll or even
working for the Germans.

Mrs. Bazzini made a simple breakfast of ham and
soft-boiled eggs with bread and olive oil. There was no
coffee, not even the ersatz coffee that Sam had drunk in
other places in Italy, but there was fresh milk. Although
it was simple, it was still delicious and enjoyable even if
Sam scandalized Mrs. Bazzini by sprinkling a pinch of
salt on his bread—he had never adjusted to the bland
Italian loaves. Once again, the Bazzinis ate next to
nothing despite repeated requests from the Americans
to join them.

When the Americans left that morning, each
soldier had a rolled blanket in his possession—Sam's
was powder blue, Beams' was lime green, and Kenton's
was a red and green-checked affair. They also were sent
with three hard-boiled eggs each, and Sergeant Kenton
carried a small gunnysack with what remained of the
ham and the bread. It was not much for three men,
but it was nearly all the food in the Bazzini larder. As
delightful as their small store of food, their clothes had
been cleaned and dried overnight next to the fire and on
a coal-burning stove. Mrs. Bazzini had been unable to
get all the stains out of the uniforms, but they felt clean,
which was an unexpected treat, and smelled infinitely
better. Sam had a roadmap marked as coming from the
Italian State Tourism Office, and each man now carried
a small knife. Unfortunately, Mr. Bazzini had no guns
to give away. The fascists had confiscated all personal
firearms, he explained.

Their goal was to move west past the village of
Dunarobba into a lightly forested area that extended
northward through the Umbrian region into Perugia

Province. After Sam had mentioned the thought of taking a boat and escaping out to sea, Mr. Bazzini had laughingly pointed out that they were in the only region of Italy that was landlocked. From the forest, they were to pick up a north-south highway that would take them toward their destination. "You can't miss it. It's the only paved road for miles," Bazzini had said. Bazzini then told them what to do.

0615 Hours
East Bank, Rapido River, Italy

"Sir, if you look right there, you'll see a spot that might work if we need to cross again. The bank ain't as steep as elsewhere so we'll have an easier time with the boats and the bridging equipment." Corporal Kulis indicated a general area with a nod of his head.

"Yeah, I see it. Any notion of the defenses across from it?" Ryan ran an eye over the distant bank but saw nothing to indicate it was defended.

"Yes, sir. There's razor wire beginning at the far bank, then a minefield, then more wire, then prepared machine-gun nests. The Krauts have got every square inch covered in one form or another. We cleared a lot of those obstacles during the assault, either directly or through artillery, but Kraut pioneers have rebuilt it all over the last few days. See them white stripes?" Kulis pointed to sets of white lines perpendicular to the river.

"Yeah, I was gonna ask you about them."

"Those mark mine-free lanes that our engineers have cleared to the river. It's white tape. Since those look kind of orderly, I reckon they were put down in the last day or so. I'd guess that's the most dangerous place in the Liri Valley right now."

"Why do you say that?" asked Ryan.

"Because the Germans cross every night like we do and they either move the tape or re-mine the cleared lanes. Sons-a-bitches." Kulis's face lost its scowl as his eyes lit up. "Hey, let's drive some of the sheep down that lane and see what happens."

"Corporal, I haven't been at this war thing for long, but I can tell you what'll happen. Either we'll lose the battalion's deposit on these sheep or the Krauts will start shooting at us. Or both. No thanks. I don't want to be shot at, and these sheep will cost us six dollars apiece if I don't return them mostly whole."

No sooner had the words left Lieutenant Ryan's mouth than things began to happen very quickly. Both soldiers froze as they heard a moan. It came from a small ditch that was filled with bulldozed brush and the detritus of war—the remains of a green rubber raft, a field grey helmet, a discarded gas mask bag. The shooting started as they moved toward the sound, and about the same instant that Lieutenant Ryan realized that the helmet was German. After hesitating for a second, he dropped his walking stick and was fumbling to bring up his M-1 carbine from underneath his sheepherder's coat when a single shot from the German side of the river impacted the dirt five feet behind the two American soldiers—the sound of the gunshot following immediately behind.

Kulis screamed, "Run!" and without hesitation, they both bolted for the small ditch covering the short distance in seconds. As they slid into the ditch, the first thing they noticed was a dead German soldier. His legs had been shattered by a mine and he was covered with dead brush. The second thing they noticed was that he wasn't dead. Ryan remembered the moaning they'd heard, and a slight movement of German's chest indicated that he still clung to life.

That was about the time that the explosions began along the river as the spooked sheep ran toward the water and tripped freshly planted mines in a lane marked by white tape. Terrified, the remaining sheep ran along the riverbank heading downstream, and thirty yards farther, the sheep ran into another minefield.

The explosions echoed through the valley, and they threw an astonishing amount of dust, debris, and ungulates into the air. Both sides, thinking that the other was entering or departing the no-man's territory along the river began a grazing machine-gun fire along the opposing banks while mortars began firing at unseen targets along the river. In seconds, the morning's stroll along the river had turned to pandemonium.

0620 Hours
East Bank, Rapido River, Italy

"What do we do with this son of a bitch?" asked Lieutenant Ryan. "He's pretty badly wounded."

Ryan peeked over the edge of the ditch briefly to watch the explosions along the riverbank, and came to the determination that their best chance to escape would be while the dust and smoke still obscured the valley floor. A small rise another fifty yards behind them would be their first objective.

"I usually kill 'em," answered Corporal Kulis honestly. "But, whaddya think that sniper was doing? Trying to keep us away from this fella, or drive us to him?"

"What? What do you mean?"

"Well, sir, maybe it was a small patrol and this guy tripped a mine and wounded another who managed to get back over the river. Or the rest of the patrol couldn't find him in the dark, and they were fixin' to get him tonight. What I'm thinking is that sniper wanted us to duck into the ditch and find him. It wouldn't have been a hard shot to get one of us from the bank. I think he missed us on purpose."

"Huh," was all that Ryan could manage in reply. Shaking his head at the strangeness of war, he turned his attention to the wounded soldier. A field tourniquet had been wrapped around his leg just below the knee. Ryan had not seen combat injuries before, but he figured that the German soldier was unlikely to make it until nightfall. He might not even make it back to an American aid station.

"What are your orders, sir?" asked Corporal Kulis. He knew what he would do—either slide a knife between his ribs and put the soldier out of his pain, or just leave the German behind and sprint to the rise behind them—but he was curious to see what the new lieutenant would do. Ryan was breathing heavily, but he appeared calm enough under the circumstances.

The new lieutenant had already decided what he was going to do, and his plan differed from his corporal's plan. There was no way of knowing what the German soldier on the far bank intended: did he successfully drive Kulis and Ryan to the aid of a comrade, or had he intended to kill one of the two Americans and just missed? In any case, Ryan intended to do the right thing by the German soldier, and make it work to their advantage. "We're taking him. I'll carry Fritz on my back. You'll have to help roll him on my shoulders while we lie here. When we get up, you go first, and I'll follow. I'll block you from the sniper, and Fritz blocks me. Think it'll work?"

"There's only one way to find out, sir. Let's do this now before things settle down."

1100 Hours
Clearing Station, 111th Medical Battalion,
Mignano, Italy

Perkin sat on the edge of his cot and sipped on a tin cup of steaming black coffee. The medical battalion was hardly rear echelon, but the amenities were far better here than those enjoyed by the troops on the Gustav Line.

The doctor had come by that morning and informed him that his hands were tied—there were no beds in Naples or Caserta for him, and he was going to be sent back to North Africa for further medical treatment. Dr. Poynter had said again that there was little chance that he would be invalided out of the service, but that the odds of him returning to his old unit were slim.

As he drank his coffee, Perkin outlined in his mind how he could change his future. Major Spaulding was his first line of defense. He was sure that Spaulding would see about pulling strings at the regimental level, although the regiment was in such chaos after being destroyed on the Rapido that it was unlikely that they could help in a timely manner. At least the regimental commander, Colonel Wranosky, had a soft spot in his heart for Perkin and would likely do what he could to help.

Perkin then thought that he might approach Major General Walker directly and ask him to intervene. Walker had served with Perkin's father in the Great War, and had personally presided over Perkin's promotion to captain several months earlier.

Perkin was an optimist by nature, but wasn't optimistic about his chances of getting the brass to intervene. Walker was a by-the-book officer of an older generation—he was in fact the oldest division commander in the army—and Perkin was not sure that family ties would suffice to get him to intervene. It might have the opposite effect where the general would use the opportunity of Perkin's wounding to have Perkin taken out of a combat role. Perkin's father had been a company commander killed at the Marne in July 1918, and Walker had been his father's battalion commander and a longstanding friend.

Perkin frowned at that possibility and tried to think of other courses of action that might hold some promise. He was friends of Lieutenant Colonel Fred Walker, Jr., the division commander's oldest son and the division's operations officer. Maybe Fred could be an advocate for him with the Old Man or they could go in and see the general together.

Perkin stood and looked for an orderly. He would have to get a uniform and a jeep if he were to go to the division's headquarters. Instead of an orderly, he saw Major Spaulding evidently concluding a conversation with Dr. Poynter. Spaulding turned and headed to Perkin's cot.

"Hey, Professor, how are you doing today?" Spaulding looked tired, and when he sat down next to Perkin on the cot, he braced his arm so that his damaged hand pointed upwards. Seeing Perk notice the movement, Spaulding explained, "It helps reduce the throbbing a little, although there's no stopping it altogether."

"What's the doc say about it?" Perkin asked.

"That it'll hurt like hell until it stops hurting. Everyone's a comedian." Spaulding reached over, took Perkin's coffee cup from him, and finished the last of his friend's coffee. Grimacing at the taste, he continued, "So, I was just talking to Dr. Poynter about you. He says that he's sending you to Africa tomorrow..."

Perkin interrupted, "I know, Bill. He told me that before breakfast. I don't understand why I can't stay here. Hell, half these cots are empty now. Look, I think I can go to Wranosky..."

"Hang on, Perk," Spaulding interrupted. "Wranosky's got enough on his plate. The word around the campfire is that he's marked for relief, and same story with the commander of the 143rd. Honestly, I guess that I'm lucky to still have a job. If we hadn't made the only beachhead to see daylight the next day, I'd be gone too. I guess I have Sam to thank for that. By the way, you can't stay here. The 142nd's being attached to the 34th Division today in their attack across the Rapido near Cassino. These cots will be filling up tonight and tomorrow."

Perkin was silent as he digested the news. The failure of the Rapido crossing was not the fault of the regimental commanders. He sighed and looked sadly at his battalion commander. "Poor bastards. There ain't nothin' right about this, Bill. We can't cross that damn river with piecemeal attacks, and it's just wrong to blame two regiments for not doing what will take a full corps or more to accomplish."

Spaulding nodded. "Yup...I know. But Clark's not going to take the blame for it, is he? In addition to the battalion and regimental commanders that he's gonna chop, I understand that he decided that one Wilbur and three Walkers in one division is too many, although he ain't made it official yet. I gather he said to some of his staff monkeys that it hurt division morale for Fred and Charlie Walker to serve under the Old Man, so they're on the black list as well."

"I'd heard General Wilbur was a marked man. So you're telling me that Clark is blaming the general's aide for the Rapido?" Perkin's indignation was building.

Captain Charlie Walker was his father's aide-de-camp.

"I think he blames all of us, Perk. I heard from some friends that the 5th Army staff is about evenly divided in two schools of thought: One school of thought is that our crossing had a low chance of success but was justified to take the pressure off the Anzio landings. In other words, we were expendable and the operation worked as well as could be expected. The other school is that, well…we're a poor division. Poorly trained, poorly led, and not up to the task. I suspect that Clark is the headmaster of the second school."

Perkin swore and glared across the tent. "I guess the Old Man is next, then," he said bitterly.

"Probably, although it ain't happened yet. I guess that when Clark can make General Walker disappear from Italy without him bein' an obvious scapegoat, he'll be gone. No corps command, no recognition of what we've accomplished, just…disappeared to somewhere else in the war."

"Aw shit, I hate to hear that. General Walker's… well, he's one of the good ones. What other wonderful news do you have for me?" Perkin's face had fallen. He decided that General Walker shouldn't be bothered with his problems now, and as he wasn't a very political officer, he didn't have any more connections above him that could help out with his situation.

Major Spaulding had come to the same conclusion as Perkin. He shook his head and said, "No more good news, brother. I've got a better picture of officer manning in the regiment and it's pretty grim. We were ripped apart as you know, but 2nd and 3rd battalions were raked over the coals as well. Both batts lost their commanding and executive officers, and every company commander in the regiment except for the CO of Easy Company was killed or wounded on the river. Unless we're looking at job opportunities; there ain't much good news...wait! That's not true. Kulis and Alex Ryan made it back from their recon a little shook up, but mostly okay."

"Eddie was shook up? That's somethin' I'd like to see," Perkin said with a faint smile.

"Naw. He was as cool as a cucumber. Ryan was the one that was shaken, but Kulis pulled me aside and told me that Alex did well under fire. Not only kept his head, they brought back a wounded Kraut corporal as a prisoner." Spaulding had been gratified at the prisoner. The battalion had received orders to cross the river and bring back prisoners for interrogation. No patrols of that nature had been successful since the Rapido attack, and Spaulding planned to use the wounded German to fill his quota.

"That's good news, Bill. He'll do fine. Look, I'm awful sorry to be leavin' you in the lurch like this..." Perkin's voice trailed off and he hung his head.

"Don't worry about it, Perk. I'd do just about anything to have you back either as a company commander or on the battalion staff, but the army always told us that no one's indispensable. So bearin' that in mind, I'm sure they'll send me someone that's better and smarter than you. Eventually." Spaulding coughed out a raspy laugh. "Well, Professor, I gotta be movin' on. I'll come by tomorrow morning and see you off. I'll bring Kulis along as well. I'm sure he'd like to say goodbye."

1300 Hours
Three Miles West of Dunarobba, Italy

They had been moving slowly all morning, and despite Sam's desire to reach their goal by the early afternoon, they had been delayed for over an hour by a slow working farmer and his young son who were repairing a wire fence on a cold cloudy day. Unfortunately, there had been no easy away around the man and the boy, so the three Americans hunkered down in the brush and watched from a distance of a couple hundred yards.

"That's about the only wire fence we've seen but if he don't use a fence-stretcher, he'll just have to repair that fence again before long," Sam opined. No one else seemed interested in discussing fencing techniques, and Beams and Kenton quickly fell asleep while Sam kept watch.

The land that lay before them was pretty country, even on a cold gray day. High hills and a light forest were dotted here and there with cleared land for pastures, and a few small farmhouses were close to the dirt road that they had been following. As soon they were on the move again, they would cross over a highway in less than a mile, and then turn north through a forest.

The countryside reminded Sam of some areas of the Texas hill country, which in turn brought forth a memory of a quail hunting expedition with his father, Old Perkin, and Perkin northeast of Boerne along the Guadalupe River during the boys' senior year in high school. The hunting itself wasn't particularly fruitful, and, Ned, the Brittany Spaniel that they were hunting with kept looking back to the men as if to say "Why are we here?" But it had been a great winter day nonetheless. Raymond Taft and Old Perkin had led the two teenaged boys over miles of hills, through mesquite thickets and along the small bluffs over the Guadalupe. They had seen as few humans as quail that day, and when they returned to their camp that afternoon, everyone was happily exhausted, except for Ned, who sulked well into the evening.

There's something about being in the wilderness, Sam reflected years later, *to take one's mind off other troubles*. Raymond Taft didn't have to think about the ranch; Old Perkin didn't worry about his students; and the boys didn't have time for mischief. The irony of his reflection was lost on Sam as the Italian wilderness brought him no relief from his current worries.

Sam watched with some jealousy as the Italian farmer and his son worked on the fence. It was good, hard, honest work, which came to a stop several times as the farmer rested on a fence post while he told his son a story. Even from the distance, Sam could see the affection between the two as they laughed over some shared anecdote or joke. Although Raymond Taft had died nearly eight years before, Sam found himself missing his father to the point that a lump formed in his throat and his eyes grew moist. Normally when Sam pined for home, he thought of Margaret, but today, his thoughts were of his father and Old Perkin.

There had never been much of a female presence in Sam's life before he married. There had been Anna, Old Perkin's second wife, whom he regarded as a grandmother, and there had been Lupe, the Mexican woman who ran the household on the ranch before he married Maggie. But the men of Sam's life had been his guides and role models, and Sam wondered what his father or Old Perkin would think of his current predicament. *What would Dad tell me to do?* Sam asked himself.

Sam had little idea what to do, where to go, or how to get out of occupied Italy. Mr. Bazzini told them where they could stay that night, but he didn't have any suggestions about what to do after that other than he would be in touch in a day or so. They certainly couldn't get by with stealing roosters or eating hard-boiled eggs indefinitely, and Sam knew that if they were to approach the Church for help, it might as well be sooner rather than later. Sam knew enough about the Church's assistance to escaped prisoners and downed pilots to understand that it was not official Church policy. Father Patrick Riley had told Sam and Perk earlier that very month that the Pope would not risk the Church's independence to help escapees—but that some priests were willing to take the necessary risks. That assertion was reinforced in a conversation with an escaped Australian captain named Fred Hardy. He had told Sam and Perkin that they made it to the Vatican with the help of a parish priest, and there they had been assisted greatly by Monsignor Hugh O'Flaherty. Other priests might not be so helpful.

What a monsignor was, or how to get in touch with O'Flaherty was a mystery to Sam, and yet the Jesuit priest seemed to be the obvious key to their escape. Sam thought that perhaps he would take the same path to the Vatican as the Australian lieutenants, Hardy and Van Deventer, by approaching a parish priest for help. But as Sam thought about it, why bother with O'Flaherty at all? He and Kenton would stand out like sore thumbs in any Italian city, so maybe their best course of action would be to hike through the Italian countryside to the Gildardino farm in the no-man's land between the armies—the southernmost terminal in their underground railroad.

Courtesy of Mr. Bazzini, Sam now had a map of Italy, and in the gray light, he traced his finger over their travels since landing in Italy five months before. He had gone from the west coast of Italy to its east and nearly back again, and he had stopped at a few places in between. The Gildardino farm was one of the places in between. It lay about a third up a mountainside in the Abruzzi mountains, and the Vatican's pipeline to freedom ran along a mountain ridge, or a series of ridges, from Avezzano some twenty miles to the northwest to the farm. A challenging route in summer, Sam reckoned that it would be nearly impossible in the winter.

Although his map wasn't detailed, he looked at the route options. Then he used a twig to measure the distance against the map's scale. It was a long way, maybe a hundred miles or more as the crow flies, and they would be headed back toward the Germans that they had left behind in Terni. There were no good options that Sam saw, and he asked himself again what would his father tell him to do? *For that matter, what the hell would Perk do?* Sam scratched his chin and puzzled over that for a second, and then started laughing to himself. He decided that Perk would most likely shack up with a beautiful Italian girl, maybe two, while personally organizing the Italian resistance.

Sam looked up from the map to where the father and son were still working on the fence. The farmer was letting his son use a pair of pliers to twist a wire, and Sam could see the father move to intervene a couple times but he stopped himself short and let his son figure out the problem on his own.

Sam nodded approvingly over the distance. His own father remained silent on Sam's problem, and Sam knew he would have to figure it out on his own.

1430 Hours
Clearing Station, 111th Medical Battalion,
Mignano, Italy

Perkin lay on his cot and stared at the tent above him. He had gotten up the hour before to go to the latrine, but the pain had kept him on his cot ever since. Even the boredom could not compel him to move around much. The pain trumped all.

Several times an hour, Perkin would gingerly run his fingers along his stitches and wonder how he lasted as long as he did before he collapsed. Adrenalin and anger, he supposed. The adrenaline was long gone, but he couldn't conceive of the anger ever dying out.

The medical tent was full of angry men. There was not a soul within its confines who wasn't personally injured. More poignantly, there was not a soul who hadn't lost a friend or even a relative at the crossing. The 36th was a National Guard division, so the loss was even more deeply felt. Many soldiers had lost friends from home and they knew that if they survived the war themselves, they would have to return to their hometowns and tell what happened to the boys on the Rapido. It was a conversation about loss and shame that no one could bear to contemplate.

Perkin thought about the conversation that he would have to have when he returned home. *What if I'm wrong about Sam? How do I explain to Maggie and Old Perk and Anna that Sam was captured or, God forbid, killed while I was safe and sound on our side of the river?*

The irony of his troubled thoughts escaped the wounded soldier as he lay on the cot staring at the green canvas above him.

1440 Hours
Four Miles WNW of Dunarobba, Italy

They had been on the move for more than thirty minutes. After the farmer and his son had returned to their home, Sam and his companions had resumed their passage along the dirt road. They had carefully crossed over a paved highway, moved into the forest beyond, and turned north.

"It shouldn't be much longer," Sam said. "Assuming that Mr. Bazzini has his distances right, it should only be about another four or five kilometers."

Lieutenant Beams replied, "He was right so far. He's aces in my book. B.G.E. stands for Bazzini's a Great European."

"I can't argue with you," Sam said with a grin.

"Hey, I was going to ask you country boys. Why did they have the cheese in a cage hanging from the ceiling?" asked Beams with his new whistling lisp.

"It's to keep the varmints out. Mice, rats…" said Sam.

"Rats!" exclaimed Beams with a shake of his head. "Oh, I hate rats! Fuck them. They're almost as bad as June bugs." An involuntary shiver shook the lieutenant.

"Whaddya have against June bugs?" asked Kenton. He had never heard of anyone with a prejudice against June bugs so severe that he'd rank the beetle as worse than rats.

Beams repressed another shiver and said, "Whaddya mean what do I have against them? I've never liked 'em. They're the dumbest fuckin' bugs in the world."

"Is that a fact?" asked Sam with a straight face.

"You know it. I was arresting a drunk in downtown Houston one night in '40, and one came flyin' straight at me. I saw it comin' but I was wrasslin' with the drunk, and it kept comin' and comin'. Just headed straight for my face while I was tryin' to get my nightstick out. I turned and then it landed on my ear and grabbed aholt of me…on the inside of my fuckin' ear for Christ's sake! My partner said I screamed like a little girl, which ain't true, but, well…anyway, in the confusion, the drunk punched me in the stomach and ran off. My partner was laughin' so hard that he just let him go. I've had a grievance against the insect ever since." Beams tried to offer a manly smile to his comrades, but the effect was lost without his front teeth.

Sam grinned at Kenton, but they said nothing to Beams who seemed grateful to not have to discuss June bugs or rats further, and they resumed their journey. They were on a trail through the woods, not unlike the one they had left the morning of the day before. The woods on either side of the trail were thick, mostly oaks and pines, and squirrels chattered at them from the tree branches above their heads. It was much darker in the woods and it seemed that nightfall was imminent although it was only midafternoon.

Sergeant Kenton had taken the point and he set a slow steady pace through the woods. Kenton was surprisingly graceful given his size and he was able to move effortlessly through the forest without making much noise. He would frequently pull aside branches and brambles for his companions, and he looked wistfully at the empty blackberry bushes that they passed.

They had gone more than a mile through the forest without talking further when Kenton held a branch aside for Beams and Sam to pass under. As Sam walked by him, Kenton said in a low voice, "We're being followed, sir. Y'all go ahead, and I'll keep an eye back here."

1445 Hours
Clearing Station, 111th Medical Battalion,
Mignano, Italy

A short bull-necked colonel walked into the tent at the clearing station and looked around. Many of the soldiers being treated in the tent belonged to him. He walked through the large tent and stopped and chatted briefly to the men he recognized. He shook the men's hand if they were capable, or patted them gently on the shoulder or leg if they were not. The colonel asked how each man was getting along, and before he moved down the line of cots, he thanked each one.

When Colonel Robert Wranosky approached Perkin's cot, he saw that the captain was staring hard into the ceiling canvas of the tent. The wounded soldier winced as he shifted his weight, and then he started as he saw the colonel watching him.

He looks like hell, thought the Alabaman who was more accustomed to Perkin's usual cocky visage. Wranosky managed a wan smile as he said, "Well, good afternoon, Professor. How are you gettin' along?"

"Fair to middlin', sir. How about you?"

Perkin struggled to sit up, but Wranosky shook his head, "Stay put, Captain. Let me fetch a chair and I'll join you for a spell."

Wranosky looked around and spied an empty stool next to another cot. He brought it over and sat next to Perkin. "Well, Perk, since you asked how I'm doing, I've got to confess that I've had better weeks."

That seemed to be a universal sentiment in the tent. Perkin replied, "Me too, sir."

"Yep, not a banner week for the home team." Wranosky hesitated and said, "Hey, um…I was sorry to see that Lieutenant Taft is listed as missing. All things considered, I hope that he was taken prisoner."

Perkin nodded. "Yes, sir. I think he was. There might could be a possibility that he escaped. Did you not hear about that?" When Wranosky shook his head, Perkin explained, "There were radio intercepts that indicated that three American soldiers from the 141st escaped after killing their guards. Based on the descriptions, I think that they were Sam, B.G.E. Beams, and Sergeant

Kenton—you know, the big red-haired sergeant from Able."

Wranosky nodded gravely. "I know the guy. I don't if escape helps them or not. Two pasty white-boys as big as them kind of stand out, don't they?"

"Yes, sir. But Sam and Kenton are both pretty capable out in the woods. I think that Beams is a city boy, but he should be fine with those two. If it's true that Sam escaped, I think that he'll do one of two things. He'll either try to lay low until we've caught up with 'em, or he'll try and work his way back via the...the, uh... damn, I can't think straight. What are those mountains in the center called?"

"The Abruzzi?"

"Yes, sir. I don't know why I couldn't recall 'em. We were there just a few weeks ago." Perkin looked puzzled for a moment and then shrugged.

"Son, we've all been through a hell of a lot in the past week. And the weeks running up to the river weren't exactly a cakewalk either. You almost died out there, and your body needs some rest. Speakin' of which, I reckon I need to be going. I just wanted to check on you and all the boys here." Wranosky's face tightened, then he said softly, "Well, I really came to say goodbye, and to thank you for all your hard work before I shove off. They haven't made it official yet, but I understand that they're sending me home. When the orders come, they'll want me out fast and I probably won't have the opportunity for goodbyes."

"Sir..." Perkin faltered for a second as he got a lump in his throat. He blinked hard and then said, "It ain't right. Nobody could have done what they asked of us. And it ain't right for them to blame us for not doing the impossible."

Colonel Wranosky nodded. He stared at a medic

who was changing a set of bandages and said after a long moment's reflection, "Perkin, we're asked to do the impossible from time to time. And we don't get a choice in the matter. But, you've been around long enough to know that sometimes what we thought was impossible really wasn't and we win. We pull it off. When we came ashore at Paestum and found a German *kampfgruppe* waiting for us, there was a voice in the back of my mind telling me that they'd asked us to do the impossible. But they hadn't. We held our ground on the beach, and we ain't been kicked out of Italy yet. But sometimes, the impossible is just that. Impossible. Just like the Rapido. So you win some, you lose some. We lost this one, but it ain't the end of the world. Not for the survivors anyway." Wranosky offered Perkin a compassionate smile as he said, "Don't let this eat you up, Perk. We took a lickin' here, but we'll win in the end. I'm being sent home because General Clark needs to let the boys know that it wasn't their fault."

Perkin said bitterly, "I ain't sure what you're gettin' at, Colonel, but it sounds like you're lettin' him off the hook."

Colonel Wranosky thought about his words for a moment, and said, "Well, I'm not, but let's look at this logically. If the division thinks it cain't handle the war, that the Germans are better soldiers, they'll never have the belly to fight again. The general has to let the troops know this ain't their fault, but we both know, he can't fire himself. And he can't fire the division, and he ain't gonna let General Walker take the heat for this either. Not yet, anyway. That'd raise too many questions, but somebody had to be held to account. So, it looks like the regimental and battalion commanders weren't up to the task. It wasn't the soldiers."

"What about General Wilbur?"

Wranosky offered a wan smile and said, "That's a separate issue. He's being fired for honesty. Not for lackin' it, but for havin' too much of it. He told General Keyes personally what fuck-ups he thought Keyes and Clark were that night. I guess he thought his Medal of Honor was a shield against another general's ego, but he was wrong."

Wranosky paused and thought about what he had just said to the young captain. He understood the political machinations at work and it left him feeling queasy every time he thought about it, which was virtually nonstop. For one of the first times in his professional career, he had no idea what the future held for him, or how he even felt about the future.

It had been less than a week since the crossing, and General Clark had awarded Colonel Wranosky the Distinguished Service Cross, the nation's second highest award for valor for his actions on the Rapido River. Now it appeared almost certain that he would be fired. It was a bitter pill to swallow, and Wranosky assumed that the medal was nothing more than a crass attempt to buy his silence. He and other field commanders were being made scapegoats for an operational catastrophe crafted by General Clark, and the politicians on the 5th Army staff apparently concluded that the DSC would be sufficient to keep him quiet—a sap to his professional vanity. If that's what they believed, thought Wranosky, they had the wrong soldier. *Or did they?* He certainly couldn't be bought off with a ribbon and a piece of medal, but even as he raged inwardly, he remained a professional soldier to his core. He didn't know if he could take on the army establishment and win. Or if he even wanted to try. The regular army was not just his career but also his home, and he had no idea how he would act after the numbness faded. He wanted to resist the tarnishing of his professional reputation—a tarnishing for no greater cause than to obscure the incompetence of higher command—but part of him assumed that he would just soldier on and let the indescribably sad politics claim him as a victim. Another sacrifice for the army after an adult life of sacrifice, he thought. But, maybe if he didn't make waves, he could get a combat command in the Pacific Theater or even in one of the new conscript divisions headed toward Great Britain and the second front. Wranosky sighed to himself again. The bottom line was that he didn't know what he would do, but he would certainly not complain to a subordinate—one of the few remaining company-grade officers who was left with the unenviable task of rebuilding the division.

"Now, Captain," Wranosky said, "before I go, I believe that you owe me something."

Perkin looked puzzled as apparently nothing came to mind. He said, "I'm not exactly sure what you're referring to, sir, although I reckon I owe you about a dozen apologies."

Wranosky grinned and said, "Funny you should say that. Back on the beach at Paestum, when you thought it would be amusing to play a joke at your then battalion commander's expense, that battalion commander, i.e., me, gave you the task of researching a particular battle and reporting back to him. Since I haven't heard a word about it, I assumed that you've forgotten. Is that a fair assumption?"

Perkin gave the colonel a wounded look, "No, sir. Gosh, I've been maligned once again. How does this keep happening to me? As a matter of fact, sir, I was planning on getting on your schedule this coming week to report back to you." He paused, collected his thoughts, and said, "It was the Battle of the Rosebud, or as some call it, the Battle of Rosebud Creek, and I'm ashamed to say that I'd never heard of it before. So, after getting homework for our misunderstanding at Salerno, I was kind of at a loss on how to research this. Not many editions of *Creasy's Battles* layin' about and the division historian wasn't much help either. I ended up writing the chairman of the history department at UT, who wasn't a big fan of mine—a misunderstanding there as well involving his daughter and...well, let's just call it an unreasonable curfew—but he wrote me back anyway. Must have been feeling patriotic, I suppose...this is what I know: The Battle of the Rosebud took place on a single day in June, 1876. If I remember right, it was the 17th. The army had moved into the Montana area to resolve the fallin' out we had with the Lakota Sioux and the Cheyenne Indians. Apparently, they were unhappy about being moved out of lands that they'd been settled on and guaranteed by treaty..."

"They didn't appreciate the economic imperative of being displaced due to gold in the Black Hills?" asked Wranosky wryly.

"Apparently not. So the army sent General Crook and two other generals in from different directions to help explain it. Converging columns. A very American approach, you know—I hope we get to try it someday. Anyway, Crook had a reputation of being the best of the Indian fighters and the Indians themselves respected Crook. They said that anyone who understood them so well must have been part Indian himself. I can't say if there's anything to that theory, but Rosebud wasn't exactly his finest hour on the frontier. His column was comprised of cavalry and infantry mounted on mules, and he had a contingent of Crow and Shoshone Indians in his force as well. They were headed to an Indian village on the Rosebud Creek to resettle the Indians there on a different reservation. They had been up since

0300, and he decided at 0800 to call a halt for a rest. A little while later, his Indian scouts reported enemy contact, and then they were attacked in force by Lakota and Cheyenne under the command of Crazy Horse and Sitting Bull."

"What happened then?" asked Wranosky.

"Well, it seems that Crook was unprepared, but the Crow and Shoshone were up to the challenge. While Crook got his men into position, the Crow and Shoshone charged the greater force of Sioux and Cheyenne—several times, in fact. Crook later said that he believed that the enemy force would limit themselves to hit-and-run attacks and that it would be a brief skirmish, but it didn't work out that way. It was actually a toe-to-toe engagement with the Indians—probably not the first one since Tippecanoe, but there certainly weren't a lot of those."

"How were the sides matched up?" asked Wranosky.

"Pretty evenly at about a thousand each, and the Indians were as well armed as they were at Little Big Horn a week later," Perkin said.

"Meaning…?"

"Meaning that the U.S. Army was outgunned by the Indians. They had repeating rifles and we had single shots."

"Okay, so, why didn't Crook end up like Custer?"

"Well, sir, let's see…first, Crook was a better soldier than Custer. Second, the odds were closer to even. Custer was dramatically outnumbered. Third, Crook's force didn't fight a static battle. They seized the high ground, they charged the Indians several times, and when Crook began a wide sweep—a flanking maneuver on the Indians' left—the Sioux and Cheyenne withdrew from the battlefield."

Wranosky nodded, "That's about how I remember

it. So, who won in your opinion?"

Perkin thought for a moment and said, "Even though Crook claimed to have won the fight, I'd say that it was a tactical draw. Casualties were about the same. The Indians vacated the field first, but Crook didn't hang around much longer himself. Strategically...I don't know. I reckon it helped the Indians more in the short run. What happened was Crook hunkered down to wait for reinforcements and didn't pursue the Indians. Had he been more aggressive, maybe Little Big Horn might have had a different outcome. Who knows? But in the long run, it made no difference to the Indian cause. Crazy Horse was dead within the year, Sitting Bull decamped to Canada, and their folks ended up on reservations. A tactical draw or even a victory, it didn't change the inevitable outcome."

Wranosky nodded, "Thanks, Perk. One last question and then I need to be movin' on: Any lessons learned there that might help us here?"

Perkin was on the verge of a flippant response about not fighting Indians, but instead, he said thoughtfully, "Well, puttin' myself into their boots, I suppose that the soldiers at the Rosebud were rattled a little. They had been beatin' the Indians skirmish after skirmish, and here they were surprised. Not just by the attack, but by the nature of the battle—the tenacity of their enemy and their tactics. But Crook's troops held their ground, and then did what Americans do best. Got around the enemy and drove them from the field. If they were shook by the Rosebud though, Little Big Horn must have had 'em truly concerned. To answer your question, I don't know...I'd guess that the chief lesson from the Rosebud and the Little Big Horn combined is, well, leadership matters. You can have a good commander like Crook get caught with his pants down but still be able to recover. And then you can have a bad commander like Custer get caught in the same situation and have no more imagination on the battlefield than to wave his dick at the Indians when they rode up to take his scalp. I guess that it's also true that the outcomes of battle aren't always what they seem at first light. Like you said, I reckon that we got licked this week, just like the army got licked in '76, but we're still here. We'll adjust as necessary, just like they did. And then we'll push these sons-a-bitches outta this goddamned country and Mark Clark can just wave his little general at the Krauts when we pass 'em by."

1450 Hours
Four Miles WNW of Dunarobba, Italy

"It's two Eye-ties, sir. They ain't country folk. They don't know how to move right without being seen," reported Sergeant Kenton in a low voice.

Sam nodded. He and Lieutenant Beams had moved forward along the trail while Kenton had ducked behind some heavy brush and worked his way back parallel to the trail. "Are they still following? Any weapons?"

"No, sir, they just followed us for a little bit to see what we were up to. They didn't have guns so I reckon that they're hiding from somethin' rather than huntin' small game."

Sam nodded again and said nothing. It was possible that there were Italians hiding in the forest, but hiding from what?

Sergeant Kenton looked Sam in the eyes and asked, "You want me to take care of them?"

Sam had already considered it and shook his head. "No. The odds are good they're hidin' from the fascist authorities or the Germans, so they're unlikely to report us to anyone. Let's move out. In a few minutes, circle back around and make sure they ain't tailing us."

1550 Hours
Clearing Station, 111th Medical Battalion,
Mignano, Italy

From the discomfort of his cot, Perkin watched the conversation between Major Spaulding and Dr. Poynter. The men were too distant for Perkin to hear the exchange but Spaulding was becoming unusually animated while the doctor listened impassively.

Twice, Spaulding nodded in Perkin's direction and once he tapped his fist into his palm to emphasize his point. That he winced as he hurt his wounded hand was not lost on the young doctor who put his hand on Spaulding's arm and then held both hands out in front of himself in a calming gesture. It didn't work. Spaulding leaned in closer to the doctor, a movement that Perkin had only seen when his friend was getting ready to become unpleasant in a superior officer kind of way.

Perkin then watched as Dr. Poynter nodded in his direction, and then both men nodded at each other and started to walk in his direction. As gracefully as possible, which was not graceful at all, Perkin rose to a sitting position on the edge of the cot, and then pushed himself to his feet.

"Good afternoon, sir," Perkin said to Major Spaulding. He had discovered that Poynter was a captain like himself, and so just merited a friendly nod. "What's going on?"

Spaulding looked for a spittoon, saw none, and swallowed as he replied, "I think we have a solution to you being evacuated to Africa—Kulis's idea actually—

but the doc here ain't entirely in favor. He did say that he'd take your wishes into account."

Dr. Poynter started to protest that wasn't an accurate representation of his views as he felt he'd been bullied into agreeing to talk to Perkin, but instead he said, "I understand that you are friends with a local Dago doctor and a local nurse."

Perkin thought he saw where this was going and he nodded vigorously, "Yes. Dr. Bonucci and his daughter, Signora Frattini. They're displaced residents of San Pietro." All the former residents of San Pietro were now displaced. The town had been destroyed in savage fighting in November.

Poynter nodded with a raised eyebrow, and said, "Yeah. Dr. Bonucci and his daughter. Look, what the major here is proposing is that we release you into Bonucci's care and that you come see me once per week to assess your progress. I told the major that I am not authorized to release you to civilian care, particularly Italian civilian care, but that I would be open to bending the rules a little bit if I could meet Dr. Bonucci and be assured that they have a clean environment to house you for the duration of your rehabilitation."

Spaulding took a step forward and interjected, "That may not be possible. Dr. Bonucci is a pretty busy man. As you know, many of the physicians of the area had been conscripted into the Italian Army, and are now scattered to the winds or interned by the Germans. Bonucci may not be able to meet you but maybe his daughter can come talk to you? I heard she's fluent in English."

Perkin stifled a smile. That Dr. Bonucci shouldn't meet with Poynter was clear to him—not because Bonucci was too busy, but because he was too blind. Perkin couldn't remember if Spaulding had actually met the Bonucci family or not, but clearly Corporal Kulis had warned the major not to let the two doctors meet.

Poynter shrugged. He had to get back to his patients. He sighed, "All right, sir. I need this cot anyway, but there's one last thing I'd like to say on the subject. Dr. Bonucci may be the finest doctor in the Mediterranean since Hippocrates, but the level of care in Italy, under their current circumstances, is going to be below the standard that you could get at the army hospital in Oran. From what I've seen of the Italian living conditions, in and around the path of the war, suggests that you have a better than even chance of picking up lice and then maybe contracting typhus. They're not talking about this much, but there's a typhus epidemic in Naples, and it can easily spread here through lice on GIs or Dago refugees. So, you're most likely gonna pick up some little critters, and I haven't even talked about your wounds not healing properly due to cold and moisture. And more than half of the Eye-tie families that I've seen are malnourished, and the whole nation under our control is dependent on Winnie and Franklin for what they eat. You'll have to take your own rations because you certainly can't take theirs, and since they're in a weakened state from the lack of proper diet, disease is rampant. I'm particularly concerned that about every other Dago seems to have some sort of persistent pulmonary disorder—acute bronchitis, pneumonia, consumption, whatever. And guess who else is in a weakened state? You are, Perkin. I'll leave the decision up to you, but I'd rather that you go ahead with medical evacuation to Africa. Now, do you still want to trust your health to some Dago quack?"

"Definitely. I'll be okay. Shoot, I'm almost ready to go now."

Poynter shook his head. "No. You're not, and let's not pretend otherwise." Poynter scratched his head and said in a resigned voice, "Against my better judgment, I'll try this as an experiment…but under two conditions. First, I don't want to wait another week to see you again. How about three days from now? Second, if you're getting worse, you're evacuated without question. These are nonnegotiable conditions. Understood?"

Perkin nodded, and when Poynter looked to Spaulding, he nodded as well. Somewhat satisfied, the doctor asked, "Now, Major, how do you propose to do this?"

Spaulding smiled. "Thanks, Doc. I've already run this by Dr. Bonucci, of course, and they're lookin' for him tomorrow. If Captain Berger can stay here tonight, I'll have a driver pick him up tomorrow morning. If you don't have room for him tonight, I'll take him back to my CP. We'll haul him out there with a cot, blankets, and C-rations for two weeks."

Poynter nodded. "Tomorrow morning. That way I can check on him one last time, and get a hot breakfast into him. It'll give me some time to put together a post-surgical kit for Dr. Bonucci—gauze, alcohol, sulfa powder, merbromin—and I'll throw in some delousing powder and a hand-pump for good measure. Good luck…you're gonna need it."

1605 Hours
Six Miles Northwest of Dunarobba, Italy

They had arrived at their destination with a little daylight to spare. Mr. Bazzini had recommended a derelict castle for them to use over the course of a few days, and derelict it was.

In a history lesson that was largely lost on the

Americans, Bazzini had explained that the castle had begun as a watchtower in the twelfth century and had once been grand but had fallen on hard times. When Sam asked if by hard times, he meant the Depression, Mr. Bazzini had replied, "No. The plague."

It certainly looked like it had been deserted for centuries. As they walked up a hill through an equally ancient and untended olive grove to the southeast of the castle, they could see that what roof the castle had once possessed was largely collapsed although remaining sections of dark brown tile still could be seen.

They studied the building for several minutes from a distance of several hundred yards, and then slowly moved closer through the olive orchard and observed again. There was no sign of inhabitants. No smoke coming from the building, no antennas or electrical or telephone wires, and the ancient ruts that passed as a road had its closest point of approach to the castle more than a hundred yards away. Sam left Beams and Kenton at the tree line and walked to the castle wall. When he crossed the road, Sam saw no signs of recent traffic in the ever-present Italian mud nor was there any sign of foot traffic approaching the castle. It seemed deserted.

The southern approach appeared to be the main entrance to the building. Less than ten windows graced the wall of the castle including three that were aligned unevenly along what Sam reckoned was the original tower. It was apparent that the castle had been built over the span of differing generations. Stone and mortar patterns differed, and it looked from the front as if there had been at least three major additions to the tower. The entrance itself did not look very grand—certainly not sufficient to adorn an edifice such as a castle. It was a simple arched doorway to what was an otherwise undistinguished and crumbling stone façade. The door itself was missing, although rusted iron hinges indicated that there had been a door in years past.

Sam looked cautiously through the doorway, and then to either side. The doorway led into a large stone courtyard that had tall brown grass growing in its corners, and debris from the ages lying throughout. At one time, someone had started a fire in the courtyard in the lee of the southern wall, and Sam saw the scorched remains of the heavy door. He walked slowly into the courtyard and looked at the burned door and the surrounding stone walls. No one had been there for a very long time.

Sam walked to the doorway and motioned for Beams and Kenton to join him, and shortly, they were exploring the castle. Beyond the old fire, there were few signs of human visitation, although birds and rodents had made a home in the castle. There were multiple floors within different wings housing a dozen or more rooms, some with at least partial cover from the elements, but no furniture remained within its confines. Sam selected a room with an intact ceiling that might have been a great room or a dining hall at one point in history, and he sat his gunny sack down on the stone floor, and then eased himself wearily down as well.

Looking up with a contented smile on his face, he said, "Boys, we're home."

1945 Hours
Six Miles NW of Dunarobba, Italy

The three hours that Sam and his companions had been at the derelict castle had not been wasted. They had gone through every room again looking more closely for signs of inhabitation or any items that might be of value. With one exception, they found neither.

In Sam's mind, the most valuable aspect of the castle next to the intact roof over the great room was a working fireplace—perhaps the largest that Sam had ever seen. By Sam's estimation, it was about eight feet wide, with no step up from the stone floor, and about three feet deep. Rusted iron remains on the stone floor suggested to Sam's imagination that great pots of stew had once been held over the fire, and his stomach began to growl at the thought. The interior of the fireplace was almost cavernous and while Sam couldn't stand upright within it, an older child or small adult could have. When Sam looked for a damper, he found that there was none, and instead of a flue, it appeared that the smoke collected in the canopy of the fireplace and then vented almost horizontally through a hole in the wall.

While Sam and Sergeant Kenton gathered wood from outside the castle, Lieutenant Beams carefully made his way up a rotting staircase to the top of the watchtower. As the castle was perched on a hilltop, he had a sweeping view of the Italian countryside for miles.

When Sam and Kenton returned with arms full of fallen olive branches, Beams reported, "We don't have any neighbors for more than half a mile in any direction. That sounds close, but there's a thick belt of trees that runs like a crescent moon between us and some little village to the north and another village to the west. The one to the north is maybe twenty houses or so. Probably over 100 people but less than 200. I didn't see any electrical or phone lines, but that don't mean they ain't there. It's a good ways. The village to the west is smaller, maybe fifteen houses or so, about a mile or a little less away. The same thick belt of trees between us and them. I didn't see any lights there either. Some smoke coming out of chimneys but not a lot of moving about. I don't think that they have enough elevation to see us if we're at ground level, so as long as we ain't hangin' lanterns from the tower, nobody's goin' to see us even if we're outside." Beams shrugged and added, "Unless, of course, they walk through the woods and onto the castle grounds."

Sam had thought for a moment and said, "As soon as it gets dark, we can start a fire in the chimney. There's not going to be any light since there ain't any windows. It's a moonless night, so no danger of anyone seeing the smoke unless they come up close. I'll take my chances on a day like this that no one's goin' strollin' about."

It had taken some effort to get the olive branches to light, but once they had the fire going, Sam was delighted to find that the olive wood burned very hot with a pleasant smell. It was fortunate that the aroma was pleasing as the vent to their fireplace was either clogged or inefficient, and the room became somewhat smoky. None of the men seemed to mind, and they each took turns standing watch while the others slept. The castle wasn't ideal accommodations, but Sam thought as he drifted to sleep that under the circumstances that it couldn't get much better.

2005 Hours
West of Mount Trocchio, Italy

His first full day in his new unit had been a full first day, thought Lieutenant Ryan. He had gone on his first patrol, had come under enemy fire for the first time, and now he was leading the twenty members of his company to a new location in the dark.

The battalion was being taken out of regimental reserve and was being deployed to the division's new line of resistance parallel to the Rapido River. The idea, as Ryan understood it, was to establish a defensive line against any possible German counterattack across the Rapido, and to set up forward areas to support the resumption of the Allied assault against the Gustav Line should that order be given.

Ryan had heard from another lieutenant that he knew from the replacement depot that additional offensive operations by the 36th Division were being drafted, and the notion scared the living daylights out of him. Ryan had skeptically asked the other lieutenant that if the full division couldn't achieve a permanent beachhead on the far bank, then what would make the higher command believe that the shattered remnants of the division would have better luck under the same circumstances? Ryan's friend shrugged and said, "I don't know, Ryan, I'm just repeating what I was told. And I was told that II Corps believes that we, well, I mean they, were just on the verge of victory and that it'll take just one more push."

Ryan wasn't one for barrack room rumors, but Major Spaulding's face had been pretty grim when he returned from the medical clearing station and issued the orders to deploy the battalion into the valley and out from the shelter of Mount Trocchio. Or maybe, thought Ryan, his battalion commander was in a lot of pain, and was exhausted.

The march in the dark was brief, and Ryan was profoundly grateful that he and Kulis had done their small reconnaissance that morning. While a scout from the 92nd Reconnaissance Squadron led them to their position, it was still good to have a working knowledge of the geography. It occurred to Ryan that perhaps that had been on Spaulding's mind when he ordered him on the mission the day before.

"Sir?" said the scout in a quiet voice.

"Yeah?" replied Ryan.

"Halt your fellas here, sir, and let me tell you about the land."

Ryan halted his small column, and he and the scout walked forward from the others..

"All right, Lieutenant. This is it. There isn't much here to hide you and your men since we're on the high ground leading back to Trocchio, so just remember that I did the best that I could. I recommend that you dig your fighting positions here and here, and maybe dig back into the slope here." The scout motioned to his left and right. "There's what's left of a vineyard here which will break up the observation pattern of your presence some, and unlike some of the vineyards closer to the river, our boys say that they didn't find any mines. There's been a helluva lot of foot traffic through here the past couple days, so I'm about half comfortable with that. Come daylight, you'll see the remains of some houses about 100 yards or so to the north, and down the slope a little. I'd guess that they were blown up by the Krauts before we took Trocchio, but they've been shelled several times since. I'm not telling you your business, sir, but I'd avoid the temptation to put an observer in there. He'll just get shelled if they see anyone moving about. Speaking of which, you're gonna be under observation from the church on the hill, and their spotters up there, so, if you don't mind me saying so, dig your holes deep...if you can. When's the rest of your company coming?"

"This is it, Corporal," Ryan replied as he looked at Mount Trocchio looming in the dark behind him.

"Oh. Okay. Well, shit, sir. You got a lot of frontage to defend with a squad, but I can't imagine them being dumb enough to try and cross to this side. Good luck to you." The scout slipped away in the dark, and Ryan walked back to his soldiers.

Chapter Four

January 27, 1944
0305 Hours
West of Mount Trocchio, Italy

It had been backbreaking work but a working two-man fighting position complete with a grenade sump was finally finished by Lieutenant Ryan and Corporal Kulis. Their original location had consisted of what seemed to be a millimeter of top soil over rock, so Ryan made the decision to move his command post to a better location in the center of the shattered vineyard. It made sense to him that if there was enough soil for grapevines, then there would be enough soil for the two-man foxhole. The answer was barely enough soil for either, but they were able to shovel enough dirt, cut enough roots, and pry enough rock to dig a ragged grave-sized hole on the edge of Mount Trocchio.

"My farm has about ten feet of the blackest, richest loam on the earth as topsoil. I could have dug this myself in twenty minutes back in Iowa," Ryan groused to Kulis as they toiled.

"Our farm is mostly clay. It ain't very rich but it's good enough. Whaddya grow on your farm, sir?" Kulis asked.

"A bit of variety. Corn and soybeans, mostly. We've got an alfalfa field and clover field for our hay, and I raise beef cattle and hogs. And of course, chickens, but those are for us. I put in a small apple orchard, but it's not producing yet."

"When you say 'we,' who else are you talking about?" asked Kulis.

"My girl and I plan to get married when I get back to Iowa, so it's for us."

"Who's minding it for you? Your fiancée?"

"What?" Ryan scoffed, "A girl run a farm? That's crazy. Naw, my dad's running it for me. It's right next to his."

"Lieutenant Taft's wife is running his ranch, and he's got 16,000 acres and about 5,000 head of cattle," noted Kulis. He'd seen his own mother run the farm many times when his father was sick or away.

"Jesus Christ! Sixteen thousand acres? I don't know what I'd do with that much land. What do you guys raise on your farm?"

"My dad's like yours; he tries a little of everything as well. He just scraped by during the Depression, you know. Pretty lean times, but at least we didn't lose our farm. He's got hogs and cattle as well but I don't much care for hogs though. We grow some cotton and corn and he's got a plot of land with sorghum as an experiment. I don't know how's it doin' though. My mom does all the writin' for the family, and she ain't mentioned it. Things must be gettin' a little better, though. She told me that Daddy bought a Farmall H. I guess he'll have sold off the workhorses by the time I get back. Do y'all have a tractor?"

"Yeah. We're in John Deere country though. I've got a John Deere G, but I like those Farmalls as well."

Lieutenant Ryan dragged over the remains of an ancient grapevine and laid it across the top of the foxhole. He surveyed their work in the light of a distant flare, and said, "Lord, I wish that I was there now...well, this'll have to do. Let's go check on the others and see how they're doing."

They moved slowly and carefully to the various sites along the high ground fronting Mount Trocchio. There were no issues with passwords, and everyone was either finished or close to finishing their foxholes. In two instances, Corporal Kulis directed the soldiers to dig their holes deeper, and Ryan was gratified that there was only good-natured grumbling in response.

Kulis was the only noncommissioned officer in the company, although there were a few soldiers who had seen as much as or more service than Corporal Kulis. If they resented Kulis's new authority, Ryan saw no sign of it. Without asking for permission, Kulis had seen that each two-man team had a veteran soldier paired with a replacement soldier. Ryan knew that wouldn't be popular as the men would want to be paired with buddies, but he felt that it was nevertheless a good call.

Ryan wouldn't have normally kept the second-most senior man in the company with him, but those were Major Spaulding's orders. Ryan was to keep Kulis close, pay attention to his suggestions, but the final authority was his own.

0930 Hours
Presenzano, Italy

Even though the drive from the clearing station to the village of Presenzano was less than ten miles, it still took half an hour to arrive at Perkin's new quarters. Perkin was wrapped in a heavy winter overcoat, and had blankets over his legs, yet he shivered the entire voyage. There was a cold moist wind blowing from the north, and the jeep swayed several times from gusts that cut relentlessly to the marrow of Perkin's bones.

Perkin's driver was Corporal Kulis who seemed unfazed by the cold, although he swore several times as he fought to keep the jeep from drifting off the road. Kulis had been up for most of the night, but seemed unfazed by the lack of sleep as well. As he drove, he brought his company commander up on the latest events.

"So, Lieutenant Ryan and I were sent to check on defenses along our side of the river last night. The battalion's got nearly half a mile of frontage along the river to defend, and we're mustering only about seventy-five or eighty right now. We had a trickle of boys come back to the companies, but we've also lost a few the past couple days. Two guys just broke down from combat fatigue, and we seem to have an epidemic of trench foot. So, I don't know how many we have exactly, but it ain't enough."

"What happened with the combat fatigue cases?" Perkin asked with a genuine curiosity. While the army didn't make a distinction between shell shock and combat fatigue, Perkin did. He thought that there was still value in the old WWI designation of shell shock and he had seen several instances of the affliction—soldiers shattered from severe barrages, whether they were of short or prolonged durations. But since the landings at Salerno, he had also seen a few cases of what he thought was more appropriately called battle fatigue—what he considered to be a state of mental and nervous collapse brought on by the cumulative and combined stresses of fear and physical exhaustion. An old veteran from the Great War had once told Perkin that, "Everyone will reach their limit…it's just a question of when." The army psychologists seemed to agree. They were warning that there would be many more cases to come as the war progressed, and they were now recommending that soldiers exhibiting the signs of combat fatigue be kept in the theater, close to their commands, and returned to their units as soon as possible.

"I don't know where they went, sir, but they'll have a lot of company if they don't pull the division soon. Major Spaulding reckons we'll all be inpatients at the Georgie Patton Clinic for Psychiatric Disorders before long," said Kulis with a grin.

"God help us," Perkin said. "So what happened last night?"

"We were moving from one company observation post to another to the west of Trocchio, when there was a mine explosion up along the river. I assume it was the Germans because we didn't have any patrols out at the time. One of our posts opened up with a .30 cal on the flash, and then they got mortared for the next ten minutes or so. Lieutenant Ryan and I just hunkered down and waited it out, and then went back and checked on 'em. It was kind of lonely out there for a minute. But the good news was that the fellas were shook up a little but no one was hurt."

"Good. How'd the lieutenant handle it?" Perkin knew that he shouldn't be asking one of the army's newest noncommissioned officers about an officer's performance under fire, but he trusted Kulis's judgment and he wanted an honest appraisal of his new lieutenant.

"Oh…about as good as you might expect, sir. I think he's regretting leaving Brownwood, but who ain't? It was a long day, what with the sheep and all. I think he'll be fine, sir." Kulis downshifted and announced, "We're about here." The jeep rocked and groaned as they made a hairpin turn heading up a steep hill, and they shortly passed a stone marker announcing the village limits of Presenzano.

Kulis pulled the jeep up in front of a small two-story stone house on the edge of the village. In front of the house was a narrow pull-off where Kulis parked the jeep, and as he stepped out of the vehicle, he handed his M-1 Garand to Perkin. "Hold this for me, sir, and I'll get the stuff."

Perkin sat the butt of the rifle down on the ground and used the weapon to help steady himself as he stepped out of the jeep. He bent over slowly and pulled his Thompson submachine gun off the floorboard and set both weapons on the passenger seat. Just then, the door to the house flew open and a teenage girl stood beaming in the doorway.

"*Ciao*, Perkin Berger!" said the teenager as she ran out to give him a hug.

"Well, ciao yourself, Stefania Frattini!" said Perkin with a broad grin.

Stefania remembered why the Texan was coming to the house and she stopped short of hugging him. She took a step back from Perkin and stood with her hands on her hips while she surveyed the much taller Texan. "You don't look so good, my friend. Where's *Cugina Orso*? Eddie will not tell me nothing."

Stefania glared briefly at Corporal Kulis then looked expectantly back at Perkin, who hesitated, and then said softly, "Well, honey, I don't rightly know. I think Cousin Bear was captured by the Germans, but I just don't know for sure."

The smile vanished as the girl's face turned grim. Her father, a doctor from San Pietro, had been taken by the Germans in October to work in a slave labor battalion on the Gustav Line, and she hadn't had any news of him since then. Remembering her manners, she inclined her head slightly and said firmly as she chose her words in English carefully, "He will be okay. All prisoners will be returned unharmed at the end of the war."

"Yes, I think they will," said Perkin. He was about to ask how Stefania was doing, when Stefania's mother, Angela Frattini stepped outside.

She was a thin, worn woman with dark circles under her eyes—the by-product of too many sleepless nights worrying about her husband and her lost home in San Pietro. But her worry lifted for a moment as she saw Perkin and Corporal Kulis at the jeep. She offered a genuine smile, and walked to where Perkin and Stefania were standing at the side of the jeep.

"I am so glad to see you here, Capitano! Please come inside where it is warm." Angela gently kissed Perkin on both cheeks, took the rifle and the Thompson, and slung them with some difficulty over her shoulder while she put her arm through his. "It's a bit crowded, but we are so excited about you being with us."

"Miss Angela, are you sure I won't be putting anyone out?" Perkin asked.

She shook her head emphatically, "No. This is the new Italy. We share what we have. It's what God wants. Let me introduce you."

Perkin stooped as she led him through the door, and as he stiffly straightened, he saw what looked like a dozen faces staring at him from a dark room. His eyes scanned the room quickly and he saw two faces that he knew: old Dr. Bonucci who stared vacantly in the direction of the door, his head canted slightly so he could hear better; and, Maria Moroni, Angela's sister—a woman who had threatened to castrate and kill Perkin in San Pietro two months before.

When she saw Perkin, Maria jumped to her feet and, lacking the medical sensibilities of her sister and niece, she fiercely hugged Perkin and then kissed him on both cheeks. Unlike her sister, Maria didn't speak English, but Perkin gratefully understood that circumstances had changed since they had first met.

"Well, hello, Miss Maria! It's good to see you again!" Perkin waited while Angela translated, and he was gratified by a pleased smile on Maria's pretty face. Without openly wincing, he painfully extricated himself from Maria's hug and walked over to Dr. Bonucci who was sitting on a simple wood bench with a girl of four or five. Perkin winked at the girl, laughed inwardly at her surprised face, and he bent over and grasped the old doctor's hand. "Dr. Bonucci, it's good to see you! How have you been, sir?"

The old man raised his head and stared at Perkin's voice through milky white eyes. He smiled and said, "I am well, my friend. Good, good. And how are you?"

"Papa," interrupted Angela, "let me introduce the captain to everyone first." The old man nodded and Angela continued, "We have three families staying here now. This is Signora Moroni. She is Maria's mother-in-law. This is her home, and we are her guests."

Perkin didn't need Angela to tell him the importance of the mothers and mothers-in-law in Italian families. He also knew that how he acted reflected on Angela, Maria, and their father. He walked over to the lady, who was of an indeterminate age between sixty and ninety, and inclined his head in a slight bow. Signora Moroni was sitting in the only padded chair in the room, and it was obviously the place of honor in the house. Perkin saw that she was struggling to stand, but he motioned her to stay seated. He slowly lowered himself to one knee, gently took her wrinkled hand,

and said in English, "Ma'am, I am very pleased to meet you. And I'm very grateful for your hospitality." When translated by Angela, this was met with a warm smile, and then the old lady spoke to Angela.

"Capitano," Angela said, "Signora Moroni said to say that you are most welcome in her house. Although many Italians have suffered during the war with the United States, she has always heard that Americans were nice people. She says that she is surprised that you look Italian except, of course, that you are tall and have blue eyes. She thought you would look more English, although to be honest, I don't think she has ever met an Englishman. In fact, she says she's never seen blue eyes before—only on a *nazar*—so she hopes that's a good omen."

Perkin gave Angela a quizzical look and asked, "What's a nazar? Like one of those blue-eyed sled dogs?"

Angela laughed and translated for the room. Most of the adults smiled and the children giggled loudly, but a middle-aged woman sitting in the corner crossed herself.

"No, Capitano, a nazar is not a dog. It's an amulet that the Turkish and some Italians wear to protect from the evil eye. Sometimes one is hung by the door to protect the house. Generally, we use a *cornicello* amulet, or if we don't have one of those, sometimes garlic or spit or a hand sign will protect you."

Perkin nodded and smiled. "I don't doubt it. Well, you learn something new every day, don't you?"

Angela returned the smile and replied sincerely, "I hope you learn more about Italians while you are here than of our superstitions." She hesitated for a second as if recognizing the irony of her next question, and then she asked, "Can Signora Moroni see your locket? She would like to very much."

Perkin saw the expectant faces around him and realized that Signora Moroni would not be the only one to ask, so he pulled a large rectangular locket from under his shirt. He turned to Angela and said, "Please ask her to take it from around my neck. I can't lift my arms over my head."

Perkin bowed before the old lady like a knight before a queen, and he could feel her trembling, dry fingers hook under the locket's chain. Signora Moroni handed the silver locket back to Perkin, and watched with keen interest as he opened it. Perkin nodded as the Moroni matriarch gasped as she saw the artwork within—the power of the little painting clutched at his heart every day when he looked at it.

The locket had been a present to Perkin from Gianina—an Italian woman that he had loved briefly before her murder at the hands of Douglas Grossmann. It was a small but powerful copy of Guido Reni's painting of Saint Michael defeating Lucifer. Gianina had told Perkin when she gave him the locket that Saint Michael was the patron saint of soldiers and that he would protect Perkin through the war. That was just hours before her death.

Every person in the room was familiar with the story. Angela and Stefania had told the other women about the American soldier from the cave in San Pietro, and how his Italian woman had portrayed the victory of good over evil on such a small ceramic tile. It was a message that met approval at the confluence of their imagination and faith, and unknown to Perkin, he was almost mystically venerated by a roomful of women that he had never met. The presence of Saint Michael in the locket added weight to the women's approval as Saint Michael was not only prophesied to lead God's army against Lucifer, but he was also the patron saint of the destroyed church in San Pietro. Did not the inscription over the shattered church door still beseech Saint Michael to *Watch Over Us Here, And Everywhere*? Both the message and the locket of the tall soldier had a powerful resonance to the women who had lost almost everything to the war and who were terribly anxious about a return to normality.

Perkin looked at Stefania who had a quiet smile on her face. Stefania knew that there was more to the locket painting—that if one looked closely at the small face of St. Michael, it looked an awful lot like the bespectacled face of Corporal Kulis—but it was a secret that she was evidently prepared to keep to herself.

1045 Hours
Six Miles Northwest of Dunarobba, Italy

Sam had walked out from the castle to the belt of trees to the west. He wanted to personally look at the villages and see if there was any German or fascist presence that he could identify. He had thought about conducting a personal reconnaissance through at least one of the villages the night before, but a cold drizzling rain persuaded him against the notion.

It was still cold and the brush through the forest was wet, but Sam was gratified to be spared more rain. For the thousandth time that winter, he thought that it seemed unfair and unnatural that the Mediterranean could be as cold and wet as it was. Sam had always imagined the weather in Italy to be similar to South Texas, but he found the winter to be far worse than anything he'd seen back home.

Sam had slept well the night before, as had Beams and Kenton. He was awakened several times during the course of the night from the sounds of the wind blowing through the castle remains, but after opening an eye and seeing first Beams and then Kenton awake and on watch, he quickly went back to sleep. The blankets given to them by the Bazzinis had been very welcome, but had done little to cut the effects of the hard stone floor, and although he was still in his twenties, Sam felt as stiff as an old man that morning.

Sam kept an eye open for wildlife as he moved slowly through the belt of trees. Acorn remains suggested that the woods were home to squirrels, although he didn't see any. Sergeant Kenton had promised to trap some, and Sam's stomach growled at the thought of roasted squirrel. It was far from his favorite dish, but he told himself that as far as rodents went, it was pretty good.

Sam's thoughts were on food and the first smell of a campfire only reinforced his reverie about a long-ago barbeque, and he turned curiously toward the smell before remembering where he was. Instinctively, he dropped to a crouch and tried to get his bearings from the smell. It was impossible in the forest. There was no visible smoke and little breeze from which to divine a direction, but it was clear that he wasn't alone in the forest.

1045 Hours
Avezzano, Italy

The priest had told him that the high temperature for the day would be -5 degrees Celsius, and it certainly seemed that cold to Douglas Grossmann. He shivered involuntarily from the brisk wind blowing down from the north, but he couldn't be happier. The priest had given him a reprieve from his solitude in the cold dark church office, and it was sheer freedom to be walking around unsupervised.

On such a cold windy day, there were few people out and about in Avezzano. Had it been peacetime, the town would have been full of skiers looking to hit the slopes near Ovindoli, but there was no money for such pursuits this year. Instead, Avezzano was as dark and gloomy as the church office, but it was still exhilarating to be outside.

Grossmann suspected that the weather might have had something to do with his freedom, however brief that might be. Father Carlo had red-rimmed watery eyes that morning, and he sounded congested. So while he might present this opportunity out of the church as a compassionate change of heart, Grossmann suspected that the priest didn't feel like running errands on such a cold and windy day.

It was a relatively simple task. He was to walk to a hardware store that was owned by one of Father Carlo's trusted parishioners and pick up a box of fuses from the owner. The unstable Italian power grid was wreaking havoc on the church's supply and Father Carlo wanted to ensure that he had enough fuses in stock to make it through the rest of the winter.

As he walked along the deserted sidewalk, Grossmann looked at the town of Avezzano, which had sustained some damage by Allied bombing raids with cleared rubble somehow making the day seem grayer, and many of the buildings that remained intact were boarded up. Other buildings had masking tape optimistically crisscrossed over the windows as a futile hedge against bomb blast and concussion. There were still a few shops and restaurants open, but they had few patrons, and when he looked into the window of a bakery, he saw only a few loaves resting on otherwise empty shelves. Grossmann was not a particularly sentimental or empathetic man, but even he was struck by the severity of wartime life in the small town. It certainly seemed that Rome and even Naples had a better wartime standard of living.

The war had clearly not passed Avezzano by, but Father Carlo had told him that the citizens of the town were afraid that the worst was yet to come. There had been some Allied bombing of Avezzano including strikes on the rail lines and highway in December and as recently as the week before. These most recent raids had been without much effect other than to strain the nerves of the town's residents. Still, while empty bomb shelters dotted the town, and German air defense crews huddled at their stations trying to stay warm, Avezzano was quiet during Grossmann's short brisk walk.

Grossmann saw some of the militarization of the town. The ubiquitous posters exhorting citizens to give more to the war or proclaiming eternal German-Italian unity were fading and peeling from the harsh winter weather. Father Carlo had told Grossmann that the Germans and their Italian fascist allies were busy stringing wire lines between the mountaintops nearby to try to prevent the A-20s and A-36s from flying overhead. Grossmann looked for the lines and the work crews but saw neither.

Out of habit, Grossmann casually checked behind himself to see if he was being followed. He saw a small man with a black overcoat with his head covered by a dark brown Tyrolean hat during two checks, but on the third check, the street was empty behind him. It was like walking in a ghost town.

1100 Hours
Six Miles Northwest of Dunarobba, Italy

Sam made his way slowly and quietly back to the

eastern edge of the woods. He had no idea how far away the fire might have been, but he knew that the smell of a campfire could travel hundreds of yards if not miles. He couldn't explain it even to himself, but it *felt* closer. He might not have been in the vicinity of any other people, but he decided not to take any chances. Whoever else might be in the forest probably valued their anonymity, as did he. Sam paid close attention to the forest looking for signs of human presence but he saw none. Other than the smell of the mystery fire, he might have thought himself alone in the woods.

Sam continued to press toward the eastern edge of the belt of trees, and then when he was close, he dropped to his stomach and crawled until he reached the end of the forest. He spent several minutes just looking at the castle remains. There was no sign that the castle was inhabited. No indication that they had spent the night there, and he knew that the smoke he had smelled had not come from the fire that they'd had in the castle—it had been allowed to die out hours earlier.

Sam shifted his gaze to the half-moon of the tree line curving to his left and right. There was no apparent path running from the castle into the woods. More importantly though, there were no faces that he could see that were looking out at either the castle or him.

Giving the forest around him a final look, Sam came to his feet and began a slow jog to the castle walls some hundred yards away. Maybe it would be best just to lay low for the day, he thought as he went through the archway into the courtyard.

1100 Hours
Presenzano, Italy

Everyone was laughing at one another. The

occupants of the Moroni house had all been deloused, and there were good-natured jokes being told in Italian about the white powder being an improvement on the dirt that they had become used to. Corporal Kulis had demonstrated the technique on Perkin first, and then he passed the chemical hand pump over to Angela Frattini before leaving to return to the company.

Angela told Perkin that in peacetime she would have been ashamed had there been lice brought into their house, but her wartime standards of cleanliness had suffered as there was no soap to be found—everyone simply accepted the lice as another burden to bear in their modern world. She also told Perkin that she had heard good things about the treatments used by the Americans, and that they prayed he would bring some when he came.

"I hadn't been given much choice," Perkin had explained. "The doctor said that there's a typhus epidemic in Naples, and he wouldn't let me stay here if we didn't delouse first. This stuff is great. It's called DDT, and it's some kind of miracle chemical. It'll take care of these little critters in our hair and clothes, and we should spray down our bedding and around the house."

"Is it safe to use on children?" Angela had asked.

"No doubt about it," Perkin replied as he watched Stefania pump the insecticide into the hair of Maria Moroni.

Maria ran to a mirror afterwards and laughed at how she looked like Marie Antoinette with her powdered hair. "*Qu'ils mangent de la brioche!*" she proclaimed in French with a mock haughtiness.

A large ammunition crate that had been filled by Dr. Poynter was being examined by Angela who then turned and exclaimed to Dr. Bonucci, "Oh, Papa! There's so much here. Much more than we'll need for

Captain Berger." Turning to Perkin, she asked, "Will they let us keep it when you leave?"

Perkin, who was about to explain that Marie Antoinette had never said, "Let them eat cake," instead replied to Angela, "Of course. No one's gonna care about this stuff anymore. What all did he pack?"

"There's more delousing powder, a box with a dozen bottles of aspirin. Several more stuffed with gauze. There are several pairs of scissors, medical tape, bottles of Atabrine, sulfa tablets, soap—my God, look at the soap! Iodine, alcohol…merbromin? I don't know what that is. Suturing thread and needles…Papa, there's enough here to treat the village for a month!"

1105 Hours
Avezzano, Italy

The owner of the hardware store was delighted to have company on such a dreary day. He had a small coal stove in the corner so he pulled two chairs over to the stove and talked to Grossmann while they drank tea with milk. Grossmann was equally delighted to talk to someone other than the priest.

"Father Carlo is a good man. He told me that you are unhappy staying in the church," said Mario Lucini, the storeowner.

Grossmann was surprised. "He told you that I was staying there?" he asked incredulously. Father Carlo had seemed too paranoid to talk loosely of such things.

Lucini nodded. "Yes. I help him with people like you. I like Americans because I have a brother in Providence. That's in a province known as Rhode Island. He works in a paper mill, or at least he did before the war. I don't know what he's doing now." Lucini smiled shyly and added, "My wife has cooked for you. Father Carlo said that you were fond of her rice and chestnut soup."

Again, Grossmann was surprised. He had been very dubious about the soup when he and the priest had shared a pot three nights before, but he had found it to be the most delicious of the meals that he'd had from Carlo's parishioners. "Yes! It was wonderful. I'd never had anything like it back home. Please thank your wife for me."

Lucini said, "It's a mountain dish. It's pretty simple but it's good in cold weather. My mama does it better of course, but I can't say anything about that at home."

"No, I would think not," said Grossmann with a smile.

"It's like my wife's sister. She has bigger tits. Of course I notice, but I can't say anything." Lucini's eyes glazed over for a moment as he thought about his sister-in-law, and then coming back to the conversation he asked, "Are you married?"

Grossmann shook his head, "No. No wife, no kids."

"You should get married. You speak Italian perfectly so you should marry a good Italian woman and take her to the States after the war. Italian women have big tits. How are the tits on American women?" Lucini asked curiously.

"Wonderful," Grossmann replied. "They're not all perfect but they range in size from chestnuts to forty-two longs. Every set's different but they all start out as God's greatest gift to man."

"That is so true." Lucini nodded his head in agreement and putting away the pot of tea, he offered Grossman a small glass of grappa.

"No thanks, Mario. I would like nothing more but I need to be going or Father Carlo will never let me out again." Grossmann shook hands with the Italian and picked up the small box of fuses.

"I'll tell him that there's no need to lock you up. He just doesn't understand how men live. I can't even talk to him about tits at all."

1120 Hours
Presenzano, Italy

Perkin's standing with the Moroni household had already been high, but with the delousing and the extravagant gift of medical supplies courtesy of the U.S. Army, it was even higher. Everyone in the house had come over and thanked him profusely with varying degrees of sociability ranging from extreme shyness to near brazen. It struck Perkin during the introductions that with the exception of Dr. Bonucci and two young boys, one bearing the unfortunate name of Benito, the occupants of the house were entirely female.

As Angela helped him take off his shirt so that she could assess his wounds for Dr. Bonucci, she told him mockingly, "You must beware, my friend."

"Why's that, Angela?" Perkin asked curiously. He realized then that he had an extensive audience for his medical examination. Three teenage girls, including Stefania, and every adult woman in the house watched as Angela eased off his undershirt and removed his bandages. Two of the women gasped as they saw the extensive stitching on his side and shoulder, and one of the younger girls nudged another and whispered. Both girls unsuccessfully repressed a giggle while Stefania glared at them.

"There are few men in this house, let alone this village. If you aren't careful, you will have an Italian bride before the sun goes down."

Perkin looked at the old lady, Signora Moroni, who was sitting in her comfortable chair with her dentures in her lap while she stared vacantly out the window, and asked, "Is she spoken for?"

Angela laughed, "Oh, so you like mature women? That will not be a problem in this village either. I will tell Papa that later. He will think it's funny." She set a wooden bench in front of the old doctor, and as she motioned Perkin to have a seat, she said to Dr. Bonucci, "Papa, give me your hand."

Stefania guided the old doctor's hand to Perkin's torso, and Perkin jumped as Bonucci's cold fingers traced the course of his stitches on his side. Bonucci probed gently at first, and then more firmly on either side of the stitches. Perkin tensed up from the pain, but didn't say anything. Stefania then guided Bonucci's fingers to Perkin's shoulder, where he again ran his fingers on either side of the stitches and probed sharply with his fingers. Bonucci then had Perkin demonstrate the limitations of the mobility of his arms and torso. After determining that Perkin could not lift his arms over his head, Bonucci spoke to the elder Signora Moroni.

Signora Moroni stood with the help of a cane and walked over to Perkin who was sitting on a bench before Dr. Bonucci. Her trembling fingers lightly touched Perkin's sutures, and then she put her nose close to his wounds and sniffed several times. Stefania had to steady the old woman as she bent over to sniff at the wounds on his side.

Signora Moroni turned to Dr. Bonucci and addressed the doctor in her Neapolitan dialect. Perkin couldn't follow the discussion that transpired, but Perkin noted that the doctor nodded several times and seemed to be in agreement with Signora Moroni, who left the room and walked slowly into the kitchen.

When the conversation, or consultation as it were, concluded, Bonucci spoke to Perkin: "I asked her opinion to be polite, but we are in agreement that your stitches are rough and will leave a wicked scar, but that it is better to leave them in place than to try to redo them. Signora Moroni did not smell any corruption, uh, infection. Nor did I, and I did not feel any sign of it either. You have considerable inflammation along your wounds, which is to be expected, and I feel that you are building up interior scar tissue along the wound on your side. No so much on your shoulder. We will want to knead away that scar tissue before it becomes permanent. It will not be pleasant, I'm afraid."

Perkin nodded, "Okay, when do we start?"

"Soon."

1125 Hours
Avezzano, Italy

Grossmann was walking back to the church with breasts on his mind. Specifically, he was thinking about Antoniette's breasts, and how much he'd like to hold them again. The storeowner was right, Grossmann mused. The priest didn't know how to live like a man, and it was wrong to force Grossmann to live in the same unnatural state.

With a subject as wonderful as breasts on his mind, Grossmann was less attentive to his surroundings as he normally would have been. Consequently, he didn't see the man in the black overcoat and Tyrolean hat until he stepped out of a storefront doorway and directly in his path.

"Excuse me, sir," said the man. "Do you have a light?" The man spoke clear Italian but with a slight German accent.

"Sorry, friend. I quit smoking and don't carry matches." Grossmann looked at the other man with some interest to see if there would be a countersign given. If not, it was likely just a coincidence.

"I started when I was twelve. Now I can't stop." Matches and twelve had been the sign and countersign. The man in the black overcoat looked Grossmann in the eyes and continued, "Major Grossmann?"

"Yes. Who are you?" The question for whom he worked was already resolved. It was a sign/counter-sign that had been established before leaving on this mission. The man in the black overcoat worked for the Abwehr—Germany's military intelligence.

"Fenstermacher. Captain Albert Fenstermacher. From the front office. Colonel von Hatzfeldt has been looking for you." Belying his earlier statement that he didn't have a light, Fenstermacher pulled out a silver case from his overcoat, and then lit two cigarettes for Grossmann and himself using an American Zippo light-er. Fenstermacher showed the lighter to Grossmann. It had a painted image of Betty Boop on its side, and was one that Grossmann had seen many times before—in von Hatzfeldt's possession.

This was unexpected. Colonel von Hatzfeldt was a disagreeable prick of a man in Grossmann's opinion. He never failed to give Grossmann a hard time, had questioned his loyalty to Germany on many occasions— an accusation that was frequently accompanied with the threat of transfer to the Eastern Front. Grossmann would have to be careful.

"I've only been gone a week," Grossmann said. "I've been locked up in that damn church since I got here. This was my first day out."

Fenstermacher smiled. Not a nasty, brutish smile like Grossmann expected of one who worked with von Hatzfeldt, but a genuine warm smile. "I know. We had a man follow you here from Rome, and I've been in Avezzano waiting to talk to you since Sunday. I've attended so many masses looking for a sign of you that I think I might convert now that I've got the rhythm down." Fenstermacher crossed himself and grinned.

"I'm stuck in the church office on a cot. I don't think that conversion is in my future." Grossmann inhaled deeply of the cigarette. It was American and tasted incredible.

A housewife walked by clutching a meager bag of groceries. She didn't spare a glance for the two men, and when she had passed, Grossmann asked, "What's the colonel want? Am I being brought back?"

"No. I don't know what exactly he wants other than for you to hold in place until he can talk to you personally about your mission."

"Personally? Am I in trouble?" Grossmann blurted out. An hour with this disagreeable colonel was worse than a week pinned up in a church office.

"What? No. Of course not. The colonel thinks very highly of you, as does the admiral." The admiral in question was Admiral Wilhelm Canaris, the director of German military intelligence.

"Oh...now that makes me sad, Albert. I thought you were a straight up guy."

"What do you mean?" Fenstermacher looked confused.

"Von Hatzfeldt hates me." Grossmann watched as Fenstermacher's face turned to amusement.

"Of course he does! He hates everyone, Major. Even me, and I've been with him since '42. But, I've sat in meetings where he's been a vocal advocate of you and your team of *Auslandsdeutsche*. He thinks that you've done a remarkable job under difficult circumstances. Yet, when he talks to you in person, you'd think you're a day away from the firing squad, yes? I'm his aide so I know. Every day I go to work expecting a transfer to the Eastern Front, but he respects your accomplishments even if he'll never say so personally. Why, I even drafted the nomination for your Iron Cross—at his direction, of course."

"Oh. Well." Grossmann didn't know what to say.

Seeing this, Fenstermacher smiled again and said, "Don't worry, he just wants to clarify some points of your mission in person. It's unusual, yes, but that's what he wants to do. Must be important though—he didn't tell me." Fenstermacher looked at his watch. "You likely need to get back to the church so I'll let you go. I can have the colonel here in two days. He's flying to Berlin from East Prussia, so I'm heading back to Rome to let him know we've made contact and to get his travel arranged. There's another front blowing in, so there's no chance the priest will want to head south any time soon. Maybe Saturday at noon, we can meet at my hotel. We can arrange to have the priest called to Rome." Fenstermacher thrust a piece of paper into Grossmann's hands with a hotel name, address, and room number marked on it. "Two last things. First, our man that followed you believes that you killed your companion on the train. The colonel wants to know why. Were you compromised?"

Grossmann thought back to his murder of Captain Mullen only a week ago. "No. We had been tasked by Monsignor O'Flaherty with taking sensitive information back to the Allied governments. My companion was an Australian officer, and was determined to do that."

"Oh. That's curious—was it military intelligence?" Fenstermacher looked at Grossmann with interest. "Or political?"

"No. It wasn't operational. It was more...more of

a political nature." Grossmann took a deep breath as he considered how much to divulge to the captain. He decided to tell the whole truth. "O'Flaherty sat us down and detailed alleged…German atrocities in the occupied territories against…well, against their Jewish populations. They were pretty graphic allegations, and I thought it best that they not be delivered," Grossmann said neutrally.

"I see. Let me ask you, sir, did these allegations include mass deportations of the Jewish populations?" When Grossmann nodded, the captain clarified, "Not to concentration camps but to extermination camps?" The friendliness was gone from Fenstermacher's tone. His face was grim and Grossmann could not divine anything from it.

"Yes. Dozens of camps. Thousands dead. Soviet lies, no doubt…"

"No. I'm afraid not," Fenstermacher said harshly. "Not lies, Major. Not thousands dead. Hundreds of thousands, maybe millions. And that's not hyperbole. Maybe more. Tens of millions. If this war were to continue for another five years, there would not be another Jew left alive between the Atlantic and the Urals. You've spent the war in Paris and Rome, yes?"

Grossmann nodded but said nothing. The subject that was being discussed was incredibly dangerous.

Fenstermacher continued without pause, "…so you don't understand what's happened there, in the east. It's not just the roundup of the Jews, we've all known about that, but their mass extermination." Fenstermacher lit two more cigarettes for himself and Grossmann, and the major noticed that the captain's hands were shaking. "Things in the east are…unnatural. I don't know how to describe it, but you've heard the stories. It's…unreal. A nightmare. A savage nightmare. Savage to the point that it makes the battle of Fontenoy seem as if it were fought by another species. The SS is doing the things that O'Flaherty alleges. And worse. They've, well, they've gone insane in the east, and they'll arrest or execute any Wehrmacht officer that interferes with them. I know it's hard to believe, but we have the documentation and I've personally heard the stories from army officers who've had to support the SS. I've seen the photographs of what they've done. It's beyond description. Beyond comprehension. Just…beyond humanity. There's no military justification for their conduct—those animals have stained German honor for the rest of all history. The old emperor, God bless his soul, must be rolling over in his grave in shame. You know, it makes a man ashamed to be a German officer, and I don't know how we will be able to face the world when this war is over, particularly if we lose. I don't know. It may be worse if we win." Fenstermacher's face was white despite the cold wind that blew through the streets of Avezzano. He shook his head in contempt and said, "This isn't the time or place for this discussion. It's probably best not to talk about these things at all because…it's not wise. I think the SS would kill us all to cover their tracks now that the tide of war has turned."

Grossmann nodded, confused.

Fenstermacher turned to go, but said as he threw his cigarette on the ground, "Obviously you can't talk about this. And there's one last thing, Major, and this comes from the top. You are not to resume contact with Miss Bernardi. We know that you are, uh…well, that you have an extraordinary relationship with her. It must stop. It seems that our interests and hers have diverged, and she cannot be trusted to support the Abwehr's agenda any longer."

1300 Hours
Able Company Command Post, West of Mount
Trocchio

In their move in the darkness to a better location to
dig, Lieutenant Ryan and Corporal Kulis had lost the
dubious protection of the slight defilade identified by
the scout the night before, but their loss was more than
compensated by the advantage in visibility. Stretched
out before Ryan lay the northernmost sector of the
Gustav Line in the Liri Valley.

To his right was the town of Cassino, and a major
battle was underway to the north of the town. The
sounds of constant machine-gun fire overwhelmed the
popping noises of rifle fire, and the booms of mortars
and heavy artillery fires echoed through the valleys.

Ryan had spent the morning with his time divided
between checking on the soldiers of his company, and
expanding the foxhole laterally. He thought, with good
reason, that the occasion might arise where his ad hoc
command post might have to house more than two
soldiers.

There was so much smoke over the battlefield that he
felt safe enough to work and move about without much
fear of being seen. His command post was roughly 1500
yards behind the river, and more than three miles from
the battle underway for Cassino.

Proving the wisdom of expanding his two-man foxhole into something like a short deep trench, Ryan and
the sleeping Kulis had been joined by Major Spaulding
and his radio operator.

Ryan and Spaulding were trying to watch the battle
in Cassino with little success. "They don't help much, do
they?" asked Spaulding, referring to the M3 binoculars.
"It looks to me like they've crossed the Rapido up there.

It's shallow enough to ford, but it's still damn cold."

Ryan stared hard through the binoculars and thought he saw tanks moving but he wasn't sure—the distance was too great and the smoke too thick. "No, sir. I can't make out much."

"Well, it's my understanding that the 34th got a battalion over the river with several tanks in support this morning, but it sounds like they're having a tough time holding the beachhead. Damn!"

A sharp crack followed instantly by a loud boom echoed off the mountains, and a column of black oily smoke rose from the scene of the battle. The machine-gun fire and the small-arms fire diminished momentarily but soon resumed.

"What do you think that was, sir?" asked Ryan.

"My guess is that was the ammo detonating on a Sherman. See? Look, you can see the flames. Poor bastards! Oh, hell! Can you see that?"

Ryan blinked hard and stared through the binoculars. He sighed, "Yes, sir, I do."

As hard as it was to make out through the distance and the haze, Ryan could see a stream of men running to the rear amid plumes of smoke and dust. The battalion that had struggled so hard that morning to form a beachhead on the far side of the Rapido had just been routed.

1445 Hours
Avezzano, Italy

For the first time since arriving in Avezzano, Douglas Grossmann welcomed the isolation of this particular mission. He had spent the last three hours sitting in the church office and chain-smoking a pack of cigarettes given to him by Captain Fenstermacher.

Thoughts raced through his head with little order or coherence, and there seemed to be few things in his conversation with Fenstermacher that made sense. While he was concerned about the impending meeting with Colonel von Hatzfeldt, most concerning to Grossmann was the directive to avoid contact with Antoniette Bernardi. What had happened to cause the Abwehr to turn against their most valuable agent in Italy? Had Antoniette betrayed the cause somehow? Was someone working against his interests in Rome or Berlin? How could he be expected to follow that order, or was it just a loyalty test of some kind?

He had very nearly turned around and headed straight for the train station after taking his leave of Fenstermacher. Assuming the trains were running, he could be in Rome within the hour, he thought, and in Antoniette's arms within two. Of course, there were even bigger assumptions—that he would be able to find her and that he wouldn't be followed and arrested for disobeying an order. Each step toward the church was a battle between his intellect and his emotions, and twice he stopped, partially turned toward the train station, only to continue to the church, his head bent against the freezing wind while his mind raced.

Father Carlo had taken to his bed with a cold or the flu, Grossmann didn't know which, nor did he care. But he was grateful that there was no one to talk to, no interruptions. He decided that his near panic was self-defeating, took a deep breath, and tried to get his thoughts in order.

He started by putting aside his concerns for Antoniette for the moment and contemplated von Hatzfeldt's upcoming voyage to Avezzano. That was the key to the whole puzzle, but Fenstermacher had left him with no clue as to the nature of von Hatzfeldt's journey.

Grossmann started with the presumption that it was of the utmost urgency to the Abwehr. Von Hatzfeldt was a senior officer on Admiral Canarias's staff—considered by many to be the admiral's closest confidant. For von Hatzfeldt to leave his duties at the admiral's side in East Prussia and risk the travel to Italy meant that the journey was of critical importance to the admiral himself—otherwise, why couldn't Fenstermacher have conveyed the message, whatever that was?

There was to be a change in mission, of course. It couldn't be anything else, but the mission to find the end of the Vatican's underground railroad had not been canceled. Otherwise, Grossmann would be on this way back to Rome and would be shortly issuing arrest orders for Father Carlo. *So, what tack, what variation in the mission, would the change take?* Was Grossmann to attempt to infiltrate the Allied command again—maybe he was to infiltrate Eighth Army this time? Maybe von Hatzfeldt wanted him to kill the Italians at the terminus in the Abruzzi. *Maybe*…although he was planning to do that in any case. Was that why he was being told to break contact with Antoniette? The Italian connection? It was possible he thought, but unlikely. She cared little for her countrymen if they weren't fascists.

Grossmann then gave that thread some thought. Antoniette was a dedicated fascist. Dedicated with the passion of youth. Her father was a friend and supporter of *Il Duce*, and while Grossmann suspected that her father's political convictions were like most Italians—subject to changes in the breeze—Antoniette was different. She was dedicated to both Mussolini and to the Führer. She was dedicated to the war effort, and had in fact contributed more than most serving soldiers. Grossmann had seen the fire in her eyes when they had discussed politics. She was a more loyal Nazi than he was…or she had been. As he lit another cigarette, he thought that maybe there had been an abrupt change in her thinking—sparked perhaps by a realization that the Allies would win. Maybe she had witnessed a German atrocity in Rome or maybe she was just ready for something, or someone, different. War brought disillusionment to all, even the victors, but more strongly to the vanquished. There was nothing more dangerous than a disillusioned youth, Grossmann thought, unless that youth was also female.

1445 Hours
Able Company Command Post, West of Mount Trocchio

Major Spaulding had left the command post to check on his other units and returned.

With a grimace as he checked his watch, he said to Lieutenant Ryan, "I want you to get some sleep if possible. We're likely to be busy tonight, so it'd be a good thing if you and Kulis can divide up the remainder of the daylight. There'll be no hot chow until we're pulled back, just C-rats."

"Yes, sir. Are we getting ready to cross again?" asked Ryan.

Spaulding shrugged, "Who knows? I keep hearing rumors that II Corps wants us to push ahead again, but the 141st and 143rd are combat ineffective, and the 142nd is under the operational control of the 34th Division. So, who knows?" he asked again. "No, I think we're here just as a roadblock in case the Germans go on the counteroffensive and cross the river."

"Does anyone think that they will?" asked Ryan. He fervently hoped not.

"Nope. That river works against us both equally—then we'd slaughter them trying to cross. Besides, where would they go?"

Ryan heard the tracks first, and he turned to their left to see what it was. Tanks were on the move. Resorting once again to binoculars, Ryan and Spaulding watched as four Sherman tanks emerged from behind the southern bend of Mount Trocchio. The tanks moved from the shelter of Mount Trocchio two abreast with two tanks in trail so close that they nearly touched the lead track. In an impressive move that reminded Ryan of fighter pilots in formation, the two lead tanks peeled off to their left and right, and the trailing tanks moved up until the four tanks were abreast of one another on a patch of high ground near the destroyed village of Pieta.

"What's going on?" asked Ryan.

"I don't know. Another demonstration to take some of the attention off of the 34th's withdrawal from Cassino, I'd guess."

The tanks had no sooner reached what appeared to be their destination than a soldier came running out of the brush waving his arms and shouting at the tankers. At that moment, the four tanks opened fire in a ragged succession, the tanks rocking back on their tracks in recoil. Ryan had seen tanks fire many times during his training in Texas and in Georgia, but he had never seen one fire live rounds at actual humans, although where those humans were wasn't exactly clear. The soldier on the ground forgotten, Ryan turned to see the impact of the rounds.

Their specific targets escaped him, but clouds of dust and smoke erupted from the far side of the riverbank opposite the crossing site of the 1st Battalion a week before. Ryan turned back to the tanks and watched as in rapid succession each tank fired ten rounds at their distant unseen targets while the soldier on foot continued to scream without effect at the tanks. The soldier suddenly twisted his body and stared at the German side of the river, his attention no longer consumed by the American tanks.

Ryan then heard the distant booms and in a flash, the soldier was gone from view seconds before the German counter-battery fire arrived. The Able Company command post was more than one thousand yards distant from the impact area, but Ryan could feel the shock of the explosions as German artillery continued to pulverize the area with great accuracy long after the tanks had withdrawn.

1600 Hours
Able Company Command Post, West of Mount Trocchio

Major Spaulding ran crouched over through the vineyard, although with the poor visibility, it was unlikely that anyone would see him. He eased himself into the trench that was serving as the Able Company command post, so as to not wake up the sleeping Lieutenant Ryan. But as he had come there to talk to the lieutenant, he had no choice. He grinned and winked at a red-eyed Corporal Kulis, and then Spaulding grabbed Lieutenant Ryan by the overcoat and violently shook him awake.

"Wake the fuck up, Lieutenant!" Spaulding barked in his command voice before spitting a stream of tobacco juice at a gnarled grape vine.

Ryan jerked awake and was reaching instinctively for his carbine when his senses partially returned. He'd been dreaming of a large Iowa thunderstorm at the

Sperry 4th of July picnic. "Huh? What'd you say?"

"I said your company was supposed to be at phase line charlie thirty minutes ago. What are you doing asleep?" Spaulding suppressed a grin.

"What?! Phase line what?" Ryan started looking for his pack, when Spaulding put a hand on his shoulder.

"Hang on there, high speed. I'm just kidding." Spaulding laughed at the confused look on Ryan's face. He reached back to his hip, pulled out his canteen and handed it to Ryan. "It's coffee. Ain't real hot anymore but have as much as you want. Sorry to wake you up. We got a mission to go over."

Ryan took a long pull of the lukewarm coffee, offered some to Kulis who declined and closed his eyes, and said, "Please don't do that again, sir. I almost... what's going on, sir?"

Spaulding took a drink of the coffee, screwed the cap back on his canteen, and said, "We're doing more demonstrations tonight. We're going to shell the far bank, and then we're going to hit it hard with machine-gun, mortar, and small-arms fire. Then withdraw, wait until their counter-fire abates, and then repeat the process. Round one goes at midnight and round two is scheduled for 0300 hours."

Ryan nodded. "Where do you want us, sir?"

"Follow me."

The two officers climbed out of the trench and moved crouching down the hill to the edge of the old vineyard. The view was fairly unobstructed and Spaulding was able to point out where he wanted the remnant of Able Company to position, and where he wanted them to mass their fires.

Spaulding spat again and said, "There ain't a lot of point to these demonstrations, but corps is hot to do 'em. I don't think that we can muster enough firepower

in our demonstration to convince Jerry that we're fixin'
to cross again, but if there's any advantage to us doing
this, it's to push them back from the river somewhat. I
don't reckon they've got a lot right on the banks in any
case, so maybe it's just meant to amuse us both. Or show
purpose or deprive them of a little sleep, that kind of
thing."

Ryan groused, "It deprives us too, you know."

"Well, hell, Lieutenant, you got so much sleep you
missed the phase line." Spaulding barked out something
between a laugh and a cough, slapped Ryan on the
back, and then directed his attention behind them and
to their left. "That demonstration earlier was another
corps ordered evolution. But that time, there was no
coordination with division. Just the corps directing
tanks into our sector to open fire and then leave.
You know what happened? One of our boys from the
regiment dead and another wounded out of the cannon
company, and two M-7 Priests destroyed. Unless we
hit something by luck over there, all we did was destroy
two valuable guns. I think these demonstrations are
doing more to us than to the Germans."

1640 Hours
Presenzano, Italy

Perkin sat with his back to the fire with a hot poultice
of olive oil, rosemary and other spices draped over his
shoulder and held in place by Stefania. It was the second
such treatment of the day, and Perkin was beginning to
wish that he had chosen medical evacuation to North
Africa.

It wasn't the poultice. The poultice not only smelled
good, it felt wonderful—a deep, penetrating warmth
that he hadn't felt for some time. It was what was coming

next that he dreaded. Angela Frattini replaced Stefania on the bench behind Perkin and the poultice was replaced with a rolled-up tea towel packed with snow. At first, the snow felt good after the heat of the poultice, and then Perkin noticed the growing discomfort and then the pain of the cold.

"Are you sure we're doin' this right?" he asked.

"Yes, of course. Do Americans treat wounds differently?" Angela asked.

"Well, I can't rightly say, but it seems that the treatment is more painful than the wound."

"It's not my fault. You shouldn't have gotten shotted, I think," Angela advised as she frowned at her word choice.

"I think I shouldn't have gotten shotted either. Oh Lord, how much longer?" Perkin asked.

Angela looked at a black clock trimmed with gold leaf sitting on the fireplace mantel. "We just started. Another fifteen minutes, and then we'll do your waist. I don't want to scare you, but this isn't the worst."

Perkin tilted his head back to look at Angela. "What's worse than this?"

"Before we go to bed tonight, Papa will knead that scar tissue. I'll have to give you some brandy first. It will be uncomfortable. And then tomorrow, we will start stretching your limbs."

"Won't that tear the sutures?" Perkin asked.

"We'll be careful, we don't want that. But you said that you wanted to return to your friends as soon as possible, and this is what we have to do. The hot and cold will ease the pain and inflammation—rosemary is very good for that—and the stretching and exercises will restore your mobility."

"Exercises? You mean like calisthenics?"

"No, something more practical. You'll see

tomorrow."

1730 Hours
Avezzano, Italy

Douglas Grossmann sat in the church office and stared at the plaster walls. At one time, it might have been painted a soothing yellow, but in the dim light of the desktop lamp, the walls seemed dark, dirty, and dingy. It wasn't soothing at all. He had paced back and forth in the office since running out of cigarettes, but he found little clarity or guidance in pacing, so he sat and thought. It wasn't helpful either. He was nauseated, but had he bothered to think about why, he wouldn't have been able to say whether the queasiness he felt originated from the events of the day or from the volume of cigarettes that he'd smoked. His dinner, brought by a trusted parishioner, was a plate of salami, cheese, and bread, and lay untouched on the priest's desk. He couldn't bring himself to even look at it. He had tasted the wine that came with his dinner, and sat it down with a grimace.

Pacing and smoking had not given him the answers that he needed. While his intellect and sense of duty told him to ignore the events of the day and remain focused on the mission, his nerves were screaming that he must do *something*. The problem was that he didn't know what to do, but he did know that if he didn't act soon, that if he didn't leave his self-imposed prison, that if he didn't get answers, he would go insane. He would have to go to Rome and find Antoniette. It was the only way.

1935 Hours

Six Miles Northwest of Dunarobba, Italy

Sergeant Kenton led the way, and Sam followed closely behind. There was no moon, and the dim light of the cloudy dusk was long gone.

Sam was an accomplished outdoorsman. He had hunted and camped all of his life, and he had had the benefit of some pretty demanding natural environments before coming into the army, including hunting deer and birds from Texas to the Great Plains up into central Canada. He could move silently, and he also had the benefit of exceptionally good hearing and eyesight. Nevertheless, he had known for years that Sergeant Kenton was the better man in the woods, and he gladly allowed the large sergeant to lead the way.

Perkin had told him once that the wilderness was in Kenton's blood—that he was a descendant of some pioneer that Sam had never heard about who had helped tame the early frontiers of Kentucky and Ohio. Although Sam was a Texan through and through, his extended family still lived in Ohio and in all of the trips that he had made as a child and teenager back to Ohio, he never saw much that suggested the pastoral state was once a treacherous battlefield between the early Americans, and the British and Indians.

Whether it was something from Ohio or something from the Kenton bloodline, Sam couldn't tell, but he was always amazed at how gracefully and silently the large sergeant moved in the woods. There was virtually no light so Kenton's effortless movement around briars and fallen branches seemed almost instinctive to Sam, who kept a light hand on the shoulder of the sergeant. Every now and then, Kenton would pause and lean back to whisper, "Watch that rock to your right, sir," or

"We're gonna slide down a few feet here."

They were looking for a creek or stream. The water that they had brought from the Bazzini's in corked wine bottles was gone. There were puddles in the courtyard of the castle that would do in a pinch, and the sky was threatening yet more rain, but if they could find a nearby source of water, Sam would be more comfortable. They still had some ham left over, which would get them through another day, and Kenton had set several squirrel snares in the afternoon. Food wasn't guaranteed, but they had done what they could.

When Kenton entered the woods in the afternoon, he had remained close to the castle-side of the trees and had not ventured very far into the forest. He had not seen any signs of people, and could not smell the smoke that Sam had detected that morning. They still moved cautiously, this time to the north, and Kenton paused several times to listen to the sounds of the forest. Beyond the normal sounds of the forest—the movement of the trees in the wind and the small wildlife—there was nothing but the distant squawking of birds to their northeast.

There appeared to be no stream running through the belt of trees. Unlike many green belts that followed a creek, it seemed that the trees were just left standing, maybe as a barrier between the castle and the nearby villages.

They came to the northern edge of the woods, and they crouched as they looked out on the village to their north from a slight elevation. If they hadn't known the village was there, they might have passed it by without seeing it in the dark. They could feel the loom of the little town, but it was completely black with no streetlights, no lanterns at the doors, and no outdoor fires. It might have been uninhabited except that every

now and then, Sam and Sergeant Kenton would catch
a brief glimpse of light as someone opened a door and
quickly closed it. The villagers clearly were living under
wartime conditions, and their windows must have had
thick blackout curtains. So much the better, thought
Sam.

They moved out of the shelter of the trees, and
approached the edge of the village. A road ran through
the narrow town, but Sam and Kenton had decided to
stay off the road, and approach the village through the
countryside. Sam had seen outbuildings from the castle
tower that suggested that some of the village residents
kept farm animals, perhaps sheep or a dairy cow, but
they neither saw nor smelled livestock as they walked
cautiously to the first house. From a distance of twenty
yards from the stone house, Sam and Kenton could see
a small glow around the window facing them, and they
knelt and took stock of their situation.

In a low whisper, Sam said, "I want to see if they
have a well or a cistern with a pump around one of
these outbuildings—they'd need something to water
their livestock—or better yet, maybe there's a fountain
in the village."

"Why's that better, sir?" asked Kenton.

"A pump might be noisy. Might attract their
attention, or wake up a dog. But these Italian fountains
seem to flow nonstop. We can just wait here until they
go to sleep, and then we'll check out the town."

"Do you reckon they might have a common well or
spring and a pump house somewhere?" asked Kenton.

"They might," Sam replied. "But I ain't seen any
electrical wires yet. This village may not have electricity."

Kenton nodded in the dark, and they lay down in
the grass and began to wait.

2150 Hours
Presenzano, Italy

The elderly Signora Moroni had turned in for the night and she insisted that Perkin sit in her easy chair. It was a comfortable, well-used, Victorian-style chair with dark red velvet with even darker red roses as the pattern. It smelled to Perkin like old people.

After dinner, which had just concluded, the interest in Perkin had waned through the house for the moment. Everyone was solicitous and kind, but the language barrier was too great for most. Unknown to Perkin, two of the teenaged girls had approached Stefania and asked her to translate so they could talk to Perkin, but the younger teenager had refused. Everyone had come by and profusely thanked Perkin for providing the dinner which consisted of a very large can of army hash that the women of the house complemented with a large flat pasta cooked with olive oil and garlic. Dessert came from another large army can, this time of peaches, followed by another glass of homemade brandy with Dr. Bonucci.

Other than the pasta, Perkin had been uninterested in the food. He had eaten enough army hash for a lifetime, but it appeared that the household had been without meat for so long, that even army hash was a treat for the Italians. Perkin poked through the crate of cans brought by Corporal Kulis and while the young soldier had brought enough food to feed a platoon for a week, the food choice clearly reflected what was available as opposed to what might be desirable. In the mix of C-rations and K-rations, there were several more large cans of hash, smaller cans of Spam, one canned ham, peaches galore, two very large cans of smooth peanut butter, packages and cans of crackers and cookies, a twenty-pound canvas bag of flour, powdered eggs, coffee, cans of condensed milk, chocolate bars, and lots of gum. Perkin noticed that none of the boxes contained cigarettes, and he assumed correctly that Kulis had pilfered the cigarettes for himself knowing that the captain didn't smoke.

While Perkin sat down with Dr. Bonucci to have his glass of brandy, he heard delighted squealing from the children in the house and the clapping of hands. Perkin raised a quizzical eyebrow at the doctor, which was missed, and then he asked, "What was that about?"

"The children are all getting a square of chocolate. It's quite a treat for them. I don't know the last time that they had sweets other than a piece of honeycomb." The old man pulled out a deeply stained meerschaum pipe bearing the carved face of Garibaldi from his coat pocket and tamped in a small pinch of tobacco. "How do you feel, my friend?"

Perkin laughed. "Much better now." The truth is that he did feel better. The combination of the hot and cold poultices seemed to be having the desired effect and the swelling in his shoulder seemed better than just that morning. On the other hand, though, his torso was almost too tender to touch, and he winced inwardly as he recalled the pain of Dr. Bonucci breaking up the internal scar tissue on his side.

"Yes. I think that you will be fine. In a couple days, you can go back to your unit."

"A couple days? Seriously? I was told a few weeks at the earliest." Perkin was delighted but skeptical.

"Yes, yes. If you were in my care in a military hospital, you would be one of many soldiers, and your therapy would be part time. Here, for better or worse, I get you all the time." Dr. Bonucci pulled a pack of matches from his vest pocket and lit the old pipe. Staring slightly above Perkin's head, he said, "It's surprising. I can picture your wounds exactly from touch. I treated many wounds just like yours in the Great War."

"I didn't know you had served," said Perkin.

"I didn't want to because of my age but by 1917, I was needed. My first battle—almost my last—was at Caporetto. In the mountains of northern Italy on the old frontier with the Hapsburg Empire." Dr. Bonucci accepted a glass of brandy from Perkin and continued, "The mountains there are worse than here. Higher, steeper, colder. I knew many men who died from exposure, and many who lost fingers and toes to frostbite. I was never hurt, even though I was too old to be in the army even then. Of course, the hospital wasn't in the mountaintops but it was still a brutal winter—just like this one."

"I'm a flatlander," Perkin said. "The mountains are beautiful, but they're no place for me."

Bonucci smiled. "You should come here in peace-time, my friend. The mountains are a wonderful place for peace, but a terrible place for war. But as long as men have lived on this peninsula, the mountains have taken their lives—these mountains, those mountains, the mountains of Italy, are filled with the ghosts of soldiers who had to fight here: Etruscans, Greeks, Romans, Carthaginians, Goths, Normans, Slavs, Moors, French, Austrians, Germans and now we have the ghosts of Americans and Englishmen. It's silly but my father told me when I was a boy that the ghosts of the mountains can never sleep, they just keep fighting their last battle."

"Well, I hope that's not true—I think they've earned some peace. Tell me, what was Caporetto like? The battle, I mean. I've read Hemingway's book...he was there. I don't suppose you met him at Caporetto?"

"Yes! Yes! He wasn't famous at the time of course, but he stood out. Not just as an American, but as a man. As he was an ambulance driver, I knew him quite well. I was still learning English at the time from a Scottish volunteer there, and I used to have a smoke and practice my English with Hemingway."

Perkin laughed in surprised delight. "You learned English from Ernest Hemingway?"

"No. I learned English from my friend Alastair Campbell, but I learned how to be understood in English from Hemingway, who said Campbell's accent was worse than mine. Ha, ha. I never read that book by the way—*A Farewell to Arms*—it was banned here in Italy. So, I taught Angela and her husband to speak English—they went to London on their honeymoon before the Depression—and they taught Stefania. But it seems that she's learned more from your corporal in a couple months than she learned from her parents. She is quite taken with him."

"That's what I understand," Perkin said. "She told me a month ago that she plans to marry him. I'm surprised it hasn't blown over yet—he's too old for her."

"No…he's only sixteen or seventeen…" Perkin was about to say that Kulis was in his twenties, when Dr. Bonucci continued, "…besides I don't think it will blow over. He's a marked man, you know. She's very strong-willed and very dedicated to her few friends. You've seen how protective she is of you?"

Perkin smiled and said, "Yes, I noticed."

Bonucci said, "She has a very small circle of friends, and you and your corporal are in it. She's an odd girl for an Italian. *Allora*…we are an outgoing race. We love to talk and be with people. We argue and we love like there is no tomorrow, but Stefania is quiet and inward looking. She only lights up around her family, and now you and your soldier...I would say she's Finnish if I didn't know better."

"Finnish? What do you mean? Why do you say that?" asked Perkin.

"The people of Europe all have distinct personalities, you know, but you can make some generalities. The southern Latin races are animated and voluble. The northern people are more reserved, and none are more reserved than the Finns. Maybe because their language is incomprehensible to everyone but themselves, but they are an inward people like Stefania. Do you know the European joke about Finns?"

Perkin said no, and Bonucci asked, "So, how do you know that a Finn likes you?"

"I don't know," said Perkin. "How?"

"He talks to your shoes and not his."

They talked about Stefania for a few more minutes, and Perkin was struck by the affection in the old man's voice for his granddaughter. He thought of Old Perkin and how much his own grandfather would enjoy speaking with the doctor, but he wanted to come back to a subject that they had passed over.

"Dr. Bonucci, what was Caporetto like?"

Dr. Bonucci sighed and looked toward Perkin with his milky white eyes. "Capitano, you know of war, so I don't need to tell you what a terrible waste war is. I was a doctor, not a real soldier so I can't talk the tactics with you. But I know we were able to hold the Austrians in the mountains. Battle after battle, they would attack and we would hold them. Or we would attack and they would hold us. Maybe neither the Italians nor the Austrians are made for war. Maybe because we are Catholic or maybe people just move slower the farther south you go, but then as now, Italians like to talk about war as if we were the Romans of old, but we don't like to fight the wars."

The old man motioned at his glass, and Perkin filled it with more brandy. Continuing, Bonucci said, "The Germans had soundly defeated Russia by then, and had a million more men to move to the west. Ha! I bet they wish they could do that now, don't you? So, they moved some down to our little fight in the mountains. Special troops called *Sturmtruppen*. The cowards hit our soldiers with mustard gas and phosgene from remotely fired launchers, and when our soldiers retreated in confusion, the Germans moved in the storm troopers. Our soldiers were routed and it was a disaster—10,000 killed and a quarter of a million men taken prisoner. The only thing that saved us were the mountains themselves."

"What do you mean?" asked Perkin.

"After the rout, it was a headlong retreat out of the mountains. The Austrians and Germans could not keep up, *come si dice*, they were unprepared for success, I think. We barely escaped. We moved our patients behind the Piave River, and in June 1918, we defeated the Austrians there. Now, that was a heroic battle! *E' meglio vivere un giorno da leone che cent'anni da pecora!* That was our motto: 'It is better to live a single day as a lion than a hundred years as a sheep!' Between the Piave and the battle of Vittorio Venuto we put an end to the Austrian Empire…" Bonucci stopped as if considering his words, and then he said, "…But to be honest, it is easier to defend against a river crossing than to make one. I think you know something about the difficulties of crossing a river under fire, yes?"

"There can't be much worse in this life," Perkin said, and to his surprise, his eyes suddenly welled up. He wanted to talk about the river, to tell the old doctor about the heroism and the finality of those two nights, but he couldn't. He wanted to talk about his fears that he might be wrong about Sam, and maybe he hadn't escaped. Or worse. Maybe it was the brandy, or perhaps the recollected melancholy of battles past over the span of generations, but the welling became a silent flow of tears down each cheek.

Even if he couldn't see his friend's stricken face, Bonucci instinctively understood. He had seen war at its worst, and he had a sense of the tragedy that the young Texan relived in his mind. Bonucci said nothing further, and there was a long silence as the two men listened to the crackle of the fire. After fifteen minutes, Angela wordlessly came into the room and helped her father to his feet. On her way out, she kissed Perkin on the forehead and he lay down on his army cot and watched the fire die out in silence as he thought about the ghosts of the mountains and valleys of Italy that he knew.

Chapter Five

January 28, 1944
0005 Hours
West of Mount Trocchio

Fifteen minutes before the start of the demonstration, the soldiers of Able Company had moved out of their prepared fighting positions and advanced toward the river. Lieutenant Ryan had done many evolutions similar to this during his training in the States, but this was his first coordinated movement at night in the war zone.

The nights remained pitch dark. There was no moon, no streetlights, and no flares. Distant fires in Cassino cast some light into the low-hanging clouds, but so little was reflected into the battlefield that Ryan felt as if he could have been blindfolded.

The presence of Corporal Kulis was reassuring. He had already moved laterally along the soldiers of Able Company and checked on the men, and then came back confidently to Lieutenant Ryan even though Ryan had advanced some fifty paces in the dark. In the few minutes that Kulis was gone, Ryan had walked into one grape vine and stumbled over a root in the dark.

Soon they reached the point that Major Spaulding had designated as their position for the demonstration. Their mission, if it was to be called that, was to simply pour small-arms fire into the enemy territory on the far banks. They would be shooting, but at nothing in particular.

Ryan and Kulis saw to the siting of the company's one surviving mortar and its sole machine gun, and then after checking the position of the remaining soldiers, they hunkered down to wait. The first sign that the demonstration was beginning was a series of deep booms far to their rear. The artillery had opened fire.

Ryan turned expectantly to the north and when the massed fires of the division's artillery arrived, the darkness turned to several points of sharp, bright light and the far bank of the Rapido was well-lit in the span of seconds. The echoes reverberated through the valley as scores, and then hundreds of rounds detonated over the Gustav Line.

The impact of the rounds on the far bank was the signal to the infantry to open fire. Ryan fired a magazine from his M-1 carbine, and then he and Kulis walked along the line to make sure that each soldier had fired. Everyone had, and as far as Ryan could see, the course of the war had not changed in the slightest.

When German artillery responded, the initial rounds were along the river where a crossing would likely be, but they did not fire a sustained barrage. After German forward observers reported that there were no indications of a crossing underway, the priority of the German artillery shifted to counter-battery fire. The soldiers of Able Company lay down on the rocky soil of the Rapido plain while hundreds of artillery rounds passed overhead in both directions, and after a few minutes, Ryan ordered his soldiers back to their foxholes. The first demonstration of the night was complete.

0100 Hours
Collelungo, Italy

It seemed like the village had finally gone to sleep. They had lain patiently in the grass outside the village waiting for the sounds to tell them that the day was done for the villagers, but the close of the day comes late in Italy. Patches of songs and laughter could be heard as they waited, and at least one family seemed to be having a disagreement as the sound of a man and woman's argument carried into the night.

"Glad I ain't him," Kenton whispered. "She seems kind of agitated."

"It's hard to tell with these Dagos," Sam opined. "They seem kind of agitated about everything."

Whatever the cause of the agitation, it died out eventually. Sergeant Kenton led the way again, and Sam moved behind him. They had seen a man standing guard on the road at the village limit chain-smoking in the dark, so they cut quietly through the fields and passed between two houses and onto what appeared to be the main road through the village near the southern tip of the narrow town. There was enough ambient light to see the shape of the buildings as they passed them by. Sam saw several pumps resting over cisterns, but they were all hand-cranked rotary pumps, and Sam knew from experience that the chains would be noisy. Especially so at night.

Periodically, they would halt and listen. The little village was quiet and Sam was prepared to head back when he heard the sounds of water ahead of them. He nudged Kenton and they moved on. After another twenty yards, the sound of a fountain was unmistakable, but it was clearly to their left.

In the dark, Sam could see nothing but felt along a stone wall until they came to a cross street. They edged down the street, and in another twenty yards, the street opened to a small piazza. Sam and Kenton crouched and looked hard through the darkness. No lights, no glowing ends of a cigarette, and no sound.

Sam stood up and headed to the fountain. It was like the fountains that he had come across in every other Italian village that he had gone through: a flow of water from some carved animal or saint into a pool. Sam bent over and tasted the water—it was ice cold and tasted clean. Both men drank until they couldn't drink any more, and then Kenton wordlessly uncorked one of the bottles and filled it from the pool while Sam did the same with their other bottle.

Sam would have liked to look around and see what was in the small town, but it was simply too dark. Time to depart the village. Half an hour later, they were back in the castle and sound asleep next to the remains of their fire.

0300 Hours
West of Mount Trocchio

Once again, the deep boom of distant artillery signaled the start of the demonstration as distinctly as a Very flare. The soldiers of Able Company crouched or lay down near the same spot as last time, and they prepared to fire meaningless rounds in this curious method of winning the war.

Corporal Kulis was relatively alert. He had fired with the rest of the soldiers three hours earlier, and then he had gone back to his shared foxhole with Lieutenant

Ryan to catch a few more minutes of sleep. Ryan had said it was okay, he wouldn't sleep any more that night. Kulis knew that the excitement and the adrenaline would diminish for the new officer relatively quickly, and before he knew it, Ryan would be sleeping nearly vertically with his feet resting in six inches of icy mud with the best of them.

Kulis normally spent his waiting time thinking about whores, but tonight was different. He was thinking about applying to West Point, and was trying to figure out how to explain to the army how he came to enlist fraudulently two years ago at the age of fifteen. He knew he wasn't the only underage soldier in the battalion, but while some recruiters turned a blind eye to underage enlistments, sometimes the field commanders did not. He was relatively certain that Captain Berger wouldn't take action on his age unless forced to, but if he put in a request to apply to West Point, his request would go up the chain of command at least to the regimental level or perhaps even higher. It was a bit of a conundrum. If he applied now, eventually, it would come out that he was underage. In fact, it needed to come out that he was underage, because with his false stated age, he was too old on paper to go to either West Point or Annapolis.

There were other commissioning options open to him, he knew. A field commission was a possibility, but he would have to be a much more senior NCO for that to happen and there would be every likelihood that he would revert to his old rank once the war ended. He could wait until he was released from active duty and attend a university like Texas A&M, earning his commission through ROTC, or he could go through either the army's officer candidate school or that of the National Guard. But as he squatted on the hill over-looking the Rapido River, Kulis decided that he wanted the education along with the commission, and that he should shoot for West Point over A&M or the Citadel. He wanted to go regular army, and not the National Guard no matter how much he loved the Gun Club. *If you're going to be a career officer, West Point it is*, he thought.

The opposing bank of the Rapido lit up once again as scores of artillery rounds began to impact. Kulis smiled in the reflected light as he thought about German soldiers dying in droves, even though he knew that the panzer grenadiers would be safe in their hardened bunkers. *The artillery rounds might drive some of the bastards mad, but it won't hurt many of them*, he thought. In general, Kulis had nothing against the average German soldier and usually he felt a slight degree of pity for any soldier on the receiving end of artillery. Nevertheless, he smiled. These were the bastards responsible for killing his friends at the Rapido, and while Kulis might sympathize to a degree with their plight, their deaths made him happy. They had a job to do, and that job necessitated the killing of many men.

Booming from the other side indicated that the Germans were beginning their return fire. If they held true to the pattern of the last demonstration, they would shell the known crossing sites again before beginning counter-battery fire against the American artillery.

This time was different. Bright lights appeared a thousand feet over the battlefield as the Germans fired star shells—parachute-retarded magnesium rounds that burned extraordinarily hot and bright until the inexorable pull of gravity brought them to the ground.

"Down! Get down!" Kulis yelled to his left and right, but most of his soldiers were already prone. None of the Able Company soldiers were profiled by the light of the flares, but as Kulis turned his attention back to his front, he thought he saw movement along the Allied bank of the Rapido River.

"Sir, do you see something about thirty yards back from the river along an azimuth towards the two o'clock position?"

Ryan stared hard in the direction that Kulis indicated and shrugged. "No. What'd you see?"

"Movement—maybe a guy low crawling towards the river. Maybe the demonstration caught a German scout out on patrol," Kulis said.

"Maybe he's one of our boys?" Ryan looked hard toward the river in the dying light but still saw nothing.

"We shouldn't have anyone out there. That all should have been deconflicted with the demonstration. We gotta open fire in any case, that's where I'm shooting." Kulis brought his rifle to his check and quickly fired two rounds downrange. Nothing happened, so he shifted his aim to a point that seemed more shaded from the flares and closer to the riverbank and fired again.

A distant figure sprang to his feet and began to sprint toward the defilade of the riverbank. Both Kulis and Ryan fired repeatedly at the target, but the fleeing man was over the bank in seconds and out of view.

"Do you think we hit him?" asked Ryan.

"Not yet, sir." Kulis jumped from his position and ran back up the slope to where the company mortar was temporarily sited. The flares began to die out while he was running, but breathing heavily, he made it to the mortar's position and began to bark out orders. When he was sure that the mortar team understood where the target was, and what Kulis wanted them to do, he stepped aside to let them do their work.

The first mortar round impacted the Allied side of the river about twenty-five yards from where Kulis had indicated, but before he could order a correction, the team made adjustments and fired again. It was closer but not where Kulis wanted it, and adjustments were made again, and the mortar fired a third round.

Kulis gave the team leader a thumbs-up and jogged back to Lieutenant Ryan's position. By the time he reached the lieutenant, the fourth round impacted the same spot, and the fifth and sixth rounds were directed to spots along the riverbank downstream from the original target, and the seventh and eighth rounds were directed upstream. As Kulis explained to his lieutenant, it was unlikely that the enemy scout would try to cross the river while American artillery was plastering the far side, so Kulis figured he would try to use the bank as cover and either move up or down the river.

"I doubt that we got him, sir, but who knows? I could take a team out and try to snag him, but I'd be afraid of being lit up by our own boys."

Ryan nodded, thought for a second, and said, "Let's get a team down there just before dawn, and we'll see if we hit anything. It looks like the demonstration is wrapping up, let's withdraw our people and head back to the CP."

0900 Hours
Presenzano, Italy

Perkin had been awake for nearly an hour, but he seemed to be the only one up in the house of countless people. He had been surprised and embarrassed when he woke up to find that the living room that had served as his bedroom was also the bedroom for many others. They had not been there when he had gone to sleep the night before—obviously, they had waited until he had gone to sleep before going to bed themselves.

He had quietly dressed, surrounded by five sleeping

women and children on the floor, completely covered in blankets. Stefania had placed her bedroll next to his cot, and he carefully stepped over her, grabbed his overcoat, and walked outside to relieve himself.

The day was shaping up to be just like every other during the gray Italian winter. A cold wind blew in from the northwest, and Perkin knew enough of the signs of Italian weather to recognize that there was a good chance of sleet or even snow. He sighed at the thought and decided that if he were going to go for a walk it would be better to do it now than later.

Since arriving the day before, Perkin had not had the opportunity to walk through Presenzano. Like many villages and towns that Perkin had seen in Italy, Presenzano was built on a steep slope and seemingly defied gravity. It rested precariously on the side of a foothill that connected to the mountain complex running to the northwest and passing by San Pietro some eight miles away. The town itself faced to the southeast and some hundred yards or so below the town's lower city limit, a valley plain met the mountains. Perkin thought for a moment why the ancient Romans would build a town on a hillside when such a nice flat plain was available, and decided that arable land was at such a premium that it had to be reserved for agriculture.

Whether it was or not, Perkin couldn't tell. The war had obviously passed Presenzano by but it had left a mark. Whatever fields had once existed on the flat landing fronting Presenzano had been shredded by the passing armies, and Perkin worried, not for the first time, about how the Italians would be able to feed themselves in the future.

The door to the Moroni house opened, and a sleepy looking Stefania peered out with a worried look on her face, which lit up when she spied Perkin. She ducked back into the house, grabbed a coat, and joined Perkin outside.

"Good morning, my friend. Did you sleep well?" asked Stefania.

"I did, thank you. And you?"

"Good, good. I miss my bed though. Do you miss yours?"

Perkin thought for a moment and said, "I haven't slept in my own bed for ages, and even then, I hadn't used it much since I left for college. Gosh, I think it's been over a year now since we left the States, and it had been months since I'd been home."

Stefania took Perkin's arm and said, "Let's walk this way. Tell me about Texas, I need to know if Eddie and I will move there after the war."

Perkin smiled and looked down at the teenager on his arm with a mixture of amusement and affection. She saw the look, laughed a rare laugh, and then said in a mock threatening tone, "Don't make fun of me, Perkin Berger! I'm serious. What's Texas like?"

"We call it God's country even though some of Texas ain't exactly picturesque, you know. Not like here. Where I come from, Texas is warm and flat and springtime is a wonderful thing. I live on the water in a town called Portland, which is in the south of Texas. There ain't a flatter place on the planet, I suppose."

"What's the food like?"

Perkin had been asked that question a lot by the Italians that he met. Food was on everyone's mind nearly all the time. "Texas is beef country. So, lots of beef and in every way you can think of—barbeque brisket, roasts, stews, steaks, ribs, whatever. But, we're also on the coast, so we have some pretty good seafood as well. Trout, redfish, shrimp...damn, I'm getting hungry talking about it."

"Do Texans eat pasta or pizza?"

"Not so much, although I suspect that there will be a lot more after the war. A lot of Texans are going to leave Italy and demand something more than army spaghetti when they get home."

Stefania laughed at the thought that spaghetti might be the only pasta in Texas. "I'd have to change that," she said. "Are the people nice?"

"Texans are generally known as very nice folk, I think. But people are people. Most are good, but some are bad. Italians are nice people, but I've met some of them who ain't."

Stefania nodded. She knew exactly what Perkin was talking about. "Do you think that there are niçe Germans, Capitano?"

"Yes, of course. But to be honest, I ain't met a lot of the nice ones so far in my European holiday. It seems like every German I've met wants to kill me. But, I think that people everywhere are largely the same. They want to be happy, want to see their kids grow up, but sometimes, people are poorly led."

"Maybe that's the way it is with Italians, but I don't know that the Germans want all that. They just want what others have." Stefania protectively grabbed Perkin's arm as he slipped on a patch of ice, and then she said, "Like my papa. Everyone's papa went and hid in the mountains so the Germans wouldn't take them. Except mine. He said he had to stay and take care of the sick and the wounded in San Pietro. He didn't run away, but the Germans took him. Don't they have doctors?" she asked.

Perkin looked down at Stefania's worried face and said gently, "Honey, I think that they needed your daddy to take care of the Italian men and boys that they took for their labor battalions. Doctors are valuable men, so

I think that your daddy will be okay."

"Most people are valuable, Perkin Berger. My papa is. The shepherd is. The farmer and the grocer are all valuable...to the people of their town. To their families. But I know that not all of them are treated well by the Germans. Did you know that the German soldiers killed two girls in San Pietro for trying to get water from our fountain? They said it was now theirs and they shot two girls. I knew them both. How can you be a good person and shoot a girl for taking a drink of water?"

"You can't," Perkin said. "Good people don't do that. Good officers don't order that."

"Do you know what happened with the husband of Signora Ocello?"

"Which one is she?" Perkin watched as a convoy of American trucks in the distance worked their way up Victory Road toward the fighting in Cassino to their north.

"Signora Ocello, she's the mother of the two annoying girls..." Stefania's face darkened briefly at the thought of the other girls. "...they are from Mignano. She's the niece of Signora Moroni. Her husband and her son and several other men from Mignano were in hiding in the mountains toward the coast. In a cave, like we stayed in a cave, but no so nice as our cave. Every day, one of them would come down from the mountain and meet his wife. She would send them food if they had food, and the men would share it. This started in September and every day, one of them would come down from the mountain. Then one day in October, the wife of one of the men begged her husband to stay the night with her and their children, and that was the day the Germans decided to raid his house. Maybe they were looking for men, but maybe they were looking for food—they would take anything in the house, and if they were really hungry, they would dig up our yards. Most families had buried food you know. Maybe they were looking for women. I don't know. So the Germans raided this house and caught this man with his family. They beat him really bad and made him take them to the cave, and they seized all the men staying there. He and another man tried to escape, and they were both shot, just like the girls. The rest were sent to work for the Germans as slaves."

Perkin was silent for a moment and then said, "Oh, Lord that's terrible. Why haven't Mrs. Ocello and her daughters gone home? Most of Mignano is still standing."

"It was her husband who was caught and then betrayed the others. Signora Ocello isn't welcome in Mignano anymore."

1000 Hours
Six Miles Northwest of Dunarobba, Italy

Sam heard a low whistle and then Lieutenant Beams' voice call out, "Sam, we have a vehicle approaching from the south."

Both Sam and Sergeant Kenton had been awake for an hour, but they had been slow to get up from their bedroll. They were currently alternating their discussion between favorite foods and baseball prospects. At Beams' warning, they jumped to their feet and began to stuff their meager belongings into the gunnysacks that had once held the ham they had finished for breakfast.

Another whistle and then Beams called down to them, "It's Bazzini and another fellow."

Sam and Kenton stopped their frantic packing and joined Beams in the courtyard. Mr. Bazzini was pulling up in a heavy truck bearing a load of dark brown coal.

The tall man dropped down from the passenger seat, while his young companion handed down two large canvas bags. When Mr. Bazzini took possession of the bags, the driver smiled and waved, and then put the truck in gear and drove back to the south.

Bazzini offered a smile and as he said hello, he shook the hands of the three Americans. "I didn't want the truck to bring attention to you. I'll walk home from here." Bazzini looked around the courtyard. "It's a good place to stay, no? Todi castle?" he asked.

"Is that what it's called? It's been very good to us, Mr. Bazzini. Thank you for telling us about it. We've slept very well since being here," Sam said.

"I wondered if you would," said Bazzini with a smile.

"Why's that?" asked Beams.

"Because it is reputedly haunted. It's what makes it safe for you."

This time, Kenton asked the same question, "Why's that?"

Bazzini pulled a bottle of dark red wine from one of the bags, and as he pulled the cork, he said, "The story is that the mistress of the castle lost her entire family—husband and sons—to the plague but lived many years after their deaths. She went insane from the grief, renounced her faith in God, and as a punishment has been forced to live as an angry spirit in our world here at this castle. She is buried in that room there." Bazzini pointed at a room that was opened to the elements. "There's a crypt under the floor."

"How's that keep us safe, Mr. Bazzini?" asked Kenton. He didn't care for loose talk of ghosts.

"Because Italians are superstitious. Most believe in ghosts, saints, spirits, evil eyes, and other nonsense." Bazzini looked amused.

"And you don't?" asked Sam.

"Of course not! I'm an engineer, aren't I? I believe in mathematics. I believe in science. I believe in the tools of man—sometimes a slide rule and a pencil and always a pick and a shovel. Despite myself, I occasionally believe in divine providence, but I don't believe in spirits— other than those that come from grapes and grain, of course." Bazzini laughed at his joke, proud that he could tell one in English. He handed the bottle over to Beams who took a long drink of wine before passing it to Sergeant Kenton. After taking his turn at the bottle, Bazzini said, "There are no ghosts here, nor is nearby Mount Subasio haunted like some think, but the local villagers believe that the poor crazy lady still inhabits these walls, mourning her lost husband and children."

"How did you come to know about this place, Mr. Bazzini?" asked Sam.

"My grandpapa was from Collelungo, which is the village on the north...the other side of the castle. He said that my brothers and I should stay away because of the ghost, so naturally we dared each other to come here—first to touch the wall, then to come into the courtyard here, and then to explore the castle. The local boys thought we were crazy. They wouldn't come near the place, nor would their fathers, the sheep. But we did. Have you found the hidden room, yet?"

Sam laughed. "A castle, a ghost, and now a hidden room. What have you gotten us into, Mr. Bazzini?"

"Maybe sanctuary. Maybe no."

1000 Hours
1st Battalion CP, West of Mount Trocchio

The 1st Battalion command post was decidedly more elaborate than the hole that served as the Able

Company command post. It had been established in a gully coming off the side of Mount Trocchio. It had the advantage of a defilade position, and engineers had carved out a small room back into the side of the gully, and covered it with wood from pallets and recovered tin roofing held in place by burlap sandbags. There was a constantly flowing trickle of water underfoot, but the worst of the elements were so far kept at bay by the improvised shelter. A chair, a field table, radios, and the battalion telephone exchange were the only modern touches to the man-made cave.

"Alex," said Major Spaulding, "we've got a quiet night ahead of us. No demonstrations planned, so keep your boys on fifty-fifty and try and get some sleep yourself."

Ryan nodded and yawned involuntarily. True to his prediction, he had not been able to get back to sleep. A drop of accumulated rain worked its way through the planking above Ryan's head and dropped onto his cheek. As he wiped it away with the back of a dirty hand, Ryan asked, "Patrolling tonight?"

Spaulding shook his head. "Nope. There are patrols scheduled along our frontage tonight, but not by us. To your right, the 2nd Battalion of the 6th Armored Infantry will be conducting patrols, and will also be laying down barbed wire in their sector. In front of us, A Troop of the 91st Recon Squadron is going to cross with one, maybe two patrols. We'll get with regiment in a minute and make sure we coordinate with those boys. The 91st just got here, but they have a good reputation from Africa and Sicily."

"Sir, any word yet on reinforcements?" Ryan had lost another man to trench foot and was concerned that his squad-sized company would disappear.

"Yes! Finally." Spaulding spit tobacco juice into the

little stream at his feet, adjusted the quid in his cheek with his tongue and said, "I'm getting thirty boys in from the replacement depot later this morning. I'll send ten over to Able Company when they get here."

"Thirty? Great! Any NCOs?" asked Ryan. Inwardly, he was disappointed that it was so few, but he didn't want to look a gift horse in the mouth.

"No idea. Probably not, but keep your fingers crossed. We may get some troops culled from the 142nd, but let's not count on it. Oh, and speaking of NCOs, I was impressed with how Kulis performed last night, and I'll tell him so when I see him. Unless we get some senior NCOs in today's levy, keep him in his role as your acting top."

Ryan smiled with some satisfaction. They had found the mangled body of a German scout twenty yards downstream from where they had seen him slide down the riverbank. Ryan had relayed the story to Major Spaulding that morning, and made sure to give the credit to Corporal Kulis. The lieutenant thought ruefully that the young corporal knew more about war, and thought quicker than the young officer did.

1020 Hours,
Todi Castle, Italy

Mr. Bazzini gave a tour of the castle to Sam and the others, and had shown them the false wall in the chapel, only a few feet away from where he claimed the unfortunate mistress of the castle lay interred. The wall opened to a small room that had no other exits. It might be a place to hide, thought Sam, *but what happened to the proverbial tunnel out of the castle?*

Bazzini had brought more food. He explained to Sam that he had gone to a small circle of trusted friends and relatives, and when they found out that it was for escaped American soldiers, they opened their larders and provided food. They had graciously given several jars of olives and mixed vegetables in jars, another small ham, several hard sausages, more boiled eggs, a small round of cheese and several unmarked bottles of red wine.

When Sam explained that they had gone into Collelungo to get water, Bazzini started to look around. "There used to be a well or cistern here…"

"The walls have collapsed into the well," Sam interrupted. They had found it their first day, but it was unusable.

Bazzini shrugged. "There is a creek in the woods to the east of Collelungo that might be the best bet for water but the village may no be safe. Maybe the village to the west, Morre, is no so safe either. There are fascists in this part of Italia, although most of the families are not political. There may be Allied sympathizers in the town council, or as mayors or constables, I don't know. But officially, everyone at every level of government supports Mussolini and Hitler. There's no other way."

Sam nodded his head. He had no intention of making contact with anyone official in any case. "What about the Church, Mr. Bazzini. Is there any help there?"

Bazzini replied, "Maybe yes, maybe no. I'm no so much a religious man, but I asked a friend who is making some questions for you. Asking some questions. *Come si dice*, uh, carefully. There is a priest in Orvieto—twenty kilometers to the west of here—my friend said that this priest will help if asked. My friend went to Orvieto this morning."

Sam looked at the others, and nodded. "Okay…if you trust him, then thanks."

"My wife and her friends are seeing about clothes

for you. It's no so easy, there aren't many Italians as big as you. They will make some if necessary."

Before he left to walk back to Dunarobba, Mr. Bazzini turned to Sam and said, "I almost forgot. The BBC is saying that your landing at Nettuno is hard fighting. German radio says you are stuck on the beach and surrounded, and will be exterminated before Monday." He reached into a coat pocket and pulled out a worn pack of Armanino playing cards. "I would bring a book or two, but all we have are in Italian. Try not to get too bored. I will see you when I have news. If you leave on your own, put your empty bottles in the hidden room. That way, I'll know you weren't arrested."

1110 Hours
Presenzano, Italy

Perkin had undergone another round of torture, or stretching as Dr. Bonucci preferred to call it, when he and Stefania returned from their walk. As painful as his treatment was, the combined effects of the hot and cold poultices, the stretching of his muscles and the massage of the scar tissue seemed to be helping. While the soldiers of the battalion remained on Perkin's mind, the absence of near combat, and the subconscious knowledge that he was out of danger also seemed restorative.

Perkin was finding out what other therapy was in store for him. The women had taken him into the kitchen after Dr. Bonucci was done with him, and he had kneaded dough while the women watched and commented in Italian. It became surprisingly difficult after a few minutes, and Signoria Ocello offered Perkin a faint smile as she moved over to help him. After his arms rested, he dutifully began to knead the stiff dough again.

There were no English speakers in the kitchen with him, and directions on how to properly work the dough were given in a torrent of partially understood Italian and through a lot of hand gestures. When Signoria Ocello stood beside him, put her hands on top of his and showed him how to push the dough away from him properly, he was struck by the fact that she was an attractive woman. A few years older than him, but attractive. He hadn't noticed that the day before. Then he noticed that she smelled nice, which was unusual. In the absence of soap, he hadn't met many people for quite some time that smelled nice.

Stefania came into the kitchen to check on him and glared briefly at Signoria Ocello before saying, "Capitano, Grandpapa has a new exercise for you out-side. You won't need your coat and you won't need her." She took a tea towel and knocked the flour and scraps of dough off his hands before ushering him out the back of the house.

"Do you like Signoria Ocello, Perkin Berger?" asked Stefania when they were outside. Her scowl was replaced with a grin.

"No, of course not. I mean she's nice and all, but no." Perkin returned the grin. "Why do you ask?"

"Because in the month that we've shared a house, she has never worn perfume or put on makeup. That's why."

"Oh. Well I usually bring out the best in people, except of course when I don't. What's my exercise?"

"Running," Stefania laughed.

"Running?"

"*Si*! Running away from women before long, I think. *Allora*, we should prepare for that." Stefania led him by his arm to the side of the house where a pile of logs lay waiting. "Eddie says you have a girlfriend. An

Englishwoman."

Perkin grinned. "Is that a fact?"

"Uh huh. He said she was a peach. I think that's good, no?"

"She is a peach—a peach is a good thing. But, I don't know if I'll see her again though." Perkin certainly hoped that he would but he didn't have high expectations.

Stefania handed Perkin an axe and set a log on the chopping block. "Grandpapa says to only do as much as you can. No more. Why don't you think you'll see her again? Do you like her more than Gianina?"

"Oh, honey, I don't know. Gianina was special, but so's Helen. But, they're different." Perkin tentatively tried to swing the axe. He could lift the head only as high as his shoulder, and when he brought it down, the blade sank into the wood and stuck.

Stefania giggled. "Haven't you chopped wood before, Perkin Berger?"

It was Perkin's turn to offer a mock glare, which made Stefania giggle even more. When he broke the axe free from the wood, and reset the log on the chopping block, he forced himself to lift the axe higher. He had the same result twice more—both from the chopping and from Stefania—and in his fourth attempt he raised the axe even higher and brought it down hard on the log. This time it split.

The movement and the violence of the swing brought forth an old memory in a rush to Perkin's mind. In an instant, Perkin was transported back to the beach in Paestum where he found himself with a heavy sledgehammer in in hands. He was on the deck of a Panzer IV and was trying to disable the tank's coaxial machine guns with the sledge. The sounds of combat and the smell of powder and exhaust fumes seemed as real and concrete for Perkin in Presenzano in January as they had that day in September in Paestum. In his mind, he watched with panic as the tank commander extended a Lugar with a trembling hand through a gap in the commander's hatch and pulled the trigger again and again. He missed and Perkin hit the hatch so hard with the heavy sledge that the tank commander's wrist was nearly severed...

"Perkin? Perkin Berger? Are you okay?" Stefania asked in a small voice.

"Huh? What's that, honey?" Perkin looked down and his hands were trembling. Not as bad as they had that morning, but he was shaking and he didn't know why.

"Are you okay, my friend?" Stefania asked again as she took Perkin's hand and peered intently into his face.

"I am...I just had the strangest, um...daydream though." The trembling was gone, and Perkin looked down at Stefania and offered a weak smile. "That was the damnedest thing."

"You looked very angry. Did I say something wrong?"

"What? No...my mind was just somewhere else for a moment. Back...in the war," Perkin said hesitantly, although he knew it was true.

"Should we go back inside?" asked Stefania.

Perkin shook his head, and picked up the axe again. He spat on both hands and swung the axe back and forth for a moment to loosen up before resuming his task. Perkin chopped wood for another fifteen minutes and his range of motion increased as his muscles warmed up and stretched. Satisfied, he and Stefania went inside, the Paestum memory fading in his mind.

1300 Hours
Avezzano, Italy

Grossmann was in an angry foul mood. The priest had flat out rejected giving Grossmann any more leeway to walk about Avezzano, and they had argued up to the point that Grossmann believed that if he pushed it harder, he would come out of character as an escaped American pilot. If he wasn't awaiting the arrival of Colonel von Hatzfeldt, he would have the damn priest arrested and be done with his mission. *Damn him*, he thought over and over.

It was clear that he wouldn't be able to make it to Rome and track down Antoniette before his meeting with Colonel von Hatzfeldt tomorrow. It was likewise clear that such a course of action was fraught with terrible peril and dire consequences for him in any case. Had there been a breach of security, if Antoniette was suspected of something, then it was likely that her apartment was being watched and her phone monitored. And the irony was that the surveillance was likely being done by his own organization, the Abwehr.

Grossmann picked up a novel and sat cross-legged on his cot trying to find a beam of light through the dirty window. The gray sky outside wasn't providing much illumination in any case, so Grossmann threw the book down in frustration and patted his pockets for a pack of cigarettes, even though he knew that he had chain-smoked them all the day before.

If he had been a different man, he might have walked into the nave of the church and sought solace there. Even the uninspiring church ministered by Father Carlo had provided peace and solace to many over the years of war, but Grossmann was not in the mood to ask God for help. He stood up and began pacing the short

length of the office, turned and repeated it again and
again as he fought the urge to scream from frustration
and withdrawal.

1530 Hours
Able Company CP, West Slope of Mount
Trocchio, Italy

Corporal Kulis jogged hunched over through the
leafless branches of the grapevines. Before sliding under
the mixture of dead vines and tin roofing that offered
their foxhole some protection from the elements, he
offered a low whistle. Lieutenant Ryan had been a
pretty jumpy sleeper ever since Major Spaulding's prank
the day before, and Kulis wanted to let him know that
he was coming in.

A hand emerged from under the tin and waved
him in. When Kulis slid into the trench, he was met
with a faint smile and a hot cup of coffee from an army
thermos. Kulis wasn't a big fan of black coffee, but he
wanted the warmth. Even with wool socks, pants, shirt,
and gloves and his heavy overcoat, he was chilled to the
bone. A cold biting wind from the northwest brought
spicules of ice blowing into his face under his helmet
and he had to resist the urge to clean his glasses every
few minutes. He had nothing clean to dry them with,
so he just endured the obstructed vision.

"Wonderful army day, isn't it?" asked Ryan. He'd
clearly gotten some sleep.

"It is, sir." Kulis placed his tin mug of hot coffee
before him and opened up a can of cold hash from his
C-rations. He found that if he took a bite of the cold
beef and swished around some hot coffee in his mouth
at the same time, it was almost the same as eating hot
food. Almost.

"Where were you at?" Ryan asked. "When I woke up, you were gone."

"We got our levy of men, sir, and I was gettin' 'em settled," Kulis replied.

Ryan looked sharply at Kulis and said, "Why didn't you wake me? I should have been there."

Kulis nodded. "Yes, sir, I thought about that. But with all respect, sir, there's a thousand things that you could be doin' at any moment of the day, but there just ain't enough hours. So until we get some more officers and non-coms in, we're gonna have to divvy this up some. You need sleep. I need sleep. They came in on my watch, so I let you sleep."

Ryan knew that there was truth in what Kulis said, but he felt that he let down the new soldiers in some way. Nodding, he said, "What'd we get? How many?"

"We got eight soldiers, sir. I guess battalion got less than we expected. Seven are riflemen, one's a medic. I was hoping to get a BAR in to replace Fratelli, but we didn't, but one rifleman's a German speaker."

"Good. Any impressions of the new guys?" asked Ryan.

Kulis shrugged, "A mixed bag, I'd reckon. They mostly look lost and scared. One bubba from Tennessee...none are from Texas by the way...one bubba from Tennessee named Hodgson looks pretty hard, but intelligent. He told me he's a broken bowl."

"A what?"

"A broken bowl."

"What's that?"

"That means when he reached fourteen or maybe fifteen, his pa broke his bowl." Kulis wiped his spoon on his jacket and put it in his pocket.

Ryan shook his head and shrugged. "I still don't follow you. So what?"

Kulis looked incredulously at the lieutenant and saw that he was serious. "Ain't y'all got poor folk in Iowa? Broken bowl means that when he reached manhood, or at least old enough to fend for hisself, his pa broke his dinner bowl and he couldn't stay at home no more because he couldn't eat. A broken bowl is someone who was kicked out of his home and family because they didn't want to feed him no more."

"Jesus Christ! Were you a broken bowl?" asked the lieutenant.

"No, sir. We had enough to get by, and my mom wouldn't have allowed it in any case. But there were plenty kids around me that struck out on their own at fourteen or fifteen. Them were some tough years down where I come from." Kulis had in fact left home at fifteen, but mostly out of boredom.

Ryan poured himself some more coffee as he listened to the freezing rain land on the top of their tin roof. Things hadn't been easy for his family during the Depression either, but there wasn't anything in his experience relatable to a broken bowl. There was some unrest throughout the state during the early years of the Depression as the stock market collapsed, then manufacturing collapsed, then the bottom fell out of the agricultural market as well. Ryan's father had owned enough land outright that he was able to sell a small farm, although for pennies on the dollar of its true value, and hold on to the money for taxes and expenses on his primary farm.

If it hadn't been for the extra land that the Ryan family owned, Lieutenant Ryan mused that maybe he would have been a broken bowl son as well. He remembered that the year he turned twelve, his father came home from selling the corn harvest and told Ryan's mother dryly that he almost took his profits and bought a bottle of whiskey. He wanted a gun more, he had joked, but the harvest didn't bring in enough cash. He had sold his corn at eight cents a bushel that year. With sixty acres in corn, and twenty-seven bushels of corn per acre, his cash crop for the year had earned him a gross of only $129. It was a year that led to widespread bankruptcies, loss of farms, and suicides.

It wasn't until the next year with the passage of the Agricultural Adjustment Act that things began to stabilize somewhat for Ryan and his neighbors. Ryan's father had told him that the problem was too much acreage in cultivation, and the farmers were growing more than an impoverished population could afford to buy, and there were no international markets to ship to either. It was self-evident to most farmers that they were growing too many crops, but equally self-evident that no voluntary scheme to limit production was going to work. The AAA paid subsidies to take land out of use and ensure the crop prices didn't fall any further. Ryan's father was upset by the AAA because it seemed wrong for a farmer to limit what he grew, but as he told his son, it was better than the shame of having his name listed in the newspaper along with all the others who were forced to accept welfare.

"Did you guys ever have to burn corn?" he asked Kulis.

"You mean for heat?" When Lieutenant Ryan nodded, Kulis answered, "No. We had enough trees on our land to get through a winter. We never bought coal like you Yankees do. We had a wood stove in the kitchen and another in our livin' room. It can get pretty cold in Texas from time to time, so we'd haul our mattresses into the livin' room and sleep there when a blue norther come through. I can remember that stove gettin' red hot sometimes when we'd burn green wood in it."

Ryan thought about the coal chute that ran to the basement of their house. He had hated shoveling coal into the furnace when he was growing up. "I knew some farmers back home who had to burn corn. It just didn't pay enough to haul their corn to the town silo, and they couldn't buy coal and had cleared their farms of wood. Sometimes the countryside smelled an awful lot like burnt popcorn in the winter."

"Oh brother, I'd like some popcorn. With lots of salt and butter," mused Kulis. "You think that farming will be tough again after the war?"

"I don't know. My dad's finally banked some money since we started building the army in '40. Most other farmers are doing better too. Hopefully, they're paying off debt and banking some for later. Let's say the war goes on another year or two and then everyone goes home. Are the jobs going to be there for ten or fifteen million vets? What happens when Uncle Sam is no longer footing the bill to feed ten million GIs? I'd think that it might be tough times again, but I sure hope not."

1700 Hours
Presenzano, Italy

Perkin and Stefania had gone out for one last walk before darkness set in. Surprisingly to Perkin, he felt better than he had since his injury and he could sense that his mobility and flexibility were returning.

The last vestiges of his fever were long gone, and he was eating with enthusiasm. Lunch at the Moroni house that afternoon had been pasta with a homemade red sauce, the bread that he had kneaded, and more peaches. He had sipped a rather hideous red wine, and had taken a nice nap before the fireplace during *reposo*. The cot that he was sleeping on was more comfortable than the ground that he was used to, even if his feet dangled over the edge. Overall, he was relaxing and he could feel his strength and energy returning. The episode earlier was puzzling, but he wasn't worried about it.

He was getting to know his Italian housemates better, and his Italian had improved over the course of a day. There were many cognates between Spanish and Italian, and if Perkin didn't know a word or phrase in Italian, he would try it in Spanish, which met with varying degrees of success. The children would hang on him until Stefania or Angela shooed them away, but outside of some occasional pain, he found that he didn't mind. Being a convalescent in an Italian home was the nearest thing he'd had to a normal life in some time.

His mind never left the war, however, and as much as Perkin was truly grateful for home cooking, a fireplace, and near constant female attention, he couldn't relax entirely. Perkin was itching to take command of the company, and he wanted to get back as soon as possible. No doubt Lieutenant Ryan, under the tutelage of Major Spaulding, would have things organized by the time he got back, but Perkin wanted that organization to have his stamp on it—not Ryan's and not Spaulding's.

He knew that personnel matters in the battalion were largely under the purview of Major Spaulding, but should regiment or division desire to put a particular officer in that billet, there would be little that Spaulding could do to stop it. Perkin certainly was looking forward to being a company commander again, particularly Able Company, but he also knew that he was the ideal placeholder for Sam—should Sam ever make it back.

Sam was on Perkin's mind when he and Stefania turned a corner and he nearly ran into a large American soldier and a smaller soldier in a British uniform. The

American soldier was a major with a 5th Army patch on his uniform sleeve, but the officer in the British uniform was in the shadow of a building and Perkin couldn't make out the trappings of his uniform other than the single crown on his epaulette signifying that he, too, was a major.

Perkin saluted and said, "Good afternoon, gentlemen." He moved to walk around the two men, but was stopped by the American officer.

"Captain, just a second if you don't mind." The officer had a northeastern accent and seemed pleasant enough as did the officer in the British uniform.

"Yes, sir, what can I do for you?"

"Could we talk for a second?" The major glanced briefly at Stefania.

"Sure." Perkin reached into his pocket, pulled out a handful of lire and handed it to Stefania. "Run ahead to the store and buy some hard candy for the kids, would you?" Perkin smiled at the delighted look on Stefania's face, and then he turned back to the two majors.

"I'm Major Sullivan, and this is Major Blair of the New Zealand Corps," the large American said by way of introduction.

"Cap'n Berger, 141st Infantry," Perkin said as he shook the offered hands.

"How long have you been in Presenzano, Captain Berger?" asked Blair.

"This is my second day, here, sir. I'm staying with an Italian family while on convalescent leave."

"Oh." The American officer seemed disappointed. "So, you don't know which units have been in this area before?"

"Sir, I've actually never been to Presenzano before, but I've been in the area since we moved up in the October timeframe. Is there a unit that you're looking for in particular?" Perkin's tone was polite, but he wasn't sure why the 5th Army staff officer didn't know the location of a unit.

Sensing this, the major explained, "I've been a liaison officer with the 8th Army, and I haven't spent much time in our own sector. Major Blair and I are beginning to..."

"We're just sightseeing, Captain," interrupted Blair in an accent that sounded Australian to Perkin.

Perkin looked at the brief concern on the New Zealander's face, and then he thought he understood. "Gentlemen, let me give you a quick overview of the area, since you're new to it all. We're on the southern slope of a massif that extends to the Cassino area. We're far enough back here that we're out of range of German field artillery, and there've been no air raids in this area that I know of since, I don't know, mid-December. Just, uh, speaking hypothetically, that if one wished to place, perhaps, a corps headquarters in the area, you would be ideally situated between Fifth Army at Caserta and the combat units in the Cassino area of operations."

Perkin saw that he had the intense interest of the two officers, and was going to say more about the placement of a corps command when he saw for the first time that Major Blair was wearing the insignia of the New Zealand Army Medical Corps. "Also, you know, we had a field hospital, the 33rd I believe, just down there," Perkin pointed to the plain at the base of the mountain. "But it was withdrawn after a freak storm over New Year's, which flattened just about everything. I ain't heard about it since, so my guess is that, well, it's probably in Anzio about now. Other than with the weather, this worked well for us...so it might be a good place again for a division or corps level hospital just down there. It's protected, but close enough to the front that ambulances can cover the distance from aid stations to here in thirty minutes or so. You've got Victory Road, I mean Highway 6, just yonder, and we're at most a couple miles from a spur line on the southbound railroad to Naples. Another four or five miles down the road that way is the U.S. 16th Evacuation Hospital, and I know that there's another one, the 95th down by Capua. Hell, this area's got so many hospitals that you can't hardly swing a dead cat without hittin' one."

Major Blair laughed at the thought, looked Perkin over, and asked, "Why aren't you in one of them? Is it standard for the U.S. Army to quarter their wounded soldiers with the natives?"

"No, sir. As it was described to me, the inn's full, and my options were therapy with a local doctor, or evacuation to Africa or the States. I was already friends with the local doctor and his daughter, who's a nurse, and the girl who's my tour guide is his granddaughter. It was an easy choice for me."

"Good for you, Captain. It's my experience that you're more likely to die in Africa from disease than in Italy from combat. Better here than there, mate." Major Blair looked at his watch and nodded at his taller American companion. "Sully, we need to be on the road if we're to get to Caserta before it gets pitch black."

When Perkin offered his hand, he asked of Major Blair, "Sir, any chance when y'all head this direction that the British 8th Field Surgical Unit will come with you?"

The New Zealander looked serious for a moment, shrugged, and then said wryly, "No one said anyone was going anywhere, Captain, but…be a good fellow and not discuss it further if you don't mind. What's your interest in the 8th?"

"I have a friend assigned there as a surgical nurse,"

Perkin said. "Helen Langley."

Blair stared at Perkin and shook his head. "I should have known. You told us your name was Berger, right? And is your Christian name Merkin or Perkerby or something odd like that?"

When Perkin nodded, and said it was indeed something odd like that, Blair said, "I suppose I've heard your name enough times that I should have made the connection. Captain, it gives me no pleasure to tell you that next to Mussolini and Kesselring, you may be the most hated man in Italy—she talks about her 'lovely American boy' so much that you'd best have bodyguards for the rest of the war. But since you've been very helpful, I'll pass along your regards to Sister Langley, and if you happen to come round here in, say, a fortnight, why not swing by and give her your regards in person?"

2030 Hours
Able Company CP, West Slope of Mount
Trocchio, Italy

In the fading light of a distant flare, Second Lieutenant Alex Ryan looked at Second Lieutenant Dan Kemper with something akin to affection even though they had never met. Kemper had reported to Ryan a few minutes before as the first officer replacement for the company since Ryan reported to Major Spaulding four days before.

Kemper was from Phoenix, Arizona, and his teeth chattered as he talked to Ryan. "So what's the deal with Spaulding? A good guy?"

"Yeah, he was the company commander here before moving to battalion. He's got a handle on this business," Ryan replied. It was an assessment that he had made based on his battalion commander's command presence and reputation with the company old-timers, as he had not really seen Spaulding handle the battalion in action.

"What about this Captain Berger? Spaulding says he's the company commander, and you're the acting company commander while Berger's on convalescent leave." Actually, what Spaulding had told Kemper was that Captain Berger was acting company commander, and Ryan was acting acting, but it had made no sense to Kemper, so he just nodded.

"He strikes me as very smart—he's even got a Ph.D. I think he's been either with Able or with battalion since 1940 or so. Corporal Kulis, Private Froman, and a few others who survived the river swear by him."

"Good enough, but do you think he'll be back soon? I heard he was pretty torn up."

"I don't know. A week, maybe two was what I was told. His cousin, Lieutenant Taft, is in the company as well," said Ryan. "But he was captured at the river. He was in command of the company at the time."

"That's a tough break." Kemper shivered as a gust of ice-cold air blew down the neck of his overcoat. He cinched his coat tighter and tried to duck down farther into the trench but it brought no warmth.

"Yeah." Ryan wanted to talk second lieutenant to second lieutenant about what he had heard about the river, about his own uncertainties and concerns, but as he was the acting company commander, he didn't think it would be appropriate.

"Alex, Spaulding told me you're in charge until Berger gets back or we get assigned a first lieutenant, and I have no issues with that, but just so we both know, what's your date of rank? Mine's November 13th, '42."

"Mine's October 2nd." Ryan was the senior officer, and he wasn't sure whether that was a good thing or not. Part of him would have been relieved had a more senior lieutenant taken over, but another part of him was grateful that he wouldn't be taking orders from another butter bar. He understood where Kemper was coming from though. He probably was unexcited at the prospect of taking orders from someone as uninitiated as himself. "Take command of 1st Platoon. PFC Froman is your senior guy. Major Spaulding says that Corporal Kulis stays with me as my senior NCO until we get a sergeant in, and then he'll go to the platoon."

"What happens when Berger comes back?" asked Kemper.

"I dunno. I'd guess that we'll have more riflemen by then, and he'll divide us up into two platoons, plus or minus. As it stands right now, we can't muster two full squads."

Ryan spent a few more minutes talking about communications and what they expected that night, and then he escorted Kemper to a two-man trench about one hundred yards to the south that he would have to himself. One previous occupant had been diagnosed with severe trench foot—a blow to the company as he had been in Able since before Paestum—and the other soldier had moved into another trench with a buddy.

Kulis joined Ryan in the command trench and after a moment of silent contemplation of a series of explosions in Cassino, Ryan closed his eyes and fell into a fitful sleep.

2200 Hours
Todi Castle, Italy

Sam and B.G.E. Beams talked quietly in the dying light of the fireplace. There was no need to be quiet as Sergeant Kenton had gone outside to check the perimeter of the castle. Sam didn't necessarily see any reason to conduct a security check, but it never hurt, and Kenton was looking for a break from the boredom in any case.

"What do you think is going on at Nettuno?" asked Beams.

"Well, your guess is as good as mine, but based on what we saw at Paestum, the Germans probably blocked their exit from the beach and they're having to build up for a breakout. I can't think of anything else that would keep them on the beach."

There was a moment of silence as each man considered what the conditions were like at the beach, unaware that history would record the landings as the Anzio landings, and not the Nettuno landings. "How much longer do we wait, Sam? I can't stand you guys anymore," Beams said in the dark.

"I know. Between Kenton's farts waking me up at night and your lisp getting on my nerves so bad that I want to knock out your remaining tooth, I don't want to spend a minute longer with either of you. Let's see what tomorrow brings. Maybe there will be some news from the priest in, what was it? Orvieto?"

"Yeah, Orvieto. Speakin' of knockin' out my tooth, I hate to even ask, but d'ya reckon they have a dentist there?"

"Teeth getting worse?" Sam had seen Beams spit blood several times over the past day.

"Yeah. I should have talked to Bazzini this morning. It's really been bothering me for a couple days, but I've been thinking that it'd get better, but it just seems worse. I've got a tooth that broke off below the gum line that I think is infected. I need to have a doc dig out the remainder."

Sam winced at the thought, and said, "I can't see

anything in this light, but I'll look tomorrow, and if Mr. Bazzini comes back, we'll see if there's a discrete doc we can go see. If nothin' else, maybe he's got a pair of pliers and I can pull it for you."

Beams sighed and said, "That'd probably be best, I feel kind of crappy. Goddamnit! All I had to do was behave myself, and we'd be on our way to Germany for the duration. Behind wire, yes, but I'd still have my fuckin' teeth, and you and Bill wouldn't be in this shithole. I'm sorry I got y'all into this."

Sam shrugged in ambivalence. The die was cast in any case. He had a great reserve for boredom, but little tolerance for restricted freedom. All things considered, he'd take his chances as they were but the risk was considerable. They could remain at the castle until Allied forces moved through the area—if that ever happened—but the longer that they remained at the castle, the greater the odds that they would be discovered. There was no doubt in Sam's mind that the German Army had already checked out the castle at least once since the invasion of Italy, and it was only a matter of time before it happened again. If they waited at the castle until the fighting rolled past them, they would be caught. But to get on the road again and try to work their way out through the Abruzzi mountains was equally risky—he rated their chances of getting out of occupied Italy as no better than fifty-fifty. Then he thought that the real qualifier was getting out of Italy alive, because if they were captured, they would almost certainly be shot as soon as they were identified and they would stay in Italy for eternity.

"Don't worry about it. There's only two outcomes for us. We'll either get out alive and be heroes or we'll be dead-ass GIs in some muddy ditch in central Italy— ain't a lot we can do about it now."

"I choose the first option, partner…hey, sounds like Bill's coming back in."

It was in fact Sergeant Kenton, who came in with a burst of cold air. Kenton was carrying a skinned and cleaned squirrel, and had a pleased look on his face. "Anyone up for a late snack?" he asked rhetorically.

As he prepared the squirrel with salt and sprigs of rosemary from a bush on the castle grounds, he said to the officers, "I headed down to that creek that Mr. Bazzini tolt us about. Ain't far—a couple hundred yards or so. I wanted to wash this little fella off after I cleaned him. While I was back there, I smelled something dead."

Beams raised an eyebrow. "Whaddya mean?"

"I couldn't see nothin' 'cause it's dark, but I could smell it. Could be anything, but it's somethin' big. Not a rodent." Kenton was sure of himself. "It might have been a dead calf or maybe a horse or somethin' but it was a powerful smell. Thought I'd go out and see what it is at dawn and check out the creek in a little light as well. If we can get the stuff from Mr. Bazzini, maybe we could run a little trotline."

"Trotline?" asked Beams. "That's fish, right?"

Sam laughed. "Yep. That's fish. You can catch just about anything on a trotline, up to and including little alligators back home. Oh brother, I'd love to have some fried fish. Or some fried gator for that matter. Damn, that squirrel smells good!"

2230 Hours
Able Company CP, West Slope of Mount
Trocchio, Italy

The critical need for good coordination between units sharing a common front had been drilled into Lieutenant Ryan from his first days in the army. It was a lesson that he had taken seriously, and consequently, that afternoon he made a point of traveling to his north to meet his counterpart on the left flank of the 6th Armored Infantry to his right. His company commander counterpart was a captain from Illinois, and he seemed fairly relaxed for someone in such close proximity to the enemy. That proximity was realistically no closer than Ryan's but he didn't feel particularly relaxed.

The captain was from Galesburg, and he had worked as an administrator for the Chicago, Burlington, and Quincy Railroad, which meant that he was as close of a neighbor to Ryan as he expected to meet during the war. The captain gave the lieutenant a cigar, and they smoked their cigars in a nicely furnished trench while talking about home.

Coordination was on Ryan's mind that night as he moved between the various trenches and foxholes of his company. He had already passed the vital information that another unit would be attempting a crossing in front of their position, and that they were not to fire at anything until the patrol leader had reported back to his 91st Reconnaissance Squadron that the mission was complete. He had already passed that information, but he was doing it again.

Lieutenant Kemper's foxhole was the last place to visit before Ryan returned to his CP to catch some sleep. He was about to whistle that he was coming in when small-arms fire erupted along the riverbank several hundred yards to their west.

Ryan turned to watch the spectacle. As he had come to expect in his very limited experience in warfare, the small-arms fire quickly escalated from the popping of individual rifles to crew-serviced machine guns and then mortars. He watched as brief flashes on the far bank indicated the locations of German infantry just as the brief muzzle flashes on the Allied bank indicated the same for the soldiers of the 91st. It looked to Ryan that the firing from the American soldiers was dropping off, which he hoped indicated that they were beginning a withdrawal under the cover of darkness.

A deep boom from back in the mountains signaled the next escalation as Ryan assumed that field artillery was joining the fight, but they hadn't yet. A bright flare sputtered to life 600 feet above the Rapido River, and Ryan could make out shadowy figures running hellbent for the safety of Allied lines. Another failed patrol.

Chapter Six

The three soldiers moved slowly toward the creek in the woods. Lieutenant Taft would have been content to leave the small expedition to the creek to Sergeant Kenton, as he was not sure that Lieutenant Beams was up to the walk, but Beams insisted.

"I gotta get some fresh air, Sam," he said. "I've been burning up all night. I think I just need some exercise and some water, and I'll be right as rain."

That Beams had had a rough night was apparent to both Sam and Kenton. He had refused any of the squirrel saying that he didn't believe he could handle any food, and he moaned through most of the night. The first moan was a long deep mournful gasp that woke Beams' two companions. To Sam's great amusement, Kenton leaped to his feet and looked about the great room with something approaching panic. After he calmed down, the huge soldier admitted with a sheepish grin that he'd been dreaming of ghosts, and he'd thought that Beams' moan came from one of the reputed spirits of the castle.

"I know it ain't very scientific of me, sir, but ghosts and clowns give me the heebie-jeebies."

"Better than a case of the vapors, I suppose." When Sergeant Kenton didn't react to Sam's joke, Sam tried an explanation. "Get it? Since we already have enough ghosts, you know? Vapors? Ghosts are sometimes called...well, never mind...but you don't have nothin' against rodeo clowns, do ya?"

Kenton shivered and said, "Not as much as circus clowns, but I wouldn't invite one over for dinner."

They entered the woods a hundred yards north of the castle and followed Kenton into the forest. "It's up this way. Only a few hundred yards."

It was well before a few hundred yards that Sam caught the scent of death. He had heard others describe the smell as sickly sweet, but although Sam couldn't have put it into words, his description wouldn't have agreed with sickly sweet. There was nothing sweet about it. The smell of death repulsed him. In the forest, it was pungent and almost overpowering, and Sam understood what Kenton meant when he had said that the smell was too much for a small animal. Sam had smelled death on this scale before, but only on the battlefield, and he thought that had the winds shifted only slightly, they must have smelled it from the castle.

"Will I smell like that?" asked Beams in a low voice.

"Huh?" Sam was turning toward Beams when Kenton said, "Oh Lord, look at that."

Sam felt himself go cold—a penetrating cold worse than the icy wind blowing from the northwest. Swinging from the branches of several towering oaks were the decaying bodies of six men—all civilians wearing the clothes of common men.

"B.G.E., what do you make of this?" Sam asked of the former policeman.

Beams walked slowly around the feet of the men, their shoes at face level. He looked at their hands tied behind their backs, and their faces, which had been worked over by the carrion birds of the forest. He turned around, vomited, and then as he weakly stood up, he froze. Beams peered hard into the forest, and said to Sam, "This ain't all of 'em."

Sam followed the trace of Beams' pointing finger and saw the shredded remains of another man tied to a tree, his head drooped down over his chest. Sam walked toward the tree and saw two more bodies lying face down on the ground, both female. Sam knelt next to them and was joined by Beams, who said after a second, "They were shot in the head from behind. This fella looks like he was shot by a firing squad—see, half his chest is missing. Six of these Dagos were hanged. It was an execution, or maybe a series of them. I don't think this happened at the same time. These females are on the ground but it doesn't look like the animals have been at 'em as much as those fellas." Beams' ashen face looked to the trees.

Kenton let out a low whistle. "I wonder who these poor folk are? Was this done by the Germans?"

"Oh Jesus…" Beams let out a long moan and started shaking. He looked imploringly at Sam—a look that Sam had never seen from the fiery B.G.E. Beams—and said, "Sammy, you need to take me back to the castle now. I'm feeling so cold that I can't stand it. I know it's daylight, but do you think we could start a fire?"

0810 Hours
Todi Castle, Italy

Lieutenant Beams collapsed on the walk back to the castle. He stopped once to catch his breath, and then a few steps later, his eyes rolled back in his head and he dropped to the ground. Sam and Sergeant Kenton took turns carrying him, and Sam had been struck by how quickly the lieutenant had gone from coherency to unconsciousness.

When they walked through the courtyard of the derelict castle, Sam laid Beams on the ground and opened the lieutenant's mouth and peered in. Even in the cloudy light, Beams' gums were clearly in terrible shape, which Sam expected to see. There was no way that they could have survived such trauma and recovered in only a week. But Sam didn't see anything more than what he expected—there was no obvious site of the infection.

Kenton put his hand on Beams' forehead and looked worriedly at Sam. "Ah shit, sir. He's just burning up."

Sam tried it as well, and felt the same high temperature emanating through Beams' forehead. "Ah shit," he echoed. "This ain't good, Bill. He's had open sores in his mouth for a week, where he ain't brushed his teeth or nothing. And we've been eating wild game, and drinking from streams and ditches."

"Let's get him inside, sir, and covered up with blankets," suggested Kenton. They carried the unconscious Beams into the great room and laid him next to the fireplace. Sam and Kenton looked at each other, and without discussion, Sam began to look for the driest wood while Kenton lit a small pile of wood shavings and kindling.

"Sam," said Sergeant Kenton who never called officers by their first name, "what do you think we should do?"

"Geez, Bill," Sam said worriedly, "I was going to ask you the same thing. I dunno. He needs a doctor, obviously. I can walk into Collelungo and see if they have one, but to be honest with you, I think the odds are about even that I'll get arrested. Mr. Bazzini said yesterday that the town leadership and police are all still fascists. If I had civilian clothes, I'd just walk through the town and look for an apothecary."

"We stand out, sir, even in mufti. Look, those executions took place only a few hundred yards from Collelungo. Maybe the, uh, victims were from Collelungo. Maybe they were shot by the Germans, and the Krauts are in the town. I don't think it's a good idea."

Leaving aside the issue of Beams for a moment, Sam said, "I don't think they were executed by Germans."

"Why do you say that?"

"All the reports that I've heard suggest the Germans execute civilians to make a point. If they killed Dago civilians, they'd do it against the wall of the town hall or in front of the church, not in the woods where nobody sees it."

"Well, who were they then?" Kenton asked.

"Hell if I know," Sam answered. "Maybe they were partisans and were shot by the fascists, although they'd most likely line up against a wall in town like the Nazis would. Maybe they were fascist sympathizers and were killed by partisans. Maybe they were the Montagues or the Capulets. I don't have any idea, and I don't really care, other than I don't want it to involve us."

"Me neither," said Kenton agreed fervently.

"Me neither," said Beams weakly. Sam and Kenton looked down at Lieutenant Beams, who had regained consciousness. Beams looked up at Sam who was kneeling next to him and asked, "What happened?"

"You dropped while we were walking back as if I hit you with Perkin's sledge. How are you feeling, buddy?" Sam looked at Beams' eyes—they were glassy—and he felt Beams' forehead. He could discern no difference.

The lieutenant was running a high fever.

"Worse than I look. Sam, I want to ask you for something, and I want your word on it." Beams seemed to have a hard time catching his breath.

"What's that?" Sam asked.

"Don't go into those villages on my account…"

Sam interrupted, "I don't think I'll make that promise, B.G.E. You need a doc and I ain't one, and neither is Bill. We don't know what's wrong or what to do." That was only about half true. Sam had spent his life in the company of tens or hundreds of thousands of animals, and had seen every disease known to man in the bovine and equine worlds. His suspicion was that Beams had septicemia—a spread of the infection in his mouth to his bloodstream. Sam had seen it in horses many times, and couldn't recall seeing it resolve successfully very often.

Beams was thinking along similar lines. "Sam, I seen a cop in Houston get shot in the gut, and they saved him—had him stitched up and released and back home with his wife after a couple days. A week later, he comes down with a fever and dies two days later from infection. The doc said his organs just shut down once that shit got in his blood."

Forgetting his concern about feuding Italians, Kenton started to stand up to go to town and drag back a doctor if necessary. "Sir, that's all the more reason to get a doc now. We don't wanna wait."

"No!" Beams voice was weak but clear. "If it's just an infection, the fever will beat it. If it's in my blood, the Dago doctors cain't fix it…you know there's no sulfa or penicillin here. Let's just ride this out to the end, okay, boys?"

1000 Hours
Presenzano, Italy

"No, no, no...tell her they're supposed to be green! Don't throw them out!" Perkin was referring to the powdered eggs that Signora Ocello was cooking in a large copper pan. Stefania was helping with the translation.

"I don't know, Perkin Berger...I've never seen eggs that color before. Are you sure they're okay?" Stefania was pretty doubtful although she restrained Signora Ocello from putting the eggs in the dog bowl outside the door.

"They're army eggs, sweetie. Everything in the army is either green or brown." Perkin let the explanation stand, as he wasn't entirely sure why the army's powdered eggs were frequently green when served.

Stefania stared doubtfully at the eggs while Signora Ocella resumed cooking them over the stove. "I don't think I can..." She was interrupted by a knock at the front door.

It was Corporal Kulis and Lieutenant Ryan. They were ushered into the house with great commotion and fanfare. Stefania ran over to Kulis's side and glared as the two Ocello daughters giggled. The soldiers were enjoined to have breakfast at the house, and although Lieutenant Ryan seemed hesitant, he allowed Maria Moroni to guide him by the hand to an open seat while she made him some tea. Kulis was taken by the hand as well as Stefania led him into the kitchen for a plate of green eggs and prosciutto cotto.

"Sir," said Ryan to Perkin. "Major Spaulding sent me. Is there a place where we can go talk privately?"

Perkin looked at the somber face of the young lieutenant and nodded. Both officers stood and walked outside. It was another cold gray day, but there was no precipitation yet.

"What's up, Alex?" Perkin asked.

"Sir, this is going to seem strange, but these are Major Spaulding's orders. First, he asked me to inquire about your health."

"Inquire about my health?" Perkin laughed. "I'm good. Tell Major Spaulding that I'm fit for duty if that's what he wants."

"He said that you would say that." Ryan's face now seemed more grim than somber. "And then he added, 'Perk's like a brother to me, but he'd rather climb a tree barefoot to lie to me than tell me the truth flatfooted on the ground.' I'm sure that's some meaningful Texas wisdom, but rather than explain it, would you humor me, sir, and please show me your range of motion?"

Perkin was nonplussed, but he complied. Careful to keep his face neutral, Perkin lifted his right arm over his head. Although it was stiff and still painful, it was accomplished fairly easily compared to just two or three days before. The massages around his wound had been excruciating but had broken up the internal scar tissue.

"Great, sir," said Ryan, although he didn't look happy. "How about the other side?"

Perkin's wounded shoulder was still very stiff, and he wasn't sure he could do it without stretching first. He raised his arm smoothly until it began to bind over his head. Then he looked down at his feet and said, "See, I can even do it on my tiptoes." Ryan's eyes naturally followed Perkin's to the ground, and then Perkin lowered his arm before Ryan could see only a three-quarter effort.

Ryan handed Perkin his M-1 carbine and said, "Please show me that you can aim it."

Perkin did as requested, although he wasn't sure he

could have held the light carbine for long. "Alex, what's this about?" Perkin asked. "Does Bill need me back now? I'm good to go."

"Sir, if you are good to go, Major Spaulding asks that you come back with us. I'm to take you back to the clearing station and get the doc to sign off on a return to full duty. We received orders this morning that the division is to resume the assault across the Rapido River tonight, and Major Spaulding wants you to take command of Able Company."

1020 Hours
Presenzano, Italy

Perkin had made the rounds saying goodbye to all the people present, and he had saved Dr. Bonucci for last. There had been tears from Angela, and surprising him, from Maria Moroni as well. Stefania had seemingly taken his impending departure in stride, but when she hugged him goodbye, there were tears in her eyes, too. Signora Moroni, the matriarch of the household, offered him an uneven and strained smile, but then she gave him the perfect present.

When he had arrived, Signora Moroni had taken the sweater that Gianina had given to Perkin before her death, and miraculously repaired it, as it had been torn by shrapnel, cut open by a medic's scissors and bled on profusely by Perkin, but there it was before him in reasonable condition. Not having brown yarn, Signora Moroni substituted a navy blue thread where necessary, but it looked great to Perkin in a Frankenstein kind of way. He was absolutely delighted.

While Lieutenant Ryan and Corporal Kulis helped themselves to freshly baked bread in the kitchen, Dr. Bonucci sat down with Perkin on a bench for a few last words. "Keep stretching your upper body, young man, and you should be fine. Come by and see me whenever you want."

"Thank you, sir, for all you've done. I didn't expect to be this good for some time. I really appreciate it," Perkin said sincerely.

"You're quite welcome, Capitano. And thank you for the gifts of food and medicine. Before you go, Stefania told me that you had an...*come si dice*...an episode yesterday." Bonucci pulled out his old pipe and filled it with tobacco as he talked.

"Yes, sir, it was the damnedest thing. Almost like I was reliving a battle from September." Perkin shrugged. It was past him now.

"If you have it again, resist it. Focus on things around you or occupy your mind...count the buttons on your shirt or name the women you've taken to bed in order—ha ha, I suspect that will keep you busy for a while. Follow a bird without losing focus, or count the panes of glass in a window and then multiply them together. Keep your mind on something else. It's not healthy to relive these things. It's not good for bad memories to take control."

"Okay, Doc, I will." Perkin reached over and grasped the hand of the old doctor before standing up. He whistled and called out, "Come on, boys, let's get moving."

They walked outside to the jeep, carrying out far fewer things that they had carried in only a few days earlier. The entire household including Dr. Bonucci followed the Americans outside to say goodbye, and they lined up in front of the Moroni house.

"Hang on, boys," Perkin ordered. "I want to prove my time here ain't been wasted." Turning to the assembled Italians before him, he sang in a clear and loud voice,

"The stars at night, are big and bright!" and the Italians clapped four times and answered with the right pitch but faulty pronunciation, "Deep in the heart of Texas!"

Perkin threw his head back and laughed, applauded his singers, and climbed into the jeep. Kulis gunned the engine, and as Perkin continued to laugh, pulled out of Presenzano.

1145 Hours
Avezzano, Italy

Major Douglas Grossmann of the Abwehr almost skipped down the streets of Avezzano. Father Carlo told him he was going to Rome, and would Douglas be all right by himself for the day? It couldn't have worked out better, thought Grossmann, unless the priest had asked him to go to Rome.

Two days of fretting were past him now. He had come to no conclusions about what was going on, but had resolved not to let his fears take the better of him. He was in control of himself, he was sure, and if Antoniette had run afoul of the Abwehr, he would either straighten out the misunderstanding or she would pay the consequences if necessary. The Norns would not weave his rope of destiny—that would be of his doing, he told himself—and with Wagner on his mind and with a burst of enthusiasm for himself and his newfound confidence, he sang *Wintersturme* to himself while he walked.

Certainly, he had some trepidation about meeting Colonel von Hatzfeldt. Regardless of what the colonel's aide, Captain Fenstermacher, had told him, he was convinced that von Hatzfeldt hated him. *Oh well, I've survived that son of a bitch before, and I'll survive him again*, he thought. He had gone through all the permutations of what von Hatzfeldt might want, and he didn't have any leading contenders out of all the possibilities.

The worst case was that von Hatzfeldt might want him to attempt to reinfilitrate the Allied command structure as he had in the fall. That was nearly impossible, he knew. Their counterintelligence in Italy was far more advanced than it had been back in the chaos of the landings, and Grossmann was undoubtedly known to Allied CI in any case.

Far more likely, von Hatzfeldt was going to tell Grossmann to kill the entirety of the underground railroad of the Allies. Probably not Monsignor O'Flaherty, but Father Carlo and the Italian civilians on the far end. Grossmann had no problem with that. Father Carlo was well-meaning, but he was clearly an enemy of the Reich as were the distant Italian civilians. Besides, even if Grossmann were favorably inclined toward Father Carlo today, he was still rubbed raw by the priest's paranoia. However, if von Hatzfeldt did in fact want Grossmann to go back to Rome to kill or arrest O'Flaherty, he would recommend arrest. It might cost him some sleep if he were to kill that magnificent, gentle man who Grossmann considered to be on a short list of people he genuinely liked and respected.

Grossmann turned down the street leading to the address that he was given for Fenstermacher's hotel. From habit, he turned to see if he was being followed. He didn't see anyone, but there was a sense of being watched that nagged at him. *Now, who's being paranoid?* Still, one didn't survive long in this business without a heightened sense of awareness and a knack for precaution. He walked by the small hotel, noted the stone building, the single arched doorway, the baloneys lining the second story, the small empty car park, and the total lack of activity. On a cold winter day like this,

this was no particular surprise.

Grossmann walked fifty yards or so beyond the hotel's entrance, took another close look at his surroundings, checked his watch and turned back. He walked into the small lobby of the hotel, and sitting in a corner reading an old copy of the European edition of *Stars and Stripes* was Albert Fenstermacher.

Captain Fenstermacher stood and offered his hand to Grossmann. There were no military salutes, no Nazi salutes or "Heil Hitler," nor coming to attention and clicking the heels together. Just a casual handshake seemingly between friends. They were omissions of protocol, of course, that were natural due to the nature of a confidential meeting in an Italian hotel, and Grossmann didn't think anything of it, until Fenstermacher nodded to the elderly man behind the front desk and introduced him as "Wachtmeister Schmidt, formerly of His Majesty's Imperial German Army."

Grossmann looked at the old sergeant major, saw a cavalryman to the core, and said with a nod, "Wachtmeister."

Schmidt returned the nod with the greeting, "Good afternoon, Herr Major. Welcome to my hotel."

Fenstermacher led Grossmann down a hallway and explained as they walked, "Schmidt married an Italian woman and has lived here since '19. He's been one of the admiral's men since '36...you know, for odd jobs, favors."

"Why didn't I know of him?" asked Grossmann, who had run the Rome Abwehr office.

Fenstermacher shrugged. "The admiral plays some hands close to the vest."

"Albert, anything that I need to know before I see the colonel? Can you tell me what this is about?"

"Sir, I'll leave it to them to explain to you what this is about. I just learned last night. I beg of you to go in with an open mind, and for God's sake be discrete." With that cryptic explanation, Fenstermacher opened the door and ushered Grossmann into the hotel's sole suite as Grossman thought, "*Them?*"

1200 Hours
Todi Castle, Italy

Sam walked out to the courtyard to meet Mr. Bazzini. He had heard the coal truck coming from some distance as it had backfired coming up the hill.

"Mr. Bazzini, I'm very glad to see you," said Sam. He felt that he had the weight of the world resting on his shoulders, and while he suspected there wasn't much that Bazzini could do, he was still grateful for his presence.

Bazzini stepped down out of the truck, and pulled down a battered suitcase. "I have some clothes for you. Let me take them out of the suitcase and I'll tell my driver to go on. I like the walk home. It's the only time I get to myself."

Sam said in a low voice, "Can you ask your driver to stay for a minute?"

Bazzini's smile was replaced with a frown as he saw the serious look on Sam's face. "Yes, of course. Is there something wrong?"

Sam first explained to Bazzini about Beams' fever, and then he told the Italian about the execution site near the creek. Bazzini's tanned face became very white, and for a moment, Sam was afraid that he was going to climb into the truck and drive off. But Sam was wrong. Bazzini spoke a rapid string of sentences to his driver, who asked some questions and then dropped down out of the truck.

"Please do tell Enrico where these crimes took place," requested Bazzini. When Sam complied and after Bazzini had translated, the driver reached under the seat of the truck, pulled out a small pistol, and tucked it in his belt.

"I thought you said you didn't have any guns," commented Sam.

"I don't. That's his. He was an airman when Italy still had an air force, and he carries that to keep himself out of the German air force. Let's see Mr. Beams." Bazzini picked up the suitcase and followed Sam into the castle.

Five minutes of looking at the unconscious Beams and they were no closer to a diagnosis. Bazzini said that he had never heard of bad teeth killing a man like this, but that he had no doubt that Beams was close to death.

"Can we take him to a doctor?" Sam asked. He was aware of Beams' request, but he wasn't going to simply let nature run its course.

"Let's see what Enrico reports, first."

Enrico was back in the castle in another ten minutes, white and slightly out of breath. He talked at length to Mr. Bazzini, who said, "This is terrible news. Enrico knew the women, and thinks that he might know one or two of the men. They are from Morre, the village to the west. Enrico says they are communists—partisans. He thinks that there may be two or more partisan groups at war with one another. Maybe monarchists and communists. Fascists would have arrested them he says. Maybe yes, maybe not."

"What does this mean for us?" asked Sam.

Bazzini spread his hands, pursed his lips and shrugged. "I think it means that we should move you as soon as we have a place for you. If these villages are at war with each other or there are armed bands here, it is not safe. Being an American won't help you if you get in the middle, I think. But, there is a more sooner problem, maybe. Mr. Beams needs a doctor. Morre has a doctor, but maybe it's no so safe in Morre."

Bazzini and Enrico had a long discussion and then Bazzini said, "Enrico doesn't know the doctor here, and doesn't think it is safe. We'll drive back to Dunarobba and get the local doctor there. He hates Germans and will not turn you in. We can maybe be back soon, but we can't drive at night." Bazzini turned to go, but another thought occurred to him, "Is Lieutenant Beams Protestant?"

Sam shrugged and looked at Sergeant Kenton, who also shrugged. "I honestly don't know. I think he mentioned his family was Irish, so I'd guess Catholic."

"I'll bring a priest as well then."

"Mr. Bazzini, any word from Orvieto? The priest there…can he help us?" Sam asked.

The Italian shook his head in disappointment. "No. Bad news. He disappeared several weeks ago, and it's believed that the Germans executed him."

1200 Hours
Avezzano, Italy

At exactly noon, the man who was responsible for the execution of the Orvieto priest, Douglas Grossmann, walked into the hotel suite. A second later, he froze and then his training took over. He snapped to rigid attention, and his arm went out automatically in the party salute as he came face to face with Admiral Wilhelm Canaris, the head of the Abwehr and the director of German military intelligence.

Canaris smiled, gently put his hand on Grossman's

arm and pushed it down to his side. "Not today, Major." Canaris looked at the confusion on Grossmann's face, smiled again, and turned to indicate a man sitting on a sofa in the suite. "You know Colonel von Hatzfeldt, yes?"

Recovering from his surprise, Grossmann looked at the colonel, who made no effort to stand up or even acknowledge Grossmann. "Herr Colonel," Grossmann said as he nodded. Everyone in the room was wearing civilian clothes.

"Yes, Grossmann. I see you are still alive." Von Hatzfeldt offered what passed for a smile—a smile that had always terrified Grossmann.

Captain Fenstermacher took charge of getting the meeting moving, "Admiral, if you would sit there, please," indicating one of two chairs pulled up next to a coffee table opposite the sofa. "Major Grossmann, there, if you please."

Grossmann took the chair to the right of Admiral Canaris. Fenstermacher poured four cognacs and gave one each to Canaris, von Hatzfeldt, and Grossmann. He set his own on the coffee table, and then opened the door and checked down the hall. When he returned, he sat on the sofa next to Colonel von Heltzfeldt. As he sat down, Grossmann noticed that he was carrying a sidearm in a shoulder holster under his suit coat.

Admiral Canaris picked up his cognac and said, "Gentlemen, I'd like to propose a toast if I may."

Grossmann picked up his glass and prepared for the inevitable toast to the Führer.

"Gentlemen," said Canaris with feeling. "To peace. May we see peace in this year of our Lord, 1944." He held out his glass, and touched it to the other glasses, as each soldier in the room murmured, "To peace."

Grossmann was struck by the magnetism of

Admiral Canaris, a trait that he shared with Monsignor O'Flaherty. The day would be momentous, of that Grossmann was certain, but he had no idea what the meeting would bring—only that he had not conceived of it beforehand.

"Douglas, do you know the role that cognac *almost* played in our history?" asked Admiral Canaris.

"Admiral, before we get started, you wanted to make Major Grossmann's promotion official," interrupted Colonel von Hatzfeldt, who reached into his pocket and pulled out a folded piece of paper and a fountain pen, and handed them to the admiral.

"Yes. Quite right." Canaris looked at the paper, read it quickly and then smoothed it out on the table. He handed the pen to Grossmann, and said, "In recognition of the excellent work you've done so far, with anticipation of more to come. We will do a more formal ceremony either back in Rome or in Berlin, maybe, but this will have to do for now. You're officially promoted to the permanent rank of Lieutenant Colonel, and you accrue all rank, privilege, and pay thereof effective immediately." The gray-haired admiral offered his hand to a surprised Grossmann, and after they shook hands and Grossmann had accepted the congratulations of all in the room, the admiral had him sign and date his promotion paperwork. Von Hatzfeldt waited until the ink had dried, and then refolded the paperwork and placed it in his coat pocket.

"Now, what was I saying, Paul?" This was to Colonel von Hatzfeldt.

"Admiral, you were speaking of cognac...," said Colonel von Hatzfeldt.

"Yes, Colonel Grossmann...are you aware of the role of cognac, or rather, the almost role of cognac in our recent history?" asked Admiral Canaris.

"No, sir. I don't believe that I am," answered Grossmann.

"The first attempt to assassinate this mad evil man—Hitler—was a bomb placed in a crate of cognac carried in his personal aircraft. Obviously, it failed to detonate." Canaris looked sad for a moment, and then he said dryly, "So, I suppose you're wondering why we're all here today, Colonel."

1215 Hours
1st Battalion CP, West of Mount Trocchio

"Perkin, I'm sorry that I had to cut your vacation short, but it's good to see you." Major Spaulding offered his hand and a smile. "Seems like the division needs your expertise again."

"What expertise is that, exactly?" asked Perkin with a grin. He was glad to see Spaulding as well.

"I ain't sure, to be honest. I think your main qualification for anything at this point is that you're able to blink and breathe." Spaulding motioned for Perkin to follow him, and they took three short steps to a desk with a map on it. Pointing to the Rapido River on the map, Spaulding said, "As Alex told you, the regiment's got orders to resume the assault. No time given yet, but we were told to be ready by this evening."

"Wonderful. What are we being told to do?" asked Perkin.

"The operational details are still being worked out. This is a II Corps plan, and it looks like they're doing a scaled down version of last week's wildly popular 5th Army plan. A two-pronged boat crossing in the vicinity of Sant'Angelo to take the town, establish a Bailey crossing with follow-on echelons exploiting the gap."

"So...the only problem with last week's failed

attempt to cross was what? Too many troops?" Perkin asked sarcastically.

"Yeah, the logic kind of drives you there, don't it? If two regiments cain't do it, let's throw a couple battalions at the problem and see what happens." Spaulding shrugged. "What'd you have planned anyway? A night at the opera?"

"I might have had a full dance card by tonight," Perkin answered with a grin. "I was kind of popular with the ladies at Presenzano. Of course, I was the only man in the town, but still…"

"You already have a girlfriend…" Spaulding started to say.

"Hey, that reminds me," Perkin interrupted. "I think that 8th Army is going to transfer the New Zealand Corps to our sector." Perkin explained his chance meeting with the New Zealand officer from the day before.

"Hmm," said Spaulding. "Maybe that explains our current orders."

"Whaddya mean?" asked Perkin.

"Pride. Corps and army staff wanna wrap this up before some foreign unit comes in and takes the credit." Spaulding shook his head. "That's a terrible thing to ask a soldier to die for…some general's pride and ego."

"That explains about half the casualties in every war since the beginning of mankind, I'd guess," Perkin said. "Do we have an order of march?"

"Not yet," Spaulding replied. "We've got a one in three chance of being the first assault echelon, so let's plan on that being the case. I want you here to help me work on that. Your lieutenants can manage the company logistics, and then when we move, I need you with Able Company as the commander. It's unfair to leave that to two butter bars."

Perkin nodded in agreement and pointed at the map. "Yes, sir. If the situation ain't changed, there's a flat on the bank here that might support our crossing, and allow for bridging equipment to come up."

1215 Hours
Avezzano, Italy

Grossmann stared at the head of German military intelligence in disbelief. Was he actually saying that he had tried to assassinate the Führer? Remembering that the admiral asked him a question, Grossmann stammered, "Yes, sir. You've got my attention. Why am I here?"

"You're here, Colonel Grossmann, because I need your help," replied Admiral Canaris.

"My help? In assassinating the…?" Grossmann's voice dropped off. This was an extraordinarily dangerous conversation. He looked at the admiral's companions. Von Hatzfeldt stared absently at his fingernails while Fenstermacher watched Grossmann intelligently. There was no sign at all of fanaticism in the room, which Grossmann would have expected from those advocating the murder of the most powerful man in Europe.

"No, Colonel. I'm not an assassin, nor am I asking you to become one. But, for years now, I've had a relationship with Allied intelligence organizations…" Canaris said bluntly.

Grossmann interrupted, "What? You're telling me that you're an agent? Of who, the British? The Americans?" Grossmann was stunned, and his disbelief came out in his voice.

"No, young man. That's not quite accurate. I work for no one but my own conscience. I don't take money from the Allies, nor do I accept tasking on their behalf. But since the beginning of the war—before actually—I've maintained, well, channels of information back to Mr. Churchill."

"Channels of information?" Grossmann repeated.

"Yes, indeed. I felt it necessary to maintain these channels because there were some things that were critical for the British to understand. Matters of some importance. Our intentions in Norway, our outline and timeline for the violation of Dutch and Belgian neutrality, our broad plans for Operations Sea Lion and Barbarossa, for example." Admiral Canaris indicated to Captain Fenstermacher to pour him another cognac, reconsidered and indicated that Fenstermacher should refill all the glasses.

Grossmann struggled to maintain his calm demeanor. The admiral had just described several acts of treason, and Grossmann knew that he was being asked to participate in it. "Admiral, sir, please help me understand," he said. "What would prompt you, one of the most decorated naval officers in German history…a man venerated by millions of Germans…to commit such…treason?"

"That is enough, Grossmann!" snapped Colonel von Hatzfeldt. "You will choose your words more carefully."

Grossmann had seen disdain in von Hatzfeldt's eyes before, but he had never seen such a burst of anger. But he wasn't going to back down. "Maybe my German isn't good enough, Herr Colonel, but I don't know any other word for it!" Turning to Canaris, Grossmann said, "Admiral, I could be executed for just having this conversation and not reporting it. I mean no disrespect, sir, but I want to know…why would you do such things?"

If Canaris felt any of the same anger as von Hatzfeldt, he didn't show it. Calmly he said to Grossmann in English, "You have every right to know, Douglas. Let me explain." Canaris lit a cigarette, leaned back in his seat, and crossed his legs, the very picture of the suave, refined intellectual that he was. Canaris collected his thoughts and said, "Do you recall what Viscount Grey said at the start of the First World War?" When Grossmann shook his head, Canaris explained, "He said, 'The lamps are going out all over Europe. We shall not see them lit again in our lifetime.' Do you know what he meant?"

"I think so, Admiral. It was a sentiment like *Sic transit gloria mundi*...thus passes the glory of the world... worldly things are fleeting," Grossmann answered.

"Almost, Douglas, although I think Grey's lament was more specific. He wasn't talking about the material matters of Europe fading—the rich capitals, the wealthy burghers. Grey, who by the way was a dear friend of Colonel von Hatzfeldt's grandfather." Canaris nodded to his dour companion. "Grey was talking about the glory of Europe. What do I mean by that? The wealth of the colonial powers and their impending loss of empire and treasure? No! The glory of Europe lay in its position as the center of Christendom...the center of world civilization...the center of reason and knowledge...the moral compass of the world. That...that...that was the light that was extinguished in August of 1914! Culture and reason and morality. Not the brute, coarse, *kultur* of the Nazis, but love and learning. Faith in God, and faith in mankind. We lost so much of that in that terrible month and the years that followed. And it didn't come back in 1918. Nature abhors a vacuum, Douglas...if we lost the light that guided us as men of reason and rationality, then what replaced the light was a darkness that is incomprehensible to the men of Grey's day."

"Sir..." started Grossmann, but von Hatzfeldt raised his hand for silence.

Canaris kept speaking, "Douglas, the Nazis—and I know you're a party member as am I—the Nazis are the darkest side of humanity and they will walk hand in hand to hell with the Bolsheviks. I saw this, years ago before the war, when they started out as beer hall brawlers in Bavaria. Street thugs. Criminals. The lowest filth tossed out of the army after 1918 where all they learned during that great struggle was brutality, and nothing of discipline and honor. Hitler is one of them. The lowest of the low. Gutter trash. Yes, he has a great mind. Yes, a relentless energy...but it's twisted and dark and perverted. No humanity. No honor. No rationality. No reason. Just an atavistic hatred. And it's this hatred which drives the man. And now it drives Germany, and through us, it is destroying the Europe that I love!"

The admiral took another cigarette out of his case with mildly shaking hands, and this time offered one to Grossmann, who gratefully accepted. After allowing Captain Fenstermacher to light his cigarette, Canaris continued more calmly, "We will lose this war. The calculations of my staff suggest that the war will be concluded in spring or summer of 1945 unless there is an unexpected catastrophe on either front. Sometime this year, the Allies will land in France to open the true second front. Maybe Pas de Calais. Maybe farther south. Maybe north. And when your cousins from America get a toehold in France, and they meet the Russians in the Rhineland or Pomerania or somewhere in between, the war will be lost. We will lose the war, and nothing that Germany can do between now and then will prevent it. And with the Allies' incomprehensible policy of absolute, unconditional surrender, Germany will be defeated like never before. There will be no negotiated peace, and millions more will die as a result. Do you remember what Hegel said of Jena and Auerstadt? He said that it was the end of history. Well, this will be worse. The peace will be worse than Versailles. The civilian casualties will be worse than the depopulation of Germany in the Thirty Years War. And, mark my words, when we are occupied by the Soviets, it will be worse than any bleak, unforgiving nightmare that we've ever had. It will be a nightmare that never ends. Our fields will be salted, our livestock seized, our mines flooded, our industry stripped and moved to Russia, our women raped, our men imprisoned, and our children left to fend for themselves. And do you know what I think, Douglas?" When Grossmann shook his head, appalled at what he was hearing, Canaris said, "We will have earned such treatment. It will be God's punishment for what we've done. It's quite ironic, really."

"How's that, Admiral?"

Canaris stubbed out his cigarette and said, "Because He has chosen atheists as the tool of His wrath."

1230 Hours
1st Battalion CP, West of Mount Trocchio

"Coming in," a southern voice called out. Then the squat form of Colonel Wranosky appeared in the gully as he slid down its side in a mini-avalanche of loose stones.

"Good afternoon, sir!" said Major Spaulding and Perkin in unison.

Colonel Wranosky was carrying a full duffel bag, which he laid on the sole table in the makeshift CP. He looked at Spaulding and then at Perkin and shook his head. "What are you two miserable sons-a-bitches up to?"

"We're workin' on a plan to win the war, sir," answered Spaulding with a grin.

"Yes, sir. We're gonna keep tryin' the same thing until we get a different result," Perkin added brightly. "How are you?"

"Fuckin' peachy. Glad to see you're back, Professor. I'd heard you were here. Did the doctors release you, or are you on independent operations?" Wranosky asked.

"They had to release me, sir. The nurses couldn't leave me alone, and no work was gettin' done," Perkin answered with a grin. "It was just a matter of military expediency."

"I can't say it'd surprise me if it were true." The smile left Wranosky's face and he offered his hand to Major Spaulding. "I'm headin' out. Clark formally fired me this morning. Not to my face of course, and not just me. It was a little bloodbath of scapegoats handed down through the Old Man—Wilbur and Walker's boys are gone too."

"Aw that's just bullshit!" said Spaulding in a rare burst of anger.

Perkin was getting ready to echo his commander's sentiments when Wranosky shrugged and put his hand on Spaulding's shoulder. "Bill, I couldn't agree with you more, but whinin' ain't gonna change it. You and the professor here are gonna have to keep things in order without me, I guess."

As Perkin shook Wranosky's hand, he asked, "Any idea what next, sir?"

"Nope. Nobody will tell me because they ain't thought that far ahead. I'm going to Caserta, and from there, who knows? I hope it comes with some leave back home to see my wife, but I'm probably headed as far away from Mark Clark's conscience as soon as possible. Payroll officer in New Guinea or Guadalcanal, I'd guess—wherever the incidence of malaria is highest I suppose." An embarrassed look came over Wranosky's face as he realized he was complaining. "Well, anyway, I brought y'all some stuff I'd been hangin' on to."

Wranosky opened the duffel bag and tossed a leather-bound thermos to Spaulding. "It was Colonel Jamison's, God rest his soul. Thought I'd keep it in the regiment. It's filled, but it ain't coffee." He reached into the duffel bag, pulled out several pair of wool socks, and handed them to Perkin and Spaulding, "I won't need them for Rabaul. I doubt I'll need these either." He pulled out two wool blankets and set them on the table. Wranosky scratched his head and said, "You can get at least one night's use out of these. The crossing's been postponed until tomorrow. Corps wants us to prepare instead for a possible German crossing to hit at the flanks of the boys east of Cassino. Since the Germans aren't going anywhere, have a good night's sleep. Well, God bless you both…so long, boys."

1330 Hours
Avezzano, Italy

They had talked for over an hour with Grossmann feeling like he was captured in a bad dream. Admiral Canaris had explained his transformation into an anti-regime conspirator to Lieutenant Colonel Grossmann in great detail. He had been repulsed by the Nazis at the beginning, he told Grossmann, but it was the invasion of Poland that had forced the admiral to turn a corner toward treason.

"The behavior of the SS was…simply inexplicable other than it had the direct stamp of Berlin on it. I've known all along that the Nazis were criminals but what they did in Poland was simply beyond the pale. We've seen the treatment of the Jewish citizens of Germany, but I think that most of us believed that the Jews were…

simply convenient scapegoats—for the loss in '18, or the days of inflation or the Depression, whatever. In the mind of Adolf Hitler, he had to have someone to blame. And why not the Jews? They were the scapegoats for Europe's ills going back much farther than the Holy Roman Empire. But as things improved and the economy began to get back on its feet, the pressure on those poor people never eased. In the early days, Hitler confiscated their wealth and their businesses, then it was their homes. He forced them to choose between penniless immigration or stay in their country in a ghetto, as penniless non-citizens. Those that had the will and the means left, but it was not enough. So Hitler and Himmler used the war as an excuse to bring extraordinary measures to bear. The enemies of the Reich were rounded up and put into concentration camps: Dachau, Buchenwald, Sachenhausen, Ravensbruck, Flossenberg..." Canaris shivered unexpectedly and said, "...and a few others. Not all who were sent to those camps were Jews. The Nazis sent anyone who was deemed undesirable: the few who still believed in the Weimar Republic, monarchists, communists, Gypsies, homosexuals. Many believed that would be the end of it, but of course, it wasn't. The concentration camps became slave labor camps, and when we occupied the lands in the east, the camps became an industry. Vast camps, entire complexes, in Poland and the Baltic states. Czechoslovakia. Everywhere we spread German *kultur* over the continent, we rounded up the national Jewry and sent them to camps."

Grossmann nodded, "Yes, sir, that's what Monsignor O'Flaherty told me."

Canaris lit another cigarette and said, "The good monsignor only has an inkling of what has happened. Beginning in 1939, the SS deployed *Einsatzgruppen* to follow behind the army. Wherever German soldiers went, the murderers were close behind. The year we conquered Poland, the SS murdered some sixty or seventy-thousand in Poland: Jews, intellectuals, politicians, clergy. The Polish Jews not murdered were rounded up and contained in ghettoes like the ones in Warsaw and Krakow—those became herding pens for what was to follow. In '41, with Barbarossa, they went insane. The *Einsatzgruppen* at first just shot the Jews, but they found that was too expensive. We were fighting a war and the SS were wasting ammunition killing, what? Russian civilians? Jewish pacifists? But we did—maybe as many as two million that way. And then we moved on to gas vans. We rounded up Jews, loaded them in the back of vans, and pumped the exhaust into the back where the Jews died of carbon monoxide. That wasn't good enough for the SS though. In '42, they opened the execution camps: Auschwitz-Birkenau, Chelmno, Sobibor, Treblinka, Majdanek and Belzec. Did I miss any, Colonel?"

This question was directed at Colonel von Hatzfeldt who shook his head and said, "Some of the smaller labor camps might as well be extermination camps. No one will come out alive. But the difference, Colonel Grossmann, is that the SS has established a system for what Berlin calls the "Final Solution" to the Jewish problem. In these camps, we, Germany, modified a common pesticide to be used on people. We thoughtfully tested it on Russian prisoners in 1941, and by 1942, we ramped up our murder to an industrial stage. At Auschwitz and Majdanek, for example, they have chambers designed to hold roughly a thousand people at a time. They send the prisoners in and tell them that they are to be showered and deloused. The doors are locked behind them, and the chemical, called

Zyklon B, is dropped into the chamber in tablet form. The tablets are activated by contact with air and it turns into a cyanide gas. They can kill a thousand people at a time in twenty minutes, and they are only limited by how long it takes to empty the chambers. An SS lance corporal on our payroll told me that when they opened the doors, they would find pyramids of bodies as the poor people would climb upon one another to escape the gas. He said it took considerably more time to untangle the bodies than it did to kill the people. The bodies were initially buried in mass graves, but these camps have huge crematoriums, so now, the bodies are burned on-site. Our reports say that the ash of the dead falls like snow in the surrounding countryside—twenty-four hours a day, every day of the week."

White-faced, Grossmann whispered, "Good God."

Von Hatzfeldt looked at Canaris, nodded, and the admiral said softly, "Yes. Good God. What we face at the end of days is up to Him, isn't it?"

Grossmann looked at Admiral Canaris and asked, "Is that why you do this, Admiral? Because of your belief in God?" He almost added that he was an atheist, but didn't.

"No, Douglas, I do this because of my belief in man. I do this to save the German people. I think it unlikely that I live to tell the tale, but should I survive, I would like to be able to say at the end of the war when these crimes come to light: 'Not all the Germans were bad. Not all of us were part of this—this greatest crime in the history of humanity—and not all of us passively let this happen. Some of us believe in the goodness of the German people and were willing to risk everything to save it.' That is what I hope to be able to say. We're a small group, Douglas, and the *Sicherheitsdienst* is breathing down our necks, but if we do nothing, who will?" Canaris stopped speaking and fixed Grossmann with his intelligent eyes. He folded his hands and with a tilt of his head, he asked the question that Grossmann had known was coming and dreaded hearing, "Can I count on you to help us save the Fatherland from itself?"

1400 Hours
Able Company CP, West Slope of Mount
Trocchio, Italy

The orders to prepare for another crossing attempt had been rescinded to everyone's great relief. Perkin listened to the reports of his new lieutenants and decided that if they had been ordered to cross, the logistical aspects of identifying and collecting the boats, the movement to the river, and the forced crossing would have been even worse than the last attempt a week before. Perkin sat on the wet ground in the lee of a large rock and offered suggestions on how his lieutenants should organize for the next movement, and was gratified to see comprehension in both of their faces.

A smoke barrage had begun and under the thick smoke cover, Perkin moved his company out of their foxholes and began to improve their defensive lines. Machine guns were re-sited to give better coverage of the approaches to the river, and Perkin assisted a team in laying out rolls of concertina wire. He went over the artillery coordinates time and time again with his young officers to prepare for the possibility of a German counterattack across the river although he thought such an action unlikely in the extreme. Still, he could see II Corps' concern: if the Germans could cross the river, and then turn hard to the north, they would hit the attacking force at Cassino on their left flank. It would be a disaster, but Perkin doubted that they would try.

There were too many variables to make it worthwhile. In his estimation, no force larger than a small patrol had a chance of successfully crossing the river until at least a corps or more had been amassed, and neither the exhausted Allies nor the depleted Axis had the troops to waste in trying.

Corporal Kulis worked with Perkin to unroll a large loop of razor wire, and he kept looking back toward the river to see if the smoke cover was blowing away. Between glances over his shoulder, they talked in low tones.

"Sir, how's your arm? Really?" asked Kulis.

"Pretty damn stiff. I can barely move it, but working helps. Don't tell anyone," Perkin answered.

"I won't. Let me know if you need me to do something." Kulis looked around to see if anyone was listening and asked, "Sir, what are your thoughts on West Point?"

Perkin looked up surprised. He smiled as he realized the gist of the question, and answered, "I think that the long gray line would be vastly improved if you went there, if that's your question."

Kulis dropped his head so that Perkin couldn't see how pleased he was, and he said, "Thanks, sir. I'm thinking about applying. I reckon that they'll be looking to bring young enlisted GIs with combat experience into the officer-training pipeline after the war. Whaddya think?"

"My daddy went to West Point, so I hold it in pretty high regard. But here's my thoughts on officers: you can go through an officer candidate school, become a ninety-day wonder, and know little about the army or the responsibilities of your commission. Those things take time, and you'll learn 'em, but you'll be at a disadvantage while you do. Or, you can go to a ROTC program, say, through the University of Texas and have a mix of civilian life and the army. But a commission isn't guaranteed. It's the needs of the army, you know. Or you can go to West Point, and get a degree in engineering or something like that. You live and breathe the corps of cadets, and when you graduate and get commissioned, you may have already had your fill of the army. But that shouldn't be an issue for you."

Kulis thought for a moment and asked, "Which road would you take?"

"Probably the wrong one," Perkin laughed. "I dunno. If you want to progress and become a general, being a ring-knocker's not the only option as General Walker demonstrates, but it ain't far from it. A bigger question in my opinion is the all-important issue of skirts. I like women, and there ain't any at the Point."

"Yeah, that brings me to my next question. Can you be married and be at West Point?"

Perkin laughed. "Why? Has Stefania proposed yet?"

Kulis grinned sheepishly. "I wouldn't call it a proposal of marriage as much as an intended plan of action complete with milestones. It don't matter—she's got plenty of time to change her mind. I was just asking."

1430 Hours
Avezzano, Italy

"What do you need for me to do, Admiral?" asked Grossmann. In case the conversation was being recorded, Grossmann avoided answering the admiral's question directly.

"I need a direct line to Allied intelligence. I need for you to make contact with and convey a message to an American OSS officer and a British SIS agent. They will meet you at the Gildardino farmhouse when the snows have melted. The Gildardinos are not expecting an Abwehr officer, so you will stay in your character as an American pilot until you make contact with your counterparts. You should mention St. Louis and they will respond with cardinals."

Grossmann was surprised. "You know about the Gildardino farm?" After Father Carlo had too much wine one night, he had told Grossmann about the family at the end of the escape route through the Abruzzi Mountains.

Colonel Hatzfeldt rolled his eyes. "Of course we know. We've known all along. Colonel Grossmann, you're just one piece of a machine with many moving parts, and not all of our intentions and actions are, or need be, self-evident to you."

Grossmann felt a retort building, but instead nodded and replied, "Yes, sir." Turning to Admiral Canaris, he asked, "Sir, why is this necessary? It seems to me that you already have lines of communication open to the Allies."

"That's a good question, Douglas." The admiral paused for a moment to collect his thoughts and then said, "We have lines back to the British via Turkey, Spain, and Switzerland. Without discussing the details, in each case we use intermediaries. No direct Abwehr – SIS connection for obvious reasons. Lately, it appears that our communiques through these three channels are not being received or are being blocked or discounted. It's our analysis that an analyst in the SIS, a man named Philby, is a Soviet agent…"

Grossmann nodded. "And what's his interest in blocking peace feelers or information from the Abwehr? That seems counterintuitive."

Von Hatzfeldt answered, "Not really. We want a negotiated peace with the West—but that's not in the interests of the Bolsheviks. They don't want a return to the *status quo ante bellum*. They want to reconquer their lost territory and shift their borders to the west. Halting now leaves too much uncertainty about the future of the Ukraine, and the old states of Yugoslavia, Czechoslovakia, Poland, etc. We could have reached an agreement with the Soviets as late as last year, but that opportunity is now gone. If we're to avoid the *Götterdämmerung*, our only hope is with the West. That means a negotiated settlement, where the German Army deposes Hitler and seeks an immediate armistice in the West."

"Do you believe that the West will abandon their Soviet allies? Is it even possible to still reach an accommodation with the British and the Americans?" Grossmann asked.

Admiral Canaris answered, "Britain perhaps. The days of the empire are numbered, but they don't yet accept the inevitability of it, even though they suspect it. The British will grasp at any straw to save their empire, and a quick cessation of hostilities might be all that's left to them. And Winston Churchill, who in my opinion may be the savior of western civilization, fears the Bolsheviks as much as we do. The Americans don't know any better, unfortunately, and I can't say with any assurance that Roosevelt will cut a deal without Stalin's concurrence. But we must try, and this is what you will do…"

The admiral looked at Colonel Von Hatzfeldt, and the disagreeable colonel laid out slowly and precisely in great detail what Grossmann's mission was to be. It chilled Grossmann to the core, and he suspected that he was listening to his death sentence.

1430 Hours
Avezzano, Italy

Lieutenant Colonel Grossmann walked out of the old cavalryman's hotel accompanied by Captain Fenstermacher. He breathed deeply, and looked at Fenstermacher.

"Walk around the grounds with me for a minute, Albert," Grossmann said.

"Yes, sir. You have some questions you didn't want to ask in there, perhaps?" Fenstermacher asked intuitively.

"I've got a million questions. But it's not the asking that I'm worried about as much as the answers." They walked down the street and into a deserted park. Shivering against the cold wind, or perhaps from nerves, Grossmann asked, "What if I had refused. Would you have shot me? Had me arrested?"

Fenstermacher shrugged. "The admiral believes that everyone should be free to chart his own course, particularly in treacherous waters. He said just those words. Colonel Hatzfeldt is, as you know, less understanding, shall we say? I don't know what he would have done. Probably nothing."

"Why's that?"

"Because you had a clandestine meeting with the chief of military intelligence," Fenstermacher said. Seeing that didn't answer the question, he elaborated, "Look, you had an American mother, and you were raised in the United States. Should you have refused the admiral and gone to, say, the Gestapo that would have already been a mark against you. If you accused the admiral of treason, he would have denied it. Whose word would the SD or Gestapo take? That of a man venerated by millions, as you said, or an American agent provocateur? He might have accused you. You had a clandestine meeting in Avezzano where you were promoted to lieutenant colonel in advance of your normal eligibility, and Von Hatzfeldt has your paperwork with a signature and date on it. Implicate him, and he implicates you." Fenstermacher laughed a warm laugh. "Douglas, if I may, it just wasn't a concern. They trust you."

"How can they trust people so?" asked Grossmann.

"Because they have to, I think. But in your case, I think that they see a survivor, not an ideologue. Ach, the writing is on the wall for the Fatherland, and I think you will want to be on the right side of, well, history."

Grossmann stopped at the honest assessment of his personality, and realized it wasn't untrue. "How long has this gone on?" Grossmann pointed to a park bench and they sat down together.

Fenstermacher pulled out a pack of cigarettes, took one and gave the pack to Grossmann. He thought for a moment, obviously weighing his words, and said, "I learned about most of this yesterday, although none of it is a surprise. I've believed that Canaris spreads disinformation with the tongue of an angel, and he has manipulated the Allies as well as our own government. It's all to a good end, but I believe he's done it for years and with an amazing success."

"How has he manipulated the Allies?"

Fenstermacher sat for a long moment savoring his cigarette and said, "In '42, the intelligence arm of the SS was preparing to arrest Canaris and absorb the Abwehr. It was very close to doing so, and it was driven by the suspicions of Reinhard Heydrich over the Paul Thummel affair."

"Thummel?"

"Yes, Thummel worked for us as a conduit to the British through the Czechs. Heydrich got wind of it, and had him arrested. The admiral played Heydrich well, but I think the days were numbered for the boss and, well, all of us in the Abwehr. So thought Von Hatzfeldt and Canaris, I believe. It's just my supposition, but I think that Canaris used his conduit in Bern, a Polish lady with ties to Polish intelligence, and through them to the British, to make it clear to the SIS that his position was tenuous in Berlin due to Heydrich. As you know, shortly thereafter, in May, '42, British-trained Czech agents assassinated Heydrich, and whether the admiral set the wheels in motion or whether it was just…fortunate happenstance, I don't know."

"Jesus Christ…" muttered Grossmann. Despite Fenstermacher's earlier assurances that he was safe from Canaris and Hatzfeldt, it was becoming less clear that was the case.

As if reading his mind, Fenstermacher said, "I know what you're thinking, sir. Let me be clear that is my assumption. I may be wrong. But I know that Heydrich was an integral part of the plan to eliminate European Jewry. He chaired a conference at Wannsee in '42 that set this 'Final Solution' in motion. He was an animal, and got what he deserved: vicious wounds and a lingering death from septicemia. Did you know he was the admiral's next-door neighbor in Berlin and that Heydrich was a protégé of Canaris back in the navy?"

Grossmann shook his head and said, "No. I didn't know. Strange twist of fate. Albert, two last things: First, can I get a pistol from you? I might need one and I can assure you it won't be found at the church."

Fenstermacher smiled and said, "I thought you might ask." He reached into his overcoat and gave Grossmann a small pistol and magazine wrapped in a flannel cloth. Grossmann looked at the pistol. It was a Walther PPK – a 7.65mm pistol that was in common usage in German police and military circles. It was perfect.

Grossmann slid the pistol into his coat pocket and said, "Second, and then I need to get back to the church. Why the order to break contact with Antoniette Bernardi? She's the best in Italy. Why not use her skills to our great advantage?"

Fenstermacher looked at Grossmann with sympathy. "Her skills are being used to great advantage, Colonel, but not by us. It came to our attention that while she worked for you, she also worked for the SS security service in Rome. Everything she did for you, everything you did for us, we believe was reported to the SD and probably to the Gestapo. Hear me carefully, Colonel...Douglas...she is not to be trusted again."

Chapter Seven

Two Weeks Later

February 10, 1944
1000 Hours
1st Battalion Assembly Area, Hill 213, Italy

Captain Perkin Bergin desperately wanted sleep, but he had tried twice in the past hour and failed. The battalion completed a road march during the dark of the night, and he had spent his morning getting the company squared away in the assembly area, and then he moved to the battalion CP and helped Major Spaulding. There had been a small but steady flow of replacements but he was still the company commander of Able Company as well as the acting S2 and S3 for the battalion. He was exhausted, but the sleep wouldn't come yet.

It was raining steadily. It had been raining steadily for three straight days. He stared out of the back of the deuce and a half at the rain, and the mud, and the mass of miserable humanity, and stood up to go help soldiers put together shelter halves in the rain and the mud.

"Sit down," a raspy voice ordered. "Them boys will get along fine without you. I, on the other hand, need you rested. You ain't had any sleep that I know of for two days. Lay down, Perk, and get some sleep." The speaker was Major Bill Spaulding, and he lay on the bed of the large truck under the cover of two muddy, green, wool blankets. This was not the first time that morning he had issued such orders, and the irritation was beginning to creep into his voice.

"Okay, okay. No need to get snippy." Perkin reached into his pack and pulled out a notebook and a pencil. He looked to see if there was an objection from Spaulding, but his eyes were closed. Perkin lay on this stomach, opened the notebook to a fresh sheet of paper, and began to write:

> *The Shittiest Place on Earth*
> *10 Feb 44*
>
>
> *Dear Pop,*
> *I had meant to be a better writer but it's been a crazy couple of weeks. I hope this finds you and Anna well. Please give her my love and tell her I miss her cooking more than I ever would have thought possible. Except her salmon croquettes. I don't miss those. Ha ha.*
> *Tell Margaret not to worry about Sam. I'll go to Berlin if necessary to get him back. Seriously, tell her I said not to worry!*
> *I'm doing okay. I can move around without much pain now, I had my first hot meal in two weeks this morning (slightly chilled with rain-water), and being an optimist, I plan on going on leave someday in the near future and seeing*

Helen. I may feel like old Methuselah, but at least I got the girl. Guess which one matters most?

I want to get you caught up with what's going on, and although the censors probably won't leave much of this in place, I'll fill in the blacked out parts when I get home.

It's been nearly two weeks since I left the Moroni house. My God, I miss those good people and that wonderful fireplace. We finally left the river valley, which I will get to shortly, and I don't think I want to see the Rapido River ever again. Maybe after the war, I'll see if it has any trout in it, but until then, f—k that goddamned river.

When I came back to the company, we were on alert to cross the river again. Why? I don't know. So we went through a great planning process, got kitted up, found our bridges and our boats and were ready to go. Felt so nervous at the prospect of crossing that damn thing again that I almost vomited but I wasn't the only one. The battalion had a few self-inflicted wounds and a rash of illnesses. Bill Spaulding put an end to the illnesses, and said that every man who could walk was going. We didn't have any in the company but I lost two guys (a new replacement and an old-timer who should have known better) my first night back. They had both fallen asleep in a shared foxhole and were bayoneted by a German patrol in the dark. No one slept for the next couple days.

The assault was canceled at the last minute, and I can't tell you how relieved I was. I'm no coward, Pop, but it would have been worse than last time—even with replacements we're *still under fifty percent manning. We went through the same drill the next night, and turned the evening into a fine demonstration for the Germans instead. We created a lot of noise, got shelled, lost an officer to a mine in an area that was supposedly cleared, and got no sleep.*

Perkin thought back to that night. The paths had been cleared to the river—twelve feet wide for two battalions to pass through. *How was that supposed to work?* Lieutenant Kemper had stepped outside of the tape to hurry along the soldiers, and had stepped on a mine. His mistake cost him a leg below the knee. The demonstrations were just short of criminal in Perkin's opinion.

Two days later, we went through the same drill again. We were alerted to be ready to cross the river that night. The plan was for the 3rd Battalion to lead the assault and we would follow. Same plan as a few days before. By this point, the planners had determined that where we had initially crossed on 20 Jan was too effectively defended, and we looked to cross directly at San Angelo. What remains of the 143rd would cross south of the village, we could cross north of the village, and we'd meet up and have a party in the town square. At 1600, it was canceled and we were told to stand down. I fell promptly asleep in my foxhole upon hearing the news.

At midnight on the 3rd (I think – the dates are a little hazy) we were ordered to report to the assembly areas, so Bill and I ran around like chickens with our heads cut off getting it managed in the dark. By the way, it was sleeting that night which gave it a wonderful Christmassy feel.

We were left in the assembly area and Bill and I went to a meeting at regiment where we found out that the plans were changing fast! The 141st RCT was told that we would not be the assault force but would cross with the 1st Tank Group and be their infantry support. I was happy to hear that… I'm not the only southern boy here finally to make peace with Sherman (ha ha, get it?).

We got tasked to conduct a patrol that night, which I led. Took my new lieutenant, an Iowa farm boy named Alex Ryan, with me. He gets to do the next one. Made it to the far side without being detected, and we went inland some 300 yards until we heard some Krauts talking in an old crumbling farmhouse. Not a lot of value in the patrol so after we exfiltrated, we shelled the shit out of the house to make the night productive.

The next day, new plans were drawn up, and they are a step closer to reality. We're still attached to the tank force, and once the 34th takes Cassino, we're to move up with the tanks along Victory Road and seize the village of Piedmonte. What we're to do there wasn't explained, but I'm sure it was a picturesque village in its glory days. I suspect it's mostly rubble now (I haven't seen a whole building since leaving Presenzano). The 34th wasn't successful in taking Cassino, so even though we were put on alert at 2140 for the entire night, we stayed put.

Perkin realized that he would never be able to send the letter. He had already gone into too much detail. He got ready to tear it out of his notebook, but decided to finish it as if through the act of writing, he could make sense of events.

We went back to our holes in the ground and we met our heroes from New Zealand. We were relieved by these Kiwis over the course of the next few days. Our hopes were really high that we would be taken off the line for refit and a little R&R, but didn't happen. The Kiwis look like good soldiers and they assured us that they would succeed where we failed—I didn't dissuade them of the notion. They'll need all the confidence that they can get to do the job ahead of them. They were decidedly sloppy about camouflaging their movements though, and consequently, we were shelled for the remainder of our time on the line.

We also got bombed for the first time. I've watched our boys drop tons of bombs on them and of course, the division had been on the receiving end of German airstrikes before, but this was my first time. Worse than artillery. Lots worse. All I can say is that the shock wave coming off a bomb is something to be experienced. Once. And hopefully never again. No casualties, but some irritated fellas on our side of the river.

Our boys are mad as hell, Pop. So am I. I think we were misused something terrible on that river, and that it was just about criminal stupidity. I haven't seen much since then to suggest that we've gotten smarter. It's a hard thing to ask a dogface to risk himself for something he knows in his heart won't succeed. It's just as hard to motivate yourself to say "Follow me" when you believe the same thing. I don't know how the trench rats did it in the first war, but I think I'm learning.

It isn't all gloom though. Bill Spaulding is a hero in my book. I can't imagine working for someone else. Every day he deals with a thousand details and never makes a mistake. He's as tactically sound as they come and I couldn't ask for more. Colonel Wranosky is gone now, and we have a new regimental commander. A Lt. Col. Henry McCauley. I don't know anything about him other than Bill says he's a good guy. That's enough for me.

We're getting a few replacements now, and not all of them are green. They transferred some boys from the 142nd to us the other day, and I got Lt. Frank McCarter back. He's become a seasoned combat leader, and I'm very glad he's back. I have high hopes for Lt. Alex Ryan as well. Alex's wide-eyed look is gone most of the time and he seems pretty steady. Of course, I still have Eddie Kulis. He's a wonderful soldier and has all the potential to be a topnotch sergeant and with a little polish, he could be a great combat leader himself as an officer. I have a new sergeant, so Eddie is now a squad leader (if only I had a squad, ha ha). My new sergeant is named Alvin Parks and he's from Seguin. Glad to have a Texan. He's not been in combat before but he seems cautiously ready.

Which is a good thing. We're going back into combat any day. Any hour. We're at a place called Hill 213, near a village called Caira near a mountain called Cairo. It's huge in a Pike's Peak kind of way. Well, maybe a little smaller. There are Frogs up there now—North Africans—in a big fight, and hopefully we're not headed that way. We're so chopped up that the only thing that makes is for us to be put into a quiet segment as placeholders.

I'm gonna close now and try to get some shut-eye. My best to all back home. Kiss all the girls for me and say hey to Texas. Love ya, Pop. Perkin

1030 Hours
Poggio Vittiano, Italy

Sam Taft was having his most enjoyable day of the Italian war. He had been in Poggio Vittiano for nearly a week, knew every single person in the small mountain village, and was currently standing on some rocks fishing out of the Lago del Salto, a four-year-old man-made lake in the middle of nowhere.

Lieutenant Beams survived his case of septicemia, and even the Italian doctor was amazed. Sam and Kenton had been certain that Lieutenant Beams had quit breathing one night at the castle, and they were talking about moving the body to another room when Beams coughed in the silence of the great room. Kenton had shrieked and jumped vertically from a sitting position—ghosts were still on his mind—but Beams had survived that night and the next day.

As expected, the doctor had been unable to provide much in the way of either medicine or advice, and Sam and Kenton had merely taken turns staying with Beams for his long periods of unconsciousness, and short periods of incoherent consciousness. During these times, they were unable to get him to eat, but they were able to get him to drink a little fresh water, courtesy of Mr. Bazzini's doctor. Two days after he had seemingly expired, Beams was conscious, somewhat lucid and hungry. "I seen Jesus," were his first words after waking up. "Or maybe Merlin. I never paid much attention at Sunday school. What y'all got to eat?"

Mr. Bazzini's intense anxiety since the discovery of the forest gallows had prompted him to seek out and find a priest willing to help, and it was thought that Beams might need one in any case. Arriving the day after Beams awakened from the near-dead, Father Michele had been a godsend to the three soldiers. The priest didn't speak English, but through Mr. Bazzini, he made it understood that he was more than willing to help the American soldiers. He asked permission to speak to his bishop, to which Sam agreed, and the next day, Father Michele came back with a mule-drawn wagon and a local farmer.

"The Catholic Church would like to help you Protestant heathens," was Mr. Bazzini's interpretation of the priest's speech upon arrival. "Don't tell anyone."

They had thanked Mr. Bazzini profusely for his help, promised to look him up when the Allied armies reached Dunarobba, and then they departed the sanctuary of Todi Castle covered in a loose mound of scratchy straw. They had been in the hands of the Church and its friends from this point forward.

Sam was the only one who had moved forward to Poggio Vittiano. Lieutenant Beams was in no condition to travel and likely would not be for weeks, and Father Michele had explained through an English-speaking parishioner that it was dangerous to move all three men at once. Looking at the two giants, Sam and Kenton, he explained, "Italian men are seldom two meters tall, and since the war, never weigh 100 kilograms or more. You have blond hair and blue eyes," he said to Sam. "And you have red hair and blue eyes," he said to Kenton. "Most Italians have black hair and black eyes. So we must move cautiously until we get you to a place where there are just friends. But I know such a place."

It had been a hard decision for Sam to leave

his companions, but what the priest said was true. Lieutenant Beams could not be left alone, and Sam didn't want to order the sole enlisted man to risk the journey by himself. Kenton had argued briefly with Sam saying the two officers should stick together, but his arguments fell on deaf ears. Kenton's passion for leaving further melted away after meeting a friendly female parishioner of Father Michele.

Poggio Vittiano was an entirely safe village as far as Sam could tell. It was the home village of Father Michele, and he was related in either friendship or kinship to every single villager. There was no risk of betrayal to the fascists as the town considered itself loyal to King Vittorio Emmanuel and Prime Minister Bagdolio as the fascists had built the lake against the wishes of the local villagers, and ancient homes and farmlands were now deep under its waters.

Sam was quartered with the village blacksmith, a young widower named Manfredo who shared Sam's twin passions of horses and fishing. Sam had no particular skills as a blacksmith although he assisted where he could, but he was a good farrier and he helped out with the horses that were brought to Manfredo for shoeing. Manfredo wasn't busy though, and they spent much of their time fishing along the banks of the lake.

It wasn't ideal fishing weather and there was a brisk breeze coming down out of the mountains, but it wasn't raining for the moment. Manfredo had an extra pole and tackle, and Sam was working along the rocks with a minnow lure. To his delight, he had already caught two large-mouth bass that were big enough to keep and he was excited at the prospect of fried fish. He had been thrilled to learn that American bass had been introduced to Italian waters over fifty years ago, and two days before, he and Manfredo caught brown trout in a feeder stream. A lady friend of Manfredo had prepared them for the two hungry men.

Communication was somewhat problematic as there were no English-speakers in the village, but one ex-soldier had learned some Spanish while serving in Spain during their civil war, and he and Sam could reach a basic understanding after a little effort. There was very little that required translation however as life in the village was simple and automatic.

Father Michele told Sam that he would return Sunday after Mass, and Monday morning, Sam would move onward to the next station in his journey—an unremarkable church in southern Avezzano.

1200 Hours
Avezzano, Italy

Lieutenant Colonel Douglas Grossmann leaned on the shovel and looked to the skies. A passerby looking at the worker in the church graveyard might have had the impression that the worker was filled with awe for the nature of his work in God's service. It was less awe and more hope. Grossmann was looking at the sky in optimistic anticipation of rain and an escape from the menial labor. He had volunteered to straighten some of the most tilted headstones in the cemetery, and he was regretting it already.

Since saying goodbye to the director of the Abwehr twelve days before, Grossmann had accomplished two things. He had finally found peace in his mind about Antoniette Bernardi, and he had eventually convinced Father Carlo to give him some independence. A parishioner of the priest was a policeman, and a friend of the Church. He was a man of Grossmann's heart: a day after being introduced to the policeman by Father

Carlo, the policeman produced a set of legal documents showing Grossmann to be a member of the *comune* of Avezzano, with the profession of laborer. He had twice come by the church and Grossmann had accompanied him on his beat in the city. It had been as if a lifeline was tossed to him, and he held on to it tightly. Too many more days closed up in the church and he might have been tempted to take the Walther and kill the priest or maybe himself. Or both. He had never felt so despondent.

As terrible as the isolation was for Grossmann, some good had come from it. He had thought about Antoniette endlessly. Over and over again. The isolation could have taken him down two roads: one leading to madness. The other leading to resolution. Unwittingly slow, but definitively toward resolution was the path that Grossmann took.

He replayed every interaction that he'd ever had with Antoniette Bernardi in his mind, and at first, his thoughts were chaotic and tended to focus on their personal relationship and his obsessive love for her. It was self-defeating, and he knew it. He had known it all along. But recognizing a problem and being able to fix it are two distinct actions that sometimes are connected by only the slenderest of threads. Grossmann forced himself to think linearly, and he began to put his relationship with Antoniette in perspective. He remembered how his Abwehr predecessor in Rome had warned him about becoming romantically involved with Bernardi: "Antoniette will be your best agent," he had said to Grossmann. "She's a dedicated fascist. Admires the Führer very much. I think she is the best we are running in all of Italy already. But, I must warn you, sir, she is unlike anyone I've met before. She has no innocence of youth…she exudes compassion, yet has none. I don't know how God could have created such a beautiful creature, yet in His greatness neglected to give it a soul. She's without modesty, entirely without scruples…a heart as cold as a witch's caress…for God's sake, don't try to seduce her yourself. I don't think that she would let you, she's too professional, but it might be worse if she did. Either way, she would dangle your desire before you for an eternity—until you either kill her or yourself in despair."

Grossmann leaned against his shovel on a dark cloudy day many months later and thought about the prescience of those words, and how close he had come to killing himself.

1515 Hours
1st Battalion Assembly Area, Hill 213, Italy

The banging continued even after Perkin ordered it to stop. An incessant pounding only inches from his head, followed by a voice saying, "Perk, I need you to look at this."

"Can't you have the medic do it this time?" Perkin mumbled.

"What? C'mon. Get up."

Perkin sat up, blinked hard several times, and held out his hand. Spaulding pulled him up and said, "Orders for tonight. I just got back from regiment. Let's go over this. We pull out at night." There was an unknown first lieutenant with Spaulding, who nodded at Perkin.

Spaulding handed Perkin the set of orders, and Perkin read them silently to himself, breaking down the components of what was called "Field Order 22." After he had read the orders twice, he looked at Major Spaulding and summarized the orders. "Okay, Bill. These are the muscle movements of the order as I see 'em: We are to move tonight with the 3rd Battalion to positions on Hill 593, where we'll relieve elements of two regiments of the 34th. Tomorrow at 1100, 1st Battalion is the assault echelon for an attack across 593 toward hills 569 and 374, which we're expected to seize and hold. Third Battalion will be the follow-on echelon, and will help consolidate our position on those three hills. Is that about right?"

"That sums it up. The 1100 assault is scheduled time-coincident with another attack by the 34th on Cassino. The idea is we take the high ground north and west of the abbey, while the 34th throws out the Kraut paratroopers in the town. We get the abbey, they get the town, and the German position becomes untenable. We'll have the 131st and 132nd field artillery in support of our assault and the 155th is standing by. Let's take a look at the map. By the way, this is Lieutenant Roberts of the 34th. He offered to come over and give us a run-down on their positions." Major Spaulding nodded at the tired, dirty, and wet lieutenant.

"Sir," said Roberts, nodding again. "Hill 593 is 1800 feet of misery. It brings you within 500 yards of the abbey, but getting to the peak of 593 is going to be a challenge. When your orders say to relieve elements of the 34th Division, understand that the 34th isn't on 593, but on the approaches to it on Snake Head Ridge. That ridge runs north and south between Mt Cassino on the bottom of the mountain complex, almost to Mt. Cairo at the top. To get you on the ridge, I'll lead your scouts along a trail in a ravine. It's the last real defilade you'll have until you come off the mountain. Almost every spot on the ridge is under observation and fire, and it's best to move at night. The trail has been demined, by engineers and by the hard way, and there are some passages that will have to be done with the assistance of a rope. The sides can get steep so make sure your men understand to stay close to the man in front of them. We've lost a lot of men from just falling off the mountain."

Perkin nodded. "We understand. We were on Mount Sammucro."

Roberts shook his head. "That experience will help, sir, but this is worse. I recommend you have your boys carry as many supplies with them as possible because resupply is challenging as is getting the wounded down from the mountain."

Major Spaulding interrupted, "Mules, Perk. Regiment is laying on some two hundred mules to move our equipment up tonight and for our follow-on resupply."

Lieutenant Roberts shook his head. "Begging your pardon, sir. But if they tell you they've got two hundred mules, you can plan on about fifty, which won't be enough to resupply two battalions."

Perkin shrugged. "I don't like mules anyway. They seem to hold too many opinions. Bill, what do we do once we've got these three hilltops?"

"We keep them. Deny their use to the Germans, and eventually, we or someone else uses them as a springboard for the taking of the abbey."

They talked with Lieutenant Roberts at some length about the tactical difficulties of fighting on the Cassino massif and when Roberts left to meet with the battalion scouts, Perkin and Spaulding talked over a shared can of cold beef stew.

"Whaddya think?" asked Spaulding.

"I think that we should have stayed in Paestum. Nice beach, warm girls, and cold beers. Remember the hotel in Agropoli and the gin and tonics?" Perkin said with a faint smile.

"I do. I'd never had one before then. Although my memory of Paestum is somehow different. I remember a hot beach loaded with German tourists and no girls or beer at all. Remember how hung over those gin and tonics got Sam?" Spaulding laughed. "He had to do a road march the next day and couldn't stop burping. Sergeant Younger told me he thought that Sam was going to fall out."

"No chance," Perkin said. "Sam would never fall out...I wonder where he is."

"I think about it all the time—let's hope he's out of this rain and safe. All right, Professor, let's take a look at the map again."

1600 Hours
Poggio Vittiano, Italy

Sam was involved in the battle of his life.

He had sacrificed a rook to no great advantage, and Manfredo had made him pay for the mistake. Yet, all was not lost—far from it in fact as Sam moved a knight forward into enemy territory endangering an Italian bishop. Sam watched as Manfredo struggled mentally with the simultaneous requirements of offense and defense, and his host put a finger on his threatened bishop only to remove it while he thought some more.

The rain had come to Poggio Vittiano, and the two fishermen had barely made it inside before the skies opened up and poured down on the small village. The temperature had dropped dramatically, and Manfredo told Sam that snow would come that evening. It didn't matter to Sam though. Manfredo's home was well built, and heated by a well-stocked wood-burning stove. There was even electricity from the dam, a modern convenience that Sam had not expected when he saw the small village for the first time.

Manfredo moved his knight instead of the bishop as he decided to go on the offense and he worked an angle to trap Sam's king. But it was apparent, and Sam was able to thwart the attack by simply pushing a pawn on the other side of the board to threaten Manfredo's other knight. Sam's counterattack seemed equally apparent to Manfredo, who contemplated his next move as he poured them both a glass of homemade cherry brandy.

Deciding that he couldn't afford the loss of the knight, Manfredo poured out a stream of invective Italian, and he moved the knight to a safer square, which inadvertently opened a lane for Sam's queen. After a two-minute bloodbath that ended with a decisive victory by Texas over Italia, the board was reset, more brandy poured, and a new game was begun as the rain turned to ice spicules.

1900 Hours
Avezzano, Italy

Lieutenant Colonel Grossmann sat at the dinner table opposite Father Carlo. They were sharing a dinner of scrambled eggs, bread, and olive oil. Father Carlo had not wanted any of his parishioners to come out on such a cold nasty night, so he had cooked the eggs himself.

"Douglas?" the priest asked.

"Yes, Father?"

"We will be leaving soon. My contacts tell me that this is the last storm of the winter, and that we will have good weather next week," Father Carlo said.

"I'm ready," said Grossmann truthfully even as he snorted inwardly. Father Carlo's contact was Mario Lucini who had told Grossmann that his almanac was never wrong.

"We're to have company on our trip," said the priest.

Grossmann was alarmed but didn't show it. "Company? Who's that?"

"One of your countrymen is to join us. I can't keep two of you here for more than a day, so if the weather holds, we'll leave as soon as he gets here. One, maybe two days, on the mountains, and we are there. I say goodbye and walk back. Easy."

It wasn't easy. The mountain trail was a challenge, and Father Carlo hadn't made the trip since last fall. But the truth was that he was ready for different company. Douglas Peabody, as Grossmann called himself, was not an ideal guest, and the priest suspected that he had been indiscrete—a young woman had come by earlier asking for a friend of hers matching Peabody's description. Naturally, he had claimed not to know anyone of that height and build, and the priest had steered the young lady away from the cemetery while Peabody worked on the gravestones. It was a shame that he had to be so deceitful—she was astonishingly beautiful.

1900 Hours
1st Battalion Assembly Area, Hill 213, Italy

Another hour and they would depart. There was no moon even though the moon was full, but moonrise wasn't until morning, and it was cloud covered in any case. It had been raining, but Perkin could hear and feel the rain turning to ice.

The battalion was as ready to go as it would be, but Perkin knew in his heart that was a meaningless measure. The once 800-strong battalion was down to about two company's strength in the aggregate—about fifty percent of its notional combat efficiency—and it had nowhere near a complete command or combat element to it. The second unit in the movement, 3rd Battalion, was in roughly the same shape. Perkin's only hope was that the Germans were as depleted as they were.

Perkin was in command of Able Company, which consisted of two small platoons plus a weapons section with a single .30 caliber machine gun and two light mortars. He had two officers in charge of his platoon, one of whom was a combat veteran and the other who had seen some shooting but had not been in combat. He had two sergeants now, neither of whom had seen combat, plus a single corporal—Eddie Kulis.

Perkin had made the decision that Kulis would stay with him, and the lieutenants and the sergeants were made aware that instructions coming from Corporal Kulis were to be assumed as coming from him. A radio operator named Fisher was assigned to Perkin that afternoon, but as communications had been sketchy the entirety of the war for him, he held little optimism in clear, concise communications.

He had also been told that he was the executive officer, operations officer, and intelligence officer of the battalion. Should anything happen to Bill Spaulding, Perkin would take command of the battalion. Despite being only a few months in grade, he was also the senior officer behind the commander of the 3rd Battalion, and regiment had directed that if something happened to both of the battalion commanders, Perkin was to merge the two units and assume command. He had told Spaulding after getting the news that his first command would be to order a truce until he got off the mountain.

Perkin stood in the lee of some rocks, which helped to cut the wind even if it did little for the sleet, and he felt the familiar weight of his Thompson on his shoulder. He had come close to leaving it behind and taking a trench shotgun instead. Many of the soldiers of the 34th that he had talked to swore by the trench guns. It was an unnerving conversation to have. Most of the fighting was done at fairly close quarters at night, and the shotguns were particularly effective at twenty-five yards or less when loaded with .00 buckshot.

Both Winchester and Remington trench guns were available with shortened barrels and bayonet lugs, but although many of the Red Bulls were fierce advocates of the shotguns, at least one officer told Perkin that the rain was making the paper cartridges swell to the point that shooters had difficulty ejecting spent shells.

His pack had been filled with extra magazines for both his .45 caliber Thompson and his Colt .45. Often, officers made it an either/or decision—usually either an M-1 carbine or the .45 pistol. Perkin had deep abiding faith in both .45s, so he carried both the submachine gun and the pistol. He also carried extra C-rations and extra hand grenades, and hoped fervently that he would need neither. He wore his wool uniform with an old pair of long johns underneath, a heavy overcoat, tailored and lined leather gloves that he bought in Presenzano, wool socks, and his jump boots that he bought months before.

Perkin was joined in the shelter of the rocks by a smiling Corporal Kulis. "Hey there, Eddie. What's got you smiling?" Perkin asked.

"Sir, we've been sitting in the same crappy foxhole for almost three weeks—feels like three years. I'm just glad to be doing something. Here, give me your cup, I brought us some coffee."

Perkin produced his canteen cup, and Kulis poured out half of his own full cup of coffee.

"Thanks. Any thoughts on the boys?" Perkin asked.

"Not really. Usual stuff. Some guys are excited.

Some are terrified. Some are cleaning their rifles and others are sleeping. No one likes the food or the company. It's like every other day in the army—another day in paradise." Kulis laughed at the old joke.

Perkin found the laughter infectious, and he laughed as well. "Ain't that the truth? Wait...what'd you say? Another day in paradise, or another day with parasites?"

"Is there a difference?" Kulis said, and they both laughed again.

As they told jokes and laughed, it struck Perkin how much he valued the little rifleman's company. Kulis and the other veterans of the battalion, and all of those who had been on the bloody river, had a special spot in Perkin's heart. Although he was no longer excited to be going into combat, he was grateful to have an old comrade at his side.

Chapter Eight

February 11, 1944
1000 Hours
Snakeshead Ridge, Cassino Massif, Italy

Major Bill Spaulding and Captain Perkin Berger
huddled behind a collection of rocks with Lieutenant
Roberts of the 34th Division. It was a question of waiting now for the assault to begin, but Perkin was still
feeling the shock of just arriving to the line of departure.

Outside of the night of the Rapido assault, the
ascent onto Snakeshead Ridge had been the longest
night of his life even though the ascent itself was largely
complete by midnight. The battalion left Hill 213 on
time and in single file. Outside of the occasional distant
flare or reflected flash off the low-hanging clouds, it was
pitch-dark. Sure-footed scouts from the 34th Division
and the battalion led the way, but it was slow moving
in the dark.

Had Perkin been blindfolded and told to ascend a
mountainside by himself, he could not have felt more
disoriented. Every soldier stumbled over rocks, caught
his uniform on the mountain gorse, or scratched his
face on the jutting granite of the mountain. First ice,

and then snow, accumulated on the rocks, making the 1000-foot climb even more treacherous, and the continual rain of the past three days loosened the mud depriving the soldiers of firm hand and footholds. Every man was to keep a hand wrapped into the shoulder strap of the pack before him, but inevitably, hands grew numb and slipped, and contact was lost between the soldiers.

Through the course of the climb, Perkin heard frequent curses inevitably followed by the urgent whisper, "Wait up!" The soldier in front couldn't always wait, and the soldier behind would try to catch up if he wasn't too disoriented. It seldom worked, and rather than one long string of soldiers heading up the defile between Monte Maiola and Monte Castellone, it became many smaller groups. Major Spaulding interspersed his scouts through the long line of men, and sometimes they were able to take control of a smaller group and keep them moving, and sometimes the scouts weren't.

Some soldiers straggled on purpose, and some simply because they were too timid to move in the dark. Whatever the cause, the movement took longer than it should have. The path up the mountain would have been challenging with packs and weapons in the daytime, but at night and in an ice and snowstorm, the word "challenge" simply didn't do it justice.

They relieved the soldiers of the 34th Division, some of whom were unable to move from the cold and the inactivity. Those men, who looked worse than the survivors of the Rapido, had their cramped muscles rubbed by squad mates and were helped to their feet and pushed or carried to the rear.

When daylight came and Perkin had the chance to visually check on his men, he was disheartened to find that about ten percent or more of the battalion had dropped out, gotten lost, or simply not made the journey.

During his quick inspection with Major Spaulding, Perkin saw a handful of soldiers without packs and helmets, and in one case, a replacement soldier who had shed his overcoat and dropped his rifle on the march. Watching the soldier shiver as the warmth of exertion had passed and his sweat began to freeze, Perkin felt a mixture of contempt and pity for the man. One of the new sergeants rolled his eyes in disbelief upon seeing the witless soldier standing before the angry officer, and led the soldier off—telling Perkin he would see to getting the man squared away.

Still, there was a lot to be grateful for: some of the men who dropped out over the course of the ascent were beginning to trickle back to their companies, and the vast majority of the troops seemed prepared for the challenges of the morning even as the weather worsened on the mountaintop.

Lieutenant Roberts pointed out the salient features of their new battlefield. "They can't see you here, but as soon as they figure out more of us came up last night, they'll start hitting this position with mortars and artillery. We've been shelled more times than you can count, but there are some covered positions here made up with sandbags and scrap wood brought up by mules. It won't help on a direct hit...but...well, you get the point." Roberts used the flat of his hand to point to the southwest. "You're on the head of the snake now, and the ridge is the body of the snake and it kind of peters out on 593—or so I think. I haven't been there yet. You'll head up this incline for another 500 yards or so. Make sure to stay to either side of the ridgeline. From there, you'll move onto the ridge leading to the hilltop. You'll be exposed at that point, and drawing fire from the south and west."

Perkin nodded. "How far is that last leg? How long

will we be exposed?"

Roberts let out a long sigh. "Well, here's the thing: it's about 500 yards, give or take. But there's a lot of rocks up there, just like this one."

"Fuck me," said Spaulding. It was sounding worse and worse. They had been lead to believe that the 34th actually occupied Hill 593, which wasn't correct. Now they found out that they had 500 yards of exposed movement just to get to the hill.

Perkin agreed.

After wishing Perkin and Spaulding good luck, Roberts left the two officers from the 141st and went to join his own unit. Spaulding sent a runner to find the other company commanders, and he sat and waited with his back to the large stone and tucked his hands under his armpits.

The weather was definitely getting worse. Temperatures were well below freezing, and the wind was blowing constant at gale force and gusting above 50 mph. Everywhere Perkin looked, soldiers were huddled in groups behind rocks trying in vain to stay out of the wind.

"We're gonna lose people to exposure today," Perkin said.

"Exposure to the wind is the least of our worries," replied Spaulding. "That 500 yards of exposure to Spandaus will finish us off first." With a shaking hand, Spaulding pulled a pouch of tobacco from the pocket of his overcoat, and stuffed a huge wad into his cheek. As soon as he had it positioned where he wanted it, he asked, "So, Professor, what history lesson do you have for me that's going to give me confidence? Who had it worse than us and was successful?"

Perkin thought for a minute and said, "I got a couple stories. One with Americans, and one with the British."

"I ain't picky. What's your favorite?"

"Well, the story of George Rogers Clark is my favorite, but I'll save it for later. I'll tell you about the Englishman first, because I think he was the toughest man who ever lived," Perkin said.

"Tougher than Sam?" Spaulding raised an eyebrow.

"Sam's a cupcake compared to Shackleton. Ever heard of him?" Perkin asked.

"Yeah, he was the arctic explorer, right? Found the North Pole or something cold like that." Spaulding was shaking harder now.

"Antarctic. It was the South Pole, and he had made a couple attempts at it and failed…"

"That's right," interrupted Spaulding. "He left Scott's team, and after Scott died and Amundsen made it, he decided to go again."

"Yeah, except since the pole had already been reached, he decided to march across the continent. It was, in his mind, the last great first of Antarctic exploration. He handpicked a crew, scraped up the financing, and set sail on the eve of World War One in a ship aptly called *Endurance*. If I remember it right, when he found out that war had broken out, he offered to return, but the admiralty or the king or someone told him to go ahead…that another prize for the Crown was more important than the contribution of the fifty-some men for the war effort. So they went on. They reached Antarctic waters in January, which was the Antarctic summer, and they promptly got trapped in the sea ice in the Weddell Sea."

Perkin used his hands to illustrate ice shrinking in on the ship and continued, "They drifted as part of the sea ice, always trapped in the pack, for over a month, and then Shackleton, you know, realized that they were trapped until spring of the next year. So, they prepared the ship for winter, hunted seals and penguins on the ice pack, and, well, just hunkered down until October of 1915—so, they'd been gone for over a year at this point, and trapped in the ice for ten months. The spring break-up of the ice pack didn't free the ship, it really didn't even break up, but it crushed the hull of the *Endurance*. So, now, they were trapped on the ice, and a long way from land."

"What'd they do?" asked Spaulding.

"Shackleton ordered that the ship be stripped of necessities, including the ship's three boats—heavy wooden 20-foot lifeboats—and they set up camp on the ice floe and watched the ship go down. They stayed there for a couple months, hoping that the drift would take them close to an island where there were stores, but they couldn't do it. The ice was too bad. Then, eventually, the ice floe that they were on began to split and break apart, and Shackleton ordered his men to the boats, where they sailed to this rock called Elephant Island. By now, which I think was April of '16, they were as far from where the *Endurance* sank as Corpus is to Fort Worth."

"Good God!" exclaimed Spaulding. "Were they rescued there?"

"Yes, but not right away. Elephant Island was uninhabited. Nothing but seals and penguins. So, Shackleton and a crew of five men set sail in one of these boats. He took enough food for a month, and in the height of the southern hurricane season, they sailed to South Georgia Island, where the Norwegians had a permanent whaling station. Next to William Bligh's journey after the mutiny on the *Bounty*, it was the most heroic voyage in a small boat ever made. They sailed 800 miles over the course of two weeks and made landfall exactly on South Georgia Island—except, when they first saw land, they were in the heart of a hurricane in a 20-foot boat in 50-foot seas—the kind of storm that sinks ships. I still get shivers thinking about it."

"So, what happened then?" asked Spaulding who was shivering himself.

"They landed, but since Shackleton had our kind of luck, it was on the wrong side of the island. They couldn't put back out to sea again, so Shackleton took two of the men, crossed a mountain range taller than old Mount Cairo there," Perkin nodded at the snow-capped mountain behind them. "And hiked into the Norwegian camp the next day. He covered some thirty miles over a mountain range in less than a day and a half."

"Did they get the boys off Elephant Island?"

"They did, but not until August, 1916. But the most amazing thing is, after being marooned all that time, and in the worst natural conditions on earth, Shackleton didn't lose a single man. Not one under his command."

"Amazing," Spaulding agreed. "I wish I could say the same. You know, Perk, I don't think I've ever heard that full story before."

"Most people haven't. But for my money, he was the toughest man ever to walk the planet—they ought to write epic tales about it. But I haven't told you the best part yet!" Perkin said with a grin.

"What's that?"

"Shackleton's advertisement for men before his expedition. Old Perkin made me memorize it. It said, 'Men wanted for hazardous journey. Low wages, bitter cold, long hours of complete darkness. Safe return doubtful. Honor and recognition in event of success.' I heard that 5,000 men applied. Now, ain't that just a poetic thing of beauty?"

1030 Hours
Avezzano, Italy

Lieutenant Colonel Grossmann couldn't stand the dark cold inside the church any longer, and decided to test the dark cold outside. The weather was wickedly cold, with terribly strong winds blowing from the northwest, but he decided to walk at least a couple of kilometers just to clear his head.

It was just a question now of enduring a few more days of boredom. If possible, as soon as he had a definitive day of departure, he was to notify the wachtmeister at the hotel. If it wasn't possible, his departure would be detected by the admiral's men, and the admiral would notify Allied intelligence through the Spanish attaché in Berlin that he was on the way. He was to meet two Allied intelligence agents at the Gildardino farm, and after the priest had returned and his mission was complete, he was to return to Rome alone. He had strict orders to return as soon as possible as the admiral was understandably anxious to keep the footprint minimized as much as possible at the Gildardino farm.

Grossmann walked with his head down because the cold and the wind were conspiring to make his eyes water. As he walked, his mind ran over his meeting with Admiral Canaris and he reviewed the parameters of his mission yet again.

Grossmann unconsciously touched the lapel of his overcoat. Stitched inside were the microfilms he was to deliver to the Allied intelligence agents—pictures of documents detailing the Final Solution, maps and photographs of the concentration and extermination camps, locations of German and Russian atrocities, including photographs detailing the exhumation of the Katyn Forest victims.

Grossmann was also to convey a personal message to the Allied agents: that Admiral Canaris was willing to work with the British and American governments to seek a negotiated conclusion to hostilities. He was to convey that German officers were prepared to over-throw Hitler and install a new, pro-western government. Canaris had told Grossmann that the Americans and British might balk at a negotiated surrender, but their terms of unconditional surrender were unthinkable.

Canaris also stressed that Grossmann was to speak bluntly about the likelihood that British intelligence had been penetrated by the Soviets, and that at least one of their analysts, a man named Kim Philby was on the Soviets' payroll. Grossmann had been directed to ensure that the American representative was aware that the British had been penetrated. Canaris didn't know the extent that SIS was penetrated by the Russians, and he wanted to ensure the channel of information wasn't terminated by Soviet agents in London.

Grossmann accepted the purity of the admiral's motives. He didn't think that the admiral was merely trying to save his skin, as he candidly admitted he himself might be doing. Canaris was risking everything in the name of honor, which was making him somewhat of a rarity in Grossmann's experience. Grossmann actually found it inspiring, even as he was deeply concerned about the future. He thought, as he walked, that this mission had led him into the company of great men— men who genuinely believed in self-sacrifice for the betterment of mankind. He had thought earlier that Monsignor O'Flaherty was uniquely inspirational, and yet a few days later, he found Admiral Canaris to be a kindred spirit of the priest. He realized that he had been in the company of greatness, and perhaps it was that greatness that was inspiring Colonel Grossmann to take great risks himself.

There was no question that the risks were immense. If he were to come to the attention of the Gestapo, his rank, his achievements would be worth nothing. He would be interrogated, tortured, and then executed. He knew that his American connection could be an asset, but it was also a dangerous liability and that he would not be given the benefit of the doubt.

Why had he decided to help the admiral? He couldn't say exactly, other than he recognized the opportunity to be a part of something wonderful, something honorable. He had felt that way during the early days of the war, when the German Army was invincible, and the Fatherland was righting historical wrongs. Times had changed. Germany was not only not invincible but was creating historical wrongs that might never be righted. Did he not have an obligation as a German to help save the Fatherland from itself, as Admiral Canaris had said?

An immense risk, but wouldn't there be an immense reward if he was successful? Wouldn't he be remembered as a man of history, just like O'Flaherty and Canaris? A man who took immense risks to warn the world of the crimes being perpetrated in the east…a man who saved countless lives to help end the world war? Sure, there might be questions about his actions in Germany after the war, but he agreed with the admiral that Germany was destined to lose the war. Maybe afterwards would be a good time to move back to California—as a man who helped end the war. Grossmann had suffered through a few minutes of anxiety over how some of his actions in the war might be perceived, particularly his role in the Naples terror campaign, and his killing of Captain Mullen. But the murder of the Australian soldier was in the line of duty, and in Naples, he was merely following orders. No one would hold that against him.

1040 Hours
Snakeshead Ridge, Cassino Massif, Italy

Perkin looked at the soldiers before him. He felt as if he was at the end of a line stretching to the beginning of history—a line of company commanders going back to before the centurions of Rome. As had his predecessors, he thought that some of the men, maybe all of the men, kneeling in the cold wind before him would not survive the day.

"All right, boys. It's almost time. Everybody know what to do?" Perkin looked at the white, pinched, faces of the men before him—some of whom he had served with since the beginning, and some whose names he barely knew.

A few heads nodded up and down. Some of the soldiers stared back blankly. Perkin grinned in spite of himself. "Come on, boys...it ain't hard. Everyone know what to do?"

"Yes, sir," came the ragged refrain.

"Okay, let's just keep it simple then. Kill anyone who ain't us. Everybody know what a German soldier looks like?" All the heads went up and down. "Kill them. Every one of them unless he has dropped his weapons and has his hands up. Understood?"

"Yes, sir."

"Everybody know what to do with a German prisoner?" Perkin saw that Kulis was about to explain what he normally did with wounded soldiers, and he said quickly, "Kulis, don't answer." Perkin was beginning to feel better. It was getting time, and the butterflies were going away.

Private Hodgson, the broken bowl soldier from Tennessee nodded, "Yes, sir. Disarm them, and send them to the rear to be collected."

"Yes. Send 'em under escort if you can, but get them out of the battle area quickly. We're not going to have a handful of Krauts under our wing if their comrades counterattack. What about our wounded?"

There was no immediate answer, so Lieutenant Ryan spoke up, "Walking wounded stay in place until we're sure we can hold the objective. We might need the firepower. One of the armored regiments down in the valley is providing stretcher-bearers. Battalion aid stations are set up over there." Ryan nodded at the collection of tents that were whipping furiously in the wind.

Perkin nodded. He had been told by one of the officers from the 34th Division that evacuation of the wounded off the mountain generally took eight to ten hours per man. He shivered involuntarily, and then said, "Speed. That's the ticket. Move quickly from cover to cover, but keep moving. Bunch up and you're dead. Stop and smoke, and you're dead. Keep going! Sergeants and lieutenants, I'm counting on you to keep the momentum going. This is going to be a fight of grenades, rifles, and bayonets. Slam into the enemy, and let's punch through them. As the Yankee devil Sherman once said, 'War is the remedy that our enemies have chosen, and I say let us give them all they want!'"

1050 Hours
Snakeshead Ridge, Cassino Massif, Italy

The time had almost arrived. In ten minutes, the artillery would open up and plaster Hill 593 with a mixture of high explosives and smoke. The German defenders along Snakeshead Ridge would be ruthlessly eliminated by blast and concussion, white-hot metal fragmentation and shards of granite, and failing that, with the blood and iron of close quarters combat.

Charlie Company would lead the assault with Baker and Able companies in trail. The artillery would fire for ten minutes before the infantry moved. Even then, the artillery would only cease for thirty seconds allowing the infantry to move forward fifty yards. Then the murderous fire would begin again, hopefully catching the German defenders as they remanned their positions. It would not quite be a rolling barrage, but perhaps it would be good enough for the Texans to move close enough to begin the hot work of pushing the Germans from the mountains.

Forward artillery observers were in place. Their communications had been tested. The artillery had every square inch of the mountain already registered—they had been firing missions now for weeks. Unfortunately, German artillery had the mountaintops registered as well. It would be a zone of horrific death—ironically in view of the serene majesty of the abbey founded by Saint Benedict centuries before.

From where Perkin crouched, he could not see the German defenders of the ridge and the hill. Their positions would become known in time, but it was the unknown that was more frightening. Perkin figured that the artillery would wreak terrible damage among the German soldiers, but a lone surviving gunner on an MG-42 would do the same to the Texans as they tried to advance up the hill.

Bill Spaulding joined Perkin and Kulis behind their rock shelter. "Goddamn, Perkin, I almost forgot!"

"What's that, Bill?"

"You and Eddie break out your canteen cups. But we gotta hurry!"

Perkin shook his head as he realized the magnitude of their omission. "I'm a sorry son of a bitch, Bill. I almost forgot too."

They dragged out their canteen cups while Major Spaulding produced a leather-bound thermos. As he poured the brown liquid into their cups, he said, "It ain't Sam's bourbon. I ain't even sure exactly what Wranosky left us—might be Scotch, could be paint thinner—but it'll have to do. Eddie, hold your cup like this and follow our lead."

Spaulding held his cup with his wrist bent at an odd outward angle, and Perkin and then Kulis followed suit. The cups were put together in a circle, and Spaulding cleared his throat and said, "To God."

Perkin repeated the toast and nodded at Kulis who did the same, "To God." Instead of taking a drink, the cup traveled to their ears for a moment as if the mysterious beverage were providing wise advice on the upcoming battle.

The cups traveled back to the circle still held at that odd angle, and Spaulding toasted again, "To country!" Both Perkin and Kulis repeated the toast and all cups moved back to their ears and then returned to the circle.

"To Texas!" The cycle of refrains and listening repeated again.

Spaulding looked at the small shivering rifleman and asked, "What should we toast to now, Eddie?"

Kulis almost blurted out "Whores," but decided that the moment required more decorum. He didn't think that there would be victory on that day, and didn't want to waste a toast on what couldn't happen, so he said, "How about Bear?"

Perkin smiled, put his free hand on the shoulder of Corporal Kulis and gave it a squeeze. He nodded to Spaulding, who said, "To Bear! May he have a safe return."

"To Bear!" But instead of lifting the cups to their

ears, Perkin and Spaulding finished the toast with a loud rolling "Roiiiiissssssster!" and each man slammed back his shot, with Kulis just a second behind the others.

"Scotch, I think," said Perkin.

"No, sir," said Kulis. "It's Bushmills. You know... Irish."

The two officers looked at Kulis with surprise, who grinned and shrugged. "What? I have a taste for whiskies."

Perkin laughed and looked back at the soldiers who were similarly bunched behind rocks—mostly seeking shelter from the terribly ill wind blowing across the mountaintop. Snow blew horizontally across the ragged stone surface, and only a few minutes ago, he felt a sensation surely like Shackleton's despair when he was trapped on the ice—there might be a safe return in his future, but it was doubtful.

None of that mattered now—the ritual was completed, and he was ready for battle.

1100 Hours
Snakeshead Ridge, Cassino Massif, Italy

The familiar boom of the distant artillery was the indication that the assault had begun. The assault elements moved to the crest of the depression that they were in, and waited for the order to move up the ridge.

For the first time, Perkin could see Hill 593 ahead of him along the ridgeline. As the rounds began detonating on the hilltop, a massive plume of smoke lifted from the mountain, only to be whipped down the mountainside from its peak. They had anticipated little help from the smoke, but nevertheless, battalion mortars fired smoke round after smoke round to the north of the hilltop with the hope that the wind would blow it over the defenders. It had little effect.

German fire was nonexistent so far. The German defenders of the mountain had dropped to the ground between inadequate sandbags, and hid behind boulders that offered little protection from airbursts. There were no reinforced trenches like down in the valley, the mountaintop was solid rock. They would man their guns as soon as the fires lifted though, and the American soldiers were aware that 500 yards was a great distance to cover under fire.

Across the Cassino massif, Perkin watched as hundreds of soldiers moved toward their objectives. Soldiers from the Gun Club's 142nd infantry regiment moved on their right toward Hill 468, and troops from the 34th Division's 135th and 168th regiments began a frontal assault toward the abbey. It was time.

Charlie Company led the way. The first twenty-five yards were the easiest. Then the automatic fire began from Hill 468 to the west. Then the company began to take automatic fire from Hill 593. Then the mortar rounds began to fall.

Perkin was bouncing on his feet watching as Charlie Company dropped to the ground and covered up to a man. He turned to see Major Spaulding yelling into a handset and within the minute, mortar fire was directed against the German mortars on Hill 593. It had no immediate effect, but a resumption of artillery fire against Hill 593 did. The flanking fire from Hill 468 continued.

The soldiers of Charlie Company began a series of crawls and sprints to find cover behind rocks, and some of the first of Charlie Company's wounded began to crawl back to the draw hiding one of two battalion aid stations, while other soldiers lay where they were hit.

Perkin gave the order to begin moving Able

Company out. Baker was headed to the left of the ridge, Able would head to the right and would be exposed to the fires from Hill 468. He had weighed the option of creating a command post for the company in the draw, and commanding the company's movement from the relative safety offered there. It would have been the textbook answer. But he had told Spaulding that he didn't have enough troops to justify staying behind, and he would move forward with the men.

Spaulding had agreed, and then stipulated, "Not in front. That's not the company commander's job. Understand?"

Perkin had nodded, and thirty minutes later, he found himself resisting the temptation to move to the front of his small ragged skirmish line as they moved through the boulders of the mountain along the side of the ridge.

They began to take fire for the first time, but not from Hill 468, which had reoriented its defense to the immediate threat posed by the soldiers of the 142nd. The fire faced by the soldiers of Able Company was small-arms fire and from their front. Perkin's machine gun in the rear opened fire on unseen German soldiers by firing directly over the heads of the soldiers of Able Company as they advanced. It bought enough time for three men from McCarter's Second Platoon to reach a mound of rocks where they immediately took shelter. One soldier pointed his rifle up at the top of the rocks should a German face peer over, and the other two soldiers lobbed grenades. Hard, sharp explosions followed, and McCarter's soldiers swarmed immediately behind the rocks. Perkin expected more gunfire, but the grenades had evidently done the job.

The advance continued slowly. It was not grand like Napoleon's Imperial Guard at Waterloo or Pickett's

Charge with long lines marching bravely into the cannons. It lacked the futile intensity of going over the top at Verdun or the Somme. The advance was small groups of desperate men darting and crawling between the cover of rocks and draws and tree stumps, and the myriad minuscule defilades offered by the rough uneven terrain.

Perkin was gratified to see the majority of soldiers moving forward—with their heads bent into the wind and the traces of snow blowing hard over the ground like angry wraiths around their feet. Sometimes the soldiers would freeze from a burst of gunfire or after the impact of a nearby mortar round. It was understandable, and it was instinctual, but to freeze on the battlefield meant near certain death. The only answer was to keep moving, and Perkin's two lieutenants and his few non-commissioned officers were doing their duty: they kept the men moving, and directed the tactical battle.

"Sir?" Perkin's radioman gave him the handset. "It's Lieutenant Ryan."

Ryan was asking for mortar fire on a position ahead of him. "There's a crab about 125 yards southwest of my position. He's set back against the hill on the other side of this rise in front of us."

Perkin looked through his field glasses and saw where Ryan's position was, estimated the range and bearing of where the *MG Panzernester*—the pillbox— would be, and Kulis passed the information via handi-talkie back to the company mortar crew.

The first round fell short—almost disastrously so— and Perkin saw Lieutenant Ryan pointing frantically toward the hill behind him and Perkin could hear incoherent shouting over his headset. Kulis made the corrections, and thirty seconds later another round fell on the other side of the little rise.

Perkin listened to Ryan on the headset, and told Kulis, "Fire for effect." They watched as the handful of rounds impacted on the far side of the rise, and then as Lieutenant Ryan and his soldiers moved cautiously to the crest and then moved out of sight over the hill.

Perkin unslung his Thompson and said to Kulis and his radioman, "Time for us to move forward. We can't see the boys from here. Let's move up, and we'll see if we can direct the push onto 593."

1200 Hours
Snakeshead Ridge, Cassino Massif, Italy

It had been a hot hour since the start of the assault, and technically, Perkin thought, they were on Hill 593. They weren't remotely close to being king of the hill, however. The Germans still held the crest of the hill and panzer grenadiers had taken strong positions through the rocks and behind a stonewall fronting the hill top.

At 1130 hours, the command post of Charlie Company had been hit squarely by a mortar round, killing the company commander, a friend of Perkin's. Perkin was now in command of both Able and Charlie companies, and his command continued to dwindle by the minute.

Perkin's lieutenants were both still alive. Perkin had moved forward, and he was going to talk to his own lieutenants and then move to his left and find the Charlie Company officers. McCarter offered a handshake and said in his slow East Texas drawl, "Well, shit, Perkin. I see we're doing better than usual," to which Perkin replied, "If this is us doing good, heaven help us."

Lieutenant Ryan was hunkered down behind a set of German sandbags and he was talking to Private Hodgson when Perkin and his companions crawled over to his position.

"Hey, Alex, what's new?" Perkin said as he offered a hand.

"This whole goddamned day is a new experience for me, sir." Lieutenant Ryan was visibly angry but wasn't hysterical.

"I understand, Lieutenant. We gotta start somewhere though. Gimme the quick rundown."

"Yes, sir. Sergeant Parks is dead as are two privates, Connelly and Rush. Two wounded and evacuated. Three walking wounded still with us. Private Hodgson is my acting sergeant."

Perkin offered a hand to Hodgson, who after a moment's hesitation took it. Perkin said with a faint smile, "Congratulations, Hodgson. What's your plan?"

Surprising Perkin, Hodgson said, "It's pretty simple, sir. Kill everyone who ain't us."

"Sir!" Corporal Kulis interrupted. "There's a lot of movement back there. I think they're beginning the counterattack."

"Get Major Spaulding!" Perkin ordered the radioman. When Spaulding came up on the radio, Perkin said, "Counterattack imminent. Enemy moving north along ridge. Enemy strength…" Perkin looked at Kulis who shrugged. "Enemy strength unknown. Request fires 100 yards ahead of our position." Kulis handed Perkin the map, and Perkin prepared the fire order and read it to Major Spaulding.

German artillery arrived to the battlefield first. It was behind Perkin's position on Hill 593. The German gunners were afraid to get too close to their attacking troops and their fire mission was deliberately long. It had little effect on the forward-most American troops, but it served the purpose of cutting off either reinforcements or a retreat back along the ridge.

The German barrage was intense but short-lived. The ground shook under their feet, and the smoke from the explosions swirled briefly and then were carried off the mountains by the intense wind.

"Get ready," Perkin called out. "They'll come in close under the barrage."

Then the firing began along the line as panzer grenadiers ran crouching toward the American position. From McCarter's area, a Browning Automatic Rifle opened up to Perkin's right and Perkin watched as two German soldiers fell less than fifty yards from their front.

There were too many people in the sandbagged pit that Ryan had been using. Perkin pulled on Kulis's sleeve, did the same with the radioman, and they darted over to the cover of some rocks to their left. Perkin saw a grenadier poke his head around a shattered tree trunk, and Perkin fired a short burst from his Thompson at him. Perkin thought the range was too far for an accurate shot with the Thompson, but the soldier slid down from behind the tree and didn't move farther.

American artillery then arrived to the battlefield, exactly where Perkin wanted it. Now it was the German soldiers caught off from retreat, and the Germans soldiers closest to the Texans moved forward quickly to escape being within the blast and kill radius of the 105mm artillery. That the fires were very close was apparent to Perkin's group as first one shell fragment slammed into a stone behind them, only to be countered by fragments fired from German guns hitting stones in front of them. Even though they had effectively been straddled by the competing artilleries of two armies, no one in his immediate group had been hit.

That was not the case up and down the line, however. Perkin could hear the calls for medics to his left and right, and the bravest men on the battlefield ran forward during the barrage to help their comrades.

Perkin would do an assessment of the wounded when the opportunity presented itself. His immediate concern was holding the line against the German counterattack. Certainly, the artillery was having an effect, but Perkin could see small personal battles going on across the width of his line. In the Charlie Company sector, where he was meaning to go next, he saw German and American soldiers exchanging volleys of grenades. The German potato masher grenades tumbled end over end while the American pineapples looked more like baseballs in flight. Soldiers on both sides screamed in pain and dropped to the ground writhing in agony.

A rifle boomed out next to Perkin, and as he turned back to his own front, he saw a German soldier drop the grenade in his hand and fall to the ground. Two seconds later, the grenade detonated and a fine pink mist was blown rapidly off the mountain. Soldiers on both sides sought shelter, and a firefight broke out that reminded Perkin of Western movies that he'd seen: men taking shelter where they could with a shot here, a shot there.

He wasn't going to play that game all day. He yelled at his radioman to get Spaulding again—between his ringing ears and the howling winds, he felt it necessary to shout. He was told that Spaulding was unavailable, and he turned to find a forward observer, and saw Spaulding running toward his position.

"Hey, Professor!" Spaulding said as he crouched next to Perkin.

"Hey, I was just calling you!" Perkin shouted. "I want to reduce our fires to sixty yards across a line like so. See that stone wall there?" He pointed to a broken rock wall running east to west.

"I can hear you fine, Perk, no need to shout. Listen,

that's too close. I'll call it in a little farther out. I want you to get Frank McCarter and have him take command of Baker Company. Jimmy Smith was hit and all they got are new butter bars. I'll head over there with him."

"All right. You got a handle on the big picture?" Perkin asked as he was figuring how to organize the remains of the company.

"Yeah. The attack on the abbey has been repulsed. The 142nd is bogged down in their assault on 468. They're gonna move up on your right in the draw between these two hills and try and flank them. I want you to keep pushing in the center with Able and Charlie, and I'll have Frank and Baker try and flank on the left."

"Casualties?" Perkin asked.

Spaulding stared at him with red-rimmed eyes and then shrugged. He said simply, "Too many, brother."

1500 Hours
Avezzano, Italy

"Four days? How can you be sure?" asked Douglas Grossmann. It was the best news that he'd had for weeks.

"All the graybeards say that tomorrow the weather breaks. We get a day or two of warming, and then we go. I'm sorry, Douglas, but your time here is coming to a close. You'll be back in an airplane before you know it."

Grossmann sighed theatrically. "I can't wait to fly again, Father, but I must say you've been a wonderful host."

"Thank you, thank you. Now…I'm off to spend the evening with the bishop. We're going to talk about the other American who's coming in, and then we are playing cards. He cheats and, Father forgive me, I let him. Oh, I have a favor to ask."

"Anything, Father." Grossmann was afraid that the priest was going to have him do more work in the cemetery, but it was something pleasurable instead.

"Please go pick up some more fuses. They keep blowing. You can have supper with Mario."

"Thank you, Father. I'd enjoy that. Can I say good-bye to Mario?"

"Of course. He's one of the graybeards who says it will be safe to go."

The priest and Grossmann walked out together, and walked until their paths diverged. Grossmann wished Father Carlo good luck with the cheating bishop, and the priest walked off briskly with a scowl.

The wachtmeister's hotel was on the way to Mario's, and despite the bitterly cold wind, it was with a happy heart that Grossmann told the old master sergeant to pass back to the Abwehr that he would be departing on Monday or Tuesday on his mission. He asked the wachtmeister if he had received any further instructions from the admiral. He had not, but he wished Herr Colonel a successful mission.

Mario was likewise in good spirits. No one came into his little hardware store, and they sat and drank grappa next to a potbellied stove while they talked women and politics. Mario's views on women were fairly conventional: he liked them all, except perhaps his wife. Regarding politics, Mario was a monarchist who thought Italy was too chaotic for true parliamentarian government. Surprising Grossmann, Mario said that he preferred a strong king and a strong prime minister, and a parliament that could be dismissed at the first sign of discord. When Grossmann asked for an example, Mario said he thought the Prussian combination of Wilhelm I and Otto von Bismarck was the most effective model for modern politics. Grossmann couldn't help but agree.

1630 Hours
Hill 593, Cassino Massif, Italy

The fighting had continued all afternoon without respite, and the men were exhausted on both sides of the shared hill. First Battalion had been able, with great sacrifice, to push its way onto the hill, but it simply could not complete the job that afternoon.

The 1200 counterattack had been repulsed with great casualties on both sides, and the Germans had tried again at 1330, and again at 1530. Each successive counterattack had been launched with an artillery barrage with the infantry following close behind. Each time, the panzer grenadiers were decimated with withering fire from the two battalions of field artillery supporting the 141st, but they still advanced. In the final instance, each counterattack was driven off with grenades, small-arms fire, and in many small desperate battles, by bayonets, knives, and fists. It was the most personal fighting of the war for most of the veteran soldiers, and a shock to the replacements who had yet to learn the names of their sergeants and officers.

Ammunition was dangerously low. The advance simply could not continue, and in all likelihood, there was not enough to repulse another counterattack. There were not enough men either. The proud battalion that marched 800 strong to the Rapido River only three weeks before was now down to ten officers and sixty-nine enlisted soldiers. In five hours of nonstop fighting, they had expended 1500 grenades.

The light was dying quickly, and orders were given for mule trains to come onto the ridge bringing ammunition, and take back the wounded. Perkin found an ammo box containing magazines for his Thompson, and another for his Colt—he had been completely out of magazines for the Thompson, and was down to six rounds for the Colt. He checked and re-checked to make sure that his trench knife was close at hand, but he hadn't drawn it yet. To his knowledge, he had killed four men during the fighting that afternoon but the toll might have been higher. He had thrown grenades until his wounds were screaming in agony, and still the Germans came.

Bill Spaulding was still alive as were Kulis, Ryan, and McCarter. The acting sergeant, Hodgson, had become Ryan's right-hand man, and the two neophyte warriors were rapidly becoming veterans together.

Lieutenant Ryan was on Spaulding's mind as he shared a large can of ice-cold pears with Perkin. "Did you see what he did?" asked Spaulding for the second time.

"I did. I ain't ever seen anything like it," said Perkin as he tipped the can up and drank half of the syrup before handing it back to Spaulding. "It wasn't like any hand-to-hand training I ever had."

Kulis who had closed his eyes but was nevertheless eavesdropping said from under his helmet, "Didn't y'all know he was some big wrasslin' champion at Iowa State?"

"No. I don't really follow wrestling. Really?" said Perkin.

"Yeah, he said he would have gone to the '40 Olympics if there'd been some." Hunger won out over fatigue and Kulis sat up and pulled out a can of hash as he observed. "You learn a lot about someone bein' stuck in the same foxhole for a week."

"No doubt," said Spaulding. "But those weren't any wrestling moves that I ever seen."

"Yeah, that was probably juju-something or other. He said it was a Jap martial art that he learned in college. He said he learned somethin' else that sounded like Sambo, but when I asked him if it were a nigger martial art, he got upset and told me not to say that. Them Yankees are touchy."

"Huh," said Perkin going back to the original issue. "I don't recall AG schools in Texas teaching animal husbandry students how to break necks."

"Well, maybe they ought to," said Spaulding. He had never before seen a man killed with bare hands, and it left quite an impression on him.

Spaulding's radio operator interrupted and held out the handset. "Sir, regiment."

Spaulding took the handset and talked briefly, ending the conversation with "Yes, sir. Understood. Out here." Spaulding ran his hand through his hair and said to Perkin, "I'm taking command of 3rd Battalion as well. They're in the same leaky boat on shit river. Perk, you stay here with our boys, while I go check on their status. Regiment says to stay in position, keep close contact with enemy forces, and be prepared to resume offensive operations on order."

2315 Hours
Hill 593, Cassino Massif, Italy

There had been two counterattacks since it had turned dark, and both had been repulsed without serious effort. Neither counterattack had the same ferocity as the counterattack at noon, and Perkin assumed that the Germans were spent as well.

They were good soldiers, he admitted to himself. There was no question about the bravery of the panzer grenadiers that they faced—soldiers from the 361st Panzer Grenadier Regiment. Their attacks had been fierce and unrelenting until they were simply pushed back by equal bravery and superior force of metal. Perkin was terribly proud of his soldiers. As decimated as they were, they had repulsed six counterattacks in twelve hours. The seemingly ceaseless counterattacks made Perkin wonder who exactly was on the offensive.

He had found a shallow slit trench that had been carved out of the dirt and rock by an industrious grenadier, and he and Kulis had fallen asleep as soon as they had lain down. They slept side by side with two blankets and shared body warmth, and it wasn't remotely enough. The temperature dropped well below freezing, and they had to endure occasional bouts of freezing rain and snow as they tried to sleep. After an hour of deep sleep, Perkin awakened during the first counterattack of the night, and although adrenaline rushed through his body, it was barely enough to get him sufficiently coherent to call for illumination rounds. After the counterattack had been beaten back, the adrenaline and the cold kept him awake longer than he wished.

Perkin moved around to the soldiers of First Battalion and checked on them through the course of the night. There was no moon, but there was enough light reflected off the clouds from the fires in Cassino that he could see well enough to move. Everyone shared in the misery equally. No one had warm food, dry clothes, or enough blankets. It was a hard night, and he was afraid that he would lose men to exposure as the night went on. He had put on the wool socks that had been a present from Colonel Wranosky, and taken his wet ones and tied them around his waist to dry. He hated that cold wet feeling with a passion but it was better than not having dry socks for tomorrow. He couldn't imagine how things could get worse.

Chapter Nine

February 12, 1944
0640 Hours
Hill 593, Cassino Massif, Italy

Major Bill Spaulding and Captain Perkin Berger had completed a predawn survey of their defenses, and this day was starting out better than the night that had just ended. The winds had dropped from gale force to a normally brisk mountain breeze. It wasn't sunny but it wasn't raining either. That alone made the day seem brighter and more optimistic.

When Perkin had awakened at 0430, he found that the poncho he had slept in had frozen to the ground. It peeled off easily enough, although it remained stiff and unwieldy for some time. He hadn't brought his notebook for letters but he resolved to remember his awakening so he could tell Old Perkin. It may not have compared to Shackleton's experience on the ice, but for a flatlander from South Texas, waking up frozen to a mountaintop was a fairly novel experience.

Orders from regiment were to stay in place, and defend the gains that they had made yesterday. It would be made easier with new supplies. Engineers had been busy through the night, as had the mule trains. Not enough supplies had made it up the mountainside to support a full battalion under normal circumstances, but more than enough had made it to supply the combined 1st and 3rd Battalions. American soldiers occupied German pits in the stone that had been blasted by engineers and dug by slave labor. Sandbags, barbed wire, wood, and steel fleshed out the fortifications, which wouldn't stand a direct hit but offered some degree of protection from artillery, mortars, and small-arms fire.

In the early morning light, Perkin and Spaulding had shortened their lines in places, and extended it elsewhere. They sprinted from position to position to check on their troops, the machine guns, and the mortar pits. Phone lines were run from company command posts, to the battalion command post and back to the regimental CP. The mountaintop was beginning to look like a spider's web with miles of Allied line already overlaying the existing miles of German lines.

Perkin was waiting for Spaulding to return from a meeting at the regimental CP. He was due back any moment. In the meantime, Perkin scuttled over to a pit shared by Lieutenant Ryan and Private Hodgson.

"Mornin', gentlemen!"

"Good morning, sir," was the rather unenthusiastic reply in unison. It looked like neither man had gotten much sleep.

"Any news for me?" asked Perkin.

"No, sir," replied Ryan. "We're just waiting for the next goddamned attack."

"You sound like a despondent cornfucker, Lieutenant," Perkin observed.

"It's 'cornhusker' and they're from Nebraska. I'm from Iowa. You got any coffee, Perk?" asked Ryan. At Perkin's repeated request, he had just started calling him by his first name.

"No, but I asked General Clark to bring us some next time he comes for a visit." Perkin laughed at his own wit, and then said, "I got some powdered coffee. Just no hot water to mix it in. You're welcome to it, though. Some guys get a taste for it cold, but I never have. How are you doing, Hodgson?"

"Middlin', sir."

Perkin nodded. "To tell the truth, me too. What part of Tennessee are you from?"

"Dayton, sir. Ever heard of it?" Hodgson looked at Perkin with hard, intelligent brown eyes.

"Of course. Scopes Monkey Trial was there, wasn't it?"

Hodgson looked surprised. "Not many know that."

"It was the trial of the century. Clarence Darrow versus William Jennings Bryan. Hard not to know it. I was hopin' it would go to the Supreme Court. My cousin's uncle was Chief Justice, and I wanted to see him agitate the country no matter which way it went."

"The boys have told me about Lieutenant Taft. So, he's President Taft's nephew? Nobody mentioned that. Great family...I have a lot of respect for Robert Taft, sir."

"Mr. Republican? I can't agree. He's an isolationist... shoot, we wouldn't have this free vacation in Europe if he'd been elected. If you wait until Lieutenant Taft comes back, you can start a two-man GOP convention in the division. It is a great family, though...Sam's actually the great nephew of President Taft which makes him the first cousin once removed, or second cousin half-removed, or something like that from Bob Taft. What'd you do before the war?"

"I'm a lawyer," Hodgson said with the stirring of the first smile Perkin had seen from the soldier.

"Really?" Perkin asked.

"Yes, sir," said Hodgson. "I passed the bar last year. You seem surprised."

"To tell the truth, I am. I heard you were a broken bowl. I haven't met many what went to college."

"I didn't. When my pa kicked me off the farm, I went to Dayton and started working at the Rhea County Courthouse as a janitor. The country judge found out I had neat handwriting, so he had me copy all his notes and decisions at night after I cleaned the offices. After a couple years of reading every document that crossed his desk, I just kind of learned the law, and, well, you don't have to go to law school to take the bar exam, so I became a lawyer."

Ryan was looking at the private in disbelief. "Why didn't you apply for a commissioning program if you're a lawyer?"

Hodgson laughed. "You don't have to go to law school to be a lawyer, but you have to graduate primary school to be an officer. To tell you the truth, I don't want the responsibility. I'm just here 'cause Uncle Sam needs me here. If tomorrow he needs me on that hill over yonder, that's where I'll be then."

0805 Hours
Hill 593, Cassino Massif, Italy

"I had a hard choice to make, Professor, and I ain't sure I made the right one," said Major Spaulding.

"If it's the field promotion that I been asking for, I don't see how that can be a tough decision," Perkin observed. "It ought to be the easiest one of the day."

Spaulding coughed out a raspy laugh. "You know, Professor, it's the damnedest thing. Your self-run campaign to be the first colonel general in the U.S. Army wasn't even mentioned by the regimental commander."

"Of course not. He's new. He needs someone to explain the merits—both of the rank and of the man. You know my feelings: it's not for me, it's for the country. If the Germans and the Russians have colonel generals, I think we should as well. I hate to say it, but I fear that you've let me down again...not to mention the loss of prestige you may be causing America."

"So your grossly unmerited and highly unlikely promotion is now a matter of great national and cultural significance?"

"It sounds kind of grandiose when you put it that way. But, yeah."

"Uh huh...maybe you can explain how over a cup of hot coffee," Spaulding said with a slight air of superiority.

"Coffee? Wonderful! So, what was the hard choice?" Perkin asked.

"They had hot chocolate back there, too. I chose coffee."

"Good call. Any hot chow?" Perkin asked.

"Not that I could smell. But I stole a donut for you from the chaplain's kit. Here...the sin transfers to you." Spaulding handed over a donut that had been completely flattened. Perkin flicked some dirt off it and shoved it in his mouth before the Lord saw him with the stolen holy donut, while Spaulding poured some coffee out of a canteen.

"You got enough coffee for Ryan and Hodgson?" Perkin asked. "Or should I go share mine? They seemed in need a little earlier."

"Share yours with Eddie. I'll take some to them in a minute. Colonel McCauley is gonna shell the shit out of the Krauts in a little bit, and he's going to mule train in soup, coffee, and ammo during the distraction."

Spaulding's face indicated he thought it was a great idea.

Perkin agreed. "God bless him! What did you find out about our future?"

"We're in defense until further notice. McCauley has a realistic appraisal of what we can and can't do. He told General Walker that the regiment is now below twenty-five percent combat effective, and that we're incapable of further offensive operations. He said that Walker told him that he didn't know of any other division in either world war that had been reduced like we were on the river and then thrown back into combat under conditions like these. He said the Old Man was furious with Clark, and that he understood why the National Guard didn't trust the regular army. I guess Clark's purge of the 36th has left a lot of hard feelings at division—and not just with the Old Man."

"I'd say the hard feelings weren't limited to the front office either. Those who knew Wranosky can't understand why he was treated like that." Perkin started to get angry himself, realized that it would serve no purpose that day, and then took a deep breath. "At least we got a good one in his place."

Spaulding agreed, "We did. Anyway, don't hang your hat on this, but Colonel McCauley thinks that we'll be withdrawn today or tomorrow. He said he's hoping the division comes off the line for refit, but he told me it won't happen right away. Instead, he's pushing for us to go into defense in a quiet section until that can happen. Division and corps apparently agree, and they're looking to move a British unit up here."

"You want me to go down and tell 'em to hurry? I could be back in a day or two."

1100 Hours
Avezzano, Italy

Grossmann walked around the perimeter of the old cemetery, looking for loose stones on its waist-high wall. The harsh winter had loosened the dab of mortar holding the stones in place, and Grossmann would occasionally find a stone that had fallen onto the church grounds and return it to its place on the wall. When he was done walking the interior perimeter, he would walk along the exterior and do the same thing.

Father Carlo, who was running an errand to Rome on behalf of the bishop, wanted him to take a bucket of mortar and permanently affix the loose stones, but he had convinced the priest that it was best to wait for a dry spell. Douglas Grossmann was destined to be the man who saved German honor, and perhaps western civilization itself. He wasn't a common laborer.

Beyond the indignity of hard work, the cemetery made him uncomfortable. He had an uneasy feeling that he was being watched. At first, he had marked it down to superstition as if all the lost souls of the cemetery were watching him—the same silliness that drove him to walk around the graves rather than over them. Then he realized that virtually every headstone bore a glass-encased picture or painted portrait of the deceased. Consequently, it seemed that no matter where he turned, several sets of eyes were on him. It was quite unlike an American cemetery and somewhat unnerving.

He decided that he wouldn't be disquieted by the field of the dead. He lit a cigarette, a gift from Mario, and leaned with his back against the wall while he stared back at the headstones. He was getting ready to flick his cigarette butt at the baleful portrait of an old man when he smelled her perfume. He whipped around, and there she was—two feet away with a mischievous grin on her beautiful face.

Even though he had rehearsed exactly what he was going to say should he ever see Antoniette Bernardi again, instead of the eloquent, indignant words he had planned, he blurted out, "Gah!"

She was breathtakingly beautiful wrapped in fur—the most stunning woman he had ever known, even when she was angry. But she wasn't angry now. His confusion and incoherence obviously delighted her, and she laughed in such an earnest and genuine way that her face was alight like a playful angel. Many times when she needed to win a point with Grossmann, she would playfully pout, and it would melt his heart. This time her laughter and smile brought so much light to bear on his misery—a misery he had thought dispelled—that his heart stopped beating altogether. It was like magic, and his pulse didn't resume until she laughingly broke the spell by asking, "Gah?"

Rather than explain his word choice, Grossmann jumped the wall as if he could walk on air, swept her into his arms and kissed her. Antoniette's arms wrapped around his neck, and the portraits of the once living stared without interest at the longest, most passionate kiss to have ever graced the cemetery.

1355 Hours
Hill 593, Cassino Massif, Italy

The artillery barrage was the worst that they had seen since the assault of Hill 593 began the day before. The German batteries set farther back in the mountains were murdering the remaining soldiers of the 141st and 142nd regiments. It was the most intense, localized barrage that Perkin had seen in the war.

Perkin and Kulis had been in the middle of checking on the spread-out platoons, running bent over, and they were on their right flank in McCarter's small sector when the shelling began. There was nothing that they could do except to flatten themselves on the hard stone of the mountaintop. Several rounds impacted fifty yards away, and the force of the blast swept over them.

"Christ! We gotta get out of here!" Kulis screamed at Perkin.

"No! Stay put!" Perkin screamed back. There was simply no place to run to—the American side of Hill 593 was being pulverized, and the thousands of shards of stone and white hot metal screaming overhead made it suicidal to stand. Perkin desperately wanted to run too, but forced himself to stay in place.

American counter-battery fire opened up very quickly, but the German fire did not abate immediately. Perkin lifted his head briefly and put it down just as quickly. Rounds that were now impacting thirty and forty yards away would be lethal if they landed any closer, no matter how flat they were. The concussion from the explosions rolled over them, and both men closed their eyes and prayed.

As suddenly as they started, the heavy explosions stopped, but Perkin and Kulis remained where they were for a few long moments. As his hearing had taken another beating, Perkin said in a loud awkward voice, "Let's get to Frank's position and into a hole in case they start again." They stood up shakily, and that's when Perkin saw the flash of gray-green uniform out of the corner of his eye.

It was a German soldier moving swiftly from the cover of boulders toward another cropping of rocks, only twenty yards away. Instinctively, Perkin whipped the Thompson up to his cheek and fired a burst at the soldier. As he watched the grenadier drop to the ground writhing in agony, Perkin bellowed out, "They're flanking! They're flanking! Goddamnit! Frank, get a squad over here!" The downed soldier was crawling for his dropped rifle, and Perkin fired again.

Two more German soldiers sprinted up the draw between Hill 593 and Hill 468, and darted past their fallen comrade and behind the shelter of the terrain. They were either trying to get behind the Texans and attempt to roll up the line, or force a breach for more German soldiers to pass through. It was just good fortune that Perkin had seen the field grey uniform as the soldier had attempted to dart between boulders .

Corporal Kulis tossed a grenade at the fallen German. If there were any additional soldiers trying to move behind them, they would have to dart between cover like the two soldiers had just done. There was a loud sharp crack as the grenade detonated following by screams from behind the rocks. Perkin and Kulis both threw a grenade over the rocks, and shortly, the screaming stopped.

Perkin was getting ready to chase the two Germans who had passed to their right and behind them when Lieutenant McCarter came running up hard with six soldiers. Not a squad but the best he could do. Perkin pointed to Corporal Kulis and three of McCarter's soldiers, and said, "Go get those two!" As the four soldiers ran off down the draw, Perkin threw another grenade behind the rocks to his front for good measure. He couldn't see what was behind the rocks and preferred not to take any chances. There was no reaction, no response, and Perkin ran crouched to the rock formation and peeked behind it. Other than two dead panzer grenadiers, he saw no one.

Three minutes later and four rounds fired, Kulis and his soldiers were back. Kulis was breathing heavy and shaking his head. "They looped back that way, sir, and got away. We didn't really have a shot but I tried. They should have run into the 142nd, but there seems to be a gap between us and them. We'd best fill it pretty quick."

Perkin looked at Lieutenant McCarter who nodded. McCarter and his men ran off to patch yet another hole along the small line. Perkin waved his radioman over but was unable to raise battalion, so he and Kulis jogged back to find Major Spaulding and inform him of the gap—both men still breathing hard and shaking from the shelling and the small skirmish.

When they got back to the battalion area, Perkin sent Kulis to round up more reinforcements while he headed to brief Major Spaulding. The battalion CP was a set in a slight gulch, and was more formalized than it had been the day before—it consisted of a tent with netting. It had no heat, cots, tables, or chairs, but it had empty ammo crates, which served as chairs and tables for Major Spaulding and the three enlisted men who were maintaining his communications and maps. There should have been a score of people from the battalion headquarters staff, but they were all manning positions along the line. Besides, while Spaulding was nominally in command of two battalions, he only had about a company's worth of men on position. It simply did not require a large staff to manage.

"Hey, you all right?" asked Spaulding as Perkin ran into the tent. "Casualties?"

"I don't know yet. We've got a more pressing issue. We aren't in contact with the 142nd on our right. The shelling was cover for an attempted infiltration, and after it lifted, we were in a little skirmish. At least three enemy KIA. We caught 'em trying to flank along the draw between the hills. I've got Frank and six guys there now. He's got a BAR with him, and I sent Eddie to have a machine gun brought up. The problem is, of course, that we weaken our center. The 142nd needs to close that gap ASAP or they'll try again."

Spaulding swore, and told his radioman to get regiment on the phone. After he had explained the situation to the regimental ops officer, he turned back to Perkin and asked, "I'll head up in a second. Hey, I had just sent a runner to look for you when the shelling started. Is there anything going on that I need to know about?"

"What do you mean, Bill? I just told you what was going on."

"No. I mean with you. Personally." Spaulding looked at his friend with an odd mixture of exasperation and amusement.

"I dunno. Am I in hot water or something?" Perkin shrugged. "I shouldn't be...I ain't had time to get in trouble. Why do you ask?"

Spaulding patted down his pockets looking for his pouch of chewing tobacco, couldn't find any, swore and looked at Perkin. "I don't know, Buddy. I was told to send you and Kulis to division HQ with your gear."

"What? I don't understand. When we're pulled off the line?" Perkin looked puzzled.

"No, now." Spaulding shook his head.

"And you don't know why?" Perkin's confusion was written all over his face.

"No, I don't know why. Regiment doesn't either. I told them I couldn't spare you, and they agreed. Colonel McCauley personally got on the horn to the division chief of staff and protested. He was told to get you down there ASAP. No excuses. And to bring Kulis with you."

"Kulis?"

"Yep"

"What the hell, Bill! I can't go! Whatever it is can wait another twenty-four hours or so until we're pulled back!" Perkin was getting angry. "Jesus Christ! What the fuck do they think is going on here? Do they know what we're doing?"

Spaulding sighed "Yeah, Perk, I think Old Man knows what's going on…so whatever it is, it must be important. Now, I don't know what it's about, but I swear, if you get laid again while you're gone, I don't want you to come back. Ever. Shit. I can't afford to let him go either, but I guess you gotta take Kulis with you."

Perkin looked for a seat, found a crate, and sat down. He tossed his helmet on the ground and ran his fingers through his hair. Suddenly, he brightened. "Do you think this is about Sam?"

Spaulding shook his head and looked at Perkin with a sad grin. "You must be tireder than I am, because all of a sudden, I'm smarter than you. How could it be about Sam, Professor? Naw…it's something else. Obviously, my first inclination was that you'd done something heinous—impregnated the daughter of King Emmanuel or peed on a tree planted by St. Peter, but I figure it's gotta be spooky stuff. What else could it be? I'm guessing that they need a man of towering intellect and minimal ego." Spaulding laughed a genuine laugh. "Which explains why they want Kulis. No telling why they want you."

1800 Hours
Avezzano, Italy

Douglas Grossmann climbed reluctantly out of bed. He hated to leave Antoniette and the warmth of her hotel room, but he had to make sure he was back at the church. If he wasn't back from Rome already, he would be soon. The priest had tomorrow's Mass to prepare for, and although he would prepare in his private quarters, he might need something from the church's office. Grossmann could claim to have been out for a walk, but he'd rather not face Father Carlo's disapproval.

Grossmann was at peace in his mind. He had come directly out and asked Antoniette about working for the SD, the intelligence arm of the SS and the Nazi Party. She had admitted to it without any evasion. It had nothing to do with Grossmann, she assured him. She had been approached by the SD to report on the trustworthiness of senior Italian officials. She wasn't even using her particular talents to collect information, she simply asked her father for his opinion.

Grossmann believed her emphatically. There was no guile or subterfuge—of that, he was sure. He knew that had she denied any connection that she might have convinced him, and she would have been supremely confident in her ability to do so. Therefore, when she admitted to a connection with the SD, he believed her.

In his mind, her admission reset their relationship to what it had been before this mission leading to Avezzano. She was not only his lover but also his partner—a valued partner—in his work. With only a fraction of a moment's hesitation, he told her about his meeting with Canaris and the others. He had explained that in their opinion, an opinion with which he concurred, the war was lost, and that it was critical to have open lines of communication back to the western allies.

Antoniette had asked some hard questions about the military situation, and then she asked for Grossmann's thoughts on the future. After he explained that the admiral's belief was that the war would be over in twelve to eighteen months, and that he agreed, she was silent for a long time. Then Grossmann noticed two tears trickling down her cheeks, as she said, "I can't believe that it has come to this—after all we've sacrificed."

They talked longer and more seriously than they ever had—about what the future meant for Europe and what it meant for them as a couple. Grossmann was gratified to hear, not directly, but subtlety, that all of her plans for the post-war were inclusive of him. It was as if she were taking Grossmann's companionship for granted, and at a completely different, permanent level of relationship. She said that they would have to start moving money now, and that they could stay at her father's villa in Gstaad until Europe was in balance again.

She seemed in complete agreement that Soviet domination of Europe would be a disaster, although she seemed equally dubious about the West's ability to stand up to the Bolsheviks, calling America and Britain "weak and timid." When he had told her of other aspects of his mission, Antoniette had shown no emotion over the extermination of the Jews. If she had, Grossmann would have become suspicious. It wasn't in her nature to empathize with the plight of others.

They had talked at great length of the dangers of the mission—the risks that he would be discovered by the Gestapo or arrested by the Americans. "It's the Gestapo that's more concerning to me. They may already be aware that something is amiss with Canaris. If they arrest and interrogate the old boy, I don't know how long he can last. However long it is, that's the amount of time we have left in Italy unless we head south," Grossmann said. It had never occurred to him that he might have to flee Italy with Antoniette.

"We'll have to be prepared for that moment, my love," Antoniette said firmly. Then she said less firmly, "What if we're wrong? What if the Allies aren't going to win? Or what if the Allies are too slow, and what we're doing somehow helps the Bolsheviks? Should we consider reporting this to the proper authorities? To, the proper German authorities, I mean. Don't you think that's what we should do?" Left unspoken was the understanding that the proper German authorities meant the Gestapo.

They had talked about the future some more, made love again, and Antoniette fell asleep in his arms while Grossmann thought hard about what to do. It wasn't just about him any longer, he had Antoniette and his future with her to consider.

When the time came for him to leave, and he climbed reluctantly out of bed, Antoniette started crying. Not silent tears like before, but a deep, body-shaking sobbing. He had never seen her so distraught. When he placed his hand under her chin and lifted her face to his, he saw that her nose was running and her makeup had begun to streak as the tears flowed down her cheeks, which broke his heart.

He sat down on the bed and held her tightly as she continued to cry. Grossmann didn't say anything—he just held her until she was done. With her head on his shoulder, and in a small voice, she said, "I'm so sorry, Douglas. I'm so afraid of what will happen—to you and to me. To my family. Our fortune. If the SS finds out that you're betraying the Fatherland, they will kill us all. Everyone. You, me, Mama, and Papa. I see it every day in Rome. Or you could be killed on the mountain, or arrested by the Americans!" Antoniette started sobbing again, "Don't go! Please don't go! Oh God, I'm begging you to stay with me."

2130 Hours
36th Division CP, Cervaro, Italy

General Walker's new aide was a captain that Perkin had never met. He'd been on a first name basis with Charlie Walker, who had been his father's aide before General Clark's reassignment.

The captain looked Perkin and Kulis over before letting them into the large house. He nodded with his head to the back of the house and said, "Corporal, wait in the kitchen. There's some hot chow and some hot cocoa back there. Help yourself. Captain Berger, follow me and I'll see to getting you something to eat in a minute."

Perkin was led into an empty sitting room, and after looking at his filthy uniform, he decided to stand. The windows had heavy blackout curtains, and the room was lit by lanterns. There was a small fire in the fireplace, and Perkin knelt by it and stabbed at the wood with an iron poker. As it began to pop and grow, the door opened and General Walker came into the room.

Perkin came to attention, saluted, and said, "Good evening, General. Captain Berger reporting as directed," and then he shook the offered hand. In the dim lantern light, Perkin studied the general. He was several inches shorter than Perkin, with a ramrod bearing, graying hair, and hawk-like intelligent eyes, which looked very tired to Perkin.

"Perkin, it's good to see you, son," Walker said warmly.

"It's good to see you too, General." Suddenly, Perkin had a lump in his throat, and he looked away quickly to the fire. He couldn't explain his emotions—other than acknowledging a deep sense of respect for a man whom he believed had been ill-used by the army.

"Have a seat, Perk. I want to talk to you for a minute before bringing in our visitors."

Visitors? Perkin thought.

"How are you doing? Have you recovered from your wounds?" Walked asked.

Perkin was surprised that the general was aware of his injuries. "Yes, sir. I got a few days in an Italian home with a local doctor and nurse. A little home cooking was all I needed."

Walker nodded. "A little sleep does wonders, too, doesn't it. I wanted to let you know that I was sorry to hear about your cousin. General Roosevelt, Teddy Roosevelt, was here on the 8th and enquired about him, and the adjutant told him that Lieutenant Taft was captured on the river."

"Thank you, sir," Perkin said.

Walker nodded in acknowledgment and said, "What was the situation when you left the hill?"

"Sir, as I'm sure you know, yesterday afternoon, the 1st and 3rd Battalions were merged under Major Spaulding's command. First Battalion was down to about the strength of a reinforced platoon, so with the addition of 3rd Battalion, we're up to company strength. We have a defensive line established along the northernmost edge of what could properly be called Hill 593. The terrain is very uneven—lots of little draws, rises, gullies, boulders—so the defensive line is uneven as well and susceptible to infiltration. We took a pounding late this morning and early afternoon, but held our line. That's about where it was when I left, sir."

"What are your thoughts on the German soldiers? What kind of causalities did they sustain?" Walker asked.

"We're facing soldiers of the 361st Panzer Grenadiers. They know their business. They're aggressive, and they were determined to drive us off the massif. In the two days that I was up there, we faced, I dunno, eight or maybe ten counterattacks. Maybe more. I would put their casualties from the counterattacks at roughly 200 dead not counting those killed in bombardments on the hilltop."

Walker nodded thoughtfully, and said, "It's the same along the entire Gustav Line. The closer we get to Germany, the harder they fight. The soldiers who faced the Afrika Korps say that the intensity of the combat is far worse here." Changing the subject, Walker said, "How are your men holding up?"

Perkin paused for a long moment as he thought through his answer. He didn't want to pile onto the general, but he wanted to give him an honest answer— he felt he owed it to his soldiers to tell the truth. He looked Walker squarely in the eyes, and said, "They're getting to the end of the road, sir. I want to qualify this as my opinion, but we should have been taken off the line after the river. There's no point in keeping us there now unless we're prepared to accept the disintegration of the division. Combat effectiveness is shot and we're only a veteran division in name—we're sending replacements into combat that don't know their squad mates or their officers' names. We're doing the best we can to spread the experienced troops around, but it's getting impossible. I hate to say it, sir, but morale is low, the men are exhausted and sick, and quite frankly, I don't know that there's a whole lot more that we can ask of them." Perkin hung his head. In the movies, he would have said, "Give us some more, we can take it." But this wasn't the movies.

Walker said nothing for several minutes, and then said, "If I don't want bad news, I shouldn't ask for it, I guess. But, well, I said nearly the same exact words to the corps commander this afternoon. He didn't like hearing it either." Walker sighed, "I'm pulling the 141st out of contact with the enemy tomorrow morning. Your battalion will be moved to a different sector of the mountain complex to just hold ground, and be a reserve force. I don't have it in writing, and if I did I wouldn't trust it, but I think the division will be withdrawn from the Cassino area of operations within the week. Maybe two at most. The plan is to limit offensive ops in the 8th Army area of operations, leave a holding force on the Adriatic coast, and move some of their divisions to the fight for the Liri Valley. When you return, we should be off that damn mountain or close to it. If we're not here, look for us at Naples or Paestum."

Perkin nodded. "Return from where, sir? What's this about?"

"I'm going to let our visitors explain—to be truthful, I don't know the details. But, anyway, good luck and good hunting if that is your mission." Walker stood, offered his hand again, strode across the room, opened the door and walked out.

2145 Hours
36th Division CP, Cervaro, Italy

The two men who walked into the sitting room after General Walker left were known to Perkin. He had been half-expecting them since receiving orders off the mountain that afternoon. Wordlessly, the taller of the two, an American named George Hill closed the door. The shorter of the two, an Englishman named Charles Ackernly walked over to Perkin with a familiar smile and an outstretched hand.

"How are you doing, my boy?" Ackernly said. He took a step back and looked Perkin over from head to toe, and exclaimed, "You look absolutely buggered!"

Perkin laughed, and said, "That may be the most truthful description of how I feel yet. Mr. Ackernly, Mr. Hill…good to see you both."

Hill smiled and said, "Good to see you, too, Perkin. Sorry for disrupting your day, but we would like to ask for your assistance." He gestured to a seat, and Perkin took the one that he'd already darkened with grime.

"Is it about Grossmann?" Perkin asked with a sense of eagerness. His previous interaction with Ackernly and Hill had been during a meeting over the New Year's holiday, where he had briefed the two counterintelligence officers on what he knew about the German-American spy, Grossmann. Later, at their request, he had led a mission to the Gildardino farm to drop off an Irish priest named Patrick Riley with familial ties to a British intelligence officer.

Ackernly shook his head. "No, old chap. I wish it were. We've heard nothing of him for weeks. No, we have something else in mind." He looked at Hill and nodded.

Hill cleared his throat and said, "Perkin, when we last met, we told you that we were on an 8th Army counterintelligence task force. That was true, but not all of the truth. I work for Colonel Donovan, whom I know you've heard of."

Perkin nodded. "You work for the Office of Strategic Services?"

"Yes, and Charles is my opposite in British intelligence."

Perkin looked at the two men seated across from him. "Okay, I'm with you so far. What do you need me and Kulis for?"

Hill looked Perkin in the eyes and said, "We've had a communique from German intelligence via contacts in

Switzerland, and they're attempting to establish a direct line of communication with us." His precise delivery led Perkin to believe that there was much more to the story.

"Line of communication on…what? Military matters? Political? Yes, it's political, isn't it? They want to put out peace-feelers, or something like that?" Perkin asked excitedly.

Hill and Ackernly looked at one another. "Before I answer, young man, how did you come to that conclusion?" Hill asked.

Perkin smiled, "So I'm right? Well, German intelligence isn't going to give us information on how to beat them, although they might feel the need to scare us about our Soviet allies. If it's political, the only thing that comes to mind is that they're planning to depose Hitler and want our help, or maybe they want recognition of a new government. Or they might be trying to get us to toss in with a new German government against the Soviets and the Japanese. Kind of do what Italy did with a twist. Is that it?"

Hill shrugged. "Probably not that extreme. We don't know for sure what they have in mind, but we believe that you're probably close. We know that the German generals, the Wehrmacht generals, are disaffected with Hitler. We're aware of the great animosity between the German Army and the SS." Hill paused and lit a cigarette. "Given the high level that this contact originated from, we think that it means the German generals are willing to overthrow Hitler, and they want a negotiated peace at the end of the day."

"Okay, I'm all for sittin' down with 'em, havin' a beer, and endin' the war," Perkin said. "But, back to my question. What do you need me and Corporal Kulis for, and how do you know this isn't a trap, another Venlo?"

Ackernly answered, "Well, the thought has crossed

our minds. But unlike the Venlo incident, where the SD proposed a fake meeting of the respective intelligence services in order to entrap our agents, this is coming from, we believe, Admiral Canaris directly. We've come a long way since '39. It's our belief that German intelligence is sending a man, bearing, well, information. And, as you said, most likely a proposal. The Germans are aware of the Gildardino farm and its role in facilitating escaped prisoners and downed pilots back to freedom. The Germans are sending their man to the Gildardino farm in the next forty-eight to seventy-two hours. We need to be there to meet with him, and we'd like for you to take us there…"

"Before you answer, Perk," interrupted George Hill, "obviously, we have assets that are capable of infiltrating and exfiltrating us. That's not the issue. Here's why we want you: you've been there before. You have the proper clearance and, both you and Corporal Kulis are experienced soldiers. But most importantly, you know the Gildardino family. Depending how this meeting runs, it may become necessary to withdraw them when we leave. This certainly puts them at greater risk than they're already in. It might take your persuasion and that of Father Riley, if he's still there, to convince them to leave their home."

Perkin thought of his time with the Gildardino family—the farmer Luigi, his sister Maria, and her son Angelo, and her two young daughters, Lucia and Gemma. In his opinion, the Gildardinos were a heroic, generous, sweet family who had taken him in as one of their own. They had taken risks on behalf of the Allies, and these risks would be multiplied tenfold as a result of this meeting—a meeting that they didn't ask for or agree to.

If the Gildardino family was in danger, the matter

was closed for discussion. "When do we leave?" Perkin asked.

Chapter Ten

February 14, 1944
0930 Hours
Avezzano, Italy

First Lieutenant Sam Taft could not have been happier. Perhaps today would be the day that the last leg of his journey was to begin. Father Michele had said goodbye to his American charge the previous night and left him with friends of the Church on the northern outskirts of Avezzano. He had been told that a priest named Father Carlo would meet him shortly and they would walk the four miles to his church on the southern outskirts of Avezzano.

His hosts that morning were a cheerful older couple whose name he couldn't remember. He had been fed a couple pieces of toast with an unknown preserve on it and a glass of milk, and he understood that was all the food they could spare. His head jerked up at a knock at the door, and the wife smiled and said something to him in Italian. It was the priest who walked in and greeted his hosts with smiles and kisses.

The priest walked over to Sam and stood before him with his hands on his hips. The priest said nothing at first, he just stood in front of Sam with his hands on his hips. He said something to the Italian couple that Sam couldn't follow, and then said in heavily accented English, "You must be Sam. I am Father Carlo." They shook hands and then the priest said, "I was told that you were a giant, but I didn't believe it. Now I do. You must be twenty-five centimeters taller than my other American. We need to get you home now, before someone sees you!"

With that, the priest turned, bowed slightly to the couple, thanked them and said goodbye. The wife whose name Sam couldn't remember made him bend over so she could kiss his cheeks. He shook hands with the husband, and with that, the priest and the American giant turned and left the house.

1000 Hours
Avezzano, Italy

Douglas Grossmann tried to read a novel lent him by Father Carlo but he had too many thoughts racing through his mind, all of them competing for attention.

First and foremost was his concern for Antoniette. He had left her two nights ago assuring her that he would be back for her, that he would find her in Rome, and they would survive whatever came their way together.

It had calmed her down, but only briefly. He had left her inn and was walking back to the church with a heavy heart when he heard her calling his name. He turned and she was running down the street after him. Grossmann had never before seen her do anything athletic, and he was struck by how graceful she moved. She had fallen into his arms and started crying hysterically again, begging him to reconsider, pleading with him to stay. He almost did.

Instead, he calmed her down. He told her again that he would be back, that everything would be okay, and that they would come out of the war alive and together. Grossmann walked her back to the hotel holding her hand, and when he told her that he would be leaving in two or three more days, he thought she would break down again. She hadn't though...but she told him through more tears that she would wait until midweek at the hotel in case he changed his mind.

He couldn't change his mind though. She would have to ride it out with him. Grossmann knew that the war was lost, and only a catastrophe in the anticipated landing at Pas de Calais would delay the inevitable. Grossmann would be the man behind the scenes that saved the West, that saved German honor, that brought peace to Europe.

That was the second conundrum he faced. Getting the credit for doing the challenging, dangerous work, without alienating either of his nationalities—alienation meaning being charged with treason or getting detained for his troubles. He would have to ingratiate himself with the American and British officers, but he had decided that he would play it subtlety. He would be bluff and manly, only doing his duty for civilization. Neither outwardly ingratiating nor standoffish.

Grossmann picked the novel up again. It was entitled *Uno, Nessuno e Centomila*, which translated to *One, No One and One Hundred Thousand*. The priest had sworn that it was Luigi Pirandello's masterpiece, but Grossmann thought that the protagonist's struggle to identify himself, or whatever the hell he was trying to do, was stupid. *You are what you believe you are*, he thought. *I'm a hero. I'll save millions of lives.*

He threw the novel on the priest's desk and picked up a mystery that he had already read. The plot hadn't been terribly complicated and he'd known the murderer from the first chapter, so it was perfect for his current state of distraction. He opened the book to a random page and tried to read as his thoughts drifted between love, treason, and heroism.

1040 Hours
Sixteen Miles Southwest of Castel di Sangro, Italy

It had been six weeks since Perkin had been at the Canadian checkpoint. He had used this very location as his point of departure for the mission to the Gildardino farmhouse in early January. Not much had changed, but the changes were significant enough that they warranted extra precautions.

They had arrived at the Canadian checkpoint earlier that morning in two jeeps, one driven by Perkin and the other by Corporal Kulis. The extra jeep was in case they needed to extract the Gildardino family from their Abruzzi farmhouse. Both jeeps carried mounted .30 caliber M1919 machine guns, and all four members of their party carried their personal weapons. For Perkin, it was his Thompson and a Colt .45. Kulis carried his M-1 Garand, and had drawn a .45 as well. The two intelligence agents carried small discrete side arms. Perkin tried to convince them to draw rifles as well, but they said that they would be unnecessary.

After making the introductions, Perkin and the lieutenant that he had met in January sat down over a mug of coffee at the lieutenant's command post. The accommodations were vastly improved over the Spartan conditions from earlier. The walls of the CP were reinforced with railroad ties and sandbags, a heavy roof had been installed, and adjacent rooms had been dug into the hillside. The lieutenant had a small library, a wood-burning stove, and all of his soldiers slept on cots or bedding purchased from nearby Italians.

The Canadian officer grinned sheepishly when he saw Perkin gaping at the luxurious CP, and said, "You know how it is, sir. Put a soldier in one place long enough and he begins to acquire things. It'll all be gone in a matter of weeks though when the spring offensives begin and we move out of here. Until then, we're staying as warm and dry as possible."

"You don't have to apologize. I'm jealous." The most luxury that Perkin had enjoyed since leaving Presenzano was a shower the day before. He was still in his dirty uniform, but at least the weeks of accumulated dirt had been washed off his body.

The lieutenant broke out a pipe and lit it while he talked. "So, since you were here, Jerry's stepped up his patrolling in no-man's land, which means that we have to as well. It's probably due to your little skirmish with the Germans last time. They're just not as friendly as they used to be, but it's still pretty tame compared to where you've been."

"What about night time patrols?" Perkin asked.

"They rarely conduct them, but they do. They don't come within small-arms or automatic weapons range— they do sweeps, make sure that we're not encroaching. Same as us."

Perkin thought for a second and asked, "Last time we were here, you offered to have a squad on standby in case we needed assistance. Could I ask for that now?"

"Sure. I'll get you with my commo sergeant, and we'll either get you onto our frequencies with your gear, or get you some of our equipment. When are you heading out?"

"Tomorrow morning before daylight. We don't need

to be there before tomorrow, and I want to minimize our time on the other side," Perkin answered.

"And your return, sir?" asked the lieutenant.

"I don't know."

1045 Hours
Avezzano, Italy

"We will leave as soon as we get back to the church. It's good weather to go." Father Carlo looked to the skies and smiled.

Sam looked as well and smiled for a different reason. He was heading home. Two days tops, and God willing, he would be back on the Allied side of the line. Good weather, bad weather, it didn't matter to Sam. He was heading home.

The priest was engaging company as they walked back to the church. He knew where the checkpoints and patrols were, and he detoured through a maze of streets that left Sam completely lost.

"My church is at the southernmost tip of Avezzano, almost out of the city itself. That makes it easy for us. We gather some food, and a blanket each, and off we go." The priest had hiked the mountain trail to the south many times, and he knew a cave where they could sleep, but they would have to leave soon. "I hope your feet are in good shape. The journey is nearly sixty kilometers, but there's a good trail most of the way."

Sam smiled. "Don't worry about me, Father. I'm a foot soldier to my infinite regret. My callouses have callouses." He looked down at his army-issued shoes— the last remnant of his uniform other than his dog tags. They were in good shape and would make the journey. All of his other clothes had been replaced by his Italian benefactors. He wore a mix of black trousers, his brown sweater from Gianina, a gray worker's coat that was very snug, and a brown fedora. He knew he wouldn't stand much scrutiny with his fair complexion and blue eyes, but he kept the hat pulled down low and kept moving with the priest.

"Do you not like being a soldier?" asked Father Carlo.

"No, sir. Not really. I'm just a rancher. That's all I want to do—just go home to my wife, Margaret, and tend to my ranch."

"A ranch is like a farm, yes?"

Sam inwardly smiled and said it was. There was no point in explaining that his ranch was about 250 times larger than the average American farm, which was big by European standards. "We all have to serve I suppose," Sam said. "But I'd rather be in an airplane than on the ground."

The priest smiled. "I would too. I've never been in an aeroplane, but I imagine it's wonderful to see God's creation from above. My other American is a pilot named Doug Peabody. He can't wait to get back either."

"Peabody? I knew a Peabody at A&M. That was the college I went to. He was from a town up north—Sherman, I think. Boy, that takes me way back…"

Sam was about to talk about Texas when the priest stopped and pointed down the long street. Two hundred yards ahead of them was a modest church, which was framed by the mountains rising up off the Avezzano plain only another two hundred yards beyond that. "This is your road to freedom, Mr. Taft. That is my church, and this road leads straight to our trail." The priest clapped his hands together and with a fierce grin on his dark face, he said, "I can't wait to get started. Let's go meet Mr. Peabody, and we'll be on our way!"

1100 Hours
Avezzano, Italy

Sam had been in some beautiful churches since coming to Italy. The grandeur of the cathedrals never failed to provoke a sense of awe in him, which he knew was purposeful. He thought that the San Gennaro Cathedral in Naples was perhaps the only redeeming feature of a city that he otherwise despised. One of the few times in Naples when he had ventured into the city on his own, he ducked into the war-damaged cathedral in order to escape the urchins, the pimps, and the hustlers, who were often one and the same. He had taken a seat in the back of the nave and simply reveled in the silence and the architecture.

Father Carlo's church inspired no awe in Sam. It was simple and modest without frescoes, carved capitals, statues, or gilded ceilings. The best it could claim were a handful of faded prints of unknown saints. It was appropriate to minister to the poor of southern Avezzano, but it would not leave a lasting impression on the tourists. Father Carlo genuflected before the altar, and smiled sadly at the confusion on Sam's face.

"Follow me," the priest said, and he led Sam through a door off the south transept and into a dark corridor leading to a heavy oak door. "The church office, library, and storeroom. It's also been Douglas's bedroom for the past three weeks." As he reached for a set of keys, he explained, "I keep it locked to keep the curious out. Douglas has a key as well."

Father Carlo inserted the key and turned it, opened the door, and walked in.

1100 Hours
Avezzano, Italy

Douglas Grossmann sat cross-legged on the floor. He had been pacing back and forth, and just stopped himself from walking outside to see if Antoniette was in the church looking for him.

He held his hand out and saw that it was trembling. Maybe it was the result of too many cigarettes, he thought. Then he corrected himself. He was queasy and uncertain. Part of him believed that his actions today would lead to his death, and part of him still saw a redemption to be taken advantage of. All of him worried about Antoniette. *Oh God, I wish I could talk to her*, he thought.

He heard voices in the corridor, and heard the key slide into the lock. When the door was opened, the priest walked in with a smile on his face. Grossmann saw a massive man still standing in the doorway, and he leapt to his feet. The massive man was a soldier that he had seen before, but he couldn't place him.

"It's all right. Don't worry," said the priest. "Douglas Peabody, meet Sam Taft." In an instant, Grossmann recognized the soldier—a Texan who had run afoul of Antoniette many months before in Agropoli. A man whose cousin Grossmann believed responsible for the torture and execution of his friend and deputy, Captain Mark Gerschoffer, in San Pietro. A man he had promised to kill for Antoniette.

Grossmann watched as the large man's face changed from a welcoming smile to first puzzlement, and then to anger, and he realized the soldier knew him as well. Grossmann reached for the Walther that he kept tucked into his waistband in the small of his back.

1100 Hours
Avezzano, Italy

Sam stood in the doorway of the office. There wasn't much room to move about with the priest and the pilot in the dark room as well as a desk and a cot. He thought he would just hang back.

Sam watched as a small man leapt to his feet, and then heard the priest tell the pilot not to worry, and then he introduced them. "Douglas Peabody, meet Sam Taft."

He had never been particularly good with names, but Sam never forgot a face. He knew Peabody, but that wasn't his name. He had seen him before, but where was it? It was coming to him and then he realized where he had seen the man: it was Agropoli, and he had been wearing the uniform of a 5th Army major and he'd been arm in arm with...Antoniette Bernardi.

Sam realized as his shock turned to anger that the man standing before him was Douglas Grossmann, the German-American officer who was wanted by Allied intelligence. Perkin had never told him all that he knew about Grossmann, but Sam had seen a copy of his high school yearbook photograph, and had an inkling of the damage he had caused. Although he didn't understand the linkage, he knew that Perkin blamed Grossmann for Gianina's death. Instinctively, Sam knew that he was there to destroy the Vatican network, and he would kill or arrest everyone involved unless Sam stopped him now.

He started to take a step into the room, and saw Grossmann move his left arm protectively across his chest while he reached for the small of his back with his right. Sam knew the movement. Grossmann was going for a gun. Sam judged the distance and decided that he couldn't reach Grossmann before he drew the weapon. He yelled, "Grossmann, no!" and took a step backwards as he reached behind him for anything to throw. He found the edge of the door, and watched as Grossmann brought the gun out from behind him and fumbled with the safety.

Sam started to reach for the priest, but he had moved into the room with his hands out in a placating manner. Sam began backing out rapidly, when he heard the priest say, "No! No!..." and then Father Carlo was shot in the throat by the man he had trusted with his life. The bullet passed through the priest, narrowly missing Sam's head, and embedded in the wall of the dark and dingy office. There was no attempt by Sam to rush the man with the gun, nor to try to reason with the German agent. In a heartbeat, Sam was pulling the door closed while the priest began a long slow-motion slide to the floor. As he slammed the door shut, Sam heard another shot. The key was still in the lock, and as Sam frantically turned it, he heard the loud pops as two more shots were fired in the office. A round thudded into the door chest high, but it was stopped by the heavy oak. The other round went through a seam, splintering the wood by Sam's hand.

Horrified, Sam backed away from the door. He turned and as he ran out of the church past the prints of ancient saints, the thought crossed his mind to double back to break Grossmann's neck—just like the last two Germans he had encountered. But he didn't. The Walther made it an unfair fight and Sam wasn't going to wait around for it to resume. He ran out of the church, got his bearings and sprinted down the street toward the mountains fearful of the shot that he would never hear, but it didn't come. A minute later, the street ended in a small park, and Sam was out of Avezzano and on a trail that was marked for hikers. He looked behind him for the first time, but no one was there.

1105 Hours
Avezzano, Italy

For a long moment, as the smoke cleared and the ringing in his ears subsided, Douglas Grossmann stared in disbelief at the dead priest on the office floor. With little warning, his legs got weak and he sat down abruptly on the floor next to the body of Father Carlo. The first shot had put a tiny hole in the priest's throat but had torn through his spinal cord on its exit. He was dead before the second shot hit him in the temple a second later. Grossmann cursed himself for moving too slowly. He had never liked the safety on the Walther, he thought in a disconnected way. Grossmann shook his head in disgust. He had not meant to shoot the priest—Father Carlo had simply got in the way of a hastily aimed shot. Well, two. It was embarrassing.

His thoughts turned to himself, and he knew he would not be the savior of Western civilization. He would not be the man to end the final solution to the Jewish problem, and he would not be able to save Germany from itself. In the span of two seconds where he fired two 7.65mm bullets into an unfortunate cleric, his life changed, and he found he was not the man he believed himself to be. He dropped the Walther, put his head in his hands and rocked back and forth on the floor, almost on the verge of tears.

These thoughts ran through his head many times and it took him several minutes to recover his wits. When he had, and he was able to move past the death of the priest, he found he didn't care about being a hero. He would find Antoniette, and deal with this matter in a different manner, but deal with it he would.

He stood, picked up the pistol, and with a shaking hand, he unlocked the church door from the inside and walked into the church. He hadn't expected to see the dead body of Taft on the opposite side of the door, and he didn't expect the American to wait around. He toyed with the notion of attempting to find Taft, but he knew that ship had sailed.

It was time to find Antoniette.

1120 Hours
Avezzano, Italy

Sam had run hard for fifteen minutes, most of it uphill. He stopped and leaned against a pine tree while he caught his breath. He had a good view down into the outskirts of Avezzano, and there was no one following him that he could see. It didn't matter, he wanted as much space between himself and Grossmann as possible. He didn't know why he wasn't being followed, and then he thought that maybe Grossmann was still locked in the office with the dead priest.

Sam wiped the sweat from his face, and as he brought his hand down, it was red with blood. It had to be Father Carlo's, but Sam checked himself over to make certain he hadn't been hurt. He wiped his face off with the sleeve of his Italian coat, and began to run up the trail again, albeit at a much slower pace.

Another twenty minutes passed, and Sam could no longer see Avezzano. It was a mixed blessing. If he couldn't see the city, then he couldn't be seen from the city. On the other hand, his shortened point of view gave him the sense that someone could come around a turn in the path and be on top of him in an instant.

He started running again.

Douglas Grossmann fretted the entire two-mile walk to Antoniette's hotel. He was terrified that he had signed his death warrant in one way or another—particularly as he had just made a terrible enemy in Admiral Canaris. Or at least he had a made a terrible mistake. Or maybe he had just been forced into a set of unfortunate circumstances by the unpredictable coincidence of meeting one of a handful of American soldiers who could identify him.

He could still salvage his career with the Abwehr, he thought. It wasn't his fault, he told himself. If he hadn't pulled his pistol, the American officer would have killed him. It wasn't his fault, he told himself again. Then he thought, *but is that the way to play it?*

His mind was still in turmoil as he ran up the steps to Antoniette's floor in the hotel. Grossmann took a deep breath, collected himself, and knocked on the door. A second later, he heard footsteps on the tile floor. The door opened, and there she was.

"Douglas!" Bernardi's cry of delight masked the infinitesimally small look of fierce triumph that passed ever so briefly across her face. The following appearance of happiness was also short-lived as she saw the look on Grossmann's face. "What's happened?"

"I changed my mind," he said. "The American that was with the priest was the soldier Taft...you know, from Agropoli."

Bernardi's face darkened instantly. "Did you kill him?" she demanded.

"No. He recognized me. I don't know how, but he called out my name. Maybe the Americans were double-crossing us," he improvised. Grossmann didn't know how Sam had recognized him, but the surprise on Sam's face told him that the encounter hadn't been deliberate. "When he recognized me, he pushed the priest on me and ran out."

"You followed him?" Bernardi asked.

"No, while the priest was blocking me, he locked me in the office. I shot a couple times through the door but I don't think I hit him. When I got out of the office, he was gone. I searched several blocks in each direction, but he was gone. I guess he got lost in the city."

"Damn!" she said vehemently. "What about the priest?"

"I killed him," Grossmann said simply.

"Good." Bernardi sat down in a chair, looked at Grossmann with concern, and said, "This changes things, doesn't it?"

"I...it does. What do you think we should do? Where should we go?" Grossmann asked. He was totally lost and uncertain.

Bernardi was not. Decisively, she said, "You have to go to Rome." Then she told him what they were going to do.

1415 Hours
Abruzzi Mountains, 12 Miles South of
Avezzano, Italy

Sam was now walking at a brisk pace. He had put a great deal of distance between himself and Avezzano, but he had no solid idea of how much. He had reached a slight bend in the ridge that allowed him to look back toward the city. There was no one on the trail that day but him, and Sam was certain that he was not being followed. An hour earlier, he had seen a lone German air defense crew several hundred feet in elevation below him but he had seen no sign of human existence since then.

He continued moving along the ridge of mountains to his southeast, and several times during the course of the day, he thought he heard the echoes of artillery fire. He believed it was coming from the west, but in the mountains, it was difficult to be sure. He pictured a map of Italy in his mind, and decided that the fighting in the Cassino area had to be within fifteen to twenty miles to the southwest.

The priest had told him that morning that two-thirds of the trail lay below the tree line but the last third was closer to the ridge itself. There was plenty of water to drink in the small streams that he crossed, but there was no food. It didn't matter so much now, but he had expended a great number of calories in his flight that day, and times looked lean until he could get to the Gildardino farm.

Sam wasn't sure when that would be. He figured that he was roughly one-third of the way there, but he couldn't maintain the pace that he had set earlier. He had told Father Carlo that his feet had callouses upon callouses, but he hadn't run in boots for some time, and his feet were already tender. He would have to a set a pace that he could maintain and one that would not lead him to sweat. Sam thought that he could hold to about a 2 ½ mile per hour pace on the rugged trail until sundown, and then perhaps one mile per hour or less thereafter.

He was soaked from sweat when he finally dropped to a walk, and he took his coat and sweater off and carried them under his arm while his body dried in the cool air. Sam was certain that the temperatures would drop below freezing after sundown, and he wanted to make sure that his body was dry before then.

2015 Hours
SS Headquarters, Rome, Italy

Douglas Grossmann fidgeted uncomfortably in the outer office. He still wore his Italian work clothes, and he felt as out of place in the richly decorated office as a real Italian worker would have. He had been waiting for over two hours, and was getting more anxious by the minute.

The lack of a proper uniform or identification proved to be a challenge. Grossmann had kissed Antoniette goodbye, and ran to a German air defense unit that he had seen earlier in his walks around the city. He identified himself as a lieutenant colonel in the army and demanded transportation to Rome.

The soldiers manning the air defense guns had stared at the slight man in workers' clothes standing before them, and had not moved. Then Grossmann screamed at them in a voice reserved for officers in the German military, and the ranking sergeant called his headquarters in northern Avezzano and asked for a car. Grossmann was forced to get on the phone and pull rank with an unhappy captain who had planned to use the sole staff car for his own use that afternoon and evening.

When Grossmann had reached SS headquarters in Rome, he had initially been denied entrance by the guards—two tall Aryan specimens who had been tempted to kick Grossmann to the curb. It wasn't until Grossmann started naming officers in the intelligence directorate of the SS staff in Rome, that the guards began making calls.

Finally, a *Sturmbannführer*—an SS major—that Grossmann knew for much of his time in Rome came down to the front checkpoint. He laughed at

Grossmann's attire, and he wasn't entirely inclined to help the Abwehr officer until Grossmann swore that it was a matter of utmost urgency that he be allowed to see General Wolff.

Grossmann's acquaintance had escorted him to Wolff's outer office, explained the situation as well as he could to Wolff's aide, and then left. Grossmann was told that the general was in a meeting, and that he might have to wait until late. While he sat there waiting, he thought about what he knew of General Wolff. He was from Darmstadt, the same as Grossmann's father—but Grossmann knew of no family connections. The general served in the Imperial Army in the Great War, and after being discharged, became a businessman in the Weimar Republic. Grossmann didn't know at what point the general joined the party and the SS, but it had to have been in the early days for him to hold the equivalent rank of Lieutenant General now.

As one of the most senior officers in the SS, Wolff obviously had political connections as well. He had been Reichsführer Himmler's right-hand man for many years, although the rumors suggested he had run afoul of Himmler for some reason—Grossmann had heard that Himmler disapproved of the general's divorce and remarriage. The same rumor mill suggested that Wolff's current posting as head of the SS in Italy was an exile of sorts from the inner power circle of Berlin. *How can this work to my advantage?*

"Colonel Grossmann?" The aide's sharp voice brought Grossmann out of his contemplation. "You may see the general now. Keep it short as he has not had his dinner yet."

Grossmann was led into an elaborately decorated office—a roaring fire in the fireplace, leather-bound chairs and sofa, dark red heavy curtains, and a rich mahogany desk and coffee table. A massive portrait of a glaring Adolf Hitler was behind the general's desk giving the intentional impression that when one spoke to the man behind the desk, it was the same as speaking to the Führer.

"General Wolff," the aide said to the general, "this is Lieutenant Colonel Grossmann of the Abwehr. He has an urgent matter to bring to your attention." The aide left the room to see about dinner for the general and himself.

Grossmann stood at attention, and brought his arm up rigidly in the party salute. "Heil Hitler!"

Wolff looked up for the first time as he automatically returned the salute, and as he said "Heil Hitler" in response, he saw Grossmann standing before him in unkempt civilian clothes more appropriate for a warehouse than an SS general's office. His surprise turned to wry amusement and Grossmann noticed that the general appeared intelligent—a trait that he did not always associate with the SS.

"Is that the new uniform of the Abwehr?" Wolff asked with a grin. Without waiting for a response, he observed, "That's what happens when you put a sailor in charge." Wolff did not offer a hand, but indicated that Grossmann should take a seat. "Now, Colonel, I assume that you would not be here so, if it were not important. What brings you here at this time of night?"

"A sailor's treason," said Grossmann to the portrait of Adolf Hitler.

Chapter Eleven

February 15, 1944
0530 Hours
Sixteen Miles Southwest of Castel di Sangro,
Italy

Captain Perkin Berger lifted his pack and placed it in the back of the jeep. Corporal Kulis was already in the jeep and was killing time by sketching the Cassino Massif from memory in his journal by the red light of his flashlight. Both men had enjoyed a good night's sleep on Canadian cots, and had just finished two plates each of hot scrambled eggs and back bacon for breakfast.

Perkin was anxious for the mission to get underway. There was always a risk in moving past one's own lines, but he had been here before and knew the terrain. Moreover, he knew the Gildardino family, and he was anxious for their safety.

He climbed into the jeep and waited for Ackernly and Hill to arrive. When they did, the Canadians would lead him through their roadblock, and he would be at the base of the Gildardino mountain in half an hour. From there, he would make a determination based on the state of the road whether to proceed by foot or by vehicle. The last time he had been here, the road was too icy for even the jeeps to use, and they had walked up the mountainside. Hopefully, the road would be in better condition today.

Perkin saw George Hill walk out of the command post, and Perkin was preparing to start the jeep when Hill shook his head and waved Perkin back inside. When Perkin walked into the warmth of the bunker, the Canadian lieutenant looked at him and shook his head as well. "As we decided yesterday, I sent a team out last night to set up an observation post in no-man's land. Not too close to your ingress route, but close enough to provide supporting surveillance and fire for your mission if need be."

Perkin nodded. They had discussed it yesterday. "Let me guess...they saw something?"

"Yes, sir. They just reported enemy vehicles in sight moving to the southeast. Let me show you where they are on the map." They walked to a large improvised wooden desk and the lieutenant pointed to the map. "Here we are. Here's our OP. Here's the Jerry position at the time of the report, and if they continue another mile on this track, it brings them to the Gildardino mountain road."

"Shit," Perkin said. "What vehicles did your team report?"

"We had a man up close to the road. He said that there was a staff car and a heavy truck like your deuce and a half. He couldn't see into the back of the truck, but he thinks maybe we're looking at a car with an officer or officers, and a troop carrier with a squad or less of soldiers." The lieutenant looked at Perkin's worried face, looked at the two civilians, and said, "I'm going to step out for some coffee. I'll bring a pot back."

"Thanks," Perkin said. He looked at Hill and

Ackernly, and said, "Last time I was here, the Germans sent a team of soldiers to the farm to confiscate fodder for their animals. We intercepted them and took their soldiers prisoner. This may be the same—a raid on the Gildardino farm for food or livestock and that could be the reason for the truck. They still had draft horses and dairy cows left if I remember right. That might explain it. But…"

"Yes?" asked Ackernly.

"I don't know if a requisitioning mission requires an early morning raid, unless they just want to catch everyone asleep. Maybe they're looking for manpower, as well." Perkin said.

"Would such a mission require an officer?" asked Hill.

"No. A corporal or a sergeant could lead this mission. I'd let Eddie do it," Perkin said.

"Captain Berger, I need to discuss this with Mr. Hill, but I would like to hear your opinion first," Ackernly said.

"Yes, sir." Perkin paused for a moment to collect his thoughts and then said, "First, let me say that I'm concerned for the Gildardinos, but they said that they have a good relationship with the German soldiers in the area. The Germans have no reason to hurt them that I know of. So far. Second, this could be an unrelated mission that just coincides in time and space with our own, although it could have a correlation to us. Third, if it is related to us, our mission could be blown, and the Germans are staging to arrest us on arrival today. Fourth, we don't have the firepower to confront the Germans like we did last time. Not unless we request the assistance of the Canadians. Fifth, any armed incursion into no-man's land or up to the farm while those soldiers are there puts us and your Abwehr counterparts at risk.

It puts your whole mission at risk in fact."

Ackernly nodded. "You have a very concise mind, Dr. Berger. Your recommendations?"

Perkin smiled. "Concise isn't the word my battalion commander uses. Look, we don't know that the Germans are even headed there. If they turn up the Gildardino road, I'd recommend that you wait and see. If it's a requisition mission, they'll be down in two hours tops and we can go up then. If it's…well…a welcoming committee for us, they won't come down until we're there. They don't come down, y'all don't go up. It's that simple."

Hill said, "I agree, but what about the Gildardinos?"

Ackernly interrupted, "Wait a minute. I'm not always on top of my Americanisms. You said 'y'all'?"

Perkin shrugged. "It's a Southernism that means 'you chaps.' Look, there may not be anything that we can do for the Gildardinos. There may not be anything we *should* do for them. I think that inserting ourselves now may put them in danger. Having said that, I don't feel good about this. It's too much of a coincidence, so I think Eddie and I should leave now on foot and take a look. If the Canadian OP reports that the Krauts have left, wait a half hour and pick us up along the way."

0600 Hours
Abruzzi Mountains, Italy

Sam stood up and stretched. He was cold and stiff and hungry. Movement would take care of the former two conditions, but he could do nothing about the latter. It would be a long, hungry day.

He had been forced to stop and sleep. He didn't know how late it had been, but he guessed about 0200. Before it turned dark, Sam found a long straight pine branch on the ground next to the trail. He had a good walking stick that helped give him balance going up and down the vagaries of the trail, but more importantly, in the dark, it helped him stay on the path. He would take a step, and then do a one-two-three probe ahead of him from right to left. He would then step to that ground and the process would begin anew. When he stopped for the night, it had been because his walking stick found no trail before him, no ground before him, and in the darkness of the night, all he could see was more darkness.

Sam had simply lay down on the trail and fallen asleep. He was tired from the exertions of the day, and the terror of walking along an unfamiliar mountain trail in the dark had been further exhausting. He hadn't been confident that he'd be able to fall asleep, he just assumed that he'd have an uncomfortable few hours until daylight, but he was asleep within minutes.

The light of dawn was enough to wake Sam, and it was then that he realized that his walking stick had saved his life. The trail had turned sharply to the left more than 100 yards before Sam had stopped for the night. On awakening, Sam was treated to a spectacular view of a valley opening directly below him. Another two or three feet and Sam would have walked into oblivion over a sheer cliff that dropped several hundred feet.

With the recognition that God takes care of little children and wandering Texans, Sam gave thanks to the Almighty, and then turned back and regained the trail. The trail's missed turn brought Sam to a sharp ascent over a rock face that raised his elevation above the tree line. It wasn't a hard climb, but when the trail resumed, he was now much closer to the actual ridgeline. It was also a much more exposed position but as Sam surveyed hundreds of square miles from his vantage, he saw not a single fellow human. But he could hear them. The sounds of humanity echoed through the mountains like the ghosts of long dead warriors—Sam could hear distant booms to his right, which he assumed correctly was from the continuing battle of Cassino. He had no optimism that Fifth Army had broken out into the Liri Valley, and his concern for Perkin and his friends came flooding back.

He was in snow now but even so, his progress wasn't slowed much. Countless generations of herders, adventurers, and mountain sheep had left a defined trail even when it was covered with a few inches of snow. It was certainly better than the night before, and Sam calculated that he would be able to maintain a two to three mile per hour pace for as long as the trail held out. That might get him to the farm in another four hours...faster if he jogged. He swore and then started a slow run.

0800 Hours
Johannistal Airfield, Berlin, Germany

Lieutenant Colonel Douglas Grossmann stepped off the plane and blinked in the bright morning light. It was much colder in Berlin, and he buttoned his uniform coat to the neck, and pulled up the collar.

He had gotten on the plane in the middle of the night. It was amazing what a concerned general of the SS could accomplish when he wanted to...even down to requisitioning his new SS uniform and dragging a tailor in to make it perfect. Grossmann had been told that if his story checked out, he was to consider himself transferred to the SD—the intelligence arm of the SS. If it didn't check out, he would be tried and shot as an agent provocateur.

Wolff had been skeptical at first. Canaris was an admiral after all. A man deeply respected in the tight ranks of the regular navy and army—but the SS had always had its suspicions. His political motivation had always been lacking.

The microfilms convinced Wolff. The data on the camps came from one of two places—from the SS itself or from an intelligence organization. It had not come from the SS. Wolff had turned white when his own intelligence officer told him of the detail and the scope of the evidence against the SS, and after reviewing the microfilms himself, he called Himmler's office requesting an immediate audience while an aide arranged a flight to Berlin for both men. News of this sort could only be delivered in person.

0800 Hours
Gildardino Farm, Italy

"I know that there's a compelling reason of strategy why we're walkin' and not taking the jeeps." Corporal Eddie Kulis observed as they waded through a knee-high stream. The water was ice cold.

"Maybe," allowed Perkin. "Maybe not. Damn this water is cold." After crossing, they sat on the bank, allowed their feet to dry, and then put on their socks and boots. "I figured that if they are in fact waiting for Ackernly and Hill—sounds like a law firm, don't it—that they'd leave a small team in place to snatch us as we came onto the mountain."

"Or kill us," agreed Kulis.

"So, a jeep is more visible and is noisy. You could see one coming for a long way off, so I thought we might come along to the east of the road and approach the house from the flanks. We can see if they come out, and if they do, Hill and Ackernly will pick us up and we'll have homemade bread for breakfast."

Kulis couldn't find anything wrong with the plan, so instead of complaining he pointed out a route that had more cover. They walked a little more, and then Kulis said, "I hope Miss Maria and the girls are okay."

"I do, too," agreed Perkin. He began to walk a little faster.

"Outside of Miss Angela and Stefania and her family, no one has treated me as nice as Miss Maria. She's a special lady." Kulis picked up the pace, and then said, "You know, I have no intention of goin' back to the farm after the war is over, but bein' at their farm felt like, well, home. Not that their mountain is like Rosebud or nothin', but it was like bein' at home somehow. And that dinner that we had with them is one of my best memories. I cain't remember havin' home cookin' that was so good, and my mom's a decent cook. Not that there was a lot to eat at home…" Kulis realized he was saying too much, and stopped talking. He thought about Maria and the girls again, and began a slow steady run.

Without hesitation, Perkin matched him.

0825 Hours
Abruzzi Mountains, Italy

Sam was getting close. He finally knew for sure that he had been on the right ridgeline all along. He could see topographic features that seemed familiar—the valley to his right, another ridgeline, a stream.

In less than an hour, he would be at the Gildardinos. He wouldn't even stay the night—perhaps a bite to eat, a discussion with Father Riley about Grossmann, and then he would be on his way. In another three or four hours, his journey would be over. *Thank God*.

As he walked along, he thought of a story that Perkin had told him about Daniel Boone. Although Sam couldn't remember all the details, he knew that after Boone had been taken prisoner by the Shawnee Indians on the early days of the frontier, he had lived long enough with the Indians to earn a degree of trust and independence. One day, after learning the intentions of the Indians to attack Boonesboro, he stole a horse and rode it until it collapsed and ran the rest of the way back to warn the fort. All told, Boone had covered 160 miles in four days. If Sam remembered it right, Boone was in his forties at the time. *I wish I had a horse*, Sam thought. *I'd be in Caserta with a steak and a cold beer by now. Give me a horse and a sailboat, and I'd be home in Texas.*

Sam felt the vibration of the aircraft before he heard or saw them. They were still way off in the distance when he saw the first glint of sunlight off a windshield or a wing tip. They were moving east to west and they passed south of him high in the sky. Not for the first time, Sam felt envy at their mobility. They could cover the distance he had left to make in less than a minute.

It seemed like only seconds after they crossed Sam's path that he heard the deep rumblings of explosions to his west. Sam stopped to look. A tall black plume of smoke and dust was already reaching skyward, and Sam assumed that they finally decided to conduct high intensity bombing of the defenses of the Gustav Line. Other deep booms told him that artillery had joined the fray, and Sam prayed that the Gun Club was out of harm's way.

Wave after wave of aircraft passed over the battle-field, and as interesting as it was to Sam, he resumed his march to freedom and scarcely looked toward the devastation being wrought to the west.

0910 Hours
Gildardino Farm, Italy

"They're poundin' the defenses along the river," opined Kulis.

"They're bombin' the abbey," said Perkin. "There won't be anything left of it when we get back."

"Why do you say that?" asked Kulis.

"I heard the New Zealand Corps commander was insisting on it. I gather he thinks that it gives the Krauts some great advantage over them," Perkin said.

"Don't you? Don't you think they've occupied it, and are using it as a headquarters or whatever? I sure as hell do!" said Kulis with great feeling.

Perkin shrugged. "I suppose that they are, but I hate to see an institution like that destroyed, 'cause you know what?"

"What?"

"It won't matter. It's only one hilltop out of two dozen that we have to take. And what happens when they're done? Panzer grenadiers move into the rubble and it's twice as hard to get them out. Same story in Cassino town. Sad to see all this destroyed," Perkin said. "Wait!"

Perkin and Kulis dropped to the ground. Over the distant explosions to their west, Perkin heard the whining engine of a heavy vehicle using its gears to control its speed coming down the mountain. A few seconds later, a heavy truck followed by a staff car emerged from the trees lining the road to the Gildardino farm. Perkin and Kulis had been getting ready to sprint to some woods at the base of the hill and begin their climb up to the farm. Instead, when the German vehicles were out of sight, Kulis turned to Perkin and asked, "Do you want to wait until the spooks bring up the jeeps or should we just head up the road?"

"I ain't waiting. Let's go."

0930 Hours
Gildardino Farm, Italy

It had taken twenty minutes at a demanding pace to climb the winding road to the farm. Periodically, Perkin and Kulis would stop and listen, and when they came to a bend in the road, they moved slowly and with caution.

The last hundred yards of the road was a majestic sweep, first to the left and then around to the right, and the road terminated in a circle before the house. Long before the two Texans reached the circle in the driveway, Perkin knew that something was wrong. The front door to the farmhouse was wide open, and the Gildardino dog, a great white beast named Scipio, lay unmoving in the front yard. The dog had been shot in the head and body.

They moved cautiously through the house, which had been thoroughly and professionally ransacked. All of the cabinets in the kitchen had been emptied, all the drawers removed, their contents on the floor. The chairs had been ripped open, and all of the modest art on the walls had been taken out of the frames. The mattresses and pillows had been cut open and feathers blew through the house. The building was empty of people, and as they finished their search of the house, Kulis whispered, "Where are they? Did they take them?"

Perkin shook his head. "I don't know. Let's check the barn." Kulis and Perkin walked cautiously out of the house by the back door, and then they found the Gildardino family.

Perkin stood in the doorway and stared. Big Luigi had been shot twice in the chest, and he lay on his back in his underwear with his eyes wide open as if he were counting the endless bombers flying overhead. His sister Maria lay crumpled against the wall of the house, where she had been executed with her youngest daughter, five-year-old Lucia. Her anguish had hardened into a death mask of grief. Farther out in the yard lay the bodies of her two other children. Her teenage son, Angelo, bore the marks of a severe beating, and then he had been shot in the head. Like all the members of the Gildardino family, he was still in his nightclothes.

Kulis walked around the carnage and shook his head in disbelief as he pointed at Gemma—the oldest daughter. She was lying face down on the ground wearing a nightgown with soft yellow flowers printed on them. Perkin gently rolled her over and her forehead was missing. She had been shot in the back of the head, and the position of her body suggested that she was executed from behind as she knelt before her executioner.

Corporal Kulis looked at Perkin with tears streaming down his face. "Promise me we'll get the animals who did this! Who could do this?"

"Douglas Grossmann," a deep voice said softly. "Grossmann's responsible for this."

0945 Hours
Gildardino Farm, Italy

Both Perkin and Kulis whirled as they brought their weapons up, but there was no need for weapons. It was Sam and he was carrying the dead body of Father Patrick Riley. The priest was wearing pajamas and an overcoat, but unlike the Gildardino victims, he had managed to put on a pair of shoes. He had been shot in the chest cavity below his armpit.

"Sam?!" Perkin stared at his cousin and then at the body of the priest and he found that he couldn't say more, and instead he moved to help Sam ease the body to the ground.

"By God, I'm glad to see you two!" Sam said, his face a mixture of pain and pleasure as he gave Perkin a bear hug. "What are you doing here? How did you know I was coming?"

"We didn't, Sam. We came here as escorts for some spooks who were meeting an Abwehr agent carrying peace feelers from Admiral Canaris." Perkin wanted to sit down and sort through things, but it would have brought him awfully close to Lucia. "Where did you find Patrick?"

"I came across his body as I was coming down the mountain. He was over there about 100 yards." Sam nodded to a copse of pine trees up the mountainside from the house. "Did you see the guys who did this? Was Grossmann with them?"

Kulis answered, "Hey, Bear, I'm glad to see you, too." He blew his breath out—he was still shook up but recovering. "We were going to drive up this morning, but couldn't. They got here first. They came up in two vehicles…a staff car and a Kraut deuce and a half. The cap'n and me were walkin' in, when they left. We couldn't see any faces. How do you know it's Grossmann?"

They heard the whine of engines and Perkin and Kulis picked up their weapons and ran to the side of the house. "Ackernly and Hill. The spooks," Perkin explained to Sam.

"Sounds like lawyers," said Sam.

The three Texans walked out to the two jeeps, and Perkin explained, "We were too late. They're all dead."

Hill swore bitterly, and Ackernly put his hand on Perkin's shoulder. "I'm terribly sorry, Dr. Berger. You said that they were decent people."

"They were. They didn't deserve this," Perkin said. "There's more. Sam says Grossmann's responsible."

"Ah yes, that's you I take it?" Ackernly said. Sam nodded and introduced himself.

Hill looked at Sam with keen interest as he shook hands, and then looked back at Perkin. "Your wandering cousin?"

Perkin nodded and made the introductions even as he thought it interesting that Hill not only knew about his cousin Sam, but also that Sam had been captured.

There was a flood of questions, and Sam explained patiently but quickly about his escape and journey across the peninsula.

"I need some time to think about this," said Ackernly. "Also, I would like to leave as quickly as possible, but I suppose we should care for the poor people here."

Perkin took charge. "Eddie, see if there's a shovel or two down in the shed. Mr. Ackernly, if you would please find a blanket in the house, so that we can take back Patrick. I'm sure his brother is still in Italy, and would like to see to his burial. And if you wouldn't mind, please keep an eye on the front. Sam, let's you and me get the shovels out of the jeeps and get started. Have you eaten anything?"

"I ain't hungry, Perk. Later."

Hill asked, "What about me?"

"You were FBI before the war, right?"

Hill nodded.

"I want you to look at the crime scene and tell me what you think happened."

1015 Hours
Gildardino Farm, Italy

"Okay," said Hill. "Charles and I talked it over and this is what we think happened. The Gestapo or the SS or whoever it was that came up this morning sent troops to surround the house. They killed the dog and kicked in the door. Father Riley must have heard the dog barking and ducked out the back door before they were entirely in place. He made a run for it up the hill and was shot under his shoulder, laterally like so, which suggests to me that he was shot on the run. Not executed like these poor people. The family was brought outside, and the farmer was likely shot next. There's not a tight pattern, and maybe he tried to intervene. They then moved to the children. They came here to capture us, so they wanted information. They tortured this young man, and when he wouldn't give what he didn't know, they executed him in front of his mother. They forced this poor girl to her knees and put a gun to her head, and demanded answers from her mother, which again, she didn't have. They executed the girl, and then the mother and the other daughter."

Perkin nodded sadly, leaned on his shovel, and said, "Those are the same conclusions that I came to."

"As for Grossmann, my guess is that Canaris thought he would be a good conduit back to us because of his American connection but we may never know. What I don't understand is why Grossmann was at the church for as long as he was before he acted. I don't know if it matters other than I'd really like to know what Canaris thought was so important. I hate to think that an opportunity to end this war might have escaped us because of Douglas Grossmann."

Everyone was silent while they digested that

thought, and then another thought occurred to Sam. "Do you think Canaris knows he was betrayed?" he asked.

"I can't say, but if Canaris doesn't know by now, he'll find out quick enough," answered Hill. "Unfortunately, we don't have an expedited line of communication back to him. That was one of the things we were hoping to establish today. If it's okay with you, I'm going up front with Ackernly to keep an eye on things and talk to him. He's pretty upset."

Perkin nodded. "We're just about done here. We'll call you up and say a few words."

1030 Hours
SS Headquarters, Berlin, Germany

Obersturmbannführer Douglas Grossmann of the SS excused himself from his escort, and went to the men's room. It had been a long night, a whirlwind twenty-four hours, and he wanted to splash some water in his face.

Reichsführer Heinrich Himmler was perhaps the most evil man he had ever met. Foul darkness emanated from him, and as he shook Himmler's offered hand and accepted his appreciation, he felt as if Satan himself was leading him to hell by the hand. He looked for a bar of soap, saw none, and washed his hands as best he could in the cold water. Grossmann stared at his red-rimmed eyes in the mirror and an image of the priest's wide, disbelieving eyes at the time of his murder flashed through Grossmann's mind. He barely had time to make it to the toilet before vomiting.

Cursing his weakness, he spat the bile from his mouth, and flushed the toilet. He was rinsing his mouth out at the sink when the door opened, and another lieutenant colonel walked in. He was one of Himmler's many aides, and he had been present at the meeting. Grossmann couldn't help but contrast the man's haughty demeanor when he met him that morning with the friendly earnestness of Captain Fenstermacher, the Abwehr aide.

Yet sometimes first impressions were wrong, Grossmann thought as the SS officer said, "Grossmann! When you're done here, come on out. The Reichsführer has decided to reward you with the Iron Cross First Class. Quite the compliment for a former army officer you know, but, well, he's just delighted. Your information has checked out and our team in Italy confirmed your story. As they were getting into place, they shot a man running out of the back of the house. Not an Italian. They said he was North European or Anglo-Saxon in his racial makeup—eye color, complexion, and features. English or American, I don't know. Damn shame they killed him but he left them no choice. He was moving fast."

Grossmann nodded. It somehow made him feel better. "Was there just one of them?"

The aide nodded, "Yes. Just the one. But it was our guy. Interrogation of the female indicated that the man we shot was waiting for someone from Avezzano. That would have been you…so, *ipso facto*, right guy."

"What happens next?" Grossmann asked. He was feeling much better now.

"What, after you're made a hero of the Reich?"

Grossmann nodded modestly. He detected no sarcasm from the officer, and he was right, thought Grossmann—*I am a hero.*

"We have placed Canaris and all the other conspirators that you named under close surveillance. We'll give them a day, maybe two, and see if they'll lead us somewhere but Canaris is too wily for that. They'll be arrested within forty-eight hours is my bet. Himmler will propose to the Führer that the Abwehr be disbanded, and that politically reliable officers and enlisted men be rolled into the SD. Are you ready?"

"Just about. I was looking for some soap to wash up with," Grossmann said.

"Here." The aide opened a cabinet, looked around, and found a tissue-wrapped bar of soap. As Grossmann washed his hands and face, the officer said, "It's hard to come by these days, but we have a small supply coming in from the east. Hurry, we don't want to keep the Reichsführer waiting. Hey, where do you want to go next? He might ask."

"Rome. My business isn't done there."

1035 Hours
Gildardino Farm, Italy

The three grim-faced men stood up straight. Their horrible task was over. Kulis, the coolest killer that Sam had ever known, had cried again as the girls were placed in the grave next to their mother, uncle and brother. He only cried for a minute, but it was enough to make the other men teary as well, and Sam had to wipe his eyes several times.

He was tired. Dead tired. But happy that he was with Perkin and just minutes away from freedom. He decided that he would man the machine gun on the lead jeep all the way back to Canadian lines, and he would kill any German that he saw. To the degree that Sam thought about such things, he had told himself that he would not let hatred consume his life during the war, but he had never felt such hatred as he felt now.

"Perk, Eddie," Sam said as he leaned heavily on his

shovel. "Let's get them other two fellas and get back to the Gun Club."

Perkin nodded somberly and Kulis said, "You don't have to ask me twice, sir. Let's go."

Kulis was turning to go, but Sam stopped him with a hand on his shoulder. He looked Perkin in the eyes, a dangerous look that Perkin had seldom seen, and said, "But before we do, I want us to swear, on the grave of these good people and for the sake of poor Gianina, that we'll find Grossmann and make him pay."

Kulis smiled a hard, grim smile and said, "Don't think that because y'all are officers that I'm going to give you the first shot. I see him first, he's dead." He put his hand out.

Perkin shook Kulis's hand and then Sam's, and said as more bombers flew overhead to destroy the ancient abbey, "I swear. I swear on the grave of this family that I'll track him down to the ends of the earth, and I'll make him beg for his life. And then I'll kill him without mercy."

Epilogue

February 27, 1944
1100 Hours
Hill 706, Italy

The morning was cool but not cold, and the sun was shining brightly. Only the continuing sounds, smells, and dangers of the battlefield ruined what was an otherwise stunning start to a new week.

The battalion had been moved into a defensive position two weeks before to another part of the Cassino Massif, and although there had been severe shelling several times since then, and bombardment from both the British and American air forces, it had not been in close combat in those two weeks.

First Lieutenant Sam Taft, the commander of Able Company, and Captain Perkin Berger, the battalion intelligence officer were standing by for the arrival of Major Bill Spaulding, who had been summoned to a meeting with the division commander at the regimental command post and had called ahead to notify his company commanders to be ready to receive new orders.

It was actually a new regimental command post.

The day after Perkin and Kulis had left the battle, heavy German artillery had found the regimental command post in a barrage during the afternoon, killing the new regimental commander and wounding the entire body of enlisted personnel in the regimental plans and operations section. It was another tragedy for a regiment that had been vainly expended in combat.

Sam and Perkin stared out over the distance at the utter devastation of the 6th century abbey on Monte Cassino. The ancient building, the mountain itself, was shattered by the more than 2000 bombs that had been dropped by the combined air forces. Everyone agreed it was a shame, but most felt that it had to be done. Perkin was not one of them.

"I hate to see that," he said to Sam for the hundredth time.

"Stop lookin' then," was Sam's laconic reply. "And be quiet about it too. It's too beautiful a day to listen to you gas away." Sam turned his face to the sun, enjoying its warmth.

"Do you think that St. Benedict could ever have anticipated this happening to his creation? It stood the test of 1400 years of history—warfare, plague, invasions—and we destroy it in four hours," Perkin asked.

Sam looked at Perkin in disgust. "Stop talkin' about it! You know, if the air force could hit their damn targets, they could have destroyed it in one minute, and not wasted the rest of the morning bombing our troops." The rumors were that the bombing of the abbey had killed more Allied soldiers than Germans.

"You know, I've spent the morning thinking about Patrick. I think he would be appalled by what we've done. We had a long talk back in January, or maybe it was way back in September—I can't remember any more. He told me that mankind needed to find a better way to resolve its differences and that faith needed to be at the core of that way. When I asked him what he meant, he told me that '…if we leave Him out, if there is no moral, Christian foundation beneath us, then war remains simply a matter of consequentialism—that an act's acceptable if the consequences are beneficial…like firebombing a city is justified if it ends the war a day earlier. I'm thinking that we can't allow sophistry like that to guide how the postwar world looks at conflict.'" Perkin shook his head in sorrow. "It was such a powerful statement that I remembered it word for word. He was a very perceptive man."

Sam agreed and said, "I wish I'd known Patrick better. Did you know the priest in Avezzano was named Father Carlo?"

"I think you mentioned it, why?" Perkin asked.

"Patrick told us that the reason that he came down from Rome in the first place was to help a dying friend— another priest named Carlo. Odd that his voyage began with the death of a Father Carlo and ended with the death of another." Sam shivered and asked, "Any word on Grossmann?"

"You know I can't tell you, but…" Perkin looked to see if anyone was in earshot. "…The word is that Canaris has been relieved of duties and placed under house arrest. I reckon he's as good as dead—if he ain't already. By the way, the OSS and MI-6 are gunning for Grossmann too, so if we ever find him, we'll have to act quickly. I don't reckon a prison cell is in his future either way."

"It better not be!" Sam said emphatically. "But we kill him. He's ours."

The whine of a jeep interrupted the conversation, and Sam looked back and saw Major Spaulding in the passenger seat of a jeep driven by a newly promoted Sergeant Kulis. The promotion of the young soldier had been the highlight of the week since they had left the Gildardino farm. The low point had been delivering the body of Patrick Riley to his brother—an intelligence officer in the British 5th Division. He reacted with barely concealed grief but with open gratitude and Sam's heart had been broken once again by the losses of the war. It was time for some good news.

This might be the time. Spaulding's face was hard to read as a wad of tobacco the size of a cat's head was distorting his visage, but Kulis was grinning broadly. Spaulding strode into the German built bunker that was serving as his command post, and said without preamble, "Listen up! Listen up! We have movement orders. Company commanders will prepare their units for immediate redeployment," and then he paused dramatically, "off the line. Thank God and thank you all, gentlemen. You've done a magnificent job in the two and a half months since we moved onto the line…and now it's time for a break."

The assembled officers broke out in applause and whistles, and Spaulding allowed it to continue for a few moments before holding his hand up for silence. To the smiling faces arrayed before him, he said, "Say goodbye to the Liri Valley, the Rapido River, and Monte Cassino. I know that you'll miss these rocks, but we're headin' back to Paestum for a month or so of refit. If we come back, I reckon these mountains will still be here and you won't have missed much. This time tomorrow morning, we'll have been deloused, had hot showers, hot food, and will be looking forward to some female companionship. Company commanders, let's make sure that passes for R&R are given liberally, and those who were on the river, go first. And second. And maybe third. Finally, gentlemen, once we're off this damned mountain for good, the drinks will be on me. That's a promise. Dismissed."

Spaulding walked over to Sam and Perkin with a huge grin on his face. He extended his hand first to Perkin, and then to Sam, and after they had shaken hands, he grabbed his thermos from his pack. "I ain't waitin' for Paestum. You boys come with me."

When they walked together out into the sunlight, Spaulding's smile faded as he looked over the devastation of the abbey and listened to the ongoing battle being waged in Cassino. He poured a stiff drink of Colonel Wranosky's whiskey into each of their canteen cups. As they clunked the cups together, Spaulding said, "I'd do a Texas roister, but I'm too damn tired. But I will say I'm glad we're back together—I couldn't do this without y'all. Now, let's get the hell out of here before they change their minds."

They downed the whiskey as each man had a moment of silent contemplation. Major Spaulding's thoughts were on the battalion, and coordinating the upcoming movement to Paestum. He might have some time for R&R in the weeks to come, but he doubted it. The battalion had to be rebuilt from scratch.

Sam's thoughts were on Margaret and home. This time of year was absolutely stunning in South Texas, and Sam found himself morosely wishing that it were the end of the war, and not just a redeployment from a battle. Today might be a day that he would spend riding the ranch, or it might even be time to sample the bay and do a little fishing. But he wasn't in Texas, and the war wasn't over. Sam shook his head, grinned ruefully to himself, and after slapping his comrades on their backs, he headed toward his company. He had work to do, and he agreed passionately with Bill Spaulding about leaving before they changed their minds.

Perkin stood by himself staring over the distance at the destroyed abbey long after Sam and Spaulding had left him. He understood much better now about a warning his grandfather gave him before he joined the army. On his grandfather's bluff overlooking Corpus Christi Bay nearly five years before, Old Perkin said, "Boys, I'm here to tell ya that war ain't glory. It is pain and it is tragedy and it ain't nothin' else." Perkin's thoughts drifted to the pain and the tragedy suffered by the ghosts of the mountains of Italy, and he wished them the rest and eternal peace they deserved. As he breathed in the mountain air and felt the last of the whiskey's burn fade in the back of his throat, he took one last look at the shattered abbey, and then his thoughts turned back to his work as well—how to find and kill Douglas Grossmann.

Author's Note

Monte Cassino was a terrible, tragic battle. The nature of the fighting was dictated by the hard demands of geography but also by limited operational vision. My feelings about Mark Clark are well known among readers of the Gun Club series, but whatever reservations I have about the leadership, I'm in awe of the soldiers who fought and endured these battles.

The 36th Division was nearly destroyed on the Rapido River, and should have been withdrawn from combat. But, as described in this book, it was not, primarily because 5th Army itself was stretched to the breaking point. There was no one to replace the two destroyed regiments, and consequently, the boys from Texas (native and honorary Texans alike) stayed on the river for more than two weeks after the crossing failed. Night after night, they were told that the assault across the Rapido would resume with them as the assault force only to be stood down at the last moment. They conducted countless demonstrations in an attempt to focus German efforts on the river and away from the assault in Cassino town by soldiers of the 34th Division and the 142nd Infantry Regiment of the Gun Club. Reading through the memoirs and the regimental after action reports, I'm not sure that much was accomplished by the demonstrations other than to deprive exhausted soldiers of more sleep. Mostly, they just endured.

The mountain assault on February 11, 1944 took place in gale force winds and an ice storm, and by the end of the assault that afternoon, the 1st Battalion of the 141st Infantry was down to ten officers and sixty-nine enlisted men—after expending 1500 grenades in a few hours of fighting. Let that thought sink in.

The battle for the Cassino massif and the Gustav Line was to continue into May 1944. The soldiers from Texas were replaced by soldiers from the United Kingdom, New Zealand, India, and a dozen other points of the British Empire. Much of the area described in this book today overlooks the final resting place of more than a thousand soldiers from Poland who died in the final battles on the Cassino massif.

The destruction of the abbey was one of the most controversial incidents of the war. There's no question that the average dogface was convinced that the Germans had occupied the abbey, and the leadership believed it as well. The abbey was destroyed on 14 February by wave after wave of American and British bombers who also dropped bombs as far away as Presenzano—narrowly missing Mark Clark's forward headquarters.

I used many of the interesting little pearls of history where I could—the use of sheep as a minesweeper along the river being one of my favorites. General Walker in his memoirs stated that on January 27, two officers, three sergeants and two locals drove 250 sheep along three miles of river frontage before being shot at on their return voyage.

I tried to touch on some of the difficulties of

military medicine at the time, not the least of which was bed availability. There simply weren't enough beds to keep up with the costs of combat. There had been an American field hospital (33rd) set up at Presenzano, which was wiped out during a freak storm on New Year's Day—those doctors and nurses were to find themselves at the landings at Anzio a few weeks later. There's also the amazing fact that a great percentage of the hospital beds in Italy were taken up by gonorrhea patients. Rick Atkinson wrote in his wonderful history of the Italian campaign, *The Day of Battle*, that during the timeframe covered in this book, "Fifteen percent of all American hospital beds in Italy were occupied by VD patients." They don't teach that about greatest generation in schools.

While Sam might not respect mules at all, they were some of the unsung heroes of the mountain fighting in Italy. Both sides of the battle were heavily reliant upon the use of pack animals to move supplies up the mountain paths, and Italian laborers and muleskinners were critical to the effort.

The plight of the Italian citizens was just terrible. On the Allied side of the line, their situation improved with time, but the Italians were heavily dependent on Uncle Sam's bounty during the long and harsh winter of 1943-1944. On the German side, it was far worse. German soldiers raided villages for men and provisions, and it was not unusual for the family larder to be emptied by marauding soldiers. It was also during this timeframe that the partisans began to emerge prominently on the scene in Italy—most often opposing the German and fascist governments but occasionally fighting one another.

Admiral Canaris was one of the many intriguing personalities of the Second World War. He was of the old school of the German officer corps, whose notions of honor differed from those of the Nazis. His break with the Nazi regime came early on as he was appalled by the conduct of the war in Poland. He established several lines of communication back to the British through Spain, Switzerland, and Turkey, and his treason against the Third Reich appears motivated by patriotism and faith. He was relieved of his duties in February, 1944, and later interned, tortured, and executed at Flossenberg concentration camp.

I've had the opportunity to walk the battlefield of Monte Cassino many times. I went through the area most recently in July 2012, with Michele Di Lonardo, a local historian in Cassino. Michele was a wonderful host and a great tour guide, and most importantly, Michele works harder than anyone I know on either side of the Atlantic to keep this history alive—he's a real treasure for those who are interested in the battles of the Gustav Line.

At the end of February 1944, the 36th Division was finished with the heartbreak of the Gustav Line. They were sent back to Paestum to refit, and receive and train thousands of replacement soldiers. In May, they conducted their second amphibious landing of the war at Anzio, where they were key to the fight for Rome. I look forward to seeing you then!

CDR Mark Bowlin, USN (Ret.)
Flower Mound, Texas
October, 2014

About the Author

Commander Mark Bowlin, USN (Ret.) is an eternally optimistic Texan who believes that one day, maybe not this season, but soon, the Dallas Cowboys will return to the Super Bowl—and as players, not spectators. He likewise holds the wholly understandable opinion that Texas is truly God's country, and that cold beer and Texas barbeque is truly superior to champagne and caviar in every respect.

Mark was a soldier in the Texas National Guard before being commissioned as an ensign in the United States Navy. Mark has lived in Wales, Japan, Italy and Iraq and served in a variety of billets—ashore and afloat—in the United States and overseas. His awards include the Legion of Merit, and Defense Meritorious Service Medal, among other personal, unit, and campaign awards.